CARRY ME HOME

WM. LEE CARTER

JD™
A JAN
DENNIS
BOOK

THOMAS NELSON PUBLISHERS
Nashville • Atlanta • London • Vancouver

This is a work of fiction. Any similarity to real life in the scenes, characters, timing, and events is merely coincidence.

Published in Nashville, Tennessee, by Thomas Nelson, Inc., Publishers, and distributed in Canada by Word Communications, Ltd., Richmond, British Columbia.

Library of Congress Cataloging-in-Publication Data

Carter, Wm. Lee.
    Carry me home / Wm. Lee Carter.
        p.   cm.
    ISBN 0-7852-7858-3
    I. Title.
PS3553.A7842C37   1995
813'.54—dc20   94-24155
                                                                              CIP

Published in the United States of America

2 3 4 5 6 —00 99 98 97 96

Swing Low, Sweet Chariot

I looked over Jordan and what did I see,
Comin' for to carry me home?
A band of angels, comin' after me,
Comin' for to carry me home!

If you get there before I do,
Comin' for to carry me home!
Tell all my friends I'm comin', too,
Comin' for to carry me home!

The brightest day that ever I saw,
Comin' for to carry me home!
When Jesus washed my sins away,
Comin' for to carry me home!

I'm sometimes up an' sometimes down,
Comin' for to carry me home!
But still my soul feels heavenly boun'.
Comin' for to carry me home!

I never went to heaven, but I been told
Comin' for to carry me home!
The streets in heaven are paved with gold.
Comin' for to carry me home!

Swing low, sweet chariot,
Comin' for to carry me home!
Swing low, sweet chariot,
Comin' for to carry me home!

Chapter 1

I HAD spent the night out on the sleepin porch. That's where I sleep most nights in the summer. Even though it's now mid-September, the nights can still be powerful hot. Most nights I don't even sleep under a sheet. Momma always asks me do I want one despite I tell her no thank you every single time. Never could understand why she insists on me havin somethin over me when it's just gonna stay hot all night. Summers in Cassville, Alabama, seem to last six or seven months instead of the ordinary three. We don't really have four seasons like other parts of the country. It seems it's summer and then it's winter, and then it's right back to summer all over again. And the winters, they don't last too long.

The way I woke up this mornin wasn't exactly what I had in mind. You see, today is Monday, September 15, 1930, the first day of the school year. My best friend, Sav, had showed up before hardly anybody else in the neighborhood was even awake. I can't quite make out why Sav always gets so jumpy about the first day of school, but he has every year since I've known him and that's all my life. Sav's family lives right behind our house. Momma says we been best friends ever since before either of us could talk. I can't picture Sav not yappin, bein that he's always got somethin to say about anything you could mention. He was excited about school startin today, but once he gets that first day behind him I can guarantee you he'll be all wore out from studyin and will go to sayin how he's ready for summer vacation to hurry up an get here again. There's a lot about Sav that don't make no sense and his goin on about the first day of school is one of them. He's my best friend anyhow.

I was layin there on the glider couch dreamin about somethin good. I never was good at rememberin dreams, but I do recall that I was havin a good time in my sleep. That danged Sav woke me up by stickin my hand down in a pail of water. I opened my eyes and there he was standin over me, grinnin like he was expectin somethin to happen. Sav is tall and skinny, so you can imagine what that grin of his looked like by the time my sleepy eyes looked all the way up his long body to his face. He looked right boneheaded from where I laid on the glider. Sav's got these great big eyes that kinda bug out, which doesn't do much to make him look any smarter.

"What in the world are you doin here, Sav? Why is my hand down in that bucket? What time is it?"

"It's almost six o'clock. Did I get ya?" When Sav talks he has this little-boy sound in his voice. It's right funny soundin when you think on it. Here's this long tall water drink of a boy who already has to shave once every five days or so, and his voice is still hangin around with the junior high boys.

"Did you get me what?"

"You know, your hand being in the water. You gotta go to the bathroom real bad?"

"What kinda craziness you talkin about, Sav? I don't have to go to the bathroom any worse than I do every mornin when I wake up."

"Shoot! I'd heard that if you stick someone's hand in water while they was asleep, it would make them need to go real bad and they'd wet the bed. Stand up an lemme look."

That Sav has a brain about the size of a nickel. That's probably about all he paid for it, too. It's a pretty sure bet he was born without one. He loves to play practical jokes on people, especially if he thinks the joke is original. "I'm not ready to get up. Come get me in an hour. Why are you so early anyhow?"

"Today's the first day of school, Leroy! Come on an get up. Let's get there early."

By then it was plenty evident that I wouldn't be goin back to sleep. Sav wasn't gonna let me. He felt like if he was excited then I ought to be, too. But I wasn't. Oh, I was glad enough to get to see some folks I hadn't seen since last June, and I was glad to be in the tenth grade. That made me just a notch closer to finishin school for good. I sat up on the edge of the glider, but I wasn't in the hurry Sav was in.

"Lemme at least get dressed and get somethin to eat. You eat yet?"

"No. I just got up and come over here."

Sav's momma an daddy would know where he was. They was probably glad to be shed of him this mornin knowin how he was on this day every year. I told him why didn't he come on in an eat breakfast with me. Actually, I didn't need to give him no invite. He was already headed for the kitchen to talk to Momma.

We got to school a good half hour before we needed to be there. Cassville High School is just a few blocks from where we live. It's this big three-story building with pretty grounds around it. Fills up the whole block it sets on. In the yard where everybody gathers before school starts, there's a bunch of large red oak trees. I doubt that anybody else really takes much notice to those trees, but I do. To tell you the truth, my favorite part of the school day is when I walk up the street and can look at the red oaks that dot the school grounds. We hung around under them oak trees with a bunch of other fellas until the bell called us in to start the year. Sav practically ran through everybody to get inside the buildin. I don't quite understand that boy.

Sure enough, Sav was just like I had thought he'd be by the end of the day. When I met him after school under the red oak tree that us boys claim as our own, I asked him how did he like the first day of the tenth grade. Thought I'd see if he was feelin about the same as I was about geometry and all. He didn't show too much enthusiasm and in fact showed just the opposite. I know I was just eggin him on by askin him to give me all the details about his classes, but I enjoyed seein him act so droopy after bein so excitable that mornin. Seemed pretty fair to me seein as he woke me up so early this mornin. Normally I treat Sav like he's my brother, but today I figured I'd help him roll around in his misery a little bit. He said that about all he was excited about now was goin to bed early tonight and sleepin until the last minute tomorrow mornin. Now that's the Sav I know.

Momma had been pressin me to go get my hair cut for a week before school started as if she thought I might make a good impression on my teachers just cause my ears had been lowered a little, so to speak. I never had gotten around to it, but this mornin Daddy said real firm like that I had better not walk in the house this evenin without a little less weight on my head. I didn't have to ask twice what he meant. Daddy isn't the type to argue with about anything. I didn't really mind havin my hair cut, but I sure did mind doin it just cause my daddy said so. Least thing he could've done was to tell me in a nicer tone of voice. Daddy generally has two ways of talkin to folks—gruff or not at all. He's hard on me due to my bein a boy. Not that he needs no excuse, but that's the one he gives. He's also plenty hard on Momma and Cody Sue, my twelve-year-old sister. I've never heard him say what was his excuse for treatin them rough, but I expect it has somethin to do with them bein female.

Here I am lettin my mind get sidetracked on thinkin about Daddy and his ways. That generally puts me to poutin and I don't like to do that to myself. Besides I had done had me a pretty good day, and I was havin too much fun ribbin Sav about him bein blue at the prospect of another whole year of school. Sav decided he had better things to do than sit around down at the barber shop waitin on me to get my ears lowered, so he said see you after awhile, and I went on by myself. The barber shop is downtown on Jefferson Avenue, just five blocks from school, so I was there in a few minutes.

As I walked in, Wimp Dickerson, the barber who owns the shop, greeted me the way he greets everybody who walks through his doors. "Howdy, pal." Everybody is his pal. I like goin into Wimp Dickerson's Barber Shop on account of the way he can make you feel good about doin somethin your daddy was makin you do. Wimp's friendly ways is probably his strongest sellin card to gettin people to come to his shop.

The thing I like most about comin to the barber shop, though, is that Woody Woodrow works there. He's a colored man who shines shoes and sweeps the hair up from the floor. Woody and I have been fast friends since I was a little boy. There isn't anyone I know who is as wise about life and the ways of the world as him. He's the one person I've always gone to when I need advice. I ain't able to go to my daddy for direction like some boys, but I'm lucky to have Woody.

You look at him and he ain't all that impressive lookin. It's right hard for me to tell how old he is, but I've heard him say he came into this world not too long after the Civil War. The reason I remember that is that he's told me before how his daddy used to tell him to be proud that he was born free. His hair is short and thin and is almost all gray with maybe just a little bitty bit of black still showin. He moves all slow like an old man would. You can tell he did his share of hard work when he was younger because the muscles in his arms are still real wiry. I wouldn't call him skinny, but he isn't too filled out neither. I like that word wiry to tell how he looks.

I got Woody to talkin one time about when he was a boy, and he told me how he could tote as much cotton as the big boys before he was even twelve years old. I bet he was tellin the truth, too. Woody probably isn't all that strong now that he's all old, but I bet he was a real worker when he was young. I used to think he was taller than he seems to be now, but I reckon he stands near six foot. Maybe it was on account of how I've been lookin up to him for all these years that I used to think of him as bein closer to ten foot tall. When you admire someone as much as I do Woody, somehow that makes him look grander than he really is. As I always do when I go into the barber shop, I walked down to the end of the row of chairs and took my seat next to where Woody keeps his things.

"Hey dare, Mista Leroy. How you gittin along today?"

"Hey there, Woody. I'm doin pretty good. How about you?"

"Fine, jes fine." You know, it's common for folks to say they're doin fine when they're asked how they been doin. Some folks just say that outta habit when they really don't feel so good. But the way Woody says he feels fine, it's easy to believe him. That's one thing I like most about that man. You can always count on him bein satisfied with the way things is. I reckon if Woody didn't feel too good and I asked him how you doin he'd say not so good. But I've never known him to be nothing but on the optimistic side.

"You go ta school today, Leroy?"

"Yeah, I did. Sure was a long day."

Woody laughed when I said that. I like the tone of his laugh. It says he knows just how I feel about havin to start another school year. "I bet it sho is hard to git back in de swing o goin ta school, ain't it?"

I kinda smiled. "It sure is."

There was probably six or eight men sittin around the barber shop although only two or three was waitin to get their hair cut. Wimp's shop is where a lot of men come to find out what has been happenin around town recently. That plus the fact that times is hard for a lot of folks these days, and it feels good to get together with other folks who are strugglin same as you so you can share your worries. Nobody would admit to that bein the main reason they come to the barber shop, but it's sure one of them.

One of the men was leadin out in a discussion about whether or not football games should be played at night under lights. The big local news is that Cassville High School would play night football for the first time ever this comin Friday at the Cotton Palace grounds. You've got to understand that people in Cassville take high school football serious. Too serious. Local folks claim that Cassville High has the best football record over about the last ten years of any high school in the whole country. I don't know who keeps track of that sort of thing, but football records and kickoff times is important to them men sittin in Wimp's place. One of the men was complainin loud. "Football just ain't football if it ain't played in the afternoon! What're they tryin to do, make it into some kinda entertainment? It just ain't gonna be the same."

A couple chairs down from him, two men was discussin somethin more serious. Least what they were talkin about seemed more serious to me than football games bein played at night. This old man named Mr. Jacobs had a stern look slammed on his face as he said, "I hear there's a real close judge's race goin on down in Birmingham. This here judge has been grantin divorces right and left to anybody what wants one. A person don't even have to prove they's a reason to get one, as if what the Bible says ain't important. They's this other fella runnin against him who wants to put some respect fer what's right back in the courtroom. I tell you, it makes me pretty doggone worried about the direction of civilization when I hear about things like free divorce an such." The man he was talkin to was just noddin away. You never know if a man is noddin like that because he agrees or if he's noddin to keep out of an argument he don't want to jump into.

Wimp was carryin on to the man in his chair about whether or not women should wear girdles. It's a wonder he ever finishes cuttin anybody's hair the way he always stops to make a point about somethin. Said he'd read in the paper somethin about how girdles is bad for a woman's health. Wimp figured that meant a woman who wore a girdle just to look thinner was squeezin somethin she shouldn't and that it could interfere with her ability to carry out her womanly obligation to bear children for her husband. I didn't quite know what to think about his argument, but I do think that women wearin girdles is goin a step too far. I know of one particular fat woman who tried wearin a girdle that was so tight on her she could hardly breathe nor walk. To make matters worse, what was pushed back in the front of her stuck out in the rear. She still looked like a load when she walked, girdle or not.

Wimp finally got around to cuttin my hair. I didn't mind the wait because I didn't have much else to do, but I wanted to go outside, bein that Woody had walked out there to set on the bench. There was somethin I wanted to talk to him about. After Wimp had got finished and splashed me with that perfumy-smellin tonic, I made my way to the bench in front of the shop and found my friend.

"Whoo, lemme takes a look at you. You sho looks right smart, Mista Leroy! Smells good, too."

I didn't really like havin that sweet-smellin stuff put on me. I don't want to insult Wimp by askin him to leave it off of me, though, so I always come out of the barber shop feelin kinda sissy like. I complained to Woody, "That stuff stings when he puts it on. Stinks, too. I don't know why he does that."

"Well Leroy, ya see, when you goes outta here an walks around town, people can smell you comin an dey's s'posed to think, 'Say, I needs to go git me a haircut jes like dat dare good-lookin fella.' Ya see, you's a walkin advertisement fo dis here barber shop." Woody grinned when he said that. He knew I felt funny, but him takin the edge off my feelins made me look at the situation different. I guess I don't mind doin a little advertisin for ol Wimp. I don't have nothin against that.

I sat down next to Woody on the sidewalk bench and was quiet for a minute. But then I brought up what I wanted to talk about. "Say, Woody, I wanna tell you about somethin."

"Dat's good. Go 'head."

"You see, there's this girl at school named Alane Sharpe who's real nice." I stopped there because I didn't know what to say next. Woody probably knew what I needed to say, but could tell I was havin a hard time findin the right words.

"You mean she a girl you'd kinda likes ta know better." That was exactly what I had wanted to say.

"Yeah, I would. I been knowin her a good while seein that we've been in school together all these years, but for some reason I've got this hankerin to get to know her in maybe a different kind of way." Woody nodded his head like he knew exactly what I was gettin at. "But I don't really know how to do it. You see her family's, well, different than mine. She's from this nice family and mine, well, you know how mine is." I stumbled in embarrassment over my words.

Woody knew my family real well. He knew about my daddy drinkin too much an my momma bein too tolerant of his ways. He was plenty aware that it was like I had a hole in my heart on account of not havin much in the way of happy family relations. You see, him and his daddy worked in the cotton fields for my Granddaddy Guillebeau just south of town back in the late 1800s. My momma's daddy was what folks called a dirt farmer, meanin he wasn't worth much more than the dirt his farm sat on. At harvest time, he hired colored folks to pick cotton for him and Woody's family was some of them. My granddaddy give up farmin a long time ago an moved into town. I believe Woody's family had moved to town a long time ago, too. Although I don't rightly know all the history, I know Woody had known my family since way before I came along. Like he always said, "I knowed you befo you knowed yo'self." So he knew what I was tryin to say when I said that about my family.

"It's kinda hard knowin jes how ta talk to a girl dat's higher up dan you, ain't it, Leroy?"

"It is. But you see, that's just my problem. Even though she knows she's better off than I am, she don't seem to hold it against me. She acts real kindly to me. Always has."

"An now dat you's gettin a little older, you'd like ta pursue things a tad further, huh?"

"Well, I'm not real sure. You see, I'm not so interested in romancin her just yet as I am in gettin to know if I'd like to romance her. That make any sense, Woody?"

"Yeah suh, it do. You's gots some powerful thinkin ta do ta decide how ta handle dat situation."

Woody was right. I did need to mull over my thoughts. I didn't want to make a dang fool of myself chasin after a girl who was higher up than me, but I didn't want to pass up on a girl I might like just because I didn't think I was good enough.

"Thanks for listenin to me, Woody. I'm gonna keep thinkin, just like you said." I got up to leave, seein it was gettin near suppertime.

Before I could get down the sidewalk, Woody called me back to him. "Say Mista Leroy, lemme ast you somethin. How old is you gettin to be now?"

"I'm fifteen. Be sixteen next June."

"You's gettin to be near an adult, ain't you?"

I grinned at the prospect. "It won't be long."

"Well, Mista Leroy, you's old enough ta start figurin things out jes like I tries to, I expect." Then he grinned at me, assumin I knowed what he was talkin about. I did.

As I turned around to leave, I called out, "See ya later, Woody." I looked back at him, and he was still grinnin. He just nodded his head at me as if to say, "You's not a boy no mo. You's becomin a man an I sees it in you."

It's them little things in life that gives you the biggest lift. It wasn't such a big thing for Woody to have said that about me, but then again it was. He's a man who I admire as much as I do anyone, even though it ain't common for a white boy and a colored man to get along like we do. He knows I judge him different than other people do, and I think he appreciates that about me. I want to be above some of the hate that you see between whites and coloreds. I know that by suggestin I could think like an adult, he'd just raised me up a notch higher than I had been before I come into the barber shop. From that day on, he wasn't just an old man I looked to for direction. I felt like we was more than just friends. We was equals. I liked that. Liked it a lot.

As I walked home, I kept thinkin about what I had told Woody about Alane Sharpe. The more I thought about it, the more I figured it sure wouldn't hurt for me to explore the possibilities with her. It didn't take just a whole lot of thinkin for me to make up my mind that I was goin to look her up tomorrow at school and see would she let me call on her sometime soon.

Chapter 2

I WOKE up at the regular time the next mornin and got myself ready for school. Sav didn't come lookin for me before daybreak like he had yesterday. Momma and Daddy had got up early, like usual. Generally, they do the same ol thing every mornin. Momma fixes Daddy a cup of coffee, the strong type, and Daddy sits there at the kitchen table like a knot on a log just waitin to be served his drink. They don't never say good mornin to each other and hardly ever talk to each other. That's the way it's been for as long as I can remember it.

This mornin things was a little different. My bedroom ain't but just around the corner from the kitchen so it caught my ear when I heard them talkin. At first I didn't pay no mind to it, but when it kept goin on I couldn't help but take notice. I heard Daddy sayin somethin about his work and Momma sayin somethin back to him. I figured that what they were talkin about musta been important, so I listened in despite I know it wasn't my business. Daddy was talkin in this low voice like he didn't care if Momma could hear him or not. "It ain't yore place to be worryin about the bills, Momma. I'll take care of that part of runnin things around here."

Now it's not all that uncommon for a husband to tell a wife that she don't need to worry none about the bills gettin paid. The way I see it, there's two ways a man can say somethin like that. He can say it in a way that suggests that he's right grateful to his wife for bein concerned about things, but he doesn't want his precious love to go worryin about somethin that he's gonna take care of. Or, he can say it a way that suggests that it ain't none of her dern business where all the money's gonna come from to pay all the bills, so just hush up about it. It was the second way that my daddy was talkin to my momma and not the first. You know what they say about the temperature gettin real cold in the Bad Place before somethin chancy is likely to happen. Well, that's about how likely it is that

Daddy's gonna talk real nice to Momma about money, or anything else for that matter.

The thing that grabbed my ear wasn't that Daddy was grumblin to Momma. That happened plenty. The odd thing was that Momma talked back to him. I don't mean she was bein sassy to him. It's just that instead of hushin up like she usually does, she kept on tellin Daddy just how worried she was.

I could hear her say, "Ira, I'm afraid we're gonna get the lights cut off if'n we don't pay the electric bill in the next couple of days. And the children need new clothes for the new school year. And look at you. You need new clothes, too."

When Momma talks back to Daddy, that means she's powerful concerned about things. Generally, when Momma worries, which is all the time, she just keeps it to herself. But when she goes to talkin about how worried she is, especially to Daddy, that tells you that she's bothered somethin terrible. You've got to understand that Momma believes it's just not her place to be carryin the family's burdens. She believes that it's the man's job to provide for his family. I knew from listenin to them talk that somethin bad was wrong in this here house. It had to do with money and with the fact that Daddy don't hardly work none. It's hard to say exactly what was gonna happen, but I just know that if Momma was willin to talk back to Daddy, somethin was bad wrong.

I try to keep out of Momma and Daddy's business as much as I can. It ain't that hard to do, actually, seein that neither one of them ever lets me in on anything to do with family matters. I reckon that little conversation I overheard in the kitchen that mornin was another one of them things I didn't need to be thinkin about. I'd try to just forget about it and hope that the money problems would take care of themselves somehow. We've managed to get through bad times in the past, and I reckoned we would this time, too.

Before breakfast I went out into the backyard and just sat there tryin hard not to think on nothin that would get me worked up before school. I didn't want to start off right here on the second day of school daydreamin in my classes. That's one of the things my teachers complain about the most to me. They probably wouldn't understand if I told them the kind of burden I lived under at my house, but then again it isn't their job to go around frettin about me.

It was pretty warm that mornin, but it was that kind of pleasant warm that you wish you could feel year-round. My dog run up to me with a rubber ball in his mouth and wanted me to play catch with him. That was about the only thing that hound dog ever wanted to do. I took it from him and held it while he run off into the yard. He got all hunched down like he was ready to track down a fierce animal or somethin. That was his way of tellin me, "Okay Leroy, I'm ready for you to throw me the dang ball." I threw it real hard at him. It bounced right in front of him and he caught it on the short hop. That dog is good at playin catch and he knows it. I've never seen a mutt what could nab a ball like he can. Playin catch with that hound was as good a way as any to take my mind off of Momma and Daddy arguin.

My dog's name is Pancho. Actually he isn't my dog. He really belongs to my daddy. Three or four years back Cody Sue was about to die to have a pet, but Momma and Daddy weren't real keen on the idea. It wasn't that they didn't like dogs. They just said that they knew that if us young'uns had a dog, they'd likely end up havin to care for it all the time, and they didn't want to have to do that. Cody Sue said it wouldn't be thatta way, that she promised to do whatever it took to look after a pet. I suppose Momma and Daddy didn't really believe her because they never made any effort to get us a dog. As for me, I didn't really care one way or the other about havin a hound around the house. Oh, I like dogs all right, but I was pretty satisfied back then to play with my friend Sav's mutt.

You talk about good hound dogs, Sav has this dog named Fang. You'd think a mutt with that type of name might be on the mean side, but Fang is far from it. I believe you could take that dog to church and tell him to sit still in the seat next to you an he would behave himself just because he was told to. That's just the kind of dog he is. Fang's biggest thrill in life comes from chasin cars. When he was young, say two or three years old, he'd get right on the back tire of a passing car and bite at it like he had a yearnin to eat rubber for his supper. Did it all day long. I could get tired just watchin ol Fang chase cars. You had to marvel at the way he stuck with it.

One day Fang got a little too close to a potential victim and wound up rollin down the street. I wasn't there, but Sav said he thinks Fang hit his head on the curb. The old lady who was drivin the car thought she'd killed the dern dog. I've never seen a dog lie unconscious before, but Sav says the spill musta knocked Fang out. At first Sav cried because he thought the ol boy had went to that great doghouse in the sky. But just like he woke up from a dream in which he was fightin a pack of street dogs, Fang jumped up from the dead and started growlin and barkin somethin awful. Sav said it was spooky watchin him carry on like that. But after a few minutes he was himself again. Just like that.

Sav thinks God must favor dogs, and that's why he let the mutt have another chance. I'm sure God probably likes hound dogs as much as the next fella does, but I kinda doubt that he had anything to do with Fang gettin an extra wind. Despite what I believed about the whole ordeal, Sav put in fifty cents when the offering plate was passed in church the next Sunday. I didn't know Sav had any money at the time. He musta been savin some for a special occasion. I reckon God savin Fang was a pretty special matter to him. I know the preacher didn't turn away the money. You know how preachers are. They don't care if an offering is give out of the good of a man's heart or if it's give to say thanks for sparin my hound dog. It all spends just the same.

The way we got Pancho was that Cody Sue got tired of beggin Momma and Daddy to get us a dog. She took care of the problem herself by gettin Daddy a puppy for his birthday. The way she figured it, no self-respectin man could turn down a puppy that had been given to him for his birthday, not even Daddy. I could tell that Daddy knew he'd been duped when Cody Sue handed him the little hound dog and said happy birthday, but to his credit, he took the gift and didn't make Cody Sue take him back. You never know how Daddy's gonna handle them kind of surprises. He's liable to say, "Git that dang thing outta here. You know I don't want to be carin fer no dern hound dog in this here house." But he didn't. Cody Sue had done something I would've never done. I wouldn't have taken the chance of crossin Daddy the way she did. I might not of got away with it, being a boy and all.

Right from the start, Pancho was really Cody Sue's dog. She'd already named him and everything. At first I was right sure I wouldn't get too attached to Pancho, he was so shy and reserved. But he came out of his shell and grew on me, same as he did the rest of the family. After Pancho had been around a year or two, Daddy asked Cody Sue one day, "What'd you pay fer that hound dog, anyway?"

She said, "Why, I didn't pay nothin for him, Daddy. Mrs. Henry give him to me. She said she already had enough dogs around her place and would I like to take him." What Daddy said next was a grand compliment, even though some folks might not have looked at it that way. You gotta know that Daddy ain't the type to say nice things about just anything. He told Cody Sue, "Shoot, I'da give ten cent, maybe twenty-five fer him." From that day on, Pancho has been the whole family's dog, not just Cody Sue's. Daddy had given his blessin on him. Lookin back on all that makes me think that things could be pretty good around this here house if Daddy would just try all the time to be like he was to Cody Sue that day. There's somethin about Daddy that's a little hard for me to figure. He's rough in every way you can name, but he gives in pretty danged easy to Cody Sue in a way he won't do for nobody else, especially if it has to do with animals.

Cody Sue pressed her luck again a year or so after she got Pancho for Daddy. She wanted a cat in the worst way. Now havin a dog was one thing, but a cat was a different story altogether. Momma and Daddy objected to havin a dog mainly because they was afraid of havin to care for the thing. Turns out, me and Cody Sue did real good at lookin after Pancho, so he wasn't a burden on Momma and Daddy to have. That and the fact that he had some personality to him. Dogs are like that. They got personality just like real people. There's mean dogs and lazy dogs. Sissy dogs and smart dogs. Junior Speakman has the dumbest dog you ever laid eyes on. You can tell it just by lookin at him. But he has personality all the same.

Cats, though, are a different breed of animal. I'm not too sure what God had in mind when he made cats. Oh, they're pretty animals all right. But they missed out on personality. Maybe God was nappin when it came around to that part of creatin cats. But if that were so, that would mean God made a mistake and I don't think we should even suggest that. It must be that God intended for cats to go around with a blank stare on their faces all the time. Maybe he was just thinkin cats could just make the world look pretty, but didn't feel like requirin them to do anything that called for thinkin. Dogs can think. But I never known of a cat to think. It just don't seem to be in them.

Cody Sue won't admit it to this day, but I'm right certain that her and Darla Yarbrough came up with a plan to get Daddy to agree to lettin us have a cat. Darla's cat had had another litter of kittens. I never knew of a cat to be pregnant as much as hers. Seemed that Darla was all the time tryin to get rid of baby kittens. She had one more kitten to get rid of and knew how much Cody Sue loved animals. It didn't take much to talk Cody Sue into agreein to take it, if she could talk Daddy into it.

One Sunday afternoon Darla showed up at our house supposedly to ask if our family wanted to take her last kitten. That's the part where I think she and Cody Sue had been connivin. I think they had it all planned out where Cody Sue would answer the doorbell and then take the kitten into where Daddy was settin and ask could she keep it. I even think Cody Sue was fakin it when she started cryin because the kitten was so cute. She said she wasn't, but I never once believed her. Whether she was fakin or not, it worked. Daddy stumbled over his words for awhile, tryin to think of some reason why Cody Sue had to get that dang thing out of the house. But with Darla standin there and her daddy bein a deacon, Daddy didn't blow up like he could've. That dern Cody Sue had got away with another of her tricks. It makes me kinda mad how she can do those things and get by with it and I know I needn't even ask.

I don't think Momma cottoned to the cat being named Guillebeau. That was her maiden name. At least the animal was called Gilly for short, but I knew Momma didn't especially want a cat named after her family. For one thing, it means that when me and Cody Sue grow up, it was now for sure neither of us would give our children her maiden name as the child's middle name. I know I wouldn't want folks thinkin I had named my child after a cat. Cody Sue might not feel the same way as me, but surely whoever she marries will feel like I do.

I can get carried away pretty easy when I sit around with nothin to do. That's plain to see. After I had thrown Pancho the ball a few times, Momma called me in to eat some breakfast. One thing I can't do without is breakfast. I always eat plenty of it, too. Momma tells me I better slow down on my eatin else I'll get fat, but that sure hasn't happened to me yet. I wouldn't say I'm the tall type like Sav is. I reckon I'm on the medium side in height, but I have to admit I'm skinnier than I'd like to be. I used to be a little runt until I hit thirteen and started growin like a weed. Momma says she thinks I've grown eight or ten inches in the last two years. Folks tell me it won't be too much longer before I start fillin out. Maybe I will one of these days and when I do, I'll do what Momma says and not eat so much. But until that happens I got one thing to say, and that's pass the biscuits.

I got myself ready for school and went outside to walk to school with Sav. Funny how he sure wasn't in the big hurry today that he was yesterday. He had used up his enthusiasm for school all at one time. Today I was the one wantin to get on to school, not so much so's I could learn, but for other reasons. One reason was to take my mind off a Momma fussin at Daddy about payin bills. The other reason was a little more on the positive side.

I had English the last class period of the day. Alane Sharpe was in that class. Like I had told Woody, I had in mind that maybe me and her could get to be better friends this year. I practically ran to that class so I could be there in time to sit down in the desk next to her. I hadn't known yesterday that she was gonna be in that class, so I didn't have much of a chance to say more than hello to her. I acted real casual like when I walked up to the empty desk next to hers and kinda surprised like said, "Well what do you know, here's an empty seat. You mind if I sit next to you Alane?" She said she didn't so I took my place.

It's kinda hard for me to concentrate on English at the end of the day anyway, but it was made more difficult due to Alane sittin next to me. She was what I wanted to be concentratin on and not the teacher. I aimed to act like I was interested in what the teacher was sayin the same as Alane appeared to be, but I doubt that I come across as too convincin. Lookin over at her every now and then, I saw that she was writin down some of what the teacher were sayin. I figured I might as well do the same but it was hard for me to decide what was important enough to write down and what wasn't. I ended up doodlin on my paper just so I'd look like I was payin attention. I got to wonderin while I was doodlin about askin Alane after class could I come over to her house sometime soon. Just the thought of that made me right nervous.

Shortly before class was let out, Mrs. Lemming, the teacher, told us that we would have weekly vocabulary tests throughout the year so as to broaden our knowledge. That seemed fair enough. After all, that's what we was at school for. She passed out a list of words and told us these were goin to be the vocabulary words for the week. As she was passin out the papers, it hit me that I could ask Alane if she could help me study the vocabulary list this Saturday, what with her being a good student and me bein known to be on the lower end of the scale. Thatta way, I wouldn't face the pressure of havin to come across like I was tryin to court her and at the same time I might get some help on my English grade.

After class, I walked down the hallway with Alane, tryin to act like I had enjoyed the lecture we had just heard, despite I could remember very little of what the teacher had actually said. "What do you think about us havin to learn all them vocabulary words every week?" I asked

"I think it's a good idea."

"Yeah, so do I." I paused for just a moment and then like the thought had just hit me I said, "Say, I was thinkin, Alane. With you being so smart and all, you think you could help me out a little on this week's word list? You know, so I could get off to a good start?" I suppose other boys feel stripped bare the way I did right then when they ask a girl for the first time if she'd like to do somethin. It's like you've just taken the biggest gamble that could be took and you may come away a big loser. Whether you wanted it thatta way or not, your intentions had just been revealed.

"Why I'd be glad to, Leroy." Shoot! That was a lot less painful than I thought it would be. I said thanks, and then started off on my way. Alane called me back and asked, "When did you have in mind us studying?" I had forgot all about the details.

"Uh, how 'bout Saturday afternoon? That all right with you?"

"Saturday would be just fine. About one o'clock?"

"One o'clock would be dandy." Shoot, if she'd said six o'clock in the morning that would've been just fine, despite I wasn't ever in any hurry to get up before seven on Saturdays. Then it dawned on me that I didn't know where Alane lived. She used to live in town but about a couple years ago her family had moved out on the edge of town where some new houses had been built. "Uh, where's your house now, Alane?"

"Just go all the way out Stuart Avenue until it ends. I'm in the next to the last house."

Hurry up Saturday and get here.

Chapter 3

I T WAS a lot longer walk out to Alane Sharpe's house than I had
thought it would be. I didn't have much reason to walk to this edge
of town too often and had forgot how far Stuart Avenue went on.
Out where Alane lived there wasn't a whole lot of houses, but the ones
that was there were nice. It wasn't all that long ago that this area was
nothin but cotton fields, but the town is growin out this direction now,
so you know what that means about them cotton fields.

Alane's house was two story and had these plantationlike columns on
the front porch where there hung a swing. It stood up on this slight hill,
which made it seem bigger than it actually was. Even though it wasn't a
big house, it was plenty nice just the same. Sure beat that old run-down
place my family lives in. Walkin up the front walk I found myself hopin I
didn't smell too strong from the long hike out there. I was kinda nervous
as I rapped on the front door.

Mr. Sharpe answered my knock, it not bein proper for a nice girl to be
the one to show her guest into the house. She was supposed to be called
for.

"You must be Leroy Evans."

I said, "Yes, sir," and shook his hand. I was kinda surprised he knew
my name. After all, I probably wasn't the kind of fella he was used to seein
out here in the nice end of town. He made me feel comfortable, though,
by the way he smiled at me when he squeezed my hand, and I was
appreciative of that. I don't have hardly any experience callin on girls, bein
only fifteen years old, but I've been around enough fathers who didn't
have any manners to appreciate one who did. Maybe if I grow up to have
girls someday I'll understand why some men act the most unkind to boys
who have an interest in talkin to their daughter. Bein concerned about
your daughter's welfare is one thing, but bein downright rude is another.

That's the way a lot of men I know are. Mr. Sharpe didn't appear to be that type, and I was relieved.

"Uh, I come, I mean came, to do some studyin with Miss Alane." I tried not to act too ignorant, but it was kinda difficult. I'll be honest and say I was intimidated by Alane's father. He isn't that big a man, but he's the stout, stocky type. His black hair was just beginnin to show a little silver. It was slicked back without one single strand of it out of place. His lower lip stuck out like a bulldog's, which made a fella like me wonder if he was meaner actin than he had just sounded when we first spoke. He looked spiffy, even though he was just wearin Saturday pants and a plain white shirt with no tie.

Mr. Sharpe is a well-respected judge in town. No tellin how long he had gone to school learnin to be a judge, but you could tell by just lookin at him that he was an intelligent man. No doubt it was hard for him to look anything but smart. It was written all over him.

Unlike Mr. Sharpe, there's some men that can't make themselves look smart no matter how hard they try. They can put on nice clothes and shave and wash, but there's still a simple look about them that just won't go away. I had an uncle who died a pretty good while back, so it's okay for me to use him as an example. I recall him gettin fixed up to go to his wife's funeral. It was one of the few times he'd ever stepped inside a church in his life and to my recollection it was the only time since I'd been around that he'd been clean and in a suit. It didn't matter how long he had washed, or what kind of clothes he was wearin, or how good Wimp Dickerson tried to make his face and hair look, he had third-grade education written all over him. I didn't want to put on that appearance in front of the judge and hoped I came across as a decent young man.

"If you'll wait in the family room, I'll go upstairs and get Alane."

Mr. Sharpe ushered me to the back of the house to a comfortable lookin room. I'd never heard of a house that had what he called a family room. I liked the way he said that—family room. I guess he meant this was where the family got together and acted like they were glad they belonged to one another. The way he walked me into the room all polite like was sure a lot different than what my daddy would've done.

We don't have a family room in my house. Not that there isn't a place where all of us sit sometimes. It's just that we don't talk together as a family. Daddy sits in his chair most every night with a blank stare on his face and a bottle in his hand while the rest of us try to busy ourselves and pretend we're halfway satisfied with the way our life is. Daddy claims he hardly ever gets drunk, but he's one of them men who has alcohol in his stomach so much of the time that I doubt he really knows what bein completely sober is like. Boy, he'd be mad if he knew I was thinkin this way about him right now.

All around the walls in the Sharpe's family room was pictures of what I would assume was family members. They was old photographs and right interestin lookin, too. I wondered if Alane knew who all those folks were. Surely she did. I don't know a whole lot about my family history except that Momma and Daddy claim there isn't much to tell. I hoped Alane wouldn't mind my askin her about her family when she came downstairs. I was already curious about all of them pictures.

"Hello, Leroy. You doing all right today? You must have had a long walk out here."

I hadn't heard Alane walk in. She's like her daddy in that she doesn't have to do much to look like she has a place in the world. She doesn't look nothin like him, though. Where her daddy's the stout type, Alane's what I'd call sleek and slender. I heard a fella say that about his dog once. I'm not comparin Alane to a dog, I just like the way it sounds to call her sleek and slender. She was dressed right plain, it being Saturday, but she looked danged pretty all the same. Alane is one of them girls that would look nice wearin a tow sack. Along with that tall and slim build, she has dark skin that somehow looks smoother than what most folks has. Her hair is deep brown, almost like chocolate, same as her eyes. Usually her hair had some curl to it, but it was straight today, not that it took away from her looks. Maybe she has this same effect on other boys, but when she looked at me I had this feelin that she was lookin way down deep inside of me. It was like she already had that way of knowin how to look into a fella's heart even though she wasn't but fifteen years old. Then again, maybe it was just them unusually dark eyes of hers that made it seem that way. It was a little on the overwhelmin side, to tell the truth, to be in a room all by myself with her. I felt like I was out of place what with me bein simple and her not. I tried to act as normal as I could, despite I had a right good case of the jitters.

"Hey, Alane. I'm doin fine. I was just admirin the photographs you got hung here in this family room. That's what your daddy called this place when he brung me in here to wait. I like the way y'all named this a family room."

Alane seemed right proud to tell me about her house. "It kinda fits the way we use it. Daddy gives me credit for calling it that. He calls the room right behind you the blue room," she said pointin to a doorway by where I stood, "because it's painted blue." She kinda laughed when she said that, as if she thought it sounded odd. "Daddy likes to use that for a reading room and study. He keeps his desk in there. The room where you came in the front door is the front room, but normally we just use it when we have company. We spend most of our time in here." She seemed pleased that I was interested in her house. I was, but I was just as interested in seein how her family lived as compared to my own. This house had comfort written all over it in a way that mine didn't.

I hope I didn't come across to Alane as bein in a daze, but all I could think to do was nod my head while I was thinkin on her home. Kinda sudden like I realized my mouth had dropped open just as wide as you please. That embarrassed me. Hopin she'd oblige me, I asked Alane, "Uh, would you mind tellin me a little bit about who these people are hangin on the walls?"

She chuckled about me sayin that her family was hangin on the walls, but I could tell she liked my request. "Over on this wall are pictures of my father's family. This is Daddy when he was a boy, and these photographs are of his mother and father and his two sisters. Then right next to them is a picture of Daddy's grandparents. I never knew them." Walkin across the room she continued, "And over here are pictures of my mother's side of the family. This is my mother with all eight of her brothers and sisters. She says it's the only photograph she knows of with all the brothers and sisters together. She's real proud of it." And as if it wasn't already in her voice she added quietly, "I'm real proud of it, too." She then proceeded to show off the photographs of other members of her mother's family. I didn't know nothin at all about Alane's family history, but I could tell she had come from good stock. She knew it, too, but not in a proud sort of way. There was an appreciation in her voice when she showed me her family photographs, like she realized that her way in life had been helped along by them what had come along before her.

I walked around the room for a few minutes just lookin at Alane's family. No wonder they called this a family room. In a lotta ways there was somethin about it where you could tell it pulled the family together. I thought to myself while I was standin there that this is what my family needed—a family room. That wasn't likely to happen, though.

Alane suggested we go outside to study vocabulary words since it was a nice day. I probably looked startled when she said that since my mind was on a lot of things other than studyin. I tried not to look too taken aback, though, and said that would be nice. I had plumb forgot that I had come to study vocabulary words with her. That was probably evident by the fact that I hadn't even thought to bring any school papers or books or anything else related to school. I wondered to myself if Alane was the kind of girl who would've been studyin anyway on a Saturday just because she wanted to learn all she could. I know I sure had never studied on a

Saturday. Not that I wasn't interested in learnin anything, it's just that school and readin and such never was my favorite thing to be doin, especially on my own time.

We went out the front door and across the street where a red oak tree towered over an empty field. There's lots of kinds of oak trees, but the red oak is my favorite. They're slow growin trees and can be real big around once they're full grown. I have to admire anything that's patient enough to do what's required to become great, even if it's just a tree. I commented to Alane on how pretty this red oak was and it was quickly evident she liked trees, too. She asked me, "Have you ever been out to Fish Pond and seen that huge live oak out there? It's the prettiest one I've ever seen. It would take several people joining hands to reach around its base."

I knew pretty much where Fish Pond was. It was out north of town by Lake Cassville. I'd been to the lake a bunch of times but didn't remember if I'd ever actually seen Fish Pond before. It was owned by a private fishin club and I wasn't the type who would go to a place like that. I kinda lame said, "Oh yeah, I think I know the tree you're talkin about," but I didn't.

Alane was kind enough to change the subject. Said we'd better start studyin our vocabulary words if we was going to learn them before the test next week. She called out several of the words and gave me the definitions of the ones I didn't know, which was all of them. I hated comin across so sap-headed in front of her, but there wasn't much way I could avoid it unless we got off on to another subject entirely. I had to keep remindin myself it was my idea in the first place to be at Alane's house studyin. At the same time I was feelin bad for bein so pig ignorant, I was fussin at myself for not thinkin of a better excuse to come callin on her. Her callin words out to me just wasn't workin.

After tellin Alane I didn't know what an amendment was, I interrupted our studyin and said, "Say Alane, do you mind if I ask you a little bit more about your family? Them pictures in your family room was sure interestin." Knowin that in order for me to keep my honor undamaged we needed to change activities, and also because she enjoyed talkin about her family, she said why sure that would be all right.

"What would you like me to tell you?"

"Well, I was wonderin. Has your family been around this area a long time?"

She was real proud to say they had. "My Great-Granddaddy Sharpe came to this part of the country from Kentucky shortly after the Civil War. He had been a colonel in the Confederate Army and came down here because he had fallen in love with Alabama during the War. He wanted to help rebuild this land."

"You mean he didn't come out here like a lot of folks lookin for a chance to just get away from an awful life somewheres else?" Our history teacher, Miss Ferguson, had told us that was one of the big reasons a lot of newcomers had made their way down here in the first place. Time has a way of allowin you to assume people showed up here because they was aimin to help somebody out, when most often they were lookin for a way out of somethin else.

"I'm sure the Civil War had caused him to feel that he needed to look somewhere else to put down family roots, but from what I know, his intentions for coming here were good. His family was one of the first to call Cassville home, and I understand they were city leaders. After him, my granddaddy came along and ran a lumberyard. He felt it was real important to give what he could in the way of time and energy to Cassville. He wanted to do just as his daddy had done to make this town a nice place to raise a family. My daddy feels the same way. You know Cassville had a reputation before the turn of the century as a real rough place, not the kind of place you'd want to raise children. It used to be called 'Shotgun Junction' by people who had heard about it."

It seemed like I remembered hearin about that somewheres. I obviously wasn't up on Cassville history quite like Alane was. Then again, I'm right certain my family didn't have nothin to do with shapin Cassville into a decent kind of town. My family has been around this area for some time, too, but I don't know a whole lot about what all they did. I'm afraid if I asked, I'd find out it was my ancestors who were the rowdy ones that had gave Cassville a bad name decades ago.

"What about your mother's side of the family?" I asked. "They been here a long time, too?"

"There's an interesting story about my mother's side of the family and how they met my father's side. My Great-Granddaddy Sharpe became a surveyor and surveyed land here in this area. My Great-Granddaddy Lyons, the one on my mother's side, was a land buyer and sold lots to people as Cassville was growing and expanding, so naturally the two of them got to know one another. They hit it off real well and, as the story goes, Mr. Sharpe and Mr. Lyons hoped that their children would like one another well enough that they would one day become family. You see, both of my great-granddaddies had grand visions of Cassville being an upstanding town and thought it would be wonderful if their families could be joined in marriage somehow since both men thought so much alike.

"It never worked out for their offspring to marry, but after both Mr. Sharpe and Mr. Lyons died, their wish came true as my mother and father got married two generations later. So in a sense, both sides of my family are tied together through Cassville's history."

I clapped when Alane finished her story since it had such a happy endin. "Your family has really meant somethin around these parts, hasn't they?" Alane didn't answer with words, but the look on her face said they had and she was rightly proud to be a member of such a fine group of folks. You know, she has every reason to be snooty about her family, them bein almost a major part of local history and all, but that isn't her way. Pride is all right if it's held in check. I never cared for folks with swelled-up pride, but the kind Alane had was just about perfect. At least the way I saw it, it was.

"What about you, Leroy? Do you know much about your family history?"

I almost dropped my teeth when she asked that question. Inside my head I was shoutin, "Don't you know not to ask about my family? You don't want to embarrass me thatta way do you? Please, let's talk about somethin else!" I sat there pretendin that I was tryin to recall all the splendid details of my family history. Actually, I was tryin to think of what might be a lie I could say and she would believe it. Not that I believe lyin to somebody is somethin you ought to set out to do, but if I let on that my family was full of a bunch of drunks and scoundrels, it surely wouldn't do me no good in Alane's eyes.

"Well," I said kinda slow like, "I know both sides of my family has been in this area for probably about as long as your family. I don't remember exactly what trade they all were in. I do know that one of my granddaddies farmed cotton. You know, I bet some of your family and some of mine knew each other way back then. That's interestin to chew on, isn't it?" She said what a grand thought that was.

I was actually thinkin more along the lines that I hoped she didn't have a way of discoverin that her ancestors knew my ancestors due to my family havin done somethin like shoot at one of her family because my ancestor had been drinkin too much. I've thought before it would be fun to go back in the past and find out what all had went on way back when, but right now it seemed to be a good idea that the past was laid away in the grave and couldn't be called up again.

I was beginnin to feel the need to move on home and said so in a polite way to Alane. I may not have known a whole lot about what to do around girls, but I knew better than to stay around longer than I was wanted. I asked could I go back up to the house so I could tell her daddy good-bye. I think that won some favor with Alane as she said that would be really kind. I hadn't met Mrs. Sharpe when I first came to the house. Probably she was takin a nap or somethin at the time. She was sittin out on the front porch swing with Mr. Sharpe when we walked up to the house. All the proper introductions were made, and then I announced I needed to go on home. There was a strange feelin inside me that wanted to get to walkin.

All that talk about family was nice, but it sure made me feel edgy about my own family. I was really hurtin about my family. I hated that I had to hide behind a lie when it came to talkin about my momma and daddy to folks like Alane Sharpe who didn't know about them. Dad gum! It just wasn't right for a boy like me to have to go livin in all that shame.

Chapter 4

THE WALK back to my house was a long one, but that was all right by me. I had plenty to think about and needed the time to get it all done. I had meant to go to Alane's house to see if I would be interested in maybe gettin to know her better. Oh, I enjoyed bein around her, that's for sure, but I come away with more than just a feelin about Alane. I come away with strong feelins about *myself*. You see, all that talkin with Alane about her family hit me right hard about just what kind of family I have. I've known for a long time that my family isn't the type to go lovin on each other, but somehow hearin Alane talk about her family and her ancestors hit me hard about what I been missin. It ain't right that I gotta suffer for what my momma and daddy's folks done way before I even came along. But that's exactly what was happenin. I was sufferin. My visit to Alane's house had done proved it to me.

I was proud that Alane had a family room and nice parents and all. You could tell just by bein around her that it had done her lots of good to be raised in such a fine home. It's not that I hadn't been in homes before where people get along good with each other. Maybe it was on account of how I wasn't able to brag any on my family that made me feel more ashamed about them than I had before. Sav's family was plenty friendly to one another and it doesn't bother me to see them gettin along in a way my family doesn't. Sav's been around my family as long as he's been livin, though, so I don't feel so ashamed around him. But after visitin at Alane's house, I was hurtin in a way I hadn't hurt in a long time.

I had a hard time keepin from bein mad durin that walk home, but I have to admit that that's exactly what I was—mad. I was mad at my momma and daddy. It wasn't that they had done nothin bad to me on purpose. Maybe Daddy did, but not Momma. Here I'd been over to a nice girl's house and the main thing I had to trouble myself with was tryin not to come across as too ignorant. I can thank Momma and Daddy for never teachin me any better manners than I got. What I got, I mostly learned from watchin other folks. Alane didn't even have to try to come across all smart and ladylike. It was bred in her. Her family, all the way back to both her great-granddaddies, had given that to her. My family hadn't give me anything of the sort.

I probably sound like I'm feelin sorry for myself, which isn't what I'm meanin to do. But maybe I do feel sorry for myself. I mean, it sure wasn't my idea to be born into a family that don't even act like they give a hoot for one another. Alane has a lot of help to get through life while I don't have hardly any.

I went to thinkin about how Alane asked me to tell about my family. I don't suppose I'd had that particular request thrown at me before, least not by anybody that I cared what they thought about me. Most all the fellas I generally run around with knows not to ask about that. That, or else their family isn't any better off than mine so it's no news to hear about somethin they already know about. Or maybe they're like me and just stay away from the subject altogether just to keep from gettin embarrassed.

Let me tell you what I know about my family. My daddy is the one who runs things at our house. Even when he's not in the house, he runs things, if you can understand what I mean. You could pretty much say my whole family is scared of Daddy. It isn't the most fun thing in the world to have Daddy be mad at you. It isn't the hardest thing to do to make him mad neither. The first memory I have of Daddy is him whippin me. He called it a spankin, but that's not what I thought of it. From my angle it was a beatin. I can't even remember right now what I used to do that was so awful bad that required a whippin to get me to stop. Momma has always said I'm a good boy, but you wouldn't know it by takin count of the number of licks I've got in my life. I know that whippins are supposed to teach you to act better. As honest as I can be, I can say that whippins don't do nothin for me except make me feel things I don't like feelin, like hate and such.

People has asked me from time to time what my daddy does for a livin. Now this may sound funny, but I don't rightly know. He's been a lot of things in his life, like a carpenter and a field hand, and even a fertilizer salesman, but for the last year he's mostly been out of work. He leaves the house in the mornins and says he's goin to work, but none of us are too sure what he does all day. I think he has a friend who does odd jobs for people. If there's enough work for two, Daddy goes along with him. He's all the time complainin about money, tellin us to turn off the electricity and watch that we don't waste food and such. I don't mind doin them things, but the way I think Daddy looks at it is that if the bills ain't too high, he doesn't have to work much.

I've only seen my Grandmother and Granddaddy Evans a few times in my whole life. When Daddy gets drunk, which happens a whole lot more often than he would admit to, he sometimes talks about how him and his daddy used to fight. And I'm not talkin about just disagreein neither. Accordin to Daddy, they was real fist fights. I've learned a long time ago not to believe everything Daddy says, especially when he's drunk, but I've got to believe there's something to the stories my daddy tells about himself and his daddy. There's bad blood between them to this day. Despite my granddaddy and grandmother don't live but maybe ten miles out of Cassville, I don't hardly ever see them.

I take it my daddy was a rounder when he was younger, but from what I understand he just gets worse with age. Folks who've known my family for a long time seem to judge all of us on what my daddy and his daddy before that did when I wasn't even born yet. It's like me and Momma and Cody Sue are tainted. That's not right, but that's the way it is. I'm not the fightin type and I try to be as nice to folks as I can be, but some people don't know me as nothin but Ira Evans's boy. That's not somethin you can say and be real proud about. I don't mean to be rude by sayin all that, even though it sounds thatta way.

Daddy flat won't go to church. That bothers Momma a lot, despite she never comments on it. It seems that he's been to church with us a time or two, you know, for special occasions like Easter or Christmas. Momma's a Baptist. Has been all her life. It seems like most of Cassville is Baptist. Daddy says he's a Christian and he don't need to go to no church just to prove it, thank you. It doesn't take a strong brain to figure out that Daddy just uses any ol excuse he can find to not go to church. Maybe I ought to add that Daddy doesn't need much of an excuse for doin nothin with the family neither. I think that's one of the reasons he doesn't go to church. Since Momma takes me and Cody Sue with her, he gets to be all to himself. I like to be to myself so I can think, but Daddy he likes to be by himself just so he doesn't have to think. Also, it gives him time to drink. I can get myself worked up pretty quick like thinkin about Daddy and his ways.

I ought to say that I'm not the kind of boy who talks back to folks too much, especially not to Daddy. For one thing it wouldn't do much good. I do what I can to stay out of his way. It's just best to do it that way. I hate havin to avoid my own daddy, but life's just easier on me when I do. You know, I love my daddy just because he brought me into this world and all, but I've gotta wonder if he loves me back. He sure isn't one to show it if he does.

Momma's the quiet type who'd do anything she could to help out a neighbor. And to her a neighbor is anyone who needs helpin. Even if I strain my brain hard, I can't think of a time when she complained about the way our life is. That's not necessarily a compliment neither. You can see it in her face that she's not especially happy with the way things is, but she won't say it out loud, least not that I've ever heard. She's always workin on somethin whether it's housework or cookin or sewin. She generally has three or four projects goin on at once. I reckon the more she's got goin on, the less time there is to remind her how unhappy her life is.

One time Momma used the word sensitive to describe herself. I don't remember the occasion, but I recall her saying she was a sensitive person and her feelins get hurt easy so would I not do what I had done again. Her bein that way probably has a lot to do with her seemin to be unhappy all the time. Bein that her feelins get hurt all easy like, Daddy's ways keep her gut all twisted up. Funny thing, though, she never says nothin to him about how his drinkin or complainin bothers her.

Momma always has this look on her face that says she's tryin hard to make it just one more day in life, but she never actually comes out and says as much. She told me one time that she thinks I'm a lot like her. She says I worry and think about things too much, just like she does. To Momma it may be a burden to be a worrier and a thinker seein as how she's got no way out of bein married to Daddy. When she goes to thinkin about how our family is, it sets her to worryin and makes her drag her tail pretty low. I like bein a thinker, though. When I go to thinkin about our family, I can get upset like Momma does, but at the same time I'm always thinkin about how my life will be better when I'm an adult and on my own. I try not to worry about things, and I sure hope I don't do it as much as Momma does. Who knows, though, maybe she's right and I worry more than I'd like to admit.

Things are peculiar between Momma and Daddy. They never hug or act nice to each other. Actually, Momma acts pretty nice to Daddy, it's just that he doesn't act too nice back to her. Let's say if she were to make something for supper just because she knows it's one of Daddy's favorites, he doesn't even say thank you and she doesn't act like she expected it. Every now and then he wants Momma to fix chittlins, which is hog innards. They smell powerful bad. I know she hates cookin them because when she does she opens all the windows in the kitchen and closes the kitchen door to the rest of the house so it won't stink so bad afterward. Despite she hates chittlins herself and can't hardly stand the odor, she does it without complainin. Now that I'm gettin older, I find myself wonderin if that's what's called bein nice or bein scared. I feel guilty even thinkin bad about Momma since she'd do anythin at all for me, except maybe stand up to Daddy on my account.

I can't say I was havin fun ponderin all them things about my family while I was walkin back into downtown, but it did make the time pass quick. It was easy for me to go on by Wimp's Barber Shop before goin home, bein that Stuart Avenue went straight into town and was just one street over from Jefferson Avenue where the barber shop was. Feelin all blue and mad I thought it would do me good to go by and see Woody. That was one thing I could count on to perk me up.

I suppose I looked worse off than I thought. Woody was sittin out on the bench in front of the barber shop. Soon as he saw me walkin towards him, he stood up from the bench and walked my way, all slow and relaxed like he generally does.

"Hey dare, Mista Leroy. You sho looks glum. What you been doin dat's got you hangin yo lip so low ta da groun?"

"Hey there, Woody. Oh, I've been over to Alane Sharpe's house. The visit set me to thinkin while I was walkin back. I guess I been thinkin harder than I realized. I look that bad?"

"Let's jes say you looks like you's troubled. What happen at dat young lady's house, Leroy? She not cotton to ya?"

"No, it ain't that, Woody. She was real polite to me. It's just that her family is so nice. That's all." Me sayin that made Woody wrinkle up his face at me.

"You not makin jes a whole lotta sense, Mista Leroy. You's sayin dis here girl an her family be's real nice, but you looks bad. It don't fit." Woody figured he'd better give me time to collect my thoughts. He had a smile on his face to let me know it was all right to go ahead and say what was botherin me whenever I was ready to talk.

"Well, you see Woody, the whole way back here I've been thinkin on how her family is real special to each other and I don't have none of that at my house. It's bothersome."

"I see. An you's tryin ta figure how can you make it better at yo home."

"That's just it, Woody. I can't. What with my Daddy bein like he is an all, it seems there isn't much a boy like me can do to change things."

"Ya mean it's like you's doomed to be unhappy so long as you lives at home?"

I thought about that for a minute. "It seems thatta way." Now that was a depressin thought. I added, "But it's not gonna be thatta way when I leave home, Woody. I'm not gonna let my family be the way we are now when I marry and have kids."

Woody nodded his head as if he agreed with me. I think he also believed I could do what I said I would do to make my life better when I was older. "Shame it cain't be good now. It sho is a shame. You still gots plenty o time afore you leaves de home."

"Yeah, I sure do." I was thinkin it was gonna be forever before I got to try livin on my own and makin my own decisions. I don't think that's what Woody meant, though.

Woody wasn't satisfied to just let me be by myself with my thoughts. We sat down on the curb, and I could tell he was studyin how I musta been feelin right then and there. I can tell you it made me feel better just knowin that Woody was that interested in me. "Ya know, Leroy, maybe dey is sumthin you can do ta make things better at yo house. Maybe dey is."

"You think so? What you got in mind, Woody?" The way his voice sounded made it seem like he had some kinda plan. If he did, I wanted to know it.

"Cain't really say. But I figures you might find it if you keeps lookin fo it. It sho appears you wants ta do somethin ta make yo house a happier place. It jes ain't hit you yet what ta do."

Woody's words come to me as somethin of a surprise. Here he was tellin me that I might could find some way to make things better at my house. I couldn't figure out what he was gettin at. I asked him, "Woody, you got somethin in mind? Somethin I ain't thought up yet?"

"Not really, Mista Leroy. I guess you could say I jes has faith."

"In what?"

"Why, in you, Leroy. In you!"

One of the things about talkin to Woody was that he had a way of makin me look at things a whole different way. Here he was suggestin that I might could do somethin about the way my daddy and momma was. It was gonna take some time for me to figure that one out. I wasn't too sure I could do nothin to change our home, but Woody said he had faith in me. I liked that. Then, I liked most everything Woody said. It was always on the positive side.

About the time I was feelin more hopeful about things, this boy named Bruno Lynch come walkin up on the sidewalk behind where me and Woody was sittin. He passed gas loud enough to wake a person up from a dead sleep. "Sorry there, Leroy. I musta stepped on a big ol bullfrog." He kicked at me and added real smart aleck like, "Watch it! There he is. Don't let him jump on you!" I didn't laugh and neither did Woody. Bruno was a pretty disgustin person if you ask me. You could just look at him and tell he was that sort of fella. He was a big boy. Probably weighed over two hundred pounds. They ain't nothin wrong with bein a big boy, but Bruno was the kinda big that had lazy written all over him. He was even too lazy to pick up his feet all the way when he walked. He waddled along from one place to another instead of walkin like regular folks. And he always slumped his body down so his gut hung over his britches.

I'd known Bruno ever since the first grade. I didn't like him then and my feelins for him haven't changed much over the years, except maybe to become more convinced that he's as sorry as I've always thought he was. Bruno's real name is Donald. I don't know who named him Bruno, but the name seems to fit. He's always been the kind to pick on other folks, especially if he thinks they're the type to be easily bothered. Guess you could say he's the bully type. Even though he isn't but fifteen, same as me, he's been drivin cars around town for a good three years. I remember him bein the talk of junior high when he drove himself to school in his daddy's old truck. Course, he thought that drivin to school made him special. Like it made him better than others. I always looked at it like his momma and daddy either didn't care what he did or couldn't control him, one or the other.

"Why don't you just leave us alone, Bruno. Me and Woody was just sittin here havin a nice talk, and we don't especially want you around to ruin things like you always do. Why don't you go bother someone else?" I was mad at Bruno, but didn't want to let him go to puttin me in a bad mood.

"Well, excuse me," he said all sarcastic like. "I guess I better just git on along an leave you an yore nigger friend to yoreselves." With those crude words, Bruno waddled on down the sidewalk and left us alone.

I was embarrassed for Woody. Even though I knew he was used to hearin that word *nigger*, it made me ashamed for one of my own kind to say it, especially the way Bruno had just done. I was ashamed for the way some white folks treat the coloreds just because their skin is dark. I didn't want Woody to go to thinkin I was just like Bruno, or that all white folks think the same way he does. I didn't want Woody to think I have anythin besides respect for him, us bein friends and all.

"Sorry, Woody. I wish he hadn't said that."

Woody was real soft in the way he talked. "You gots no control over folks like dat dare boy, Mista Leroy." I know he didn't blame me, but I figure every time Woody or any other colored man heard the word *nigger* it had to do something to them on the inside.

"Woody, why do you think folks are like that?"

"Well, Leroy, de way I figures it, everybody likes ta be in control o sumthin, even if'n it's jes makin people mad."

"What're you talkin about, Woody?"

"What I means is dat everybody has dey own little piece o de world an dey likes to have some say in what happens in it. You take dat dare boy Bruno. He must figure dat de onliest way he can make hisself feel impotant is ta make other folks look unimpotant. Ya see what I mean, Leroy?"

"You mean he picks on people and calls them names because he wants to feel important?"

"Dat's how I sees it, Leroy. It don't make no sense, do it? But ya see, when you looks at it like dat, it keeps ya from gettin down on his level." Woody cocked his eye at me and came about as close as he ever comes to talkin bad about somebody else. "Ya know, Mista Leroy, dat dare Bruno ain't on too high a level." Then he laughed. His laugh wasn't the type that meant he held a grudge against anybody. Instead, it was the type that suggested he couldn't be hurt by the words of someone who thinks like Bruno. That made me feel a lot better. Woody bein hurt was about the last thing I wanted to see.

We had our little laugh and then sat there on the curb for a minute kinda quiet like. I got to thinkin about what Woody said about people likin to be in control of their part of the world. I'd never thought much about it, but I guess it was true. I wanted to know more about what he thought on that subject. I also wanted to change the subject from Bruno to something else.

"Woody, you know what you were sayin about people bein in control of their part of the world. You think I do that? I mean, you think I probably act that way with my family?"

"We all does, Leroy. Jes think 'bout it. All o us decides some o de time ta do things or not ta do things 'cause we wants ta have some say in what gonna happen next. You take de way you handles yo family. You makes some o de decisions you makes 'cause you hopes to make sumthin happen. Dat or you wants ta keep sumthin from happenin. One or de other."

We didn't say much else for the next little bit. Funny thing, when Bruno had showed up actin crude like he always does, my heart had sunk down some because I couldn't stand the sight of him. But if he hadn't showed up, I wouldn't have heard what Woody had to say about the way we all like to be in control of our little piece of the world. If he doesn't serve no other useful purpose, maybe Bruno stirs things up enough to make me think about things I wouldn't have thought about.

Woody got up to go back into the barber shop when Mr. Minniefield walked in. He was the kind who always liked to look nice and wore expensive shoes. Woody said it was back to work for him which meant he figured Mr. Minniefield would want his shoes shined. I had got what I needed from talkin to Woody. That man could sure set me to thinkin. I got to wonderin how I could go to controllin things better in my corner of the world

Chapter 5

EVERY FIRST Sunday in October, Johnston Avenue Baptist Church has what they call Homecoming Sunday. The idea is that everybody who used to be a part of the church but has moved away is given a special invite to come home, so to speak, for a visit. The part I like best about Homecoming Sunday is the dinner on the grounds that follows the church service. Right in front of where the chapel is there's a big yard where they set out this long row of tables filled with food that's been cooked up by the women of the church. Most everybody brings fried chicken along with their favorite vegetables and desserts. There's hardly ever anything on them tables that doesn't look good to me, except maybe the brussel sprouts from Mrs. Thigpen's garden that she brings every dad gum year. You'd think she'd quit bringin them since her dish is always left practically full. But she doesn't quit tryin to unload them. Maybe her husband makes her take a big bowlful so he can get shed of as many of them tasteless things as he can.

Even though I've never left Cassville and come back, I always feel somethin special about Homecoming Sunday. Could be that it reminds me that I do have some folks that I belong to, that bein my friends and all the old folks at the church. There's this old man at the church named Mr. Weatherly who's never had any kids, despite he really loves little children. I'm not saying this to brag, but I've been one of his favorites ever since I was a little boy. Even though I'm gettin on up pretty big now, Mr. Weatherly still takes a shine to me. I don't really know why he just asks this of me on Homecoming Sunday, but he expects me to come sit with him in his regular pew on that day. I used to like doin that when I was little because it made me feel important. I still do, but now I like it for a different reason. I enjoy sittin by Mr. Weatherly because of the good it does to him instead of just what I get out of it. That may sound a little on the gushy side, but that's how I feel.

The church service seems pretty long to me on any Sunday, but it seems to last about twice as long on Homecoming Sunday. About halfway through the sermon I start to thinkin about whether to pick out a chicken leg or a breast. I move on down the table in my mind and think of what kind of vegetable dishes I might pick out. I almost always get me some baked beans. I like the kind that have the juice baked out of them and are on the dry side. I figured that today I'd look to see if anybody brought some fried okra. You know, some days you just get a yearnin for certain foods, and today I was hankerin for some okra. I hoped I could get some black-eyed peas, too. That sounded good. Black-eyes is probably my favorite vegetable. Then there's dessert to think about. This lady named Mrs. Delaney always makes the best cherry pie you could eat so I figured I'd get a piece of that. You were supposed to wait until you finished your meal before you went to get your dessert, but I never did seein that I might have to settle for whatever was left over. It's probably a sin to be thatta way and I ought to be ashamed for it, but I'll have to be honest and say I never have felt much guilt about it.

The preacher finally got through sayin what was on his heart. Once the service was over, I said real polite like to Mr. Weatherly that I enjoyed sittin with him and Mrs. Weatherly and hoped to see them outside at the dinner on the grounds. I made my way to where Sav and another one of my friends, Ernie Chambers, was and told them come on let's go get up near the front of the line.

There's this certain big lady at our church named Mrs. Turnipseed who I think sits by the back door every Homecoming Sunday so she can beat all us boys to the servin table. If the truth was known, I think she slips on outside when the preacher asks the ladies who was goin to be hostesses to go on out and get things ready. Lord knows nobody has ever seen Mrs. Turnipseed offer to work. I don't think she even cares that folks think she's lazy. When us fellas got to the table, she was already at the front of the line ready for somebody to say the blessin so she could commence to eatin.

"Howdy, Mrs. Turnipseed. You look real nice today," said Ernie real polite as if he meant it, which he didn't. Me and Sav wanted to urp when he said that to her.

"Why thank ya. Y'all boys as hungry as I am?" I can't say that this is what she meant, but I would swear by the way she said her words that she was challengin us boys to a duel to see who could eat the most food, her or us three fellas. Let me tell you, she'd have won if we'd had that kind of contest. Boy could that lady eat. And it didn't matter to her who saw her neither. There was this one time at Sunday night church when Mrs. Turnipseed pulled a fried chicken leg out of her purse durin the sermon and chewed on it while the preacher preached. She claimed the doctor told her it was a good idea for her to keep somethin on her stomach. By her own report, she is said to have a sensitive stomach or somethin like that. At least havin chicken to gnaw on kept her from sleepin through the sermon that night like she usually did.

There was this other time when Mrs. Turnipseed was at the church for a meal when she leaned over and asked this other lady, "Honey, would you pass me that extry cherry cobbler down there?" Now you're not gonna believe the reason she gave for askin for that cobbler. She said, "My doctor says I need to eat more fruit." And she said it without even flinchin! I suppose she thought everybody would agree with her that whether she ate cherry cobbler or fruit straight from the farmer's market, her doctor would be proud that she followed his instructions.

Just after grace was said over the food which we was about to partake, Bruno Lynch joined us boys in line. Actually to say that he joined us ain't exactly accurate because that would suggest we wanted him around, which wasn't the case. He butted in line is what he did. He just walked up and said, "Hey fellas, get outta my way. I'm hungry." There was somethin about dinner on the grounds that seemed to bring out the worst manners in some folks, meanin Bruno, of course. I said so to Sav, and he reminded me that Bruno didn't have any manners except the bad type. Boy, Sav was right on that one.

We all tried to ignore big Bruno as best we could. That boy sure could make me mad. He finally got far enough ahead of us in line so he couldn't hear us talkin about him. I turned around to Sav and Ernie and asked them, "Why does Bruno even bother to come to church? It sure don't do him no good."

Ernie said somethin I hadn't thought of, but he was probably right. "Maybe he comes so's he can learn what's a sin and what's not. That way he can know if he's breakin as many rules as he can." We all laughed when he said that. But, you know, sometimes I have to believe that maybe that's why some folks come to church. There's people like Bruno who come to church and still don't act no better. Not that you're supposed to go just to learn a bunch of rules, but you'd think you'd learn a few anyway. Bruno didn't seem to. Or at least you couldn't tell it by the way he acted.

We got our plates filled up and went and sat up against the chapel buildin so we could sit in the shade. It could still be pretty warm out in the sun, even in October. Once we were finished eatin, Sav told me and

Ernie to look at what he had. He pulled a sack full of balloons outta his pants pocket and said real sly like, "I brought these so we could liven up this place." What he had in mind was us fillin them balloons with water and throwin them at whoever looked like a good target. Sav was always thinkin of what to do to get a good laugh. As if he was lettin us in on his battle plan, he added, "I got this here idea. We could go around to the back of the church and get up on the roof of the chapel. That way we could hide and people couldn't see us. Then we could toss these little bombs down in the crowd and watch what happens." It didn't take a whole lot to talk me and Ernie into goin along with his plan. In fact, I think Ernie was a little jealous he hadn't thought of it first.

We went next door to the church to the McQueen's house to borrow their ladder and water faucet and then filled as many balloons as we could carry. In order to have a bunch of bombs, we each pulled out our shirttails so we could use them to carry our load. Goin around to the back of the church, we climbed up to the roof of the chapel. Ernie went up the ladder first. If you've ever tried climbin a ladder while holdin a dozen or so balloons in your shirttail, you can appreciate how hard it is to manage. Ernie handled the job pretty good, although he did let one drop accidentally on Sav's head just as Sav was about to follow him up the ladder. Sav yelled, half laughin, at Ernie and accused him of doin that on purpose. Now I'm not takin up for Ernie and sayin he's not the type who would do somethin like that, but I know he didn't drop that bomb on purpose. He looked at it as wastin a perfectly good balloon that coulda been used on a girl or something.

While Sav was carryin himself up the roof on his knees, he fell forward and lost all of his balloons. And I mean every blessed one of em, too. Several of them busted on him and the rest rolled off the roof and busted on the ground. You can imagine how that perturbed him. "Dad gum! Hey Leroy, lemme have some of your balloons."

When me and Ernie saw what had done happened to Sav, we just about lost our balloons on account of laughin so hard. Here we were gonna use these bombs to soak some other people and Sav looked like he'd just been baptized, he was so wet. And I'm talkin about the Baptist kind of dunkin baptism, not the Methodist sprinklin type.

"Shut up, Sav! You want everybody to know we're up here? That's what you get when you get greedy and try to load up with too many balloons. We told you you had too many, but you wouldn't believe us, would you?" I was fussin at Sav, but he knew I was just kiddin around.

"Hey, I'm the one who brought these balloons in the first place. Y'all gimme a couple of yours." We did.

It's funny how people on the ground don't bother to look up, but even if they had, we were able to hide on the back side of the roof. We had the steeple to hide behind, too. We looked around to see who would make a good target to throw at. We figured it wouldn't be such a good idea to toss our bombs at a bunch of adults. They wouldn't think it was too funny to get splattered with a water balloon.

"Where's Bruno? I'd love to throw one at him." Ernie was saying what the other two of us was thinkin. We looked around and spotted Bruno standin over the dessert table right next to Mrs. Turnipseed. Neither one was payin attention to the other, but both of them was standin there eatin whatever looked good to them, which was just about everything.

Sav said, "Looks like a couple o pigs at the feedin trough." We figured it wouldn't be too smart to throw that near the table. Might get the food all wet.

"Where's a bunch of girls?" I asked. Off to themselves was a group of girls, includin my sister Cody Sue. They were just sittin there eatin real quiet like and talkin. I don't understand what it is about girls, but they sure do live a borin life. I couldn't just sit around talkin and gigglin. It's a lot more fun to be doin somethin. Maybe it was because I was layin up on top of the chapel so close to the steeple or somethin, but I had this urge to say a prayer right then and there and thank God I was a boy and not a girl.

I said to Sav, "Look over there. You think you can hit that bunch of girls?"

"I don't know. They may be too far off."

Ernie apparently didn't care to talk about whether the girls was too far off or not. Without sayin nothin, he just stood up and heaved a bomb as far as he could in their direction. It splattered right in the middle of them and sent girls runnin and screamin in every direction. As soon as he threw it, Ernie jumped back down on the rooftop so we wouldn't be seen. Of course, we were hee-hawin pretty hard and congratulatin Ernie for such a fine performance. It's pretty hard to laugh without makin much noise, but we tried to be as quiet as we could.

I crawled over to one side of the steeple so I could look around it. When I stood up to take a peek, Cody Sue spotted me and pointed right at me yellin, "There they are, up on the chapel!" She then took off runnin like she was gonna tell somebody on us. I thought that as long as we had been spied, I might as well take the chance to unload at least one balloon. I stood up and heaved a bomb at Cody Sue. Just like I had launched a load from a plane in The Great War, that balloon hit Cody Sue right square on her shoulder. It couldn't have hurt her, but she sure squealed like it did. Served her right for tattlin on us.

We left our ammunition sittin up on the roof and headed for the ladder. Just as we were crawlin down, Mr. Cotton, the church janitor, walked up and real casual like said, "Well boys, I caught you. You fellas outta know better than to do that at the dinner on the grounds." To make a painful story short, our mommas were told what we had done, as if they didn't already know. Mr. Cotton figured they could take things from there.

What my momma did was tell Daddy when we got home. That made me mad. For one thing, he whipped me harder than I needed to be whipped. I was also put out at Momma for even bringin Daddy into this whole mess. He wasn't even at the church so I figured it wasn't his business what I had did there. The way I see it, she should've fussed at me herself and then dropped the whole thing. She didn't see it that way, though. Probably the thing that made me maddest, though, was that Daddy seemed to hold a grudge against me just for havin a little fun. It's not like he'd never done anything wrong in his life. You'd sure think it, though, the way he got all worked up over me.

I went to my room that afternoon to think. Actually, I was sent. I had been told to go to my room to study on what I had done and how I wouldn't do it again. I didn't care to think about what I had done. What had happened was over and done with. I'd had fun doin it, too. We hadn't thought about it before we did it, but the chances of our gettin caught were pretty good right from the start, and sure enough that's what had happened. I was willin to live with that. I can't say I wouldn't do it again neither. Throwin balloon bombs was fun. I'd been doin it ever since I was little, and I imagine I'll still be doin it when I'm grown-up, too. Daddy just doesn't know how to have fun. I sure know I don't want to quit having fun when I get old like him.

Why couldn't Daddy have just laughed about Ernie sprayin that group of girls and me hittin Cody Sue with such a fine heave? Didn't he know that all he was doin by whippin me was makin me hate him even more than I already did? I shouldn't use the word hate because a boy's not supposed to hate his own daddy. But I can sure say I wasn't feelin too fond of him right then.

When I get to thinkin like I was that afternoon, my feelins go all over the place. I've already said how I was mad at my daddy for bein so hard on me over what I thought was a pretty small matter. You may find this hard to believe, but at the same time I was mad, I went to feelin sorry for Daddy. Here he was practically forty years old and I couldn't hardly remember what it looked like for him to have nothin but a hard look on his face. Surely when he was a boy he'd done some of the same kind of things I do. Maybe not, though. To hear him tell it, his daddy was even harder on him than he is on me and he didn't never have any time for fun. Could be that instead of lettin Daddy horse around with his friends like I get to do, my granddaddy made him work all the time. I doubt that Daddy really thought much about it, but he may have believed that he was bein a whole lot better to me than my granddaddy was to him. Daddy wasn't the kind of man to think about why he did certain things. He just did it. I think his childhood took all the feelins out of him and he couldn't feel nothin no more.

Here I am thinkin again about how I don't get nothin but frustration from my momma and daddy. Boy, this house can be one depressin place. Just a little while earlier I'd been at the dinner on the grounds havin me a good time and the next thing I know I'm in my room with a sore rear end. I didn't even have the chance to tell Daddy my side of the story. That wasn't allowed. Whenever I had done something wrong, Daddy tried to make me feel as bad as I could feel. At least it seems that's what he had in mind. When I was little, that's just what I did, too. I felt bad about myself most all the time. I still feel pretty low a lot of the time, especially when I'm at home. But I feel a lot madder now than I remember feelin as a little boy. Maybe I was mad then, too, but just didn't know it. Probably I was too flat out scared to be mad at Daddy back then. The way I used to think, if I was mad at Daddy, he'd find out about it some way and I'd get another whippin. Funny how your feelins plays game with you when you're little. I reckon they still do, except now it's just a different kinda game.

You'd think that me bein fifteen and all, I wouldn't feel so mad over gettin a whippin for tossin balloon bombs. I couldn't help but feel thatta way, but I'll be dad gum if I was gonna give in and let any tears come outta my eyes. That'd be the same as givin in to Daddy, and I wasn't about to do that. I thought to myself that I need to find Woody tomorrow and talk to him.

Chapter 6

I WAS pretty sore the next mornin as I walked to school. My caboose was plenty red from from the whippin I'd got, if you know what I mean. Worse than that, though, my emotions were a pretty sore sight. I didn't get a very good night's sleep on account of it all. Kept wakin up feelin all mad at what had happened that afternoon. I still feel that Daddy was wrong to have done me the way he did. And I'm still not sorry that me and Sav and Ernie had been havin fun up there on the roof of the chapel. I didn't like feelin this way, but dad gummit I just wasn't about to let my daddy tell me how I ought to act when he don't know nothin about me. I'm his son, and he hardly even knows who I am.

Usually I go by Sav's house and walk to school with him, but on this day I didn't feel like bein around nobody. It sure was hard to turn my mind to things like geometry and biology and such when all I had on my brain was hard feelins toward Daddy. I reckon I am like Momma in that things eat away at my insides pretty easy. Thank goodness I got Woody to talk to. Momma, she ain't got nobody like that to help her out. You know, even though Momma doesn't talk hardly any about her feelins, that sure doesn't mean you can't tell they're there. One look at her an you know she's not too happy. But I don't think she knows she's showin her feelins so strong to everybody. She probably thinks that if she doesn't talk about what's inside nobody will never know. Maybe I'm more like my momma than I think, just like she says. Maybe I keep too much to myself and figure that nobody knows the difference. I may be showin how I feel more than I think I do, just like Momma does. That's not what I mean to do, but maybe it's so.

As I was lettin my thoughts go ramblin around in my head, I turned the corner up Johnston Avenue and headed for Cassville High School. Like always, I noticed the red oak trees in the school yard, but they didn't speak to me the way they usually do. Them red oaks in the school yard that was just beginnin to change colors. On a normal day that excites me, but it didn't grab me today. I reckon I was more depressed than I had thought.

Gettin up close to the school, I looked around the grounds to see where some of my friends were standin. Young'uns are like adults in that they like to stand in the same place every morning before school, just like adults like to sit in the same pew at church every Sunday. I looked over to the tree where Alane Sharpe and all the other girls usually stand and sure enough there she was. I was about to go over and say good mornin when I saw that she was talkin to Royce Blackwell. They looked like they were enjoyin their talk so I decided I'd be in the way if I walked up. Mind you, I wasn't just tryin to be a gentleman by goin to the boys' red oak tree. I stayed away on account of how awkward I knew I'd feel standin there watchin the two of them go on over each other.

I didn't know quite what to think about Alane talkin to Royce Blackwell. I had been knowin for some time that Royce had an eye for her, so seein him standin next to her didn't surprise me none. Part of me wanted to be jealous while the other part of me said I don't care if he does talk to her since it's a free world. Royce wasn't the kind of boy that you would have hard feelins over. He was the mild type who was friendly to pretty much everybody, me included. Him and his family were fairly new in town. I think they'd been in Cassville maybe two years. I wasn't sure what kind of work his daddy did, but it musta been good work since Royce always looked nice and carried himself around like somebody who come from good stock.

Me and him had been in a couple classes together, and I know he's smart. He's probably about as smart as Alane. Funny that the smart students hang around together just like the dumb ones prefer each other. Myself, I don't like bein around the dumber kind. You know, the less smart you are, the more you show it by the way you act backwards and all. I know I'm not exactly the most intelligent fella around, but I'm not as ignorant as I might appear to be neither. Then again, I don't fit in with folks like Alane and Royce when it comes to makin grades. I can't help but think that if I'd had it good in life like they had, though, I'd somehow do better in school. I bet neither of them had to drag a sack full of feelins behind them as they came to school like I had today.

The more I thought about it, the less I cared that Royce had been talkin to Alane. Just because they were talkin didn't mean he was sweet on her or nothin. Besides, despite I kinda preferred Alane over other girls, I hadn't made any intentions known about her so it wasn't like he was steppin onto my territory, so to speak. Then again, if somethin was to grow between Alane and Royce then I might never have a chance to make a move on her. Shoot! I didn't want to think about all that. I had enough on my brain without worryin about girls. I decided to just live with it that Alane was talkin to Royce. At least she was talkin to a nice boy.

School was worse that day than most Mondays. I fell asleep in my history class and embarrassed myself in geometry when I got called on while my mind was a couple hundred miles off. The school day finally ended, and I made my way over to Jefferson Avenue and Wimp Dickerson's Barber Shop. I had a lot on my mind to tell Woody.

Just seein Woody sittin on the bench out in front of Wimp's made me feel better. There was somethin about the way he looked that let you know he was feelin all peaceful inside. I don't know that he was aware of it or not, but he had this smile on his face most all the time. Here Woody was a fella who didn't have hardly nothin. He was downright poor and I suppose he didn't have any education, but he was a happy man.

The way Woody greeted me made me feel good. "Why looky dare. If it ain't ma frien, Mista Leroy! How you doin today?" His smile looked like the sun to me, all bright and warm like.

"Hey there, Woody. I'm pretty good, how 'bout you?"

"I jes couldn't take it if I was doin better. Naw suh, jes couldn't take it."

I plopped down on the bench by my friend and let out a deep sigh. "Boy, I'm glad today is done with."

"You have a hard day at school today, Mista Leroy?"

"I guess you could say so. My mind wasn't really on studyin today."

"Oh? How's dat?" You know, Woody never pressed me to tell him things. He would just let me decide how much I wanted to say, and then I'd say it. I liked that about him.

"Oh, I had a hard time at home yesterday and that's been on my mind."

"You wanna tell ol Woody 'bout it?"

"Yeah. It's funny that the day started out so good and ended up so bad. You see, yesterday we had Homecomin Sunday at the church and then the dinner on the grounds after church."

Woody's eyes lit up. "I bet you likes dat dinner on da ground, don't cha?"

"Boy, that's the best part. You should've seen all the food stretched out on those long tables. There was fried chicken and all kind of vegetables and salads and desserts like you wouldn't believe." Woody showed me with his eyes that he would've enjoyed that feast as much as I did. "Anyhow, after we'd ate all we could, me and a couple of my friends had some balloons and filled them up with water and got up on top of the chapel. It was sure funny. My friend Ernie dropped one on Sav's head and then on top of that, Sav was tryin to carry so many balloons, he slipped while he was crawlin up the roof. What didn't hit the ground busted all over him. It made me think he'd been baptized, he was so wet."

Woody laughed. "I bet you boys was havin sum fun."

"We sure were. We was laughin so hard, it's a wonder one of us didn't roll off the roof just like them balloons did. Anyhow, we spotted this group of girls and ol Ernie chunked a balloon that splattered on the ground right in the middle of where they were settin. One of them was Cody Sue. She saw me peekin from behind the steeple and hollered, 'There he is,' so I figured I'd sling one at her just for tattlin. You should've seen it, Woody. I bet she was a hundred feet off, and I hit her right on the shoulder while she was runnin."

"Miss Cody Sue didn't like dat, I 'spect." He was still smilin thinkin about how us boys had been havin fun, but he was also thinkin about how Cody Sue musta felt when she had got splattered. That was sure somethin I hadn't done.

"Naw, neither did Momma when she heard about it. Course, she had to go tell Daddy and then he give me a whippin. That's the part that made me mad."

"Oh?" Woody was still listenin. He didn't think I was ready yet for him to do much talkin.

"See, I didn't figure it was none of his business to be punishin me since he hadn't even been there. Besides, you know he'd done his share of horsin around when he was young like me. He whipped me too hard. I think he likes it when he gets to hit me. Woody, I could swear he enjoys it."

"Ya think so?"

"Sure seems thatta way. Sure does." I sat quiet for a few minutes. So did Woody. You know how it is when two people sit there and don't say nothin, but you still feel like the other person understands you anyhow? That's the feelin I got from Woody at the time, like he understood me.

Woody spoke up next. "Kinda hard ta know jes what ta think 'bout all dat."

"That's what it seems to me. You know, Woody, last night I was really hatin my daddy. I know you're not supposed to hate, but I was."

"Dat hate, it be's a powerful feelin." I was glad Woody didn't get on to me for sayin I hated my daddy last night. He could have, but he knew that's how I musta been feelin so he didn't tell me I shouldn't have felt like I did.

"Sure is. I felt kinda guilty, but then again, I felt why shouldn't I hate a man who likes to hit me. Seems like that's the only time he even talks to me, when he's mad at me."

"Now dat probly makes you all de mo mad."

"What do you mean, Woody?"

"I mean de fact dat he don't spend no time wit ya lessin he's gettin on to ya. Dat sho do make a boy mad."

What I had actually said was that I was mad that my daddy whipped me and that's the only time he says much to me. But the way Woody put it made me think on it a different way. He was right. I was mad that my daddy never did nothin with me. He never had. I can't say what I'd do if my daddy said come on let's me and you go to the Orpheum and see the picture show. I don't know of any fifteen-year-old boy who's had a heart attack, but that's probably what would happen to me if my daddy said that. Come to think of it, it would feel so odd, I'm not sure if I'd want to go with him.

"You know, Woody, I wouldn't know what to do if my daddy changed and started actin like a daddy is suposed to act."

"Kinda odd, ain't it? Here you'd like yo daddy ta be different, but if'n he was, ya might not even recognize de man. Ya ever notice how folks has a hard time wit changes, Mista Leroy? Even when dem changes is good, we don't know what ta do. It's jes like we's used ta de old way and has a hard time makin adjusments ta de new way. Dey's a lot o things about people dat don't make jes a whole lotta sense."

I sat and thought about what Woody had said. I found myself wonderin if he'd had some hard times in his life. Surely he had. Most everybody has had hard times. As much as I'd talked to Woody all these years, I'd never asked him much about his past. I knew some about it, but not a whole lot. "How come you never had kids, Woody? You'd make a fine daddy for someone."

Woody got this faraway look in his eyes like my question had took him back to a long time ago. "I got's me a son, Mista Leroy."

That surprised me. I didn't know Woody had ever been married. And I sure didn't know he had a boy anywhere around town. "You do? Where's he livin?"

"He's up dare wit Jesus an de angels, Leroy. Up dare wit Jesus." My heart sunk as I heard Woody say them words. I'd never knew he had a son to die on him. He'd never even suggested he'd been through anything like that before. Course, I'd never asked him about it neither.

I asked real quiet like, "What happened, Woody?"

I don't think Woody minded tellin me, but he waited a second before he started talkin. It was hard to tell if he was just thinkin or tryin not to get all emotional. But then he spoke up. "Well, ya see, Leroy, when I wuz a young man, I wuz workin on a cotton farm down near Asa, jes like my daddy used ta work fo yo granddaddy. I didn't have nuthin, like I still don't have nuthin. But I did have de mos prettiest wife you ever seed. Lawd, she wuz pretty. Looked like she had stars fo eyes, Leroy. We wuz both young, hardly twenty, I 'spect. Well, suh, she wuz gonna have dis little baby an I wuz real proud dat I wuz gonna be a daddy. Wanted me a boy. Gonna name him Willie Mayso Woodrow, after my daddy. Dat be'd his name, ya know.

"When de time came fo her to have de baby, sumthin went wrong. My wife, she jes couldn't stop bleedin an she couldn't have de baby. When little Willie Mayso come ta dis world, he'd already died. His momma, she died, too. Went to heaven together. De two people in dis whole world I love de mos, and dey die together."

Woody still had the same faraway look on him, but there was a little smile on his mouth, too. I know I would've had a hard time smilin after I had done thought about what he had just told me. It was like he was thinkin on what it would've been like if his wife and little boy had made it through all that. I sure wish they had. Woody deserved better.

I didn't know what to say. I just sat there thinkin about Woody havin his wife and son die on him on the same day. That must of been awful. "Uh . . . I didn't know, Woody. I'm sure sorry."

"Ya know, Leroy, I used ta say, well dat's what God meant fo me ta have, but I don't thinks dat no mo."

"You don't? What do you think?"

"Well, suh, the mo I thought 'bout how bad I felt losin my wife an baby like dat, the mo I figure the good Lawd mus know how I feels. I figure he wouldn't do dat to me jes ta test me. The Lawd's not dat hard, Leroy. Don't you believe it when folks tells you dat God's testin ya or tryin ta punish ya by lettin bad things happen. God grieves jes as bad as you an me grieves when hard times comes. Probly mo. When my wife an boy die, I feels right shore dat God weren't ready fo dem. He took em, but he sho didn't wanna take em from me right yet."

The way Woody was talkin was different than what you heard preached in the church. Most any preacher I'd ever listened to said that bad things happen to punish folks for some sin or to see just how much faith they got. I'd never heard anybody say how God grieves as hard as a husband does when a baby and a wife dies all of a sudden like. But, you know, that sure makes more sense to me. I can feel a whole lot closer to a God who feels along with folks than one who just lets bad things happen just to test them. Or worse, makes bad things happen on purpose.

"That's different than what a lot of folks think, Woody."

"Maybe mos folks has a hard time figurin things out, Leroy. De way I looks at it, mos folks goes round thinkin dat God thinks like dey thinks, but I don't rightly imagine dat's de way things is. I doubts dat God 'spects us to like everythin dat happen in dis ol world. He jes wants us ta know he understans an dat it's all right ta lean on his shoulder from time ta time."

We sat quiet for a few more minutes. I liked doin that. It gave my thoughts time to settle down so I could understand them better. I got to thinkin about how what Woody had just said fit what I was goin through with my daddy. I spoke up and said, "I never really thought about it before, but I guess God don't really like that I have to live the way I do with my family bein the way it is and all."

"Ya mean, you don't reckon dat's what de good Lawd had in mind fo ya?"

"I wouldn't imagine so, would you?"

"Naw suh, I wouldn't. I sho wouldn't. Family, dat's supposed ta be de mos special people in de whole world. Ain't s'posed to be dat family don't like one another, naw suh."

"You mean you think I shouldn't go around hatin the way things is at my house?"

"Naw, Leroy, dat's not what I's suggestin. Kinda hard not ta feel what you feels. I's jes sayin dat ain't de way God meant fo it ta be, dat's all."

I got to feelin guilty thinkin thatta way. "You think it's my fault?"

"I cain't see dat you's to blame fo yo daddy an yo momma bein de way dey is. Maybe dey's some things you could do dat's differnt, but I cain't say you's de fault fo everthin dat happen around dare."

That made me feel better that I wasn't gettin the blame, least not from Woody. "You sayin my parents are more at fault than I am?"

"Well, adults ought ta know mo dan chilluns, but ya got ta remember dey may o had a hard time growin up, jes like you's havin. Only dey didn't figure things out like you's tryin to. Dat's de main difference I see, Leroy." There was somethin about the way Woody said things that made me sure he didn't hold any judgment against nobody. Not many folks are like that. I know he didn't agree with the way my folks handled things, but he didn't say nothin to suggest that he would've held hard feelins against them if he'd been me. I had a hard time thinkin thatta way, but I sure wished I could somehow learn to.

We talked a little more, and then Woody said it was about time for Wimp to close up the shop. I told Woody thanks for takin the time and he said it weren't no problem, that he liked talkin. Said it like he meant it, and I figure he did. I felt stronger than I had when I first walked up from school. It was a good thing we had that talk cause I was gonna need all the strength I could muster with what was about to happen to my family.

Chapter 7

WHEN I got home, I walked through the back door into the kitchen, just like usual. Momma was standin over the sink fixin supper. She was peelin carrots, but I noticed her kinda whimperin. I looked around to see her face, but she turned it away from me. "You all right, Momma?" I asked.

"I'm all right, Leroy. Now go on to your room. I'll have supper ready directly."

I knew Momma was lyin to me. She sure wasn't all right. She was cryin. There's one thing about Momma and that is that she hates more than anything for anyone to see her cry, so I done what she asked and left the kitchen. I headed lickety-split for Cody Sue's room to see what all she knew about what was wrong with Momma. If anybody would know, it'd be Cody Sue. She made it her practice to be in on every little thing that went on in this house, and anywhere else for that matter.

I found Cody Sue and kinda hushed, but firm like, asked her, "What happened to Momma, Cody Sue? She's in the kitchen cryin. You know what's wrong with her?"

"She's upset I reckon." Cody Sue was braidin the hair on a doll of hers. Just sat there like she didn't hardly know what I was talkin about. Dad gum, was that all she was gonna tell me? She didn't need to be so secret like. It was my Momma same as hers. I had every bit as much right as she did to know what in thunder had set Momma to cryin. She probably didn't see it thatta way, though. The way her brain works, she probably felt like if I wasn't there to see it, then it was none of my business. Of course, she wouldn't be seein it thatta way if the shoe was on the other foot and she was the one doin the askin.

"Don't be so pig-headed, Cody Sue! Momma's bothered and I need to know why, so just tell me whatever you saw happenin." I was tryin to stay quiet so as not to arouse Momma's suspicions that we were in here talkin about her, but Cody Sue was makin it danged hard on me. I don't mind sayin that I was pretty derned perturbed at my little sister.

Cody Sue stared at me with this smug look on her face. "Some things is private, Leroy. Don't you know that yet?"

"Course I know that, but it's my business as much as it is yours."

Cody Sue could tell I was gettin mad at her. I don't know if she thought she'd better not push her luck with me or if she figured she was through horsin around, but she gave a big sigh and said, "Okay, I'll tell you but you gotta keep it to yourself. I don't want Momma to think I'm tellin all I know." I didn't bother to tell Cody Sue that Momma and everybody else that knew her was already right certain that she went around tellin folks everything she knew. And everybody knew that if she didn't know all the facts, she just made somethin up. Twelve years old, and that girl was already a champion gossip.

"I promise."

Cody Sue set down her doll and leaned towards me as she began to talk in a low voice. You'd think she was tellin stories around a campfire the way she opened up her eyes real big and put all this expression on her face. I had this urge to tell her she didn't have to put on no show for me, just tell what was wrong with Momma. It didn't take much, though, for me to figure that wouldn't do any good. I listened carefully to what Cody Sue had to say.

"Well, you see, Daddy was already home this afternoon when I got in from school. I come in the back door and heard Momma and Daddy back in their room arguin. And they weren't just arguin the way they usually do. It was worse. Momma was sayin somethin to Daddy about why didn't he at least go out and look for a job. She said he should go down to the R.C. Cola plant and see if they might have some work. She thought she'd heard they had hired a couple folks just the other day. Daddy got all mad and started yellin at her, sayin for her to just shut up and if she didn't like the way he worked hard why didn't she just go right out and find herself a job. He was really yellin, Leroy, and cursin, too! Momma told him to quit talkin like that. She was kinda beggin him to quit, but he didn't pay no attention to her. You know how Daddy don't listen to nobody when he's mad. He just kept on hollerin and tellin Momma she should've married some rich fella if she didn't care for him. And you know what Momma said? She said she wished she had! That made Daddy real mad." Boy, once Cody Sue got to goin, she really told it all. She was right worked up about the whole ordeal.

I was tryin to picture the scene in my mind. It was pretty unusual for

Momma to be tellin Daddy what he ought to do. She musta been feelin right desperate to have even tried to reason with him. One thing about Daddy is that he's stubborn. Nobody ever even bothered to try talkin to him even if they were convinced they was right and he was wrong. A person could have a better talk with a jackass than with Daddy. That's how stubborn the man is. Another thing about Daddy is his pride. There's no doubt that Momma hurt his manly honor by suggestin that he needed to go down to the R.C. Cola plant and ask for a job. Daddy wouldn't admit that he needed a regular payin job, even though it was plenty obvious that he did. Besides, he didn't like askin nobody for nothin. The way he looked at it, if the folks at the R.C. Cola plant had wanted him to work for them, they'd send word. I know that don't make any sense, but that's how he sees things. All I can say is that the way he thinks is pretty peculiar.

"Boy, I bet Daddy was sure enough mad. What'd he do when Momma said she wished she had of married someone else?"

"You ain't heard the half of it yet, Leroy!" Cody Sue had done got herself lathered up and was now enjoyin the fact that she got to be the one to tell me about Momma and Daddy's fight. "When she said that, Daddy musta pushed her because I heard Momma hit the wall and Daddy was yellin about what would she feel like if he wasn't around. He asked her would she go out and find herself another man. Momma didn't say nothin the whole time Daddy was screamin for her to answer him. She was probably scared half to death, Leroy. He finally got finished hollerin and said he was leavin. He stomped right by me. I don't think he even saw me. I reached out my arm when he went by to try to get him to stop and simmer down. He just slapped at me and didn't say a word. You should've seen how hard he slammed the door when he went out. Made the whole house rattle!" Cody Sue was practically out of breath by the time she finished talkin.

Boy, oh boy. This here story was a whole lot worse than I thought. That musta been some kinda fight they had. Daddy wasn't the type to shy away from an argument, but usually Momma didn't say nothin much back to him, so their fights generally didn't last too long. Sounds to me like she waited a little too long this time to decide she better hush up.

"What'd you do then, Cody Sue?"

"Why, I didn't do nothin! I didn't know what to do." Figures. Cody Sue isn't the world's best at knowin how to begin pickin up the pieces when things start fallin apart. Course, I shouldn't be so hard in judgin her. I wouldn't have known what to do neither.

"Where's Daddy now?"

"I don't rightly know, but you know what he usually does when he gets mad like this."

I knew exactly what Cody Sue was talkin about, and she was probably right in her thinkin. Daddy usually went over to Red Howard's house and got loaded. Red was this sorry fella who made his own brand of liquor with his brother, who was just as sorry as he was. Them two Howard brothers was the type who made sure the policemen had something to do. They stayed in jail as much as they was out of it. You know the kind. It's hard for me to imagine how two people can grow up actin so much like wild coyotes, but that's the kinda folks them brothers is. Red has this scraggily lookin beard. Sav's daddy says if he had a mule whose face looked like Red's, he'd shave his rear end and teach it to walk backwards. I hate it when Daddy's been around them on account of how they rub off on him.

"Why don't we go in the kitchen and help Momma out," I suggested.

"But what if Momma don't want us in there? You know she don't like us seein her when she's all upset."

"I know, but sometimes you just gotta do whatever you can to let someone know you care about them, whether they're cryin or not. C'mon."

Me and Cody Sue walked into the kitchen. Momma's eyes was pretty red and puffy, but she had gotten ahold of herself a little better than when I first come in the door. Neither me nor Cody Sue said much, but we helped get the dishes out and the table set while she put the biscuits in the oven. Tryin to make Momma feel better, I said as nice like as I could, "You know, Momma, I don't say it much, but I sure love havin biscuits every night. They're my favorite part of supper." I know that probably wasn't the right thing to say, but I didn't know how else to let Momma know that I was feelin sorry for her. If I'd come right out and said I wish Daddy hadn't got all mad and pushed her and left the house to go get drunk, she would've had a fit just because I knew what had happened. Besides, we weren't allowed to talk about them things to her. She said they was adult matters, not things for children to fret about.

"Thank you, honey. That's right nice of you to say so." She tried to smile and added, "They's not much I like better neither than good hot biscuits. Y'all are bein helpful and I 'preciate it." You gotta hand it to Momma for tryin to act pleasant.

It took about ten minutes to get everything ready to eat. Momma said for us to come sit down and let's say the blessin. Cody Sue asked were we gonna wait on Daddy. I looked at her real hard to try to motion to her with my eyes to just hush up about Daddy. Everybody in this house knew exactly what he was out doin and there was no need bringin it up. But Momma said real polite like that she didn't know when Daddy was gonna be comin home and she would save him some supper to eat when he got here. Momma asked me to say grace. I can tell you, it's right hard to say thank you to God for your food when there's a whole lot of other things that you ain't so thankful about at the same time. I give it my best try, though, and figured God knew what was really goin on inside my brain, just like me and Woody had talked about. I suppose God wasn't feelin so grand himself right then, neither. It sure wasn't his choice for Daddy to be out loadin himself up.

Not that we're the kind of family that generally has a lot to say to one another around the supper table, but the silence at the table burned a little extra that night. Usually the silence just meant that our family relations was in its normal sad shape, but tonight it said that our family was strugglin even more than usual. And let me tell you, it really hurt.

As we were sittin there in the kitchen, me and Cody Sue and Momma, I got to thinkin about Alane Sharpe and her family. I wondered if they were out there on the edge of town eatin supper right about now. Or maybe they had finished supper and were in their family room enjoyin talkin to one another, doin whatever it is that families do when they care about each other. I found myself wishin I was in that house at the end of Stuart Avenue bein a part of her family instead of here in town bein in my own. That sounds disrespectful, which isn't what I mean to be. I just wish I had what folks like Alane Sharpe had, that's all.

Usually it's Cody Sue's job to help clean the kitchen after supper, but tonight I pitched in just as a way of showin Momma I understood that she was havin a hard time of it all. Momma didn't thank me nor Cody Sue, but I'm sure her mind was off on somethin else besides manners. She told us that she'd be back in her room if we needed her. Usually she went in the front room after supper to work on whatever project she had goin on. I expect she went to the bedroom tonight because she hadn't gotten out all the cryin she needed to do.

About nine o'clock I was gettin myself ready for bed when I heard the back door get thrown open. It sounded like it had been slung off its hinges. Daddy was home. It was quickly plain that he was drunker than usual. Lord up in heaven, if there's a time we need you to get us outta a mess, it sure is right now. You know as I think about it, I look back on what me and Woody talked about outside the barber shop earlier in the day when he told me about his wife and boy dyin on him and how he expected God was hurtin as bad as he had hurt over that incident. It wasn't really fair for me to ask God to get me outta this mess our family was in. It sure wasn't his fault for all that had happened. He was just as disappointed as I was in Daddy. In fact, even more seein that he made Daddy and all. Maybe what I really needed to be askin for was a sharp mind so I could keep remindin myself that no matter what Daddy done that night, it wasn't a reflection on who I was, even though that's what everybody seemed to think.

Daddy hollered out, "I'm hungry! Where's my supper?" He plopped himself down at the kitchen table like he expected to be fed right then and there. Momma fell all over herself gettin into the kitchen. She was rushin around tryin to fix Daddy his meal real quick. I know for a fact she wasn't hurryin out of kindness. She just didn't want the yellin to get any worse than was necessary. I went in and tried to help out by talkin to Daddy, just to keep him from bein so hard on Momma.

"Daddy, Momma's fixin it as fast as she can. I'm helpin, too. You must be hungry, bein that it's late and all." I don't think Daddy heard a single word I said. He was really drunk. He was the kind of man who could drink quite a lot of alcohol and still walk a pretty straight line. The fact that he hardly knew that he was sittin in his own house was a strong sign of just how hard he'd been suckin that bottle. He didn't pay me no attention and kept gripin at Momma to hurry up and get his supper on the table and it better not be cold. Boy the words that flew out of his mouth was pretty bad. His language wasn't always the best, but it wasn't like a sailor's neither. But on this particular night, he could've put a shipload of sailors to shame. Momma was embarrassed for us kids to have to hear him go on like that. I was embarrassed that she had to admit to anybody that he was the only man she could find to get herself married to.

Daddy's supper was finally warmed up and set down in front of him. First thing he did was put a biscuit in his mouth. No sooner had he put the thing in, he spit it right back out on the floor. "Dern biscuit's hard! I ain't eatin no hard biscuits!"

Momma tried to explain, "They's hard because . . ."

"I said I ain't eatin no hard biscuits!" Just as if one little hard biscuit was the last straw on the ol camel's back, Daddy blew up. He lifted up the edge of the table and threw it to the floor, sendin his food and everything else all over the kitchen. He took the glass of ice tea that was in his hand and heaved it up against the wall near to where Momma stood, shatterin it and soakin Momma. She screamed at him to please stop, but he couldn't hear nothin except the rage inside him that told him to keep on with his fit.

Cody Sue, cowerin near the kitchen door, was in Daddy's way as he headed out of the room. "Get outta my way, you little good-for-nothin.

Cain't you see I'm tryin to get through that door!" That set her to cryin loud and hard. Tell you the truth, Cody Sue was probably carryin on on account of bein scared to death and not so much because of havin her feelins hurt by Daddy.

Momma called out after him, "Ira! Don't talk to her like that! She wasn't doin nothin to hurt you!" She should've saved her breath cause Daddy didn't hear a word she said. He went on back to his bedroom and was throwin things around, makin a big mess of things. Momma always tried to keep the house cleaned up, but it was clear that Daddy wasn't thinkin of her. He was throwin and breakin whatever he could. After a few minutes, which seemed like hours, Daddy stomped back into the kitchen with a bag full of his clothes.

"Where you goin?" Momma asked.

"What do you care? You done said you wished you'd never married me. Well, here's yore chance. I'm leavin. And don't come lookin for me. I won't be in no better mood the next time you see me neither!" I was in shock already, but then as if he wanted to leave with everybody hatin him as much as possible, he looked right at me and said, "You can let this here little half-sized punk take care of things around here." He proceeded to spit on the floor like he was riddin himself of whatever bad taste he had of our family and left.

Me and Cody Sue and Momma was stunned. We all stood there in the kitchen as if we'd been frozen in place. I sure didn't know what to say and neither did Cody Sue nor Momma. Momma finally started to pick up the table. I went over an helped. I looked at her to see if she was cryin. I was surprised that her eyes was dry. Maybe there weren't none left in her since she'd spent most of the evenin cryin. Without sayin a word, the three of us cleaned up the mess Daddy had made. Boy, his and Momma's room was a wreck. A lamp was broke and a couple of smaller glass ornament type of things was shattered. Clothes and papers had been slung everywhere. Me and Cody Sue picked up what we could and Momma told us she'd take care of the rest. The whole time we worked nobody said anything. Who could've thought of somethin to say right then anyhow?

I went into my bedroom and laid down on my bed. Just stared at the walls wonderin how in thunder all that happened could've happened like it did. I guess I shouldn't have been surprised. Seems like it had been a long time comin. The way we all tippy-toed around Daddy, it was like we expected him to explode at any time. Well, he finally did. I couldn't help but wonder where Daddy had gone and what he was doin right then. I wondered if he was still mad or if he'd cooled down a little by now. Course, as drunk as he was he may not even know what he'd done or where he was now. Boy was he ever drunk. Worst I'd ever seen him.

I expected maybe Daddy would show up back home late tonight or for sure he'd be back tomorrow. I found myself hopin he stay gone, though. I sure was sick of livin the way we had as long as I'd been alive. Maybe Daddy didn't want to come back. Who knows, he was probably just as sick of our family the same as the rest of us. It'd suit me if he didn't come back. I had been tryin hard to ignore the little comment he'd made at me when he left. I know he was talkin drunk talk. But I couldn't help but think that maybe what had happened was that the alcohol had loosened up his thoughts enough that he said what he'd been thinkin about me all along.

My mind drifted back to Woody and me's conversation from this afternoon one more time. I tried to remind myself that what Daddy had said was somethin that I had no control over and that God was hurtin worse than I was over Daddy's behavior. I sure wanted to believe that, but then I'd see this preacher in my mind standin behind a pulpit tellin about how God don't let nothin happen that we don't deserve. Boy, if that was so, I must be some kinda sorry person. Was I that awful? I tried to go to sleep, but I couldn't. Along about midnight, I decided I wasn't goin to school the next day. I'd had a hard enough time concentratin today after all the goins on followin the dinner on the grounds on Sunday. They's no way I could make it through school tomorrow. I was plumb spent.

Chapter 8

GOT up about the usual time next mornin. I hadn't slept much, but I didn't want to stay in bed neither. It was like I wanted to see if a new day would make any difference in the way things were. You'd think I would've slept hard last night seein as how I hadn't slept hardly any the night before, but I didn't. I don't know why, but I pretty much expected Daddy to be settin in the kitchen when I walked in, drinkin coffee like he usually does. Momma was fixin breakfast for me and Cody Sue and was her usual quiet self. I didn't say nothin when I walked in the kitchen and neither did she. It was like all the hurt would just go away by itself if everybody kept their lips buttoned about last night.

I watched Momma as she went around the kitchen. She was always busy and had this look on her face that said she had to hurry up and get one thing done so she could move on to the next job. It was like she was never finished doin all that needed to be done. Momma generally had this hard look on her face. You know, there's a lot of different kinds of hard looks a person might wear. My daddy has the hard look that alcohol can paint all over a man. Momma's look was hard, but it was from worryin and frettin about things instead of drinkin. They was both hard lookin, but they had come about it in different ways.

I've always thought Momma could've been a pretty woman if life had of treated her a little better than it had. She looks like life has been rough on her, and I suppose it has been, at least it has for as long as she's been married. She's thin like a broomstick and looks kinda peaked most of the time. I never did understand what it was about livin a hard life that makes the skin under a person's eyes look dark, but that's what had happened to Momma. Folks say that a woman like that has bags under her eyes. Probably they're bags full of feelins that don't hardly ever get emptied out. She seldom smiles, which makes her baggy eyes look even droopier. I don't think about such things a lot, but I don't believe Momma sleeps much. She's always up when I go to bed and up when I get outta bed. But she never acts tired or complains about not gettin enough rest. Course, Momma never complains about nothin at all hardly.

I found myself wonderin what Momma would look like if she was happy. Probably she'd wear clothes that was more colorful. One of my favorite teachers at school is this lady named Mrs. Buckner. That woman always dresses up like a dog's dinner. The way she looks seems to match the way she feels. She looks like she would be a lotta fun and acts the same way. My momma is just the opposite. She wears clothes that are all drab lookin. Never wears any makeup neither, not even when she goes out of the house. The way she looks matches the way she acts, same as it does Mrs. Buckner. Momma looks like she wouldn't know fun if it grabbed her and tickled her, and sure enough she acts the same way. I wish my momma wasn't thatta way.

Cody Sue come draggin in the kitchen and sat down at the table. "Where's Daddy?" I reckon she expected him to be home by now, too. The way she asked it was like she had maybe forgot about last night.

"Don't know where your daddy is," Momma said real gruff like. Even Cody Sue could figure out that Momma didn't want to discuss things no further. "You young 'uns need to get off to school soon as you eat some breakfast."

"I ain't goin to school, Momma," I informed her. It wasn't like me to be the smart alecky type and I didn't mean to come across that way, but I expect that's how Momma took it.

I'd never before seen the hateful look that was comin from Momma's eyes when she turned around an looked straight at me. "Young man. You *will* go to school, and you will *not* say nothin to nobody about what happened in this here house last night! You understand?"

"Yes, ma'am."

I still didn't plan on goin to school. Had too much on my mind. Probably it was just as well, I thought, to get outta the house, though. With Momma bein this upset I sure didn't want to be around her all day. Before you know it, I'd be actin like her and I wasn't about to let myself get that mopey today. I wasn't too proud about Daddy's temper tantrum neither, but I wasn't gonna just give up on livin on account of him. Momma, on the other hand, appeared ready to give up the ghost.

Sav come by my house and asked was I ready to get on to school. I told him I was skippin. He would've gone with me, but I said I was gonna go out to the Cotton Palace grounds where the annual fair was gonna be startin up on Friday. Said I figured they'd need some help gettin things set up and I might make myself some extra money. Actually, that would've been a good idea, but I said it because I knew Sav wouldn't want to be around no work. It was my way of gettin him to go on to school without havin to tell him I didn't want him around.

I didn't do nothin at all that day. Least nothin that amounted to anything. I did go out to the Cotton Palace and look around while folks were settin up for the fair, but I didn't offer to help. I made my way down to Rock Springs in McAllen Park, which is right off the Indian Tear River a little ways out from downtown, and sat around most of the day. I usually spend time like that thinkin and such, but to tell you the truth, I was too tired to even think that day. It must have been useful to me, though, because I was ready to get back to livin later in the day, whether Daddy was home or not. Before I went back home, I decided I'd go back by the Cotton Palace grounds again and watch them folks set up their show things a little longer.

The Cotton Palace Exposition and Dairy Show was one of the big events in Cassville every fall. Seems like every year they added somethin new to make this year's show better than the last. This year they was havin a terrapin derby. I had a hard time seein how that could be too excitin, but I figured I might look in on it this weekend after the fair started just to see what it was. Mostly, though, it was a bunch of daredevil stunts, and rides, and shows, and craft exhibits.

On Saturday me and Sav went to the Cotton Palace. Sav got all excited about the Cotton Palace every year same as he did the first day of school. That boy could get all of a tizzy over somethin easier than anybody I'd ever known. Once we got inside the grounds, though, it wasn't long before he was actin bored and askin me what did I want to do next. He was hopin we'd come across some pretty girls that we could spend some time with.

My heart started pumpin a little stronger when we spotted Alane Sharpe and one of her friends walkin around by themselves. So did Sav's, but for a different reason than mine. Just seein a familiar face that was a girl excited him. As for me, I wasn't excited over seein just any girl's face, only Alane's. I figured Alane's parents must be pretty close by since they probably weren't the type to cut their daughter loose at a place like the Cotton Palace. Parents have a way of worryin about their daughter gettin lost or hurt when they're on their own at a fair. It's like they're afraid their girl might have a little fun, and they don't want to allow that. That's just one more reason I'm sure glad I'm a boy. We casual like walked up to Alane and her friend, Virginia Bledsoe, and said hello and wasn't it a surprise to meet up with them out here. It was a surprise to them, I suppose, so we weren't lyin when we said that, but we had been hopin and plannin for this kinda meetin.

"Why, Leroy Evans. How are you doing? You know Virginia, don't you?" I said oh sure I knew Virginia while Sav stood there with this dumb lookin smile on his face. It was sure obvious to me that he didn't know how to talk to girls. For all his blabberin about wantin to meet up with a girl, he sure didn't act like a boy's supposed to act around a female. I wasn't just a whole lot more experienced at these matters than he was, but I knew enough not to stand there and look like I'd just come in town from the piney woods and had never laid eyes on a female before. I wanted to punch Sav and tell him to get that look off his face, but I figured this wasn't the place to be doin that. I'd have to talk to him about his manners later on.

Bein the polite type, Alane started to introduce Virginia to Sav. "Virginia, you know . . ." She stopped in mid-sentence and got this bamboozled look on her face. Lookin at Sav she kinda giggled and said, "You know, all I know is that people call you Sav. What is your real name?"

Sav acted like he couldn't answer her question. I've been in situations before when people has asked me a hard question and I couldn't think of the right answer to save my life, like the time Alane was askin me to define all them vocabulary words that day up at her house. This was another situation entirely, though. Sav had just been asked what was his name and I honestly believe he forgot. I answered for him. "His name is Alvin."

"How did you get the name Sav as a nickname for Alvin?" Alane asked. She was still lookin in Sav's direction, but it was plain to me that Sav wanted me to answer this question, too. Like he'd just been throwed another hard one.

"Oh, you see, his last name is Vickers. One day us fellas were playin when we was real little and Ernie, you know Ernie Chambers, don't you?" Alane and Virginia both nodded. "Well, Ernie said to Sav here, 'Hey Alvin, you got any of that Vick's Salve?' All us boys laughed when he said it and started callin him Vick Salve. The name got shortened to Sav and there you go. Ol Alvin had himself a new name." Sav had this look of relief on his face that I'd come through for him again.

Alane said it was funny and interestin how people got their nicknames. I said, "You know, since you brought it up, that is interestin. I know this man named Skinny who's as fat as one of them prize-winnin pigs over in the barnyard buildin. They say he was a skinny fella when he was a boy. When he got big and changed his shape, nobody saw the need to change his nickname." I just kept on ramblin, which is somethin a lot of boys do when they're nervous. "I know these two twin boys, one's named Bob and the other's Bobby. They called the smaller one Peanut. I don't even think they look like brothers, but they swear they're twins. Now why would a mother want to go and name her twin boys practically the same name?"

Alane and Virginia were laughin at the way I was goin on, so I figured I might as well keep it up. "I even know this fella who's called Corn. They say that's 'cause he's all the time crackin these cornball jokes. They started out callin him Cornball, but it got shortened to Corn. Some folks just call him Corny." I started to tell them girls about this friend of mine who's called Whizzer because he's all the time havin to relieve himself. Goes to the bathroom more than anybody you ever saw. And he'll do it practically anywhere he pleases. He even still wets the bed, and he's almost fifteen years old. Lucky for me, I caught myself before I told that one. I didn't want to come across as havin no manners at all.

"I like the way you can make people laugh over something like nicknames," said Alane. I took advantage of the fact that Alane was enjoyin my company and asked would she and Virginia like to walk around some with me and Sav. They said they could for awhile, but they had to meet her momma over at the Crafts Buildin in a little bit. I still wasn't quite sure where I stood in my relations with Alane. A good part of me liked her and wished I could be more than a friend to her. But I had to keep remindin myself that she was a whole lot higher up in the world than I was and that I didn't have no business even wishin for a girl like her. Besides, Royce Blackwell had his sights set on her and I knew I was no match for him. His family had everything mine didn't. I didn't stand a chance with Alane up against him.

While we were walkin, Alane got to talkin about her momma and daddy. I suppose it's natural for a girl to talk about somethin she has no need to feel ashamed of. I liked hearin about her folks and all, but I didn't feel I could add nothin to the conversation since I had nothin to say about my family. I wanted to change the subject when she got to sayin what all her momma and daddy were doin lately, but I couldn't. Then she did it to me again. She asked me about how my momma and daddy were doin and would they be comin out to the fair with me sometime. Said she'd enjoy meetin them. Good Lord! What was I gonna say to that? Seemed like she was determined to force me to publicly announce what kind of family I lived with.

I suppose Sav felt obliged to me, what with me answerin them questions about his name and all. Actually, what I had did for him was bail him out of a mess where he didn't know how to strike up a conversation with a girl. He could've answered them questions, but he was just actin awkward like, so I had helped out. Now here I was the one actin awkward, and Sav knew why. I hadn't really talked much to him about my family bein the way it is, but he knew. He'd been over to my house plenty enough to know what my daddy was like. I hadn't even told Sav about my daddy leavin the house five nights ago, but he knew Daddy was a steady drinker and wouldn't keep a regular job. Sav's daddy had even tried to be neighborly to my daddy, but didn't get nowhere with his effort. Probably, he'd told Sav to be nice to me seein how my daddy wasn't too friendly and all. I don't know that he actually had told Sav that, but I wouldn't doubt it. Anyway, Sav knew I needed help at the time and stepped in.

"Uh, well Leroy's parents ain't the type who like to get out and do things, are they, Leroy?"

I wanted to be honest and say that my daddy liked to get out and go get his snoot full, but I just said, "Nah, they're just the type that likes to stay at home. I don't even know if they'll come out to the Cotton Palace this year or not." Actually, they hadn't been to the Cotton Palace in six or eight years ever since me and Cody Sue was old enough to go with someone else, so it was a pretty sure thing they weren't comin this year. That plus the fact that we still didn't even know where Daddy was. Momma said she figured he was out in the country with his brother, but she didn't know for certain since we hadn't even heard from him.

"That's too bad," said Alane. "I'd really like to meet them. They must be nice folks. I'll bet you have a fine family."

You know, I had always figured I showed everybody how my family was by the way I acted. I can generally tell when someone new comes to school if they come from a good family or not just by the way they look and act. Most of the time I'm right, too. I figured people could tell that about me, too, and wouldn't ask me about my folks. I can tell you I sure know who to ask and who not to ask about their momma and daddy. Either I do a better job of hidin the way my family is than I give myself credit for, or Alane isn't as smart as I thought she was. I'd like to think she was givin me a compliment by sayin she'd like to meet my folks. I reckon I could just give her credit for thinkin I was a pretty nice boy and then leave it at that.

I didn't like goin on this way with Alane. I figured if I was gonna have any chance at all at bein friends with her, I might as well be honest with her. No need in me goin around pretendin to be from good stock when I knew better. The way I figured it, I ought to go ahead and tell her how things really were in my home. That way if anything was to develop between me and her, like I was kinda hopin it would, she'd know what she was gettin into right from the start. That was the only fair way to do things. Sav got to talkin to Virginia about somethin else in a minute so I was able to tell Alane, "Alane, I think I'd like to tell you about somethin."

"Why sure, go right ahead," she said polite like.

"Well, you and Virginia got to get back to where your momma is, so maybe this isn't a good time. I don't know when I could talk to you, but I'd like to soon."

"I'll be coming back here to the Cotton Palace with my parents tonight. Daddy's going to be a judge of one of the shows at the crafts exhibit. Will you be here tonight?" She sounded right anxious to see me again. That give me a lift, I'll sure say that.

I hadn't planned on comin back to the Cotton Palace grounds tonight. Usually Daddy doesn't let me do a whole lot at night, but he wasn't around to tell me I couldn't. I knew Momma wouldn't mind me gettin out again. "Why, uh, yeah, as a matter of fact I am gonna be out here tonight. Maybe we could meet somewheres."

"Why don't I meet you at the Crafts Building at about seven? Maybe we could talk some then." I said that would be great. When me and Sav was walkin home a little later, I told him I was gonna meet Alane back at the Cotton Palace at seven. He tried to rib me about bein sweet on her. I kinda laughed with him, but I wasn't really worried about him thinkin I was sweet on Alane. I was wonderin how in thunder I was to explain to a girl just what my family was like.

Chapter 9

ME BEIN a Baptist, I don't know what it's like to go to a priest for confession. That must be some kind of experience for a Catholic to go through, havin to sit in a little booth and tell the man on the other side everything you've done lately that's bad. I don't know if I could do that. I have to admit I'd probably tell the priest a lie about how good I'd been. Surely there's a bunch of Catholics that does that. It would be pretty hard to convince me that it doesn't matter to them what the priest thinks about them. But then they'd probably feel guilty for tellin a lie while they was givin a confession. Nothin against Catholics, but I reckon it's a good thing I was born a Baptist.

The preacher at my church says that Baptists don't like talkin about sin. Says they go hightailin it the other way when the subject is brought up. He tells this story about how at the end of a Baptist service this preacher said, "Now we're gonna end the service a little different today. I want every one of you to think on a sin you've done committed this past week, and then I want some volunteers to stand up and confess their sins. It's good to confess yore sins, ya know. Now who's gonna be first to confess a sin?"

This woman stood up and says, "Brother Preacher, I confess that one day this last week I slandered the name of one of my best friends."

The preacher blasted out, "Well Sister Thelma, yore wrong to slander yore friend, but yore right to confess yore sin! Now who's gonna be next?"

A man stood up and shy like admitted, "Brother Preacher, one day this last week I went in a store, and I stole some goods."

In an even louder and more damning voice the preacher yelled, "Well Brother Clyde, yore wrong ta steal, but yore right to confess yore sins!"

And then as if he dared anyone else to tell it all, he glared down on the congregation and asked, "Now who's gonna be next?"

This man stood up and real unashamed like said, "Well, Brother Preacher, one day this last week I got drunk as a fish and went down for a visit at the cathouse." Everybody in the whole church gasped and waited for the preacher's reaction.

The preacher leaned on the pulpit and kinda embarrassed said, "Hoo wee, Brother Floyd! I don't believe I'da confessed *that* sin."

The preacher who told that story liked to say that's how us Baptists are. We don't like to talk out loud about the really bad things we was into. This was one of them times that I could sure understand what the preacher was talkin about. I felt like I was a Baptist goin to the Catholic confession booth to say things a Baptist wouldn't normally talk about. Not that I'd been drinkin or visitin the wrong part of town and such, but I didn't normally tell folks anything about my family.

This whole meetin with Alane Sharpe was my idea, though. It wasn't like I was bein forced into somethin where I didn't know what I was gettin into. All the same, I felt kinda funny as I headed off to met Alane. I hoped she'd be understandin. I walked onto the Cotton Palace grounds and went into the Crafts Buildin and roamed around awhile lookin for Alane. There was all sorts of items to look at and admire. My favorite thing to do was to look at the quilts that had been made by ladies from all over the county. I couldn't begin to have the patience to set still for hours at a time workin on a single quilt. My momma had made a few quilts in the past. I wish she'd enter one of them in the fair, but she doesn't have the gumption to do somethin like that. I admire a person who can do all that stitchin. It would be a whole lot easier to just enter some homemade jelly or preserves at the exhibit, but not everybody takes the easy way out.

Off among the art exhibits, I spotted Alane and her parents. All of them had a nice look about them. I wondered what they thought of when they saw me, if they thought here comes that pitiful lookin boy. I hoped not, but I couldn't say what they might think. I had tried to come dressed neat lookin tonight so I wouldn't embarrass Alane, but I don't know if the way I looked was good enough to go braggin about. I didn't really want to have to talk to Mr. and Mrs. Sharpe, even though I knew that was the proper thing to do. If I was goin to make the right kind of impression on Alane and her family, I knew I had to do what was proper, so I walked right up just like it was what I had been lookin forward to doin.

I stuck out my hand to the judge. "Hello, Mr. Sharpe. Mrs. Sharpe. Alane. Y'all enjoyin the exhibits?"

Alane was real cheerful when she said, "Why, hello Leroy. Momma,

Daddy, you remember Leroy Evans, don't you?" They said they did and treated me like any person would want to be treated. I appreciated that about them seein that they may not have wanted their daughter runnin around with a boy whose family ancestors may have caused trouble to their family ancestors.

We talked for a minute about how this was sure a fine exhibit this year and how Mr. Sharpe would be a judge for one of the contests. I said somethin stupid about that made perfect sense bein that he was a judge and passed out sentences all week long anyhow. As soon as I said it, I wished I could've swallowed them words, seein as how I didn't want them thinkin I was too blubberbrained. They didn't act like they thought less of me and went on talkin about the exhibits. Alane then asked her parents could she walk around with me a little to look at all the different things in the hall. Her parents said it was all right, so long as we was back in about an hour.

As we went walkin off Alane said right off the bat that she was glad I had come because she was interested to know what I had to tell her. That made me kinda nervous. I suggested that maybe we could step outside where there weren't so many folks around. One thing about Alane is that her and her family know everybody in Cassville and it's hard to keep a conversation goin without her bein interrupted by somebody who would come along and say hello and how you doin. We went outside the buildin to a bench and sat down. It wasn't what you'd call cold outside, but it was cool. I had on a thin jacket, but Alane had on a heavier coat. Not that I would've tried to snuggle up to her, but I thought it wouldn't have done no good what with her bein so wrapped up in that big coat.

We got comfortable and I commenced to talk. "Well, you see Alane, this afternoon when you asked me about my family, I didn't really know what to say. The same thing happened to me a couple weeks ago when I was up to your house and we was studyin and got to talkin about your family. You asked me about what was my family like and I kinda danced around the subject because I didn't know what to say then neither. I just figured I ought to let you in on what things are like at my house, just so you'd know."

Alane didn't say nothin. I couldn't tell if that meant she was interested in what I was saying or if it meant the exact opposite and she wasn't a bit interested. I collected my thoughts and nervous like kept goin. "You see, you come from a real nice family and my family, well, it just ain't like that. You got this family room in your house, and we don't have nothin like that. I mean, we got a front room in our house where the family all sits, but it isn't like your family room where y'all probably sit in there and enjoy bein with one another." I wasn't sure if I was makin any sense at all. Sometimes my words get all jumbled up and I don't know if I'm talkin English or French or what.

"I see. I didn't know that. What made you want to tell me?" The look she was wearin suggested she wasn't judgin me, and I was thankful for that.

I felt like a hobo who was talkin to the daughter of the President of the United States. I kept on explainin. "Well, you see, whenever you and me talk it's easy for you to talk about your family because you got nice parents. Not that I don't think my parents aren't nice, they're just . . ." I couldn't think of what to say. Actually, if I was to be truthful, I'd have to say my daddy wasn't that terribly nice to be around. Momma was a different story. She was nice, even though she pretty much kept to herself and wasn't the sociable type like Mrs. Sharpe.

"You don't have to say what they are, Leroy. I think I know what you're trying to get across to me."

"You do?" Boy that was somethin, because I sure didn't know where I was goin with my words. I was glad she was followin my thinkin.

"I'll try to be more understanding and stay away from talk about my family or your family. If it makes you feel bad, then we can just talk about something else."

"No! That's not what I mean. I don't want you to think you can't talk about your family around me. In fact, I kinda like it. I enjoy hearin about what goes on at your home. I like seein your momma and daddy and bein around folks that's nice like them. I don't even mind you knowin about my family bein the way they are. In fact, I wouldn't mind bein able to tell you more about what things are like at my house. It's just that I felt I was almost lyin when I was pretendin to you that my family is a lot like yours. That's all." Alane nodded her head. I stared off, and she was polite enough to let me think for a minute before she broke the silence.

"What is your family really like, Leroy?" The way she asked that question let me know she wasn't interested in findin out somethin she could go off and gab about to her girlfriends. It was more like she was interested because she really wanted to know who I am and what kinda lot I come from.

"That's kinda hard to say." I was pretty hard-pressed for an answer to that question. I thought a minute and then said, "You see my daddy drinks an awful lot. A lot of nights he just sits at home doin nothin but drinkin. Sometimes he goes out and goes over to a friend's house and I'm sure they drink over there. Some evenins he's all right and doesn't drink at all, but that's not much. He'll even go several days in a row every now and then without drinkin, but you know he'll always go back to it."

"What about your mother?"

"Oh, she don't drink. Daddy's the only one."

Alane almost laughed. "No, I mean, isn't it hard on your mother to take care of the family and do all the things a wife needs to do to make sure the house is cared for?"

"Oh. Well, she does all right, I suppose. She's always busy doin somethin around the house. She takes care of payin most of the bills and that kind of thing. That's the hard part. Daddy don't work real regular and so money's kinda hard to come by most of the time. He doesn't seem too worried about it neither. Momma worries about everything."

"What is your daddy doing for work now?"

I hated to admit to Alane that Daddy wasn't even at home right now, but I didn't want to start pretendin all over again. I'd already told her more than I had told any other girl. Actually Woody was the only other person I had really talked to about all this. A couple of my friends knew about my family's ways, but boys don't usually ask much about such things. "You see, Daddy got pretty drunk earlier this week and got mad and left. He hasn't been home all week. We don't rightly know where he is, but Momma says he's probably out in the country stayin with his brother."

Now what was she gonna think? Here I'd told her that my drunkard daddy had got mad and run away from home. I felt bad when it had happened, but now I felt really ashamed of what I had just said. It was like I was tellin all the secrets my family kept about just how rotten things could be at my house. Momma sure would be upset if she knew what I was sittin here talkin about.

The kind of bad I was feelin now was different than what I'd been feelin all week. While I'd been bein mad at Daddy for bein like he is to me and Momma and Cody Sue, now I was mad that he made me look like I was made of the same mold that had shaped him. He was an embarrassment to me.

"I'm sorry, Leroy." Alane fell silent for awhile. It was hard to read her. I wondered did she feel sorry for me havin to live the way I do or did she feel sorry she had made friends with someone with my kind of home life? My life is sure different than hers. That was plain to tell. With every detail I had given so far, she had been kind and acceptin of what I had to say. But the deeper I went into tellin about my family, the closer I figured I was comin to the limits of her tolerance.

"Well I guess that's about all I got to tell you." I figured I'd said enough.

I was through talkin unless she had any more questions she wanted to ask. Now I would just have to wait and see did she still want to be friendly with me or if she was ready to say so long it's sure been nice knowin ya.

"Do you think it can ever change?"

What? My family change? I'd never thought of that. Maybe I used to when I was little, but I had quit hopin for things to get better around the house for a long time. I figured Alane would want to know did my daddy ever hit my momma or me and Cody Sue. I was already wonderin what I would say if she asked me that one. But I'd never thought about what she just asked. Could my family ever change?

I kinda chuckled as I said, "I doubt that one. You don't know my daddy. He don't do nothin unless he thought of it first. And it's pretty safe to say he hasn't given much thought to givin up his drinkin or workin a regular job or actin different around the house. In fact that's one of the things that set him off earlier this week. He got real drunk after Momma got onto him about not havin a regular job and not carin for the family. It's not like Momma to say anything about how Daddy doesn't do much to help out the family. Naw, it's not too likely Daddy's gonna change. But I figure I'll do things different when I'm older and have my own home. I guarantee I ain't livin the rest of my life like this."

Maybe it was because Alane doesn't live with a drunk daddy, but she didn't let go of the idea that things could be different for my family. "You never know, Leroy. You just might be the one who could cause your family to make changes. Maybe your daddy would listen if you talked to him. I know my daddy listens to me when I tell him about something that needs attention. It's natural for parents to care about their children and to want to do what's right for them. That's what my daddy says. He tells me he likes it when I tell him about things he might not have noticed."

I was becomin pretty convinced now that Alane didn't understand me too good because here she was tellin me to do the things that worked for her. I knew it wouldn't do no good to say nothin to Daddy about his ways. Momma and Cody Sue and me all know we just had to learn to live with whatever he decided he was gonna do. Might as well, because he's gonna do it anyway. Look at what happened the other night when Momma got onto him for not workin steady. Daddy got so drunk he probably doesn't even know that he overturned the kitchen table and threw things all over his own bedroom. And then he left home. Not that I care a whole lot that he's gone, but there sure isn't much chance for improvin his attitude when we don't even know where he is or when he's comin back, or if he plans to come home at all. Talkin to Alane's daddy is one thing, but gettin through to mine is another job altogether.

"That's a nice thought. I'm sure glad you can go to your daddy. Mine ain't so easy to get through to. Thanks for the suggestion, though. You've been real nice to listen to me." I figured there wasn't much use in me tellin Alane what I really thought about her suggestion. If I'd said it was useless to even think of sayin somethin to Daddy and then expectin him to just quit drinkin like that, it would have been embarrassin to her. She was just tryin to be nice.

It was about time for Alane to get back to where her parents was. I said so and we went into the buildin to look around for them. When Alane saw them across the way, she said there they are and I said well I guess I'd be goin on home. Somehow I felt that if I looked at her momma and daddy in the face, they'd know what all I had just told their daughter, like I was walkin around with naked feelins or somethin. I waited to make sure she got with them all right and then made my way home through the dark night.

It began to drizzle on me while I was walkin, but that seemed to match my mood pretty close. I didn't feel upset toward Alane or nothin like that. In fact, I figured she must have understood some of what I was sayin because she was nice to me and all. I just felt kinda let down when she went to tellin me what I ought to do to try to change things, that's all. I didn't really need nobody to tell me what I ought to do. I already knew what I ought to do and that was to just wait until I was an adult and then make somethin of myself the best I could. Oh well, at least I did what I had set out to do and that was to quit pretendin that I'm somebody I'm not. Who knows how Alane would treat me from now on. I'd just have to wait and see.

As I walked home I kept thinkin on the words she said. "You never know, Leroy. You just might be the one who could cause your family to make changes." Them was right painful words for me to think on. Right painful.

Chapter 10

I WAS walkin down by the Tennessee River a couple evenins later right after supper. Wasn't doin nothin besides just thinkin. Ol Pancho had decided to come along with me. I like it when I don't have to do nothin except just think. Daddy says its dangerous when I do such, but I'd probably bust if I couldn't get off to myself now and then, specially with all that had been goin on lately. The Tennessee River was only about a half mile from my house. I know it don't make sense that the Tennessee River run split through Alabama, but it did. It flowed right through town. When we was boys, me and Sav liked to come down here and see could we skip rocks all the way across to the other side of the river. We never did make it, but we kept on tryin all the same. Now I liked comin down here just to have a place to be all to myself.

I don't always pay attention in school, but I like it when we study about Cassville history. It seems that Cassville was first found by a bunch of Indians. Who knows how long they'd been in this here territory before this place actually became a town. One of my teachers said it was a long time, but I don't remember if she said how long. The good fishin in the Tennessee River was one of the main reasons the Indians decided to live here. I know one thing and that is that there's a bunch of big ol catfish in the river.

While I was walkin along the riverbank that evenin tryin to forget about my family, I pretended I was an Indian boy and Pancho was my Indian dog. I looked down at my mutt and tried to imagine him wearin an Indian dog headband. That made me laugh. I threw out my imaginary line tryin to bait a big catfish. It's odd to think that an Indian boy and his dog might have walked along this very bank actin the same as I was. Them Indians was called the Creek Indians. I don't know what the Indians called this place, but somewhere down the line it got named Cassville. Seems like it was named after some French fella, but I think somebody spelled the ol boy's name wrong. I suppose we have to accept that not all French folks were good spellers, same as not all us modern folks are good spellers. Somebody apparently wrote the name down the wrong way one day and it stuck. Anyhow, that's how Cassville got its name.

I was enjoyin thinkin about the old Creek Indians and pretendin that I lived here centuries earlier when I spotted Woody about a hundred yards down the way. He was sittin on the bank watchin his bob, just in case he caught one of them big yellow catfish. Woody liked a lot of things, but there wasn't nothin he liked better than fishin. Actually, when I say Woody liked fishin, I don't really mean he liked catchin fish. He didn't like catchin fish as much as he liked settin on the bank doin nothin. "Afta all," Woody would say, "Dat's what fishin is. Settin dare lookin at de watta." Catchin a catfish was probably just a nuisance to Woody. He liked to sit uninterrupted and think more than I did. He was good at it, too.

"Hey dare, Leroy," called Woody when I got close enough for him to notice me. "Whatcha doing out here walkin all slow and doin nuttin?"

"Hey there, Woody. Oh, I'm just out here thinkin and talkin to Pancho here. I was thinkin about the Creek Indians really. You know, wonderin what it musta been like livin in an Indian village a long time ago right here in this very spot. Me and Pancho was actin like I was an Indian brave and he was my Indian hound dog. That's all."

The thought of me pretendin to be a Creek Indian struck Woody funny and made him chuckle a little bit at what I was tellin him. "Well come set a spell wit me. I was jes doin some o my own thinkin." I went and sat down next to my colored friend. Pancho plopped down on the bank, too. I don't know what it was about Woody, but just bein around him made me feel real proud. I was proud in lots of ways. For one thing I was proud that he was the kind of man I could say anything to and he wouldn't look at me funny or laugh at me. That was important to me. For another thing, I was proud because I could prove that a white boy and a colored man could be friends. You know, there's still a lot of folks who look on the Negroes as if they're, well, not like regular people. A lot of colored folks don't like any white folks for that very reason. Can't say that I blame em. But I was proud of Woody because he wasn't that way and he liked me just the same. He didn't hold it against me just because I was born white, and I didn't hold it against him just because he was born colored. I was proud that me and him were friends.

I'll tell you another thing. It also made me feel proud that Woody likes givin me advice. But he does it in a way that doesn't bother me. A lot of adults think they have to drape their words in a bunch of judgment. You know, the way a preacher gets on to you and gives you advice all in the same breath and then goes and calls it a sermon. Woody doesn't do it like that. He knows when I'm ready to hear from him and when I'm not. It's like he can become me for awhile and judge for himself when the time has come for me to be talked to and when I need to go ahead and make a foolish mistake. I wish more adults had that mind about them. I know the world would be a lot better off if God had made more people who thought the way Woody did. But I guess if he had, folks like Woody wouldn't have nobody to help out. You gotta believe that God knew what he was doin when he made us the way he did.

We sat there awhile saying nothin, just enjoyin watchin the river roll on past us. I hadn't told Woody yet about Daddy leavin the house. I wanted to, but I was pretty wore out from thinkin about all that. I also wanted to talk to him about when me and Alane had that talk Saturday night at the Cotton Palace. I figured that rather than bring all that up just yet, I'd just enjoy sittin with Woody. To tell you the truth, I was tired of thinkin so hard these last few days. We could talk about serious things the next time.

While we was sittin there Woody spat some tobacca juice down into the river. I laughed at him and said, "Dad gum, Woody! What are you tryin to do, flood the river? I never seen anybody let that much spit outta their mouth at one time."

Woody laughed with me. He was the kind of man who could laugh with anybody, even if it was about himself. "Dis here tobacca's right juicy, Leroy. I jes chaws on it til I gots so much in ma mouf dat I hafta spit if I's gonna be able ta talk. You want some?"

I took one look at that hard plug he was holdin out in his hand towards me and said, "You mean that ol stuff? I don't expect so. That's nasty." I wasn't meanin to come across all rude. It's just that I wasn't anxious to suck on none of that stuff. He smiled and put it back in his pocket.

"I reckon I used ta think it wuz nasty, too, but it sho is good when ya gets used to chawin it. Specially when you's fishin." He spewed out some more juice into the river. I think Woody was just showin off how good that tobacca was.

"What's that tobacca called, anyhow, Woody?"

"Dis here's called Taylor Made. It's my fishin tobacca. I spits it on my worm. De catfish likes it, ya know." He tugged on his line as if to ask all the catfish down under the water, "Ain't dat right out dare?"

"You think I'd like that Taylor Made, Woody?" I don't know why, but all of a sudden I got right curious about takin a try at that tobacca. I look back at that question and wonder why I couldn't have come up with the right answer real quick, but I didn't.

"I cain't say, Mista Leroy, you not being a tobacca chewer an all. But you never knows. Ya jes might like it." Woody knew I wanted to try it, but didn't want to get the blame if I didn't care for it, or if I got sick or something. He was a gentleman in that way. He felt it was only right for a man to make up his own mind and not do somethin just because somebody else said so.

We sat there a little while longer. A catfish nibbled at Woody's line. Probably took the bait, but Woody didn't even bother to check. That's what I mean about him lookin on fishin as a time to sit and rest more than a time to catch fish. I broke the silence and said, "Say Woody, you think I might try a little bite of your Taylor Made? I'd kinda like to see if I like it." I poked at him and added, "Besides, it may help me catch a big ol catfish next time I bring my line down here."

"Like I said, you may not likes it like I does, but you's sho welcome ta give it a try." He reached in his pocket again and pulled out his plug which was wrapped in foil. "Jes take a bite o dis."

"How much?"

"Well suh, I takes 'bout dis much," he said showing me about how much he generally bit off. "It makes fo a moufful at fust, but after you chews on it awhile you can manage it real easy. Least dat's what I does."

I took off a big ol plug of that Taylor Made. It about made me gag. "This stuff tastes rotten!"

"Dat's jes what I said when I fust took some tobacca, but it ain't rotten! Jes bought it fresh dis monin." Woody was tryin pretty hard not to laugh at me. I guess I should've been appreciative for that. On the other hand, maybe he was thinkin that if he laughed at me right off, I'd spit the whole wad out and his fun was over. He was probably holdin off just so he could see what might happen next.

This was one of them times Woody could tell I needed some advice. "Jes push it back in yo mouf an draw on it. Ya don't wanna chew it. When you gits enough juice, jes spit. Dat's all dey is to it."

I tried takin Woody's instruction, but the tobacca plug was so hard, I had to chew it just to soften it up so I could push it back in my mouth easier. I musta swallowed some juice in the process even though I was tryin hard not to. I spat a couple times, tryin to get the hang of what I was doin. Despite I acted like I thought you was supposed to act while chewin tobacca, Woody couldn't keep from laughin. In fact, it wasn't long before he started rollin on the bank, clappin his hands. I'd never seen an old man carry on like that, and said so. "What're you laughin at?" I mumbled. "Hadn't you never seen a fella chew tobacca before?"

"Not like dat, I sho hadn't! Why boy, you looks like an ol heffer chewin at de cud!"

I wanted to laugh with Woody because I imagine I did look right funny what with not knowin how to chew tobacca the right way and all. I tried to muster a smile, but I couldn't. I was feelin too green to do much of anything. Course, that made Woody laugh even harder. I was glad to see him have such a good time. I just wish it didn't have to be at my expense.

I went along for maybe fifteen minutes chewin on that Taylor Made. Woody kept tellin me, "Now don't chew quite so hard, Leroy." Maybe it was because I felt the need to be doin somethin with that great big wad in my mouth, or maybe it was because I was just not smart enough to learn proper tobacca chewin technique, but I never did get the hang of drawin on the plug the way it's supposed to be done.

"I hate to say it Woody, but I'm feelin a little peaked."

"You sho looks bad, Leroy." Woody's side was bound to be hurtin by this time, as long as he'd been laughin. The way I felt right now, I was hopin his side did hurt. Not that it was his fault I was feelin terrible. It just seemed like somebody else ought to have been sharin the discomfort I was feelin. I guess I ought to admit that by now I was holdin Woody at least a little responsible for my bellyache. I suppose I was thinkin he deserved a little bit of my sufferin. I feel bad now that I look back on it, but that's how I honestly felt at the time.

I stood up to move on along. Figured I'd had about all the fun I cared to have at one time. I spat out the wad of Taylor Made and reached my cupped hands over into the river to get a little slurp of something that might wash the taste out of my mouth. I figured dirty river water couldn't have been any worse than what had already been in my mouth. When I stood up from the riverbank, I plopped straight back down onto the grass. Woody knew exactly what I musta been experiencin and correctly guessed, "Yo world is spinnin all 'round, ain't it, Leroy?"

"Whoo-wee!" That's all that come outta my mouth. While layin there on my back, I recollect thinkin that I didn't know the sky had so many colors in it. I also didn't know it whirled around quite like it was right then. I waited for the world to catch up with me and decided I'd better get on home. I don't think I hardly even said good-bye to Woody. I do recall hearin him clappin as I walked along the riverbank. I'm glad he was havin such a good time, 'cause I wasn't.

Pancho stuck right close to me. I think that ol hound dog knew I might need him, so he stayed ready just in case. I had to stop a couple times along the way to blow beets, as they say. I'd had a pretty good supper that night and hated to lose it what with Momma goin to all the trouble of fixin it for me and all. Didn't have much choice in the matter, though. You can't keep it down when it decides its comin up is what I'd heard old folks say before. Boy, that's the dern truth.

When I walked into the house, Momma was in the front room sewin, I think. To tell the truth, I don't really remember what Momma was doin. I wasn't in much of a position to be payin attention to them kind of small details. I felt obliged to spend a couple minutes talkin to her before I went to my room. I didn't want her to suspect I had been up to somethin no good. I didn't feel guilty at all about what I had did, but Momma would've seen it as mischief. If she'd known I'd been chewin tobacca, she would've thought up some kinda punishment, as if gettin sick to my stomach wasn't enough to keep Taylor Made outta my mouth in the future. The way Momma worries about things, she might even have thought I'd had some alcohol if I let on to feelin woozy. After battlin with Daddy over his practice all these years, she had swore not to let me develop the same bad habit. If she had thought that's what I'd been doin, I would've really got it. So I felt obliged to sit down and talk awhile just to let her know everything was all right. That sure was a long couple of minutes, but I finally found my way to my bed and laid down.

It's kinda odd what takes your mind off of your troubles. I had headed over to the Tennessee River just to walk and be by myself awhile. I didn't intend to forget about my troubles by chewin Taylor Made and gettin sick. That's what had happened though. It didn't take long for me to get to sleep. I'd pretty much emptied my stomach and felt a little better. I needed the rest. Funny how I came about it.

I figured I'd be all right tommorow when I went to school and that maybe some day I'd tell Sav and Ernie about how I had chewed tobacca. I'd make it sound like it tasted real good so they'd want to try it. That way I could be the one to get a good laugh. I needed to find a reason to laugh that night. Things was fixin to get all dramatic like again and I'd need to start usin my brain for thinkin. I didn't know about that while I laid there in bed with my bellyache. It's a good thing, too. For the first time in a good while, I got a good night's sleep.

Chapter 11

HAD a headache the next day when I woke up. Didn't know you could feel hung over after chewin tobacca, but I suppose that's what I was. Momma acted surprised like when I asked for some hot coffee for breakfast. When I explained that I had heard some old men say it was supposed to turn off cold that day and that I was wantin to be warmed up before I went off to school that satisfied her, and I got my coffee. I had no idea what the weather was supposed to do that day, but the warm drink made me feel better.

My studies had took a beatin the last few days what with me not feelin all that perky and all. I would have liked to tell my teachers that the reason I wasn't payin much attention in class was on account of my daddy leavin home and the misery it had been givin me and my momma and sister. But if you ask me it isn't a teacher's place to have to listen to my woes. Besides, that was just an excuse for not doin all my work and I know it. All the same, I bet any of my teachers would've had a hard time concentratin on their job if they'd been through the same as I had lately.

I told Sav while we was walkin to school that I was goin to try extra hard in my classes today because I needed to get some work done that I'd been neglectin. I explained how I wanted to go off to college one of these days and had better start gettin serious about my learnin. I figured today was just as good as any to start preparin for what lied ahead of me. While I was talkin, Sav gave me one of them looks like he thought my shovel wasn't full of dirt or somethin like that. No matter what he was thinkin, I was ready to quit slumpin through life. I want to worry about things that I know is gonna do me some good. Gettin all stewed up about my family hadn't been helpin me out any, that's for sure.

It probably would've been a good day for me, too, if it hadn't been for Bruno Lynch. That dad gum Bruno can ruin the best of a boy's intentions and he sure ruined mine. Before school us fellas was standin out under the boys' oak trees like usual. On cool mornins we usually find some reason to run around a little just to help stay warm. One of the fellas, I think it was Leslie Carson, had brought a football with him despite it's against the rules to bring balls and things like that to school. Them kinda things are supposed to be a distraction to your education so we've been asked to leave them at home. I say asked, actually we've been told to leave things like footballs at home. I never did understand the reason for that rule because about all you hear bein talked about at school, at least at Cassville High School, is football. In this town that seems to be more than a notch or two higher than readin and arithmetic and that sort of thing. Anyhow, we were outside horsin around and playin with Leslie Carson's illegal football when Bruno come up behind me and for no reason tackled me. I didn't even have the ball. He just whacked me 'cause he felt like stirrin up trouble.

I got mad real quick like. "What're you doin, Bruno? We was just throwin the football. We ain't playin a dad gum game! Besides, even if we were, I didn't have the ball and you know it." I probably would've been smart to shut my mouth right there, but I was pretty aggravated at the way he had run up behind me and jumped on me without no warnin. Besides, it doesn't take too much for me to get sore at Bruno. The sight of him usually sets me to thinkin things I probably shouldn't admit to. "Get your fat double-gutted self offa me!"

Bruno weighed a whole lot more than I did and just laid there on top of me laughin. Of course, me hollerin like I was didn't make him in no hurry to oblige me. "What's the matter, you too little and skinny to get me off you?" I didn't like the way Bruno was tauntin me.

"Get off, you tub o lard! Just get off. I can't breathe!"

I shouldn't of said that neither. Bruno liked that he was makin me mad so he kept on layin there, diggin me in the side with his fat knee. He had grabbed me with one arm around my neck and was chokin me. By this time all the other fellas had gathered around and was yellin and carryin on. Not many of them cared too much for Bruno neither. He's the kind who can make enemies real quick like. He never has much nice to say to anybody. The other fellas was hollerin for Bruno to get up and let me have a fair chance at him. Somebody pulled at Bruno enough for me slip out from under him. I jumped to my feet and before you knew it, I had my fists up and was challengin Bruno to fight me. "If we're gonna fight, then let's fight fair!" I've said more intelligent things than that in my life, but I was mad and that's what came out of my mouth. Besides, he wasn't gonna let me alone, so I figured I might as well do what I could to defend myself.

That's all Bruno wanted to hear. He lowered his head and lunged at me, buttin me in the stomach just like a bull who was takin a swipe at a red cape. He caught me off guard, knockin the breath outta me and sendin me back down to the ground. He jumped on me again, but this time he wasn't content to just play around with me. He wanted to hurt me. Not that I didn't want to hurt him, too, I just wasn't in the best position to do nothin about it. He was, though. He slugged me good a couple times, and I was thinkin I was about to get thrashed when he was pulled off of me.

I looked up from the ground and towerin over me was Mr. Higgins, the school principal. Mr. Higgins is a big, tall man anyways, but I swear he looked at least eight or nine feet tall from where I was layin. He's a good two hundred and fifty pounds, and I mean it's a hard two-fifty, not the blubbery type. I couldn't see all of him, but I could tell he was mad by the way he stood there with his fists clenched and cocked on his hips. He looked like one of them fellas who must of caused Cassville to be called Shotgun Junction way back in the late 1800s. If I'd thought about that at any other time, I might have laughed, but I didn't think Mr. Higgins would understand me laughin right then. He didn't look like he was in that kind of mood.

"Get up, son." I pulled myself up. There's no doubt I was a sight to see what with my clothes all dirty and hair messed up and breathin heavy and all. I wanted to shake Mr. Higgins's hand and say thanks for rescuin me from big Bruno, but I didn't think that was appropriate neither. He stood there glarin first at me and then at Bruno. Boy can that man stare hard. I started feelin guilty right there on the spot. I don't know why I felt thatta way, seein as how it was Bruno what started all this ruckus, but I did.

Like he was a little kid tattlin on someone for pickin on him, Bruno whined, "Mr. Higgins, Leroy's the one who piled into me like he wanted to fight. We was just playin some football and he got all mad and started fightin." He would've kept on noisin about, but Mr. Higgins stopped him cold.

"Donald, I'm not one bit interested in what you've got to say right now! You were fighting the same as Leroy here. Both of you, get on up to my office with me right now!"

I picked up my books and followed Mr. Higgins into the school. Bruno walked along beside me. I hated to have to be that close to him. My anger turned to shame fast, though, when we walked right past the girls' red oak tree where Alane Sharpe and some of her friends was standin. I noticed that Royce Blackwell was standin in the group with her. She probably thought I looked like a common criminal bein led away to the gallows like we'd learned about in history. Somehow that would've been a little easier to accept at the time than havin to march right past Alane lookin all sorry and dirty like I did. I wanted to stop and explain things to her, but instead I put my eyes on the ground and stuck close to Mr. Higgins.

We had to sit just outside Mr. Higgins's office waitin on him to call us in for our punishment. He likes to make his victims sit for a little while before bringin them in to let em have it with his paddle. Just sittin in a chair next to Bruno was enough of a penalty for me. I knew better than to sit there talkin big about what I'd just done, but Bruno didn't. I tried to ignore him tellin me how he had whipped up on me. I told him to stuff a dirty sock in his mouth, but he didn't seem to listen to my advice. That boy just doesn't know when to quit. I honestly think if I'd agreed, he would have kept on fightin right there outside Mr. Higgins's office. That's about how smart that boy is.

"Donald, come in here! Shut the door behind you." I was glad Bruno had to go first. That way I could get some idea of what to expect when it was my turn. I couldn't hear all that was said, but I could tell that Mr. Higgins was gettin onto him pretty hard about bein in another fight. His voice was comin through the walls pretty good. Bruno musta offered some limp reason for why he had jumped on me, but it didn't appear that Mr. Higgins appreciated what he had to say. It just caused Bruno to get yelled at that much harder. I have to admit I enjoyed that part. Bruno deserved whatever he was gettin in there.

Things got quiet in Mr. Higgins's office for just a second, and then I heard a loud boomin sound that was obviously comin off of Bruno's big ol ham hocks. Whack! Whack! Whack! Ouch, that hurt me to think about gettin licks. If Bruno got them, I was sure to get some, too. I started sweatin when I thought about me gettin the same punishment as what Bruno was gettin. I was glad that old bully had gotten his, but I didn't really feel deservin. On top of that, Mr. Higgins was said to be able to send a big boy right into the next county with his hard licks.

The door opened and Bruno walked out. Looked like he was tryin not to cry. Boy wouldn't that be somethin to see this fella who thought he was the toughest thing in Cassville come walkin in class with tears hangin under his eyes. That was another one of them times I wanted to laugh but didn't, seein how it didn't seem to be such good timin.

"Leroy, your turn! C'mon in here." I gulped. The way he said it was my turn musta meant it was now my time to get what Bruno had got. My rear end didn't have near the paddin his did. Boy was it gonna hurt. I sure hoped I didn't cry. If I did, I was gonna ask Mr. Higgins could I sit in his office a minute before I went back to class. I at least wanted to be able to show myself as a man in front of my classmates, not like a whipped puppy.

Mr. Higgins almost laughed when I came in on account of how scared stiff I looked. I don't mind admittin I was about to fill my drawers. That's not the kind of paddin I was wantin to put in my britches. Mr. Higgins sat there behind his desk, lookin awful powerful like. "Relax, Leroy. I'm not going to bite your head off. In fact, you're not even in trouble. I want to talk to you, that's all. Why don't you close the door behind you." I sure was surprised at how calm he sounded. It was like a different man was in here than what I'd heard yellin at Bruno. I sat down across from the big man and quiet like waited for him to speak again.

"This is your first time to visit me for disciplinary reasons, isn't it, Leroy?"

"Yes, sir."

"It's not like you to be getting in fights. What happened?"

I knew Bruno had been in here a few minutes earlier just lyin away about how I had started everything. I also had heard how Mr. Higgins let him have it for soundin so whiny. I wanted to tell the truth and let Mr. Higgins know I hadn't started no fight, but I didn't want to sound whiny neither.

"Well, as best I can recollect, a few of us fellas was horsin around out there and Bruno decided he wanted to join in and he come up and tackled me from behind. I got mad and I showed it. I know that wasn't the right thing to do and I'm sorry, but I sure was mad at the time."

Mr. Higgins laughed again. What in thunder was makin him laugh like that? "You fellas call Donald 'Bruno,' don't you?" I nodded. "It probably doesn't take much for him to irritate you, does it?"

"No, sir, it sure don't."

"Well Leroy, don't worry about what happened out there this morning. I know that fight was all Donald, I mean Bruno's, doing and not yours. You were doing what most any other boy would've done. Just don't make it a habit, you hear?"

"Yes, sir." I guessed right then that I wasn't gettin licks. Knowin that sure made me breathe a lot easier. My insides settled down, too.

I thought Mr. Higgins was about ready to send me back to class when he spoke up again. "I don't mean to be prying into personal matters, but I think I might know why you got angry so quickly and got into a fight. I heard your daddy left home a few days ago. Tell me Leroy, what's been going on down at your house?   Y'all heard from him?"

How'd he know about that? I didn't know too many people kept up with what went on at my house. At first I didn't know what to say. "Um, well, yes, sir, Daddy's been gone for a week or ten days now. We ain't heard from him. He left pretty mad. Momma says we'll hear from him whenever he gets over bein mad."

"How's your momma doing? She must be pretty broke up over all this."

"She is. I guess you could say we all are. That is, me and Cody Sue and Momma."

"Leroy, I've got some relatives that live out in Cow Pens where your daddy's brother lives, so I know that's where he's staying. Did you know that's where he is?"

"Momma said she figured it."

"I understand your daddy is pretty bothered about what happened and hopes he'll be coming home soon. He doesn't know if he's welcome to come back, though. Can you tell me how your momma feels about things, son? I'd like to help out if I can."

Shoot, I didn't know what to say. How could I tell anybody how my family felt when nobody ever talked about that kinda thing around my house? "Well, Mr. Higgins, I don't rightly know how to put it. I know my momma's all upset, but she doesn't talk about it a whole lot. That's just her way. You can tell her feelins is all washed up by the way she's been actin, though."

"I don't want to pry where I don't belong, but do you feel like telling me what's the problem between your momma and daddy?"

"Well, the problem's mostly with my daddy. Momma says he drinks too much and won't work enough to make ends meet around the house. She's right, too."

"Is there a lot of fighting going on?"

"No, just the one. It was a pretty good one, though. Mostly they don't get into it like they did that night."

"Well, Leroy, if you think it would be all right, I might send word to your daddy through my relatives that you're doing fine and that you said to tell him hello. You think that would be proper?"

"You won't tell him about me and Bruno gettin into that fight, will you?"

"Not a word." I sure appreciated that. Daddy might come home just to give me a whippin for fightin. That sure wouldn't make a whole lot of sense, hittin me because I'd been fightin. I guarantee you Daddy wouldn't think on it thatta way, though.

"Thank you, Mr. Higgins. That would be just fine."

I left his office and went on into class. By now word had spread through school that me and Bruno had been fightin. I didn't especially want the reputation of bein a fighter, but there wasn't much I could do about it that particular day. It's odd how things turned out after bein in that fight. I was glad to hear from Mr. Higgins about where Daddy was. It kinda surprised me to hear that he was bothered by what he'd done that night. He sure never showed that kind of feelin around none of us at home. Hearin it made me kinda miss Daddy. Dad gum, I didn't figure I'd be thinkin thatta way any time soon. The way I had been seein it, it was his fault things was the way they was and him gettin mad and leavin was on account of his drinkin and not anything the rest of us had done.

Here I'd come to school today figurin on puttin my mind to my studies and before I even got to class I had gone right back to thinkin about Daddy and Momma and all that had been happenin at home. At lunchtime, I heard from Sav that Bruno had been doin some thinkin, too, but it was about somethin entirely different. I was now his sworn enemy, and he aimed to get me after school this afternoon.

Chapter 12

AFTER HEARIN that Bruno was gonna be lookin for me that afternoon, I took my time gettin my things together once school let out. I wanted to give that crude fella time to think he must of missed me when I come out of the buildin so he'd go on home and cool off. Maybe by tomorrow he wouldn't have it in so bad for me. Sav looked me up after my last class so we could walk home together. I told him I needed to go by Mrs. Tisdale's room to pick up a couple of biology assignments I hadn't done so I'd just talk to him later. Said maybe I could come over to his house later that evenin.

I did what I said I was gonna do and went by Mrs. Tisdale's class and talked to her for a little while. Mrs. Tisdale is one of them teachers I like a lot, and I think she likes me, too. She has this reputation for bein a mulish type of teacher what won't budge when it comes to lettin students have extra time on assignments, no matter what their excuse was. She wasn't never thatta way with me, though. In fact, she's just the opposite. I apologized for bein slow gettin my work done in her class and she was nice about lettin me have more time to make up some of the work I was already supposed to have done turned in. We talked for a little while about how I liked biology, and I let on like it was one of my favorite things, even though it isn't. That took up a fair amount of time, so I figured it was safe to go on outside.

You know, I hadn't stayed around too long after school had let out for the day—maybe fifteen minutes. It's downright amazin how fast a buildin as big as Cassville High School can become so deserted once they say y'all can go on home. I stood at the top of the school steps before I headed home just to see if trouble was waitin for me. Didn't see nothin.

Just to be on the safe side, I figured I'd walk home a different way than usual, in case Bruno was waitin for me along the way. Instead of goin down Ninth Street like I usually do, I went down Eighth Street. It was a straight shot down Ninth Street to near my house, so I was still goin in the right direction, just one block over. After a couple of blocks, I pretty much forgot about Bruno and tried to put my mind back on my studies. I hoped to get a lot of work done at home that night. I suppose I should've been payin better attention to where I was goin because several blocks from my house Bruno spotted me and headed my way. I didn't see him until he was practically standin in front of me.

"Hey, your rear end achin, Leroy?"

I was kinda startled, but I didn't want to let on that I was. I didn't know a whole lot about how you were supposed to act to a fella who was tryin to hard talk you, but I knew it wasn't the right thing to act all scared. That would just make the other fella want to fight all that much more since he'd figure he could win. "It ain't no business of yours how my behind is feelin. If you don't mind, I'm on my way home. I got things to do". I didn't want to tell Bruno I hadn't got it with Mr. Higgin's paddle like he had. That wouldn't have gone over so big with him.

"Like what, study?"

He said that like only sissies want to learn anything. It was plain that Bruno didn't care much about learnin, but I didn't want to act like I was interested in goin around actin as ignorant as he does so I just said, "As a matter of fact, that's what I was gonna do tonight. I don't aim on bein dumb all my life. You might, but that's not what I wanna do."

I shouldn't have said anything that would give Bruno an excuse to hit me. It wouldn't have taken much anyhow, but it was those words that set him off. He charged at me sayin, "You sayin I'm dumb? I'll show you just how a dumb boy can fight!"

I figured I might as well do all I could to defend myself. I didn't want to wind up under Bruno like I had this mornin. There wasn't nobody around to pull him off of me this time around. I kicked him right in the stomach as he got to me. That slowed him down a little bit, but not enough to stop him. He started for me again and just as he reached for me, I dodged to the side and tripped him. I hoped he'd just quit, but he didn't. He sure had it in for me.

"That's enough, Bruno! I ain't interested in fightin all day. You got your licks in this mornin." He didn't say nothin back, but headed right straight at me again. Guess he didn't care too much for what I'd said about us quittin all the fightin. It was plain he wasn't done. He grabbed me this time, and we both fell to the ground. We tussled around, rollin all around for a couple minutes. The only sounds bein made was the gruntin both of us was doin. Boy oh boy, was that Bruno one heavy load. I had got pretty mad by now and was fightin with all that was in me. I was holdin on pretty good, too, but bein that Bruno probably weighs seventy or eighty pounds more than I do, it was hard for me to do much damage to him. I think things was just about to get worse for me when a voice yelled out, "What are y'all doing? I thought you finished fighting this morning at school!"

That got Bruno's attention and as he looked up, I slipped out from under him and jumped up. He stood up, too, but didn't come after me. We was both sweatin and breathin heavy. Royce Blackwell walked up to us and looked Bruno square in the eye and said, "Don't you know when you've had enough? Get out of here before my daddy comes home! He doesn't especially like it when people use our front yard as a boxing ring."

I can't really say why Bruno listened to Royce like he was an adult or somethin. Royce isn't any bigger than I am. He sure doesn't look like the type who could back up any words he'd just said. I didn't know at the time that Royce's momma had heard the racket and stepped out onto the front porch. Bruno could see her whereas I couldn't. Whatever the reason for him hightailin it, I was glad when Bruno walked on off. I didn't even mind him sayin, "I ain't through with you yet, Leroy Evans!" Long as he was leavin, I didn't care what he said.

I brushed myself off and picked up my things. Royce bent over to help out. "Thanks, Royce, for comin out. I didn't know this was your front yard. I think Bruno was just about to wear me out. You come out at about the right time."

Royce and I knew each other a little bit, you know, enough to say how you doin to one another. I'd never really had a full conversation with him. Not that I'd ever had a reason to think poorly of him, but he was still kinda new in town and we'd just not had much reason to become friends. "He's not much of a fella is he?" Royce asked, speakin of Bruno.

I kinda laughed. "Nah, he seems to like to make trouble everywhere he goes. He's been thatta way ever since the first grade. I don't know what's got into him lately, but he seems to have it in for me. I'm sorry you had to see all this and that it happened in your front yard and all. That's the second time he's come after me today. I don't want to get the reputation of bein a fighter. I only fight when I have to."

Royce was real kind in the way he talked to me. "You didn't have much choice in it. I'd heard at school that he was mad because he got licks. Guys like him need to find someone to blame for the trouble they cause and I guess you were the one he chose. You want to come in and catch your breath for a minute?"

I didn't know what to say to that question. Here was the fella who acted like he was interested in the same girl I was interested in askin me would

I like to come into his house. That didn't feel right to me. Maybe he wasn't aware that I liked Alane seein as how I hadn't exactly made my feelins known to everyone.

Royce spoke again when I didn't say nothin. "Alane Sharpe told me today when she saw what had happened that she knew that you weren't the type to fight and that that other fella must have started things with you. She was embarrassed for you when Mr. Higgins took y'all into the school."

She was? Alane Sharpe was talkin to other folks like she knew what kind of guy I was? Shoot! I figured she was thinkin by now that I was pretty low down bein that I got in fights at school and all.

"Alane Sharpe said that about me?"

"Yes. Said you were a real nice fella and she wished that other guy would leave you alone. You know, I think she's a little fond of you. At least, it seems that way when she mentions your name."

Well how about that. Here was the guy who I figured was hornin in on my chances of gettin kinda close to Alane Sharpe tellin me that she thought I was a pretty good fella and that maybe she liked me. I didn't mind that Bruno had found me this afternoon after all. Else, how would I have found out from Royce what she was thinkin? I said I figured I was all right and that I should get on home. I shook Royce's hand and thanked him again for showin up when he did. I wanted to thank him for givin me the good word on Alane, too, but kept my mouth shut.

It wasn't too much farther to my house. I went on in the back door, hopin Momma wasn't in the kitchen so I could go clean up before she discovered what kind of shape I was in. She was there in the kitchen, though, and saw me soon as I walked in.

"Leroy, why you all dirty? You look like you been in a fight!"

Quiet like I answered, "I'm dirty because I *have* been in a fight, Momma. Two of them, in fact."

"What on earth have you been doin today, Leroy? It's not like you to be thatta way. What's done got into you?" Somehow when Momma gets on to me it isn't near as bad as when Daddy does. Her fussin is more the worryin type. When Daddy fusses, he means to put you in your right place. I didn't mind tellin Momma the truth about the day. Besides, I wanted to tell her what Mr. Higgins had told me about Daddy.

"Oh Momma, you know that Bruno Lynch? I don't know what his problem was today, but he seemed to have it in for me. He jumped on me while some of us boys was throwin a football before school and then started it again after school. I guess he figured it was my fault he got licks for that first fight and wanted to get me for that. It was his own fault, but I don't think he figured it thatta way."

"Licks! Did you get licks, too, Leroy?" Funny how I said all that and only one word stuck in Momma's mind. Licks. That was the only word she'd heard me say. That shows what kind of worrier Momma is.

"No, ma'am. I didn't get no licks. Mr. Higgins just took me in his office and talked to me real nice like. Guess what he told me while we was talkin Momma?" I didn't wait for her to make a guess. I was ready to change the subject. Talkin about an ornery fella like Bruno isn't my idea of pleasant conversation anyhow. "He said he's got relatives up at Cow Pens what knows Uncle Amos, and they told him that's where Daddy is stayin."

Momma sat down like I'd just told her somebody had died. You know ever since Daddy got mad and left, nobody has hardly even mentioned his name. Just a time or two Cody Sue has slipped and said somethin about him, but mostly it was like all three of us had forgot who he even was. Just mentionin him put Momma in a dither again, I could tell. I looked at her while she sat there at the kitchen table and wondered what was she thinkin. Maybe she was relivin in her mind what had gone on a week ago Monday night. If she was, that was probably gettin her all mad again. Or maybe she was sayin thank you to God that she knew for sure that's where he was and that he must be all right. For all we knew he could've left town and gone somewhere where we'd never see him again. I wonder how Momma would feel if she never saw Daddy again. I know there's been plenty of times I've said to myself that I'd do just fine if I never saw the man again. Surely Momma had thought the same thing seein how he's even harder on her than he is on me or Cody Sue. But he's my daddy and her husband and no matter how we feel about him most of the time, it would be at least a little bit on the sad side if we never saw his face again.

"That wasn't all he said, Momma." Momma looked up and with her eyes said well hurry up and spit out whatever it is I had to say. I kept on. "He said that Daddy was feelin right bad about what happened that night he left and wondered would we even let him back in the house if he showed up here again."

Momma kept her thoughts silent, but threw back her head a little and got this look on her face that said, "Hmph." Hard to read what she was thinkin. That was sure one private woman. Maybe I just wasn't too good at readin females. I couldn't read Alane too good last Saturday at the Cotton Palace, and I wasn't doin so good right now with Momma.

Cody Sue musta heard us talkin. Our house is pretty small so you don't have to be right in the same room as someone else to hear what all they was sayin. "You say Daddy's up at Cow Pens?" Now there's one female

I don't have much problem figurin out. Right now she was bein snoopy and tryin to be in on all that was goin on in the world. I doubt she was not so interested in knowin about Daddy as she was just not bein in the dark about things.

"Yes, Cody Sue, that's where Daddy's at. Mr. Higgins at school said so. He's got relatives up there what knows Uncle Amos." I probably sounded impatient the way I talked to Cody Sue.

"So, is he comin home pretty soon?"

"Who knows?"

Momma butted in kinda rude. "Cody Sue, your daddy's comin home whenever he sees fit. You know he ain't the type to do anything under no timetable exceptin his own. Until he does, there's no use frettin about it." There was a sharp tone in her voice. She didn't like it that we might get off on talkin about Daddy and his ways or how she must be feelin about things or anything such as that. I know she wanted to stop our conversation before it went any further. She'd done heard all she wanted to hear. But as long as the subject had been brought up, I had a couple more things I wanted to ask about. I figured Momma might not like it, but I wanted to know because it had to do with me.

"Momma, what're we gonna do about payin the bills if Daddy don't come home and find some work soon?"

Momma went quiet again. I looked at her like I was an adult sayin to a child that I demand an answer. I knew I couldn't say those words out loud, but nobody could keep me from thinkin them. Finally she revealed, "I been doin somethin about all that. I got me a few houses to clean startin this week. That ought to help out until we find out somethin more from your daddy."

One of the words you could use to descibe Momma is proud. She has never worked for money before because she doesn't think it's a woman's place to be providin for the family. The way she sees it, her job is to stay home and take care of her family by fixin the meals and keepin everything in the house in order. Most all women I know think thatta way. It's becomin a little more common for women to be workin for money, but not much. Momma's the kind that believes that only women who have to work in order to put food on the table should work. Well, that's pretty much the situation we're in at the time. They isn't no money comin in the house with Daddy settin up in Cow Pens doin nothin.

Her sayin she was tryin to find some payin work was the same as admittin she'd give up on Daddy. Maybe she still believed he was eventually comin home, but she must of been pretty sure he couldn't be counted on to provide for his family once he got here. The way I figure it, Momma must of been feelin right desperate for some time now. That's why she had got on to Daddy before he got so drunk and blew up. And for sure that's why she'd gone out lookin for work while me and Cody Sue was at school. I guess she was hopin she wouldn't have to tell us about her needin to work until she couldn't keep us from findin out. It was the same as admittin that our family had sunk pretty low.

Her sayin that and worryin the way she was made me feel right bad. "Momma, you think I need to be lookin for some kind of work I could be doin?" I figured the least I could do was offer to help out. Maybe I could look around for some odd jobs. I know a couple fellas who cuts wood for folks with fireplaces. With it gettin close to winter, maybe I could work at somethin like that if it would mean payin the bills.

"That ain't your responsibility, Leroy," Momma said proud like. Then she added as if she'd just remembered her manners, "Thank you just the same."

I went on to my room and got cleaned up. I was dirtier than I had thought. I was startin to feel kinda sore, too. I bet I'd be stiff in the mornin. Fightin and rollin around with a fat boy on top of me isn't what I'm used to doin. We ate supper in silence that night. Right after we ate, Momma cleaned the kitchen and told me and Cody Sue she'd be in her room if we needed her for anythin that night. Course, that meant one thing and that is that Momma needed to do some cryin. I got mad all over again at Daddy and hoped he was feelin real bad out there in Cow Pens. He'd sure made a mess of things around here. Despite what Momma had told me, I figured I needed to do somethin to help out with money around here.

Chapter 13

THE NEXT Friday afternoon I waited until pretty close to five
o'clock and went down to Wimp Dickerson's Barber Shop. Five
o'clock is the time Wimp closed up the shop, and I was hopin to
talk to Woody. It was a few minutes before five when I walked through
the door.

"Howdy, pal."

"Howdy, Wimp. You doin all right today?"

"Sure am. You know how Fridays is around here, though. Busy day.
Tommorow's Saturday and it's gonna be even busier then." I said
somethin about how I reckoned that was good seein how that's what paid
the bills. He laughed and agreed with me. He's practically always in a good
mood. I like comin into his shop.

Several men were sittin around in the chairs along the wall doin nothin
in particular. Cassville High was playin a football game that evenin and
a couple of them was chatterin on about that. There was still a lot of
opinions flyin around about whether or not it was right to be playin
football at night. That sure did set a lot of folks in this town off. I was
kinda amused by it all myself.

One man, I believe it was Mr. Spradling, was goin on and on to the
man sittin next to him about how a bunch of teenage boys had been caught
knob knockin the safe down at the Atlas Lumberyard over on
Montgomery Avenue. Knob knockin is when you knock the knob off the
safe and reach right in and take whatever you want. Mr. Spradling was
sayin, "Why would a bunch of hoodlum boys want to go in there and steal
a bunch of paint. It ain't like they was plannin to go and do some work
on anybody's house or nothin. There's only one thing that teenage boys
think about these days and that is what can they do that will cause trouble

to someone else. Them punks is gonna force people to put locks on their buildins just to keep safe."

He didn't seem to care that I was standin no more than three or four feet away from him while he was goin on about how teenage boys was hoodlums and punks. Hope he didn't put me in the same category as the fellas who knob knocked that lumberyard. They may have been hoodlums, but I'm not. I thought about tellin Mr. Spradling so, but I know he was just runnin off at the mouth. It wouldn't have done no good anyhow. He would've thought I was bein smart with him.

Woody was over in his usual spot puttin his things away. He looked up when I come his way and smiled. "Why dare's ma ol frien Leroy! How you doin today, Mista Leroy?"

"Hey there, Woody. I'm doin pretty good, I reckon. I always feel pretty good on Friday afternoon seein how I don't have to go to school for two whole days."

Woody laughed. "I knows jes what ya mean. Sho feels good."

I sat down in the chair at the end of the row. Woody and me talked mostly about nothin for a few minutes. I had a whole lot I wanted to tell him, but I figured I'd wait until he was ready to leave and see would he like to walk down to the river with me. He lived over on the other side of the river on the east side of town so it was convenient for him to walk that way. After Wimp closed up and Woody was ready to head on home, I asked, "You mind if I walk a spell with you, Woody? A lot's been goin on lately, and I'd like to see what you think about it all."

"Why, dat would be jes fine, Leroy. You tell ol Woody whatever 'tis you likes."

We walked pretty slow down Jefferson Avenue and I started to talk. "I guess you hadn't heard about all that's been goin on over at my house the last couple weeks. I was gonna say somethin to you about it the other day when I saw you down at the river, but we got to chewin tobacca, so I never got around to it."

Just the thought of that evenin set Woody to laughin again. This time I didn't mind laughin with him since I didn't have no sick feelins to hold me back. "I sho hadn't never seed nobody chaw on tobacca de way you wuz dat evenin, Leroy. No suh. Dat was sum sight. You sho made ol Woody laugh hard. Ya knows my side wuz hurtin de next day, don't cha?"

"I didn't know that, but you hafta admit it served you right for lettin me chew that ol stuff." Woody laughed, but he sure didn't come out and admit that he was guilty for none of what had happened. I suppose he wasn't.

"Is dat what you wants to talk ta me 'bout, Leroy? You wants sum more o dat Taylor Made?" Woody joshed me and reached in his jacket like he was gonna give some more of that chewer's delight.

"I don't think I'll ever want any more of your Taylor Made. That's for sure." We laughed some more and walked a little ways farther before I brought up my business with Woody. "I hadn't told you, but it's been near two weeks that my momma and daddy got into it and my daddy left home. We ain't heard a word from him, but we know he's stayin up at Cow Pens with his brother."

I could tell Woody was already tryin to become me as he was thinkin on what I had said. It was evident by the way he looked and the way he talked. "Dat sho mus be troublin yo family. Dat's not what a young man likes ta see happen."

"It has been troublin us. Funny thing is, nobody talks about it. Cody Sue don't understand a whole lot, but I know she's affected cause she's quieter than normal. Momma's all tore up. She goes back in her room sometimes and doesn't come out for the whole evenin. That means she's back there cryin. I want to ask her about it all, but I'm scared to. I'm 'fraid she'd just get all mad at me or somethin."

"Sum people has a hard time sayin what dey feels, don't dey, Leroy?"

"Yeah, they do. I have a pretty hard time, too, but I can't help but think about it. It'd drive me crazy if I didn't come out and say what's inside of me." Woody nodded. He didn't say nothin, but I could tell he was still thinkin. I asked him, "Why do you reckon people are like that, Woody? Why does Momma have to be so secretive about everything? Don't she know it just makes it worse?"

"Hard ta figure sum folks. Seem like dey'd see dat it don't do no good keepin all dat hurt and cryin inside, but dey don't. Some people gets convinced dat dey doin demselves a favor by keepin all silent. You sees it different, don't ya, Leroy?"

"I just know if I'm thinkin somethin, I do a whole lot better if I just go right ahead and talk about it."

"But some folks dey thinks jes de opposite. Dey thinks dat by not talkin 'bout it, it gonna jes go away . . . but it don't." We walked a little more and Woody added, "De whole family dat way, ain't dey?" When he said that, he wasn't sayin he thought my whole family was no good. He was just lettin me know that he saw how frustrated I was with em, that's all.

I sighed. "The whole family. I don't know if it'll ever be any different. I don't think it can be." When I said that, I got to thinkin again about what Alane Sharpe had said about me bein the one who just might be able to cause changes in my family. I was still bothered by what she had said and thought I'd run it by Woody and see what did he think. "Woody, you remember me tellin you about that girl Alane Sharpe?"

"De judge's daughter? Yeah suh, I do."

"Well, seems like whenever I get a chance to talk to her, she's all the time bringin up her family. Can't say that I blame her cause she's got good folks. But when she says somethin about her parents, then she's all the time askin me somethin about mine. It was like she figured my family and her family was alike. For awhile I just let her go on, but I got to thinkin I might as well be truthful and let her know that my family and her family, they're a whole lot different. So I had me a talk with her the other day and let her in on how things really is around my house."

Woody was interested in what I was sayin. "What'd she say?"

"Well, when I told her about my daddy bein all hard on everybody and drinkin too much and about Momma bein too timid about Daddy's ways, she said somethin I'd never thought about. Said maybe I'd be the one in the family who might make things different." I went silent. We had got to the river now and Woody said why didn't we sit on the bank for a minute if'n I didn't hafta hurry on home. I wasn't in no hurry so we sat down.

Woody commented on what I'd said. "I bets you's been thinkin right hard on what Miss Alane done said. She'd done said somethin different dan what mos folks woulda said."

"I sure have been thinkin. Funny how your mind works when you go to thinkin."

"How's dat?"

"Well, you see, at first I thought that Alane she didn't know what she was talkin about. I figured why didn't she come stay around my house and see how things is. Then I'd like to ask her if she still thought I might could go changin things."

"But dat ain't what you's thinkin now?"

"I don't rightly know. You think maybe there's somethin I could do to make things different around my house?"

"You mean if dey was, you'd give it a try? Hmm. Let's think on dat one." We sat there for a minute and then Woody asked, "You come up wit sumthin?" It was like Woody was a teacher who knew the answer but didn't want to tell me so I could figure it out myself.

"Tell me what you think about this, Woody. What if I was to stand up to Momma and tell her she needed to start lookin after herself and us kids a little better than she had been. I could've done that a couple nights ago, but I figured I better not."

"You knows yo momma pretty good. What you think would come of it?"

I thought hard for a minute. I tried to imagine Momma perkin right up when I said that and sayin, "You're right, Leroy, I do need to start takin up for me and you and Cody Sue." That didn't seem likely.

"It's hard to say. Momma's not the type to speak up for herself. She likes to just keep on doin whatever we been doin until she just has to change things. You know, she's started workin for folks cleanin their houses. She sure didn't want to, but she figured she'd let things go about as far as she could what with us not knowin when Daddy's gonna show up at home. It's not like her to want to hire out, but she had to."

"You mean, she likes things ta stay jes de same, no matta how bad dey is."

"Up until it gets to where she's pretty much forced to do somethin. That's right."

"Den sayin ta yo momma why don't she do sumthin might not be de bes thing. She might jes ignore you, reckon?"

"Yeah. Probably she'd just ignore me or tell me there wasn't nothin she could do." I stuck my chin down on my knees.

"Discouragin. Sho is discouragin. But you's probably thought dat ain't de onliest thing could be done."

I almost laughed at what I was about to say. "You know, I think all the time about what it's gonna be like when I get old and have my own wife and young'uns. My family ain't gonna be the type what just sits around and don't talk to nobody. Alane Sharpe has this room in her house they call the family room. I think they sit in there and talk to each other and enjoy bein a family. That's what I'm gonna have when I get my own house—a family room."

Woody seemed to agree with me. "Now dat sho would be nice ta have you dis room where everybody in de house dey come together an enjoy one another." He bobbed his head up and down like I'd just said somethin I ought to hold on to.

"What I'd like to do is say to my family, 'Look here, we got us a room in our house where we all sit, but we don't act like we even know anybody else in here. From now on this here room is gonna be a family room 'cause that's what we are, a family.'" After I had said all that, I kinda chuckled. I added, "I figure there's just two chances of that happenin—slim and none."

Woody didn't say nothin, but he sure was studyin hard. I stared out at the Tennessee River. It was pretty this time of the evenin. It was gettin a little cool, but not so much that I was feelin uncomfortable. The way things are around here in the fall, it'll get just a little bit cold for a couple days and then warm right back up. Earlier in the week it was a little on the chilly side, but not so much now.

My thoughts just roamed around kinda empty like in my head. For a minute I'd think about what me and Woody had been talkin about and then I'd move onto another thought. Just mentionin Alane's name had made me wonder what she was doin right now. Probably at home gettin ready to go to the Cassville High football game that night. I figured she went to them games, but I wasn't much for that sort of thing. My thoughts left again and went out to Cow Pens. I wondered if Daddy was drunk. His brother drank pretty bad, just the same as he did. Ran in the family, I guess. I sure wasn't gonna carry on the tradition, though. I'd already figured out that much.

I kinda shook my head and then looked over at Woody. He still had that same serious look on his face. Forehead was all wrinkled up, he was thinkin so hard. I remembered how Woody had told me a long time ago that thinkin was probably his favorite thing to do. I asked him one time what did he do at his house at night bein that he lived alone and all. He said he had lots to do to keep him busy and when he got finished doin it all, he took the opportunity to just think. Said it makes a man live a lot longer to think regular. Like I've said, I don't know how old Woody is, but he's gettin on up there. All the same, though, he doesn't look like he's gonna be slowin down anytime soon. Maybe all them years of thinkin was payin off.

"You sure are thinkin hard, Woody."

He turned in my direction and smiled that warm kind of smile that he has. "You set me ta thinkin, Mista Leroy. You sho did."

"What'd I say that made you think like that?"

"What you wuz sayin 'bout dat dare family room. Dat make a whole lot o sense to me. Sho do. Lot o sense."

I figured I ought to correct Woody and let him know what I really meant. "Oh, that. I was just talkin. I don't think there's much way that would happen at my house. Why, Daddy's not even home right now. Everybody figures he'll be back soon enough. But even when he comes back, that old front room will go right back to bein just a room we sit in. Not much else." Woody shook his head like he understood me. But at the same time, I don't think he agreed with what I was sayin. "You see what I'm talkin about, Woody?"

"I sees it. Sho do."

"What do you think?"

"I thinks you jes might have sumthin dare, Leroy." He kinda smiled again when he said that.

"Shoot, Woody! You mean you think I ought to go and tell my family that we need to be doin more talkin to each other instead of just sittin there at home doin nothin?"

"I ain't sugesstin dat's how you ought ta do it. I's jes sayin you's got a powerful lot mo good ideas dan you thinks you does. Maybe you's gonna figure yo family out befo you gets old enough ta leave home. Maybe so."

I shook my head like I agreed with what Woody was sayin. It wasn't that I didn't like what he had said. It's just that I stay confused most of the time when I think on my family's ways, that's all. We got off the subject of my family, and I told Woody about me havin two fights with Bruno Lynch in the same day. I told him how we had ended up fightin in Royce Blackwell's front yard and how Royce had told me that Alane Sharpe had felt right bad for me bein in all that trouble with Bruno. Woody laughed with me as I told him how I sure didn't know what I would've done if I hadn't got out of both them fights the way I did. He said he didn't see me as the fightin type and would've liked to have been there just to see that side of me.

It was gettin pretty dark by now so I figured I'd better get on home before Momma started worryin about me. I say start worryin about me, she was probably already worried about me, that bein what she does most all the time. Woody walked a little farther down the way with me before he turned around to get on back to the Suspension Bridge so he could go on to his house. "You keep on thinkin, Mista Leroy. You's gettin good at it."

I said I would. The way he said that, though, it was like he expected me to figure out a way to do just what Alane Sharpe had suggested I might do. Maybe I would look for some ways I could do some changin around our house. If Woody didn't think I ought to give up, then I wasn't ready to neither.

Chapter 14

A T THIS time of the year, it doesn't get light in the mornin until about seven thirty or so. Normally I'm up by six o'clock to get ready for school, but on Saturdays and Sundays I sure do like to sleep until it's light outside. I was gettin me some pretty good horizontal exercise, too, when I heard all this commotion outside. This vehicle was honkin loud outside my window and somebody was yellin. At first it was hard for me to tell what was goin on out there, bein that I'm generally not too alert first thing in the mornin. Then I recognized the voice. It was Sav. What in thunder was he doin out in front of my house this early on a Saturday mornin? Doesn't he have any better sense than to make all that racket in front of my house while I was tryin to sleep? I came up with the answer to that question real quick like.

"Hey Leroy! Get up! Come out here and look at what I got me!"

I flung open the window and hung my head out. There was ol Sav sittin behind the wheel of a beat-up-lookin truck just grinnin as big as a fella could grin. He looked like he was a king sittin up on a throne. I'd never seen a boy sit up so tall behind the wheel of a truck before.

"What're you doin, Sav? Didn't you know I was tryin to get me a little sleep?"

"It's time for you to get up! Come on out and lemme take you for a ride in my new truck. How do ya like it?" I didn't answer. I wanted to run out there and take a look at what Sav was drivin, but at the same time I didn't want to act too excited like 'cause then he might not get the message that I was irritated at him for wakin me up on a Saturday mornin. Course, he wouldn't have got that message anyhow. He was too excited to be thinkin about how he was botherin me. Besides, I was right curious to see his truck. I put on my clothes real fast and run out to the street where King Sav was waitin.

"Looky here at what you got! Where'd you get this thing?"

"Me and my daddy went and got it last night. She's a real peach, ain't she?"

I didn't have the heart to tell Sav his new truck wasn't exactly what you'd call pretty. It had a bunch of dents in it and the paint was gone in spots. It was a stunning sight to him, though, so I sure wasn't gonna be the one to tell him different. "She's right nice. I didn't know he was gettin you this thing. Why didn't you tell me about it?"

"I didn't know about it myself until we went and got it. Daddy got to talkin with this man a couple days ago who wanted to get rid of his truck. The man wanted a hundred and fifty dollars for it, but when the fella told Daddy he'd take a hundred and thirty, why we went ahead an got it. We couldn't pass up a good deal like that."

"Is it yours?"

"Not yet, it ain't. But Daddy says I can have it if I can come up with sixty-five dollars. He said he'd pay for half if I'd pay for half. Shoot, I gotta find some way to make some money so's I can buy this thing from Daddy. What do you think of it?"

I'd already told Sav once that I liked his truck, but I suppose when a fella's got a new vehicle, he likes to hear people brag on it, even if he has to keep askin folks what they think. "It sure is a fine machine. That's awful nice of your Daddy to do all that for you. Let's take her for a spin." I ran around to the other side and pulled on the door handle. It wouldn't budge.

Kinda sheepish like Sav explained, "You got to reach in and open it from the inside." Then he added, "I'm gonna tell folks that's one of the special features about this here truck." He laughed at his own joke. I figured that was a pretty good idea, though. Might as well look for somethin good to say about your brand-new truck, even if you got to make up somethin to make your truck appear to be special.

Sav ground the gears while he was lookin to put it into first and hollered, "Like ol Ernie always says, 'If you cain't find em, grind em.'" Sav laughed again as we pulled off with a jerk that like to broke my neck. I didn't know about that boy havin him a truck. He might be dangerous to everybody else on the street. It was for sure a danger to me to be ridin with him.

One thing about the streets in Cassville is that they're bumpy. Seems like every time we get in the car with Daddy, he goes to complainin about the bad streets in town. He'd say, "You'd think they dug out potholes when they laid these streets just so's the taxpayers would have somethin to gripe about. Don't see why them city planners didn't see to it that we had better streets around here. That's they job. Ought to fire every danged one of em for makin a mess of this town like they has." If the city planners had set out to make the streets bumpy just to make folks mad, they'd sure done their job right on my daddy. Course, it didn't take much to get him to go to bellyachin.

"Hey Sav, did you hear that they've hired this fella from Birmingham to come up with this plan to fix all the streets in Cassville? They say it's gonna take care of all of Cassville's street problems from here on out."

"Amen to that one, brother. Ol Fang's gettin tired of chasin trucks down beat-up streets. He wants smooth pavement to run on. It's better for his knee joints, you know." Sav laughed at the thought of Fang havin some say in the conditions under which he'd be willin to chase trucks. Boy, that Sav was sure in rare form today. Not that it took all that much to get him excited anyhow. He was just extra jumpy today. His good mood rubbed off on me, as a matter of fact. I was enjoyin the ride about as much as he was.

Just the mention of Fang set me to thinkin. I wondered if Sav's own dog would chase him when he drove down the street. "Hey, Sav, pull around to your street and see if Fang'll chase after you." Sav liked that idea and give it the gas as we went in front of his house. You would've thought the noise would scare Fang, but it seemed that the ol hound wasn't bothered at all. He jumped up and sprinted around to the back of Sav's heap and commenced to barkin as if he was sayin, "Git offa my street you danged ol truck!"

Sav hung his head out the window and hollered, "Hey Fang, it's me, your master! You wouldn't bark at me would you?"

I'll be dad gum if that old dog didn't stop dead in his tracks. I looked back at him as he cocked his head to the side with this puzzled look on his face. Amazin how dogs can have all this expression on their face. "Did you see that dog of yours, Sav? He don't know what to do. I think you made him feel right guilty about chasin your truck." We both laughed hard about his hound dog. I sure do like dogs, 'specially that one.

"I'm gonna have to tell Fang what my license plate number is so's he'll know when it's me comin and won't feel like he's got to chase me off the street." Sav thought that would probably solve the problem seein how smart his hound dog was. I was inclined to think he was right, too.

We rode around our neighborhood a few minutes before Sav took me back home. If there was anybody else in our end of town tryin to sleep late that mornin, they were bound to be awake by now. To Sav, it was like he was drivin a royal carriage, but to anybody else, his truck was just a loud ol bone-shaker.

I like to broke my neck again when Sav stopped his truck, but he didn't even seem to notice the jolt. I was about to say thanks for the ride when he hopped out of the truck and said, "C'mon Leroy, let's go get some breakfast." I knew that meant he was invitin himself to enjoy whatever Momma was fixin up that mornin. She wouldn't mind, seein how she always fixed plenty. Besides, she liked Sav the best of my friends anyway and enjoyed havin him around the house.

Sav walked right in the back door like it was his house. "Howdy, Mrs. Evans. You see my new truck?"

"I thought that was you, Sav. Where on earth did you get that truck?"

"Got it just last night. I gotta come up with some money, though, to pay my daddy for my share in it. Thought me and Leroy might go into business doin somethin to make ourselves some money." That was the first I'd heard of that idea. Sav had bought a truck and already had me figured as a business partner. But I didn't mind the thought of lookin for some work to do. Despite Momma had told me it wasn't my place to be providin no money for runnin the family, I figured I could stand to look for work 'cause we needed the extra cash.

"What you got in mind, Sav?" I asked.

"You ever done any paintin, Leroy?"

"Some."

"It ain't too hard. All's you do is scrape off the old paint and slap on some fresh paint and there it is all nice lookin." Sav had this way about him that made hard work sound a little bit too easy. Paintin wasn't my favorite thing to do, but if we could get us some jobs lined up, why I'd be willin to give it a try.

"How we gonna go about gettin us some paintin jobs, Sav? You thought about that part yet?" I know I was bein particular, but the way I see it, it don't hurt to ask for details, especially when your business partner is Sav.

"Oh, yeah. I hadn't thought much about that." It only took him about a half-second, though, to come up with a plan. "What do you think about this here idea?" he asked as he unfolded his strategy. "We could write us up some advertisements and then go out and pass em around. Hey! I even got another idea." Sav's mind was churnin. "See, we don't want to hafta carry around all them ladders and things you got to have if you're gonna paint a whole house. Besides, that'd take more time than we got. I figure we can tell folks we just paint fences. Thatta way, all we'll need is a paintbrush and some paint and we'll be in business. We could just ask the customer to provide us the paint and then all we'd have to do is show up with a paintbrush and get to work makin us some money. How about that?"

I thought on it a second. Sounded okay to me. If we could get us a few fences to paint, we could work after school and on Saturdays. Probably wouldn't take too many fences for us to make enough money for Sav to come up with his sixty-five dollars. I'd have me some money, too. "Well, when do you want to start lookin for fences to paint?"

"Why not today? I figure we could write up some advertisements and then go out and hand em out to folks and see can we line us up a couple of jobs." Sav asked Momma for some paper and wrote down what he figured ought to be put in our advertisement:

> *Alvin Vickers and Leroy Evans*
> *Fence Painters*
> *We will paint your fence*
> *Average-size fence $6 + paint*
> *Big fence $10 + paint*

Sav shoved the paper in my direction and real proud said, "Look at that. Don't it look real good? Makes it look like we's real businessmen. You think them prices is fair enough?"

I said I didn't rightly know seein that I'd never been paid by nobody for paintin a fence, but it sounded pretty fair to me. I figured out in my head about how long it would take to paint a fence and told Sav, "I reckon we could make forty, maybe fifty cents an hour paintin fences. That ain't bad at all."

Sav said let's get started makin up some advertisements so we could go out and try to drum up some business. When that boy gets excited about somethin, he doesn't waste no time with his plans. We porked down some bacon and grits and biscuits and set out to write ten advertisements apiece. Before long, we were back in Sav's truck headed out to the nice houses where we thought our chances of gettin some business was better.

I had somethin in mind besides paintin fences when I suggested that we ride straight down Stuart Avenue and deliver some advertisements. I remembered that the house right next to Alane Sharpe's house had a picket fence and figured maybe it needed a fresh coat of paint. I liked the idea of workin right next to Alane's house. I figured that for sure it would give me a chance to talk with her some.

The house at the end of Stuart Avenue was our first stop. Me and Sav walked up the stone walkway to the house and knocked on the door. You would've thought Sav was an experienced door-to-door salesman the way he talked when the lady opened up the front door. I mean, you ought to see him when he gets all in an uproar like he had this mornin. He sure is a funny fella.

As soon as the door flung open, Sav used his best high-pitched salesman voice and went straight to workin on a sale. "Mornin, ma'am! I'd like to introduce myself and my partner here. My name's Alvin Vickers and this here's Leroy Evans. We's students at Cassville High School and we's out to earn some money by doin honest work for folks. We have us this business where we paint fences." He handed the lady one of our advertisements and give her a chance to read it. She looked it over and seemed interested. Least, that's the way she appeared to me.

"Just a minute, boys." She left us on the porch while she went back into the house.

I do believe Sav was pretty doggone close to wettin his pants. Pokin me, he whispered, "I think we got us a big ol catfish on the line, Leroy. She's gone in the house to fetch her husband." I didn't hardly notice what he had said to me. I was starin off next door at Alane Sharpe's house, wonderin which room was her bedroom and what she might be doin right now.

"Huh?"

"Shh. Here he comes now." Sav stood up a little taller and nudged me as if to say straighten up. I wanted to laugh when I looked over at him and saw the big grin on his face, but I didn't seein how it wouldn't be good for business for one partner to be makin fun of the other. I tried to look nice, but I also tried not to look as simple as Sav did.

The screen door to the front porch opened and the man of the house stepped out on the porch with us, holdin the advertisement Sav had give his wife. He was wearin an old pair of pants with no shirt and no shoes like he hadn't got himself ready for the day yet. He wasn't shaved neither, but despite he looked kinda rough, he was nice. "You boys lookin for some paintin to do?" We shook our heads. Let me put that another way. I shook mine and Sav wagged his up and down like his head was Fang's tail when he was about to get him some table scraps. "Y'all know how to scrape off the old paint where it's peelin?" Our heads bobbed again. "Well, I reckon my fence is the big kind. If you'll work for eight dollars instead of ten, I'll let you fellas paint my fence."

"We sure will," I said real fast before Sav could say anything. Me and him hadn't talked about what we'd do if someone tried to jew us down on our prices, but I was more than willin to bend a little. Specially for whoever lived next door to the Sharpes.

The man stuck out his hand. "Name's Thompson. You boys be willin to start workin today if I can get the paint?" I shook hands with Mr. Thompson and then Sav did. I hoped Sav remembered to give him a good hard squeeze. I'd always heard you was supposed to grip a man's hand real firm if you was closin out a deal.

"We can be back whenever you'd like. We can start today and then come after school until we get the job finished." I'd taken over the task of makin all the arrangements. I didn't figure Sav would mind. I didn't want Sav thinkin I was bein all pushy, but I didn't want to lose the job neither. Him bein all excited like he was, there's no tellin what he might have said that would make Mr. Thompson have second thoughts on givin us the job.

Mr. Thompson said, "You fellas give me a chance to go out and get some paint, and I'll see you back here in about an hour."

Boy, that was easier than I'd thought. Here we'd been to one house and we already had us a job workin for eight dollars. And the location wasn't bad neither.

Chapter 15

MR. THOMPSON gave me and Sav a couple buckets of paint and some paint thinner like we would know what to do with it and left us to do our work. 'Course, we acted like we did know what to do, but as soon as he was back in the house, I asked Sav, "How much of this stuff you supposed to put in the paint?"

"I don't know. Just a little bit, I figure." He started stirrin the paint with a stick and told me to pour a little thinner in the bucket. If someone had looked out there on the street and seen us workin off the back of Sav's truck, they probably would've thought we was professionals. I was glad they couldn't hear us talkin, though. They might have thought otherwise.

"Dad gum," I said, "this paint smells awful strong, don't it? Gives you a headache just to take a whiff of it."

Sav agreed with me. "No wonder so many painters drink the way they do. I'd wanna be drunk most of the time, too, if I had to smell this stuff all day long." Boy, wasn't that the truth. We both got a pretty good kick out of what he said. I thought to myself that I better do what I could to make sure my daddy didn't never get a job as a painter. He didn't need no further reason to go to drinkin. Each of us got a bucket of paint and took one of the old sheets Momma had give us to keep from gettin paint on the ground. I hadn't thought of that, but Momma said it was only right for us to keep our customer's yard clean while we worked. It was just one more thing that made us look like we knew what we was doin.

I told Sav why didn't I paint the part of the fence that ran between the Thompson's house and the Sharpe's house. I suggested that he start on the other side across the yard. I knew good and well if we was to work right next to each other what would happen. I'd end up doin all the work while Sav would've sat there talkin the back leg off of a donkey.

Sav give me this look and grinned. "You ol dog, you." He knew exactly why I wanted to be on the side of the yard closest to Alane's house. I don't think he noticed it, but I was workin under a big elm tree, too. His side of the yard was out under the sun. It wasn't all that hot, but I still preferred workin under the shade than in the sun. That made it nice and comfortable for me. Sav went across the yard and we both set out to scrapin and paintin.

It's times like this when I go real quick to thinkin about things. I'd been tryin harder in school and I think I was passin most everything. We'd been studyin about the French Revolution in my history class, which had made me think about my ancestors way back on my Momma's side of the family. I wondered if any of them had been killed in all that fightin over there in France. Momma's name was Guillebeau before it become Evans. Her ancestors was from France, and as far as I knew they didn't come over here to the United States until about 1800. That would've meant some of them was right smack in the middle of all that revolution. You know, it was probably likely that some of them Guillebeaus had got killed durin all the fightin. I know our history teacher, Miss Ferguson, said a whole bunch of folks did. She told us once how many it was that got laid under, but I don't remember what she said the body count was. Besides, who in thunder goes around countin the dead bodies durin a war anyway? I've always been right suspicious of how these history books come up with the number of people who died in a particular war.

I don't know if other people think much about their ancestors like I do, but I figure it's a shame how people can live out their whole life and then just a couple generations down the road, nobody remembers hardly anything about them. Maybe they'd have their name written down in the family Bible, but besides that, they were forgotten about. That set me to speculatin on what people would remember about me once I had to hand in my dinner pail and wasn't here no more. Just think, here I was out here doin all this work for half of eight dollars and maybe it wouldn't make any difference to nobody a few years from now that I'd even been alive. Kinda scary to be thinkin thatta way.

I figured life didn't have to be for nothin, though. Might as well make the most of what I've been give. I'd been ponderin a lot about the talk I'd had with Woody the other evenin. Every time I talked with him, he gave my brain somethin to chew for several days, it seemed. The more I thought about it, the more I was convinced he believed Alane Sharpe was right when she said I ought to try to make some changes in my family. I look at Woody as bein right up there next to God when it comes to bein smart. When Alane had first suggested what she had about me makin some changes in my family, I just figured she didn't know what she was talkin about since she didn't really know my family. But Woody, he knew my family. His daddy had worked for my granddaddy a long time back so he knew my momma's side of the family real good. And my Daddy comes in to Wimp's barber shop to get his hair cut, so he knows him, too. He knows what both of them is like and can put himself in my place real easy. It wasn't like he was talkin off the top of his head when he hinted I ought to think on how I can look at my family different.

I didn't know how I was gonna do it, but I thought that I would look for some way to do just what Woody believed I ought to do. Might get my head bit off, but what difference would that make? Like I said, a few years from now, there might not be a soul on this earth who even knew anything about me, except that my name was written in the family Bible. Why not go ahead and try to make some changes that might help out whoever comes along next after me. That's what somebody in Alane Sharpe's family had done. Maybe she didn't think about it, but look what it'd done for her.

Doggone, just thinkin about Alane made my heart run just a little bit faster. I wonder how your heart could know when your brain had thought about a girl and start to runnin like it did. I sure have a lot of questions I'm gonna ask when I get to heaven, and that's gonna be one of em.

After me and Sav had been workin about an hour, we took a break to eat the chicken Sav's momma had sent with us. They had eat chicken the night before, so what we had wasn't too old. I know some folks don't like to eat leftover chicken. They complain about it bein cold and greasy. As for me, I kinda like it thatta way. We had us some biscuits from the Vickers's last night's supper, too. "What do you think, Leroy? Looks pretty good, don't it?" I think Sav felt about the same as me about the feast we was about to have.

We dug into lunch and went to talkin about our work. "This here job ain't so bad," I said. "We ought to be able to finish the whole job by next Saturday as long as the weather doesn't turn bad on us." We sat on the back end of Sav's truck while we ate. I looked over at my partner and saw him smilin real broad. I knew what was on his mind. "Thinkin about this here truck again, ain't you?"

He patted it like he was lovin on Fang. "Sure is a jewel."

About the time we finished our chicken and biscuits, Sav said, "I wonder why we ain't seen nothin from Alane or her folks. You'd think they'd been out some by now."

"That's what I'd of thought, too. Guess they're busy inside." I was feelin a little disappointed that Alane hadn't come outside. It was a right nice day, so it wasn't the weather keepin her in. "For sure she'll come out here sometime this afternoon."

When we went back to work, I figured Sav would lean over and give his truck a little kiss, but he didn't. Boy was he proud of that thing. I figured that after he'd had it for awhile, I might ask him could I drive it. I was sure he wouldn't mind, but what with it bein all brand new to him, I didn't think right now was the time for me to be askin to have fun with his truck.

Sure enough, about a half hour after lunchtime, Mrs. Sharpe come out the front door and watered some plants she had growin in the front yard. I worked a little harder when I saw her come out, just so she'd know I wasn't the lazy type. Didn't do no good, though, since she hardly looked over my way.

I stood up after a minute and called over to her, "Hey there, Mrs. Sharpe." She looked up at me. Before she could ask who I was, I reminded her, "It's Leroy Evans. You doin all right today?"

"Well, hello, Leroy. Yes, I'm doing just fine. Looks like you've got quite a job."

I walked over in her direction. "Yes, ma'am. My friend and I are paintin Mr. Thompson's fence for him. We've decided to be partners in fence paintin. You know, so we can earn some extra money. Sav's daddy bought a new truck and Sav's gonna pay for half of it, so he needs the money. I plan on savin mine." I went on to tell her all about how Sav had been to my house early that mornin to show me his new truck and how he took me for a ride before most of the neighborhood was even awake. Mrs. Sharpe had this little smile on her face as I was talkin. You know, when you're kinda nervous, you get this idea that you have to talk a lot just to keep the conversation movin along. Least that's the way I get when I'm feelin jittery. I caught myself yappin and stopped real quick. "Sorry, Mrs. Sharpe. You probably didn't want to hear all that. Sometimes I just get carried away when I'm talkin."

"That's just fine, Leroy. I'm enjoying listening to your story." I'm right sure she meant what she said, too. Mrs. Sharpe was a real lady. You could tell by the way she carried herself. Stood up straight and proud like. My momma kinda hangs her head a lot when she stands, but Mrs. Sharpe acts like she didn't feel the need to drag herself through life. She was wearin her Saturday clothes, but to me she looked plenty good enough to be seen out in public. I liked the way she didn't wear a whole lotta makeup and jewelry. She was sure enough pretty and didn't have to spruce herself up like some women seemed to feel the need to do. If you looked at her face, it was almost like you was lookin right at Alane. Both of em had the same dark eyes that spoke real kindly to you. There was this smoothness about her face that let you know that she was a gentle person inside, too. This may be a peculiar way to describe a woman's face, but to me it looked almost affectionate, it was so soft and smooth lookin. Alane's was the same way. Both of them had that long dark brown hair, almost black. Alane generally lets hers hang down while her mother tied hers up on top of her head. I've seen some women who pull their hair back so tight it makes you worry that they might stretch somethin the wrong way. Mrs. Sharpe had her hair fixed all soft lookin in a way that fit what I thought she probably acted like most of the time. Everything about the woman said she was a first-class lady. I'd only met her a couple of times, but I really admired her.

"I'll tell Alane you're working next door. Maybe she can bring you and your friend some cold water in a bit."

"Why that'd be right nice." Boy would it ever be nice! I told Mrs. Sharpe I enjoyed talkin to her, but I better get back to work and went on back over to the fence. I was gettin to where I kinda liked paintin.

Sav had seen me talkin to Mrs. Sharpe and walked over my way when she went back in the house. I told him, "She said maybe Alane could bring us out some cold water after a while. I don't know about you, but I'm right thirsty." We laughed. Sav knew that I sure would like to talk a few minutes to Alane. You know, I ought to admit that by this time I have more than just a little bit of interest in her. The last time I had come out here to study with her, I was mainly testin to see if I even wanted to get to know her a little bit better. I guess the way my heart was actin up was its way of verifyin that I was gettin sweet on her. I wasn't ready to tell Sav all my feelins about her yet. He'd talk too much. Dad gum, I wish I was a little more high-class. It would be hard to imagine a girl like her havin the same feelins for me as I was havin for her.

I sighed. "Well Sav, we better get back to work. Don't you figure?" He said he didn't really want to, but he guessed so. I reminded him to just keep lookin over at that truck when he found himself gettin tired. I think sayin that helped his spirits out.

Like I said, it wasn't all that hot out, but I honestly was feelin thirsty. Just thinkin about cold water can make you want some. Course, if I was honest, I'd admit that just thinkin about who might serve you some cold water could make you thirsty, too. After about a half hour, Alane come out of her house carrying two big glasses of water. I said hello to Alane and wasn't that nice of her to bring me and Sav a drink. I looked over to where Sav was to call him over to get his glass and doggone if his lunch hadn't made him feel sleepy. He was leaned up againt his side of the fence restin his eyes, as they say.

"Looky there at Sav. I think he had too much lunch. I hope Mr. Thompson doesn't look out and see him like that." Alane laughed at the sight of my workin partner.

"Momma told me you and Sav were working out here. Do you know what she asked me when she came in?" I said I couldn't guess what it might have been. "She asked me if Sav was really his name, and I explained to her how he got it." She laughed when she said that. I mean, her laugh sure sounded pretty.

"Your momma probably thinks we're a couple of common folks." You know, it doesn't bother me at all that my friend goes by a name like Sav, but I reckon it does sound a little on the odd side to folks that hear it for the first time. I don't know why, but sometimes folks who ain't got nothin much in life get these peculiar soundin names give to them. Sav isn't that type. I know he's gonna be somebody one of these days, but you wouldn't guess it by hearin his name.

"I don't know that Momma thinks that. She seems to think you're a right polite young man. Daddy's in the house and he said it's good to see young men who are willing to do honest work in order to help pay their way." Well now, hearin that sounded pretty good to me. If Mr. and Mrs. Sharpe had done pegged me and Sav as a couple of fine young men, then we ought to be right proud.

I explained to Alane how I had been goin about doin my work. Showed her my scraper and told her what it was used for and even gave her a demonstration. Then I had her smell the paint and asked her wasn't that the strongest smellin stuff she'd ever whiffed. She agreed with me that it did smell awful. We went on for awhile talkin about nothin. I finished my water and said I guess she ought to just take Sav's glass back on in the house since it didn't look like he was feelin too thirsty right now. Alane headed back to her house, when it struck me to tell her what I'd been thinkin about.

"Say, Alane!" She turned back around. "I talked to my friend Woody the other day about what you said about my family." She looked puzzled. I should've known she hadn't been thinkin on her words the way I had been. She'd probably forgot by now about the conversation we'd had that night at the Cotton Palace. "You remember how I told you about how my family is and you said maybe I'd be just the one who might ought to try to make some changes?"

"Oh yes, I remember. You've talked with someone else about that?"

I forgot she didn't know Woody. I'm sure her daddy would know who he was seein that he got his hair cut at Wimp's, but she wouldn't know him. "Woody's this colored man what works down at Wimp's Barber Shop. Me and him's been friends for a long time. I talk to him about a lot of things and I was tellin him about that talk me and you had. He said you might just have a good idea. All that's set me to thinkin about things and I just thought I'd let you know it's been on my mind."

Alane walked back over to the fence. "Have things changed?"

"Naw. It's still the same. In fact, my daddy's still out in Cow Pens. We figure he'll come home one of these days. I don't rightly know what I ought to do, but maybe I should think about doin somethin to make things better around my house."

"Well, Leroy, I still think you can think of some way to make things brighter. You're not like a lot of boys who would just give up and let things go on without at least trying to do what you could." I wondered how she could know that about me. I was glad she had stock in me, but I didn't know where she'd come up with all this confidence that I could do things nobody else had bothered to even try with my family. Shoot, I didn't even have no confidence in myself. All the same, I was glad she felt the way she did and said so to her.

After Alane went in, I went over to Sav and kicked him. "Wake up, Sav. Your brush is gonna get dry."

"Huh?" He didn't even know what day it was.

"Wake up. You don't want Mr. Thompson comin out here seein you sleepin on the job, do you?"

Sav jumped right up and went back to work like he hadn't missed a lick. "What're you talkin about me sleepin? I ain't been sleepin. That part of the fence was about to fall down and I was just pushin it back up." He looked at me outta the corner of his eye like I was the only one who knew his secret. I went back to work and back to thinkin. I didn't know, but I needed to be thinkin right hard. Things was gonna start buzzin at my house pretty soon.

Chapter 16

ME AND Sav was makin good time on the Thompsons' fence.
A couple more afternoons of paintin and we'd be done. Kinda
hated to see the job end, to tell the truth. Alane Sharpe had got
to where she came over and kept me company while I was workin. That
made me believe she was for sure takin a likin to me, at least I hope that's
what it meant. I can tell you it made the time pass a lot faster havin her
around. I even think I worked a little harder because of her. In fact, I'm
right certain of it. There's somethin about havin a girl watch you that
makes a boy want to work a little extra hard. Call it showin off or
whatever, but that's the way it seems to be.

Sav let me off at my house at just about dark one evenin after we'd been
workin. I hadn't hardly got out of his truck when Cody Sue spotted me
and come runnin lickety-split with this desperate look about her. "Leroy!
Hurry! I need you!"

"What in the world's wrong, Cody Sue? Somethin wrong with
Momma?" The way that girl was carryin on, I thought there must of been
some kind of predicament inside the house.

"It's Gilly!"

Now I know it ain't polite to roll your eyes when someone tells you
what they're upset about, but I had a hard time gettin worked up over
that cat of hers. I don't have what you'd call a lot of respect for cats
anyhow. I was polite enough not say this out loud to Cody Sue, but I
wouldn't have been upset at all if she'd told me that animal had eloped
with some alley cat from down the street. My heart wouldn't have stopped
workin to hear that. Cody Sue was all in a lather, though, and I wasn't
gonna make things worse for her by talkin ugly about that cat of hers.

Gilly has his own way of gettin on a fella's nerves, at least he has a way
of gettin on mine. Seems that he decided a long time ago that he was a

part owner of our house, not that he's ever made a contribution to the family or nothin. He seemed to feel that he was entitled to special liberties. The way that varmint looked at it, that meant he ought to be able to come and go as he pleased in and out of the house, you know, the way people do. Every time I'd open the back door to walk out, there was Gilly hidin around the corner waitin for his chance to slip in the house. Even when I thought I was sure he wasn't anywhere around, here he'd come sprintin like greased lightnin right past me on into the house.

Made me mad the way he'd run from you when you told him to get out of the house 'cause it wasn't his. I don't know why I'd even bother to say anything to him. Cats don't understand plain English the way dogs do. Cody Sue says he's just ignorin me when I talk to him like that. You can't convince me that there's anything besides rocks and maybe a little green moss in between a cat's ears, though. Cody Sue has never accepted the plain truth that cats are practically at the end of the line when you go to listin animals accordin to which ones are the smartest. They're right down there with snails and grasshoppers. I realize that's my opinion and I don't have solid proof of it, but you can't make me believe otherwise.

I sighed. "What's the matter with Gilly?"

"He's stuck up on the roof and won't come down."

Good Lord! I looked at Cody Sue and just about cackled because of the look of panic that was smeared all over her. "What's he doin up there? Don't he know how to get down? Cats can climb. Just let him climb down whatever way he got himself up there." Seemed like a pretty simple solution to me. If the danged cat wanted to get down off the roof, he could just decide which way he was gonna do it and then he could go to climbin. You can imagine, though, that Cody Sue didn't take the situation that lightly.

"I've tried that! He's scared and won't come down. I told him when you got home, you'd climb up there and get him. He's around on the back side of the house waitin for you."

Dear God, give me patience with this girl. I don't know how everybody else is when things like this come up, but I can tell you how I was doin. I was pressin myself hard to decide whether to laugh or cry, whether to help out Cody Sue or tell her to go call the Fire Department cause I wasn't gettin involved. Thinkin about a cat sittin up on the back side of the roof whinin, "Leroy, Leroy, come get me offa here!" was what I'd call plumb ridiculous. I went around to the back of the house with my little sister, but I'm gonna be as honest as I can and confess that my attitude smelled bad. About the only positive thought I could come up with was that Gilly chose the back side of the house to do his whinin and not the front. Least the whole town wouldn't see me fetchin a half-witted cat off the roof. Don't you know the fellas would hoot if they saw me climbin up on the roof just to help out a pitiful little kitty cat.

I shinnied up a hackberry tree that grows right up next to the house and reached for Gilly. Stupid cat moved a couple feet in the other direction. Now if that doesn't say somethin about what kind of games this here cat was up to, nothin does. I looked down at Cody Sue and knew just by lookin at her that I might as well go on up and get Gilly. She wasn't gonna quit pesterin me until I did. I got on the roof and picked Gilly up. I could swear he was wearin a smirk on his face.

"You'd make a fine playmate for that German shepherd down the street," I whispered in his ear. It didn't make any difference that I'd said that to him, though. I could feel my own breath comin out the other ear.

After I had got Gilly down, I sat on the back steps by Cody Sue. She was holdin her cat and strokin him like he had just barely got away with his life. I suppose that made me a hero, but she didn't say nothin about that part. Tell you the truth, I was glad I had did what I did, not because I had went to feelin sorry for Gilly. It was good to see Cody Sue all satisfied now. After all, she was my only sister and I didn't mind doin her a favor now and then, as long as it didn't become a habit for me to go runnin after her empty-headed cat. After we'd been sittin there a couple minutes, Cody Sue asked right outta the blue, "Leroy, you think Momma's ever gonna be happy again?"

"What do you mean, Cody Sue?" Her words threw me back a speck.

"I mean I'm gettin tired of seein her cryin and actin sad all the time, ain't you? I want her to get back to bein her usual self again."

The way I looked at it, Momma didn't never seem to be what you'd call happy. Maybe there were times that she didn't drag as bad as usual, but I wouldn't call that happy. Despite how I saw it, I knew what Cody Sue was gettin at. "Yeah, I'm gettin pretty tired of it, too. Momma's havin a hard time of it these days."

"When you think it's gonna quit?"

"Hard to say, Cody Sue." In all honesty, I was a little surprised that Cody Sue had even said what she did. I figured she hadn't noticed much change since Daddy run away, 'cept that he wasn't around to gripe and complain at everybody. Least, she hadn't acted any different. I asked Cody Sue, "You havin a hard time with things bein the way they are, little sister, what with Daddy bein gone and all?"

That was all it took to get the tears rollin down her face. Her lower lip stood out as she shook her head up and down to answer me. I put my arm around her and held her. I think she liked that. She didn't get held much the way a little girl ought to be held. Daddy isn't the type to do that sort of thing and Momma's always too spent to be givin out affection. It's a downright shame, 'cause Cody Sue's really a good girl, the kind that's easy to love on. Here I'd thought she had been plumb blind to what all had been happenin around here lately, but I reckon she has feelins she doesn't know what to do with, same as the rest of us.

"When's Daddy comin home? Soon?" I don't know why Cody Sue thought I'd know all the answers to them kind of questions. She must of figured my guess was as good as anybody else's bein that I'm fifteen years old and was supposed to know a whole lot more than her.

"I bet it'll be soon."

That night as I laid in bed, I did some heavy thinkin about Cody Sue and how all this mess with Daddy was botherin her. Here I go talkin like I'm all grown up and she's this little girl, but I suppose I should've known she would be grieved by the way Momma and Daddy done things around here. If I was hurtin about family relations, I should've guessed she'd be reelin, too. I finally got my heart to quit achin so I could get on to sleep. Lord knows, I needed the rest so I could be ready for the next day's school.

I had got to where I was brave enough to stand under the oak tree where Alane Sharpe and her friends stood before school. It helped that Sav also wanted to stand under that tree with me on account of how Virginia Bledsoe was always there with Alane. They're best friends, just like me and Sav is, you know. Ever since that time we all walked around together at the Cotton Palace, he'd kept his eye on her. Me standin under their oak tree gave him the excuse to join us so he could make time with Virginia. I reckon you could say we helped each other out in that way.

We were standin there the next mornin when I saw Mr. Higgins walk out on the steps that lead up to the school. He was strainin his eyes as he looked all over the school yard. I wondered what in the world he was up to when his eyes stopped on me and he motioned me to come over to the steps with him. I told Sav I had to go and left him there with Alane and Virginia and some of their friends. Sav got this terrified look on his face that said, "You're not leavin me here by myself with all these girls, are you, Leroy?" His confidence run away from him at the same time I left. I would've laughed to myself if I hadn't been so curious about what Mr. Higgins wanted with me.

"Come into my office with me, Leroy." Mr. Higgins led me down the hallway into his office. I don't think he realizes just how long his legs are. He was stridin down the hall casual like while I had to work to stay next to him. "Have a seat," he said as he took his place behind his desk. I put my rear end on the edge of the chair across from him.

"I do somethin wrong, Mr. Higgins?" My mind had already gone to racin, wonderin what in thunder I had done that would land me back in his office. I hadn't been in any more fights with Bruno Lynch. Ol Fat Boy had pretty much left me alone since our last tussle on Royce Blackwell's front yard. There were other things that popped in my mind that Mr. Higgins might be wantin to talk to me about, but I wasn't too sure which one it might be. I wasn't the bad kind of student, but you can understand that I didn't run away from mischief neither. If he had told me to go to confessin right then, I probably would've told him some things that was goin on around school that he would've liked knowin about. Good for me and a few other fellas that's not what he wanted.

"Oh no, Leroy, it's nothing like that." He sat there like he was tryin to figure out what to say next. "I was wondering what you've heard from your daddy." When he said that, he leaned up in his chair like he expected me to fill him in on some news.

I didn't have nothin to hide, so I told him, "We still haven't heard nothin, Mr. Higgins. I've seen a couple people who's seen Daddy, and they tell me he's doin okay, but we ain't talked to him or nothin." Mr. Higgins leaned back in his chair like that wasn't what he expected to hear from me. "Why? You heard somethin from your kinfolks about my daddy?"

I didn't get no answer to that question. Real curious like, he changed the subject. "I was just wondering, Leroy. By the way, how're you doing in your classes these days?"

"I think I'm doin better. Least I hope I am."

"I've been keeping tabs on you since we talked last. I didn't know if you were aware of that or not." I wasn't exactly aware of that, but most any student has this funny feelin at least some of the time that he's bein watched more than he'd like to think. You can tell the ones who feel eyes hittin em in the back, specially when we're takin a test. They're the ones who look up all of a sudden to take a quick peek around the room to see if anybody's takin notes on them. Them are the ones you can almost bet is lookin for a way to cheat because they can't come up with the answers. I know cause I've been there before.

"No, sir, I didn't know."

"Your teachers know something's wrong with you. A couple of them have said so to me. I haven't said anything to any of them about what you've told me. I think they're trying to make an effort to help you out any way they can. You're a smart young man, Leroy. I'd hate to see you be turned away from a good education because we didn't try to help you out the best we could."

I was pleased to hear him say them things to me, but I wasn't gonna let

Mr. Higgins get too far away from that question he asked about my daddy, so I changed the subject on him just the same as he had done to me. "Why'd you ask if I'd heard anything from my daddy, Mr. Higgins? You know somethin I don't know about?"

Dang if he didn't sidestep that one, too. "I was just wondering. That's all."

It was time for school to start so Mr. Higgins told me to go on to my class. The way he was actin, I believe he knew that my daddy had plans to come on home. That's what I figure. It was sure evident that he was hidin somethin. Adults ain't a whole lot better than little kids when it comes to coverin up secrets. Boy did that day drag by slow. Every time I looked at the clock, it seemed like it had took a tick backwards instead of forwards. When the school day finally ended, I hurried on home. For the last few days I'd hung around after my last class so I could speak a word or two to Alane before she left the school grounds, but today I had this feelin that Daddy would be at the house when I got there. I can't explain the feelin I had, but I needed to get home fast.

I walked in the house expectin to see Daddy sittin there. He wasn't anywheres to be found, though. Momma had been out cleanin a house, but was home now. "Leroy? That you? You and Sav gonna go paint some more this afternoon?"

I'd plumb forgot about that. "Yes, ma'am."

I can't explain why I had felt excited about Daddy maybe bein home, but I was. Maybe I'd read too much into the way Mr. Higgins was actin this mornin. I suppose he was just curious and wanted to get an update on how things were at my house and that was all. I was surprised at myself for feelin the way I had all day. Boy, I sure hope someday somebody can explain to me why I feel all up-and-down inside. Doggone if these feelings ain't the oddest thing I ever tried to figure. Woody says I'm gettin pretty good at thinkin, but it's times like this that I'm not so sure I agree with him. I got into my paintin clothes and waited for Sav to come get me. We didn't have much to do on the Thompson's fence and ought to finish today.

I was glad that Alane came over to talk to me while me and Sav worked. I figured it would do me good to talk a little bit to her about how I'd felt today. "Hi, Leroy. You sure got away from school quickly this afternoon. What was the rush?"

I figured I could tell Alane at least a little of what I had been experiencin today. She knew enough about my family by now that she'd probably understand. "I don't know what was in me today, but I had this queer feelin all day long that my daddy would be home this afternoon when I got in from school. When Mr. Higgins called me to his office first thing this mornin, he acted like he knew somethin that I didn't. You know, he's got relatives what live in Cow Pens where my daddy's stayin, and I reckon they tell him about my daddy's goins on. I hurried home halfway expectin him to be in the house. He wasn't there, though."

I know Alane didn't know what to say. How could a fifteen-year-old girl who come from good stock know what to say to a boy whose daddy was a drunkard. She couldn't have possibly felt what I was feelin. Not that she wouldn't want to. I expect she musta thought I was odd for goin up-and-down on my feelins the way I was. She just sat quiet and didn't say nothin. I felt foolish for even entertainin the thoughts I had been ponderin all day. To Alane's credit she didn't make matters worse for me by tryin to tell me how I should've felt. At least she knew when she was better off by not sayin nothin.

I worked slow that afternoon. Just didn't have much in me. We did finish the job, though. Sav was sure proud to have some money to give his daddy for his truck. I normally would've been excited about my four-dollar share, but it just didn't do nothin to me today. I think I was beginnin to feel the wear of Daddy's absence same as Cody Sue had been. Alane could probably tell my mind wasn't anywheres near Cassville that afternoon and went on back in her house long before we left.

I didn't eat much supper when I got home that night. I set the money I had got on the bureau in Momma's room without sayin nothin to her. I hoped she'd find some use for it. Lord knows, she needed it. I had some studyin to do, but I figured it could wait until tomorrow. After all that Mr. Higgins had said to me this mornin about my teachers wantin to help me out with my work, here I was quittin on my homework before I even got started. Made me feel a little ashamed of myself. I thought maybe I could get up a little early in the mornin and do some of what I was settin aside tonight. Maybe a good night's rest would perk me up a little bit. That was my plan anyhow.

When I got up the next mornin, I walked into the kitchen like usual. I'll be dad gum if Daddy wasn't sittin at the kitchen table drinkin a cup of coffee.

Chapter 17

MORNIN, LEROY."
  I was plumb froze. Just flat didn't know what to do or say. I reckon I had lots of choices of what I could've said or did right then, but I didn't know which one to take. I could've said, "Daddy, what the Sam Hill do you think you're doin waltzin back into this house after puttin us through tarnation for the last month? You ought to be downright ashamed to even show your face in this here house after the way you treated Momma and after you said what you did about me that night." That was one choice. Boy, don't you know that one would go over real big with Daddy. I didn't think I wanted to go to complainin the first minute I saw him.

On the other hand, I might could run over and hug Daddy's neck and say, "I'm glad you're home. Despite I was hurtin and confused while you was gone to Cow Pens, I'm sure glad you're back so's we can be a family again." I didn't feel as comfortable with that choice as the first one. Choosin that would've felt downright awkward to me. Somehow it didn't seem to be the right thing to go huggin Daddy's neck after what we'd been through. He might think I wouldn't care if he up and did the same thing all over again if I went and hugged him. Still, there was a part of me that sure wanted to go grab hold of him and squeeze.

I guess I had the choice to act like he was the boy and I was the daddy. I could have said, "Now listen here, Ira. There's somethin you're gonna need to learn and that is that if you want to be part of this here family, the least you can do is to stay put here with the rest of us instead of headin out to stay with your brother just because you're mad." I tossed that option outta my mind as soon as it popped in my head. That was too much like the first choice. Daddy would've come right after me if I'd talked to him like I was his elder. He sure would've.

Maybe I could do whatever Momma had done when she first seen Daddy. I looked over at her to see if I could catch an idea of how she must be feelin. Shoot, it looked like she was doin what she done every single mornin. She was mixin up some grits over the stove and had some biscuits in the oven. She didn't act no different than she ever did. I bet she hadn't said hardly nothin to Daddy when she first saw him. Didn't ask for no apology nor tell him he better not come in here thinkin he could just act like he had before he left. I couldn't do that. How could I act the same as I always did when I'd never felt this way before?

"Mornin, Daddy." That was all I had the guts to say.

I sat down in the chair across from my father and stared at him. I tried, but I wasn't able to read his eyes. He has this way of hidin what he feels behind them heavy eyebrows of his. Funny how Daddy looked different to me. Maybe it was because I hadn't seen him in practically four weeks. Seemed like he was five years older than what I had remembered. He always had this weathered look about him, but this mornin he sure looked whipped. He had that same red tint to his face that heavy drinkers has, but his eyes were heavier than usual. He forever wore bags under his eyes, just like Momma did, but now it looked like they weren't just the same old bags, they was full of somethin. Emotions, that's what they was full of. For the life of me, though, I couldn't read them.

"Mornin. How you doin?" I didn't know why I said mornin again, but I felt like I needed to say somethin and I reckon that's all that come to mind. My voice was barely above a whisper. I hated actin so weak and helpless, but dad gum it I just didn't have no strength in my voice at the time. A whisper was all I could muster.

Daddy nodded his head at me. Just barely moved it. He didn't say nothin. Maybe he didn't know what to say neither. I wondered if he was feelin the same as me. Or maybe he didn't have nothin he wanted to say to me. The last time he had seen me he had said I was a little half-pint punk of a man. Course, he was drunk then and may not have even remembered it, but he had said it just the same. Maybe he couldn't talk cause he was holdin a grudge against me.

My throat was so swollen it hurt. I almost felt of it to see if the knot I had inside was stickin out like it seemed to be. It was like I had swallowed a baseball. That's how big it felt. Momma set a plate in front of me. "You want two or three biscuits with your grits, Leroy?"

I wanted to say, "Momma, don't you see who's sittin across the table from me? How can you ask me about how many biscuits do I want when Daddy's just got home? Throw my biscuits out back for Pancho to eat. I don't want none. No, wait a second. Let me take them words back. Keep my biscuits in the oven until they're hard as rocks since Daddy don't like hard biscuits and then throw em at him as hard as you like. You'd like that, wouldn't you, Momma?"

"Two biscuits is all I'd like, Momma."

Shortly after I'd started eatin, Cody Sue come stumblin into the kitchen rubbin her eyes. She wasn't nearly as shy about showin her feelins as I had been. "Daddy!" she screamed as she ran and jumped into his lap. She planted a big one on his cheek. "You're home! Leroy said you'd be home soon!" She looked over my way like she thought my crystal ball must of been magic since I'd said two days before that Daddy's probably gonna be home soon. Shoot, I was just sayin somethin to try to calm her down at the time.

Daddy's reaction to Cody Sue wasn't a whole lot different than what he'd showed me. He kept a straight face like he didn't want to let on to what he was thinkin. If he smiled, it sure wasn't much of one. For the life of me, I couldn't figure why he was bein so secretive about his thoughts. He barely put his arm around Cody Sue and for sure didn't give her what I'd call a hug. The least the man could've done was say, "Howdy kids, I'm glad to see you, and I been missin you while I was gone." But he didn't say nothin of the sort. In fact, he didn't say nothin at all. It sure was strange seein him sittin in the kitchen actin like he was. It was like nothin else I've ever felt before.

Course, I told Sav about Daddy bein home while we were on our way to school. I hadn't talked a whole lot to him about this whole mess, but I figured he'd like to know. Told Alane, too, when I saw her before school. She acted happy at first, but when she saw how queer I was actin, she got quiet and just said she hoped I could start doin whatever I was gonna do to try to make things better at home. I guess that was her way of remindin me of that talk we'd had back at the Cotton Palace when I first told her what my family was really like.

The man I wanted to see most that mornin, though, was Mr. Higgins. Not that I was all that close to him or needed advice on how to act and such. I had Woody for that and didn't want no other adult takin his place. But I did want to ask him did he know yesterday when he talked to me that my daddy was comin home. I went inside the school buildin early and found him sittin in his office.

"Mornin, Mr. Higgins."

"Leroy! How you doing this morning? Have a seat. You need to see me?" Funny how yesterday he acted like he was wantin to pump me for information. Now I was wantin to do the same to him.

"Yes, sir. I just wanted to let you know that when I got up this mornin my daddy was home." He nodded his head as if to say that's what I thought you was gonna say. I kept right on talkin and said, "Mr. Higgins, I just gotta know if you knew about all this when you had me come in here yesterday mornin."

I don't know why adults feel this urge to hold back what they think from kids, but it was plain to me that Mr. Higgins didn't want to tell me what all he had been up to yesterday. But just like a little boy who was feelin forced into confessin somethin, he went ahead and told me. "Yes, Leroy, I did know something yesterday and was trying to find out from you what had been happening in your family. Actually, I was concerned and that was why I called you in."

"What was there to be concerned about?"

He fidgeted around again before he told me, "Well, you see, Leroy, my cousin who knows your uncle had heard that your daddy and his brother weren't getting along too well. It seems that your uncle was ready for your daddy to either start working and pay his way or move on back home. From what I know, it was getting real bad between the two of them. I understand they had had pretty strong words with one another and a threat was made against your father if he didn't move out of your uncle's house."

"A threat? What kind of threat?" Mr. Higgins squirmed like he felt he had already done said too much and didn't want to say no more. "Mr. Higgins, you're talkin about my daddy and my uncle. I already know what kind of men they are. I've seen just about every kind of fightin there can be in that family, so there's not much you can tell me that'll surprise me." He nodded his head like he could understand what I was tryin to say. What I was really sayin to the man was, "Dang it. It's my family so don't go holdin back none of the details. Just spit it out!"

"Okay, Leroy. It is your daddy, and you've got every reason to want to know. It seems that he and his brother were awfully drunk about three days ago and got into a pretty good brawl. Your uncle took a couple of shots at your daddy and told him to leave and never come back. I didn't know if your daddy had been hurt or not. That's why I called you in here yesterday. I was concerned for your father and for you. You can understand what I'm saying, can't you, Leroy?"

"Yes, sir." I understood all right. I also knew he probably couldn't understand what I was feelin right then. I didn't know hardly nothin about Mr. Higgins nor his family, but from what I'd seen, he was a pretty decent fella. They wasn't any reason for me to suspect that he had come from a family that was anything like mine. I could be wrong, because you never knew what a fella's family life is like. It's just that he didn't appear to be the kind who would know exactly what it was like to be in a family like mine.

"Is there anything you and I can talk about, Leroy? I want to help any way I can."

"No, sir. You've done helped a whole bunch just by fillin me in on what you know. I'm real appreciative to you for that."

"I hope what I told you hasn't upset you, Leroy. That certainly isn't what I intended to do. I just felt you had the need to know."

I was embarrassed, but not surprised by what he had told me. My embarrassment was over the fact that the way my daddy and his brother acted might make folks think I was just the same as them. "No, sir, I ain't upset. None of what you said is surprisin to me. It's happened before. Who knows, but it sure could happen again."

"I suppose you ought to run on to class now, Leroy." I shook my head and thanked him again. He stood up and stuck out his hand and squeezed mine. As I headed out the door, he added, "Leroy, thanks for telling me about your daddy. I just want you to know I'm here to talk with you if you need me. And if you need any extra help with any of your classes, let me know and I'll be sure that you get what you need." That was nice of him to be that thoughtful, and I told him so. In my mind, though, I knew I wouldn't need to call on him. I'd do the best I could in my classes. Besides, how could I tell my teachers the reason I'm not doin so good in school right now is that I didn't do my homework on account of I been havin to deal with the doins of my drunkard daddy?

So Daddy and Uncle Amos had got in a fight and Uncle Amos got so mad that he fired his gun at Daddy and told him to get out and don't come back. Dang, that musta been some kinda tangle. Not that I would've enjoyed seein it, but somehow I found myself wishin I had been there to see what had actually happened. Musta been somethin. Daddy had to have been mighty mad for him and his brother to get into it the way they did. Didn't really surprise me that Uncle Amos shot at Daddy. He was a pretty sorry man.

I tried to remember what I could about my daddy and his brother. Daddy didn't have much to do with his family, despite all of em lived right around Cassville. He had two brothers and three sisters. I'd only met each of them a few times and didn't have what you'd call regular family relations with any of em. I suppose it's a fact that if your daddy doesn't get along at all with his brothers and sisters they isn't much chance of you havin much to do with em neither.

I can only remember one time that Uncle Amos ever even set foot inside our house. And if I recollect correctly, he was drunk then. From what I've heard, he drinks just about as bad as Daddy does. In fact, I think he may even drink more. All three of the boys in that family were drunks and I think a couple of the sisters hit the liquor pretty hard, too. This isn't nice to say and I know it, but to me they just isn't much worse than a woman who's a drunk. Not that men drunks are any better, but it seems even worse when a woman gets attached to a bottle.

Why, even when Daddy talks about Uncle Amos, which isn't often, he never mentions his name without referrin to him as my drunk brother, or my brother the sot, or things like that. It's like Daddy is sayin now if you want to look at a real drunk, don't look at me, go look at my brother. I think Uncle Amos is the worst of the whole Evans lot. He had four or five kids, I don't remember which. They're all older than me. Uncle Amos had got married and had his first child when he was just sixteen years old. I know that what little I was around his kids, they were as mean as he was, even the girls. I never really considered that I was missin out on nothin by not gettin to know my aunts and uncles and their children. I always looked on it as some kind of blessin. Shame that's the way I had to look at it, but that's how it is.

Now I know my teachers must've thought I was the laziest boy they'd ever seen in school that day, 'cause I didn't hardly lift my head up off my desk. The only class where I even tried to look like I was interested in what was goin on was my English class. And it wasn't on account of Mrs. Lemming sayin nothin that was interestin that kept my head up off my desk. It was havin Alane Sharpe sittin across from me that kept me halfway alert. Despite my head was runnin about like the Tennessee River with thoughts and feelins, I couldn't let on in front of her how dizzied I was.

I kept tryin to figure out the real reason Daddy had come home. Mr. Higgins had said that this fight between Daddy and Uncle Amos happened three days ago. That could only mean that there had been two nights where he wasn't at his brother's house, but he wasn't at our house neither. When I had first walked in the kitchen this mornin and seen him, one of the things I thought was that maybe he finally decided he was ready to be back with his family. I even thought that his showin up back home could be his way of sayin that he was ready to make up for what all he had done that was wrong and was ready to try and be a husband and a daddy. Now I wasn't so sure of that.

I suppose it's normal for a boy to look on the bright side of things, especially when life around the house had been so dark for the last month. Actually, I guess I should say it's been dark around the house for all fifteen years I'd been around, but the mood has been midnight black the last month. It was downright hard, though, for me to be what you'd call a hopeful fella.

If Daddy only came home on account of his brother threatenin him with a gun, what would keep him from leavin again whenever he got a mind to? 'Course, where would he go this time if he left? He didn't have much of a place to go the first time when he went to Cow Pens to Uncle Amos's house. Now, he didn't even have Uncle Amos to go to. And if Daddy and Uncle Amos had been fightin because they had been drinkin real bad, then it didn't sound too likely that anything would be different any other time.

Even though it had felt odd havin Daddy gone for a month, I was glad we weren't havin to put up with all the hard talkin that came outta Daddy's mouth when he was drunk. And even though me and Momma and Cody Sue hadn't exactly got to where we spent the evenins enjoyin each other's company, at least the tension wasn't as thick on the nights where we all sat in the front room doin our usual nothin.

If my mind was runnin in circles before today, it was totally garbled now. I was flat ready to explode, that's for sure. Whenever I talked to Woody, things seemed to get straightened out a lot quicker than when I tried to undo the mess by myself. That's where I was headin soon as school was out.

Chapter 18

I T WAS one of them drizzly and muggy afternoons. It wasn't really all that warm, but it was so humid you felt like you couldn't hardly breathe. This time of the year we're just as liable to have dirty weather like we have today as we were to have the sunshiny type. Odd how the weather seems to match your mood so much of the time. Or maybe it's the other way around. Whichever, I was feelin heavy and muggy inside just like it was outside. I made my way down to Wimp Dickerson's Barber Shop right after my English class let out.

"Howdy, pal." Wimp never changed. You know it's nice havin things in life that you can count on and Wimp sayin howdy pal when you walked through the barber shop door was somethin you always knew would happen.

"Hey there, Wimp. Doin okay today?"

"Hair's been a flyin around here today. Yep, I'm doin pretty good. If it was any better the dogs would be comin in wantin to pay for a haircut." I was glad to see that Wimp's mood was better than mine. He made me smile when he said that about dogs comin in for haircuts. I could just see ol Pancho and Fang settin in a chair next to all them other old men waitin to get their ears lowered. Kinda humorous when you go to thinkin about it.

One of the men sittin in the barber shop just passin the time of day heard what Wimp had said and piped up with his opinion. "The day they start givin haircuts to dogs is the day I'm gonna quit gettin mine cut at all." I guess he thought it was pretty low-down for men and hound dogs to be put in the same category together.

"Now don't you talk too fast, Fred, about lettin your hair keep growin," Wimp warned. "You might just like to know that up in New York City and some of them other big cities they has people who got no other job than to cut a dog's hair." Fred acted like he either didn't believe Wimp or was too old-fashioned to agree that maybe dogs do need a haircut now and then.

I made my way down to my usual spot at the end of the row of chairs so I could sit by Woody. He was busy shinin a man's shoes when I come in, but he looked my way and gave me that smile of his that said how you doin Leroy. I raised my eyebrows back at him and grinned. I liked watchin him shine shoes. There's a real art to what he was doin. I mean, he could really make that rag pop when he went to puttin the final buff on a man's shoes. Too bad I didn't never wear nice shoes. I'd have wanted Woody to shine them so I could look extra good. All I ever wore was old brogans and it didn't matter much what they looked like. I'd knock the dirt off on Saturdays so I wouldn't look too dirty when I went to church on Sunday, but that was about as close to a shinin as I ever got.

Woody got through poppin his rag and collected a little money from the man he'd made to look good and then strolled on outside in front of the barber shop. I followed him on out there. The bench was all wet from the drizzle so he just stood under the overhang up against the buildin. I stood next to him and stuck one leg up on the wall behind me just to get comfortable.

"Sho is messy out here t'day."

"It sure is. Least it ain't cold."

Woody's smile rained down on me. "Dat's de way I likes ta look at things. If things looks like dey's bad, it's bes ta jes think o what it could be like. De way you say dat it's not cold, it don't seem to matter much dat it's all wet." It's like Woody was congratulatin me for lookin on the bright side of things, even though I wasn't really feelin too sparky.

I figured I'd jump right in to what I needed to talk about. I didn't want to waste no time chewin the fat today. Not that I didn't like doin that, especially with Woody. I just had a lot on my mind and wanted to let go of some of it. "Well, Woody, there's a lot been happenin lately. Thought I'd tell you about it."

Woody smiled at me with that warm smile of his. "Dat's jes what you said de last time you wuz by here."

I couldn't help but give a little laugh. "It was true then and it's true again today—a lot of things has happened, and I don't know what in the world to think about it all. Almost enough to make a fella laugh."

Woody finished that thought by sayin exactly what was runnin through me. "It's enough ta make you laugh if you can keep from cryin, right Mista Leroy?" Boy he hit the nail on the head that time.

"Yeah, that's sure right."

"Well tell ol Woody all 'bout it."

I started talkin and boy did I need it. "Well, it all begun this mornin when I got up and went in the kitchen and there Daddy set at the kitchen table."

"Ya don't say." Woody was already tryin to imagine what that musta been like. I could tell that's what he was doin.

"He was sittin there like he'd never been gone at all. Drinkin coffee. He said good mornin to me. That was about the only thing different about him this mornin. Usually he doesn't say nothin to me, but this mornin he at least said that."

"I expect yo false teeth 'bout dropped outta yo mouf, huh Leroy?"

"Boy, I'm tellin ya. They sure did. I was plumb paralyzed. I couldn't think of what to say nor what to do. I didn't know whether I should go over there and thrash him for what all he'd put me and Momma and Cody Sue through or if I should go hug his neck."

"Kinda hard ta know jes how ta handle sumthin like dat, seein how it ain't every day dat you has ta make dem kinda decisions."

I shook my head back and forth over the whole situation. Just talkin about it made me think how ridiculous it was for a boy to have to be puttin up with such nonsense. "It was like I was a statue, Woody. I just stood there like this." I made my body rigid and took on my best statue pose. I grinned after holdin it there like that a couple of seconds. Woody smiled with me. Bein able to smile about them kinda things somehow helps you feel better, even if it isn't really no laughin matter.

"Yo brains jes plumb froze up, I 'spect."

"Yeah. That must of been what it was like with Momma, too, when she first saw him. She was goin around cookin breakfast and actin like normal. I wasn't there whenever Daddy first come in the house, but I bet she didn't know what to say any more than I did, so she probably just didn't say nothin. Just tried to act normal, as if that was easy to do. Least that's what I figure she did. Cody Sue, she went and jumped in his lap, but after squeelin for a couple minutes, she went right back to bein the same ol Cody Sue. Daddy hadn't showed hardly no sign at all that he even knew me and Cody Sue was in the room with him so I guess she didn't know what else to do except act like usual."

We stood there for a minute. Woody always seemed to know when I needed to collect my thoughts and never rushed me to talk. He knew there was a lot more in me, but waited until I was ready to go on instead of tryin to drag it out of me. While we were standin there, Mr. Youngblood, the woodshop teacher from school, walked into the barber shop. "Hey there, Mr. Youngblood," I said.

"Howdy, Mr. Evans." He did that to everbody at school—called them Mister or Miss whatever their last name was. Sav said that was because he didn't want to have to learn the first names of all the brothers and sisters that come through the school. He could just learn the last name and not worry about the rest of it. It saved his memory from workin so hard.

I went on talkin to Woody about my story. "I learned a couple things while I was at school today that has really made me go to thinkin, and this is the part I can't figure out."

"Oh? What'd you learn, Leroy?"

"You see, the principal at the high school, Mr. Higgins, has these relatives that lives up at Cow Pens where Daddy was stayin with his brother. He heard from one of his cousins that Daddy and his brother had been gettin along pretty bad on account of how Daddy wouldn't do no work nor hold up his fair share around there. Sounds to me like he was just doin what he always does at our house. The only difference is that my Uncle Amos he wasn't gonna just sit around and act like he didn't notice it the way Momma does. He told Daddy to start workin or get out of his house. Before Daddy left, they both got real drunk and got in this fight where my uncle tried to shoot Daddy."

"How 'bout dat."

I said yeah it was true, accordin to what I'd heard. "Now here's the part where I don't know what to think. You see that happened three days ago and how come Daddy didn't come home until this mornin? What was he doin those other two days before he finally showed up at our house?"

"Makes ya wonder jes what yo daddy wuz thinkin. You'd think dat he'da come right on home once his brother had done shot at him an throwed him outta de house."

"That's what it seems. You see, when Mr. Higgins had this talk with me a couple weeks ago, he said somethin about how he heard that Daddy wanted to come on home, but didn't know if we would want him back and that's why he was takin his time."

"Hmm." Woody had that look that said he was studyin hard. I didn't expect him to tell me all the answers like Cody Sue expected from me, but I liked it when Woody went to studyin. Even if he couldn't give me every answer, he at least could help me figure out what I might could do.

"You got any ideas of what it could be that was makin Daddy stay gone them extra two days?" I was interested in what Woody thought might have been runnin through Daddy's mind.

"Could be a couple o different things. Supposin yo daddy he think he gonna get throwed outta yo house by yo momma. Dat coulda keep him away. Or else, meybe he weren't right sho if he wuz ready ta come home. Could be he wuz 'fraid he'd hafta quit drinkin if'n he do. Or meybe he's confused as everbody else. Ya never knows what's runnin through a man's mind. Ya jes cain't say. What you thinkin, Mista Leroy?"

"You're right. Could be a bunch of different things that kept him away for them two days. See, I figured he was stayin out there in Cow Pens on account of bein ashamed of carryin on so that night he tore up the house. Mr. Higgins sayin he'd heard that Daddy wanted to come home but couldn't bring himself to do it is what made me think that. But I don't know, Woody. I don't know if he wanted to be home or not. He sure wasn't actin like it this mornin when I walked in the kitchen."

"I bet you been studyin on it all day, ain't ya, Leroy? Cain't come up wit no answer no matta how hard ya thinks. Frustratin. Downright frustratin."

"I guess I'll find out what the whole story is some day. Don't you reckon, Woody?" I was hopin he'd give me a promise that one of these days things would make perfect sense and my life would be just a normal ol life. He didn't give me any such empty promises, though.

"Dey's lots o things where we never knows what really happened, Leroy. Lots o things. Sumtimes de bes thing ta do is jes find out what ya can and den make up yo mind what to do wit de infomation you gots. It ain't exactly de way it's 'sposed to be, but sumtimes dat's all life gives ya." Woody was always so down to earth. Me, I wanted to know everything what had happened and everything a man was thinkin and feelin. It just about drove me plumb crazy not knowin all the particulars. But Woody was right. Sometimes you just have to take what you got and do the best you can with it. I didn't have near enough information about Daddy to suit me. Maybe I'd pick up a few details here and there, but I expect I was just gonna have to decide how I was gonna act now that he was back home. That was about the only good choice I had.

"That's the hard part, Woody."

"How's dat, Mista Leroy?"

"Figurin out what you're gonna do with what life's done thrown at you."

"Yeah, suh, it is. Dat's de hard part. Seem like we wuz talkin 'bout dat one other time befo." I knew which time Woody was talkin about. He was talkin about when he acted like he agreed with what Alane Sharpe had said about maybe me bein the one who might change some things in my family. Woody bringin that up was basically his way of askin me what was I thinkin about that now.

"I reckon I ought to be honest and say that before today I hadn't really given a whole lot of thought about what I might do different. This mornin when I tried to think of what to say to Daddy when I walked in the kitchen, I was kinda put out with myself for comin up empty-brained. I knew he'd be back one of these days and had figured it'd be pretty soon, but I didn't think I'd be so dad burn numb when it happened."

"Now dat it has, though, you gots some time ta do some plannin." Woody looked square in my eyes and added, "Dat's both good an bad. Ya see what I'm a sayin?"

I knew exactly what he was sayin. That meant that if I was gettin tired of actin the same old way with my family, now was my chance to act different. That was the good part, that I had a chance to do somethin I'd been thinkin I wanted to do. The bad part was that I didn't have anybody I could fault if I just did what I knew Momma and Cody Sue were gonna do, which was to go right back to actin the same old way with Daddy.

"You know, Woody, it's like you're in cahoots with a drunk when you just go on acceptin the things he does and just say to yourself oh well that's the way he is. I just flat refuse to do that any more."

"An ya know what else, Mista Leroy? De man who do de drinkin, he know it, too. Ain't got no reason ta change cause nobody 'spects him ta change."

"Kinda odd how it works, but I suppose that's what happens. I know it is, 'cause that's the way it's been at our house all this time."

"You's a smart young man, Leroy. It do me good ta see a man think de way you thinks."

Gettin a compliment from Woody sure felt good. If he told me he thought I was a smart young man, then I must be since Woody didn't say nothin he didn't think was true. I knew Woody probably needed to be gettin on back in the barber shop. I told him I was gonna go on home. He said he'd like to hear from me again pretty soon. I promised I'd come look him up and let him know what all had been goin on. Before I left, Woody said somethin that set me to thinkin even more.

"Jes remember, Mista Leroy, dey's a good man inside o everyone, yo daddy, too."

"You think so, Woody?"

"I been 'round too long ta think any different. Yeah, suh, I think so."

Now there was a thought I'd never had come into my brain before. There's a good man inside of everyone. Huh. Even my daddy has a good man inside of him. Boy oh boy, he must be hidin deep down in him. It's sure sad that a boy would think thatta way about his own daddy, but I hadn't been given much reason to see it any other way. Daddy acts what you'd call bad most all the time. He's a hard man. Every now and then he'll surprise you with something nice, but it never lasts more than a minute or so.

I trusted Woody, though, and knew he must be right. There's a good man inside of everyone, even my daddy. That sure was a hard one to understand. I was gonna try to look for him, I suppose, but I didn't have a whole lot of hope of findin him. I can tell you one thing, though. I had made up my mind I wasn't gonna just sit around that house and act like I'd always been actin. I still didn't know what in the world I was gonna do different, but I was aimin to think of somethin. And soon.

Chapter 19

DADDY HAD been home now for five days. I was still feelin right peculiar about him bein home after havin been gone for a month. It's odd, because I felt funny while he was gone, too. I was sad because our family wasn't all together under one roof, but at the same time, I was relieved that there wasn't the usual agitation hangin in the air as there is when Daddy were around. No matter how hard I tried to feel normal, I found myself either feelin bitter or guilty, and I didn't like neither feelin. I had always been taught that a boy was supposed to honor his momma and daddy. Says so right there in the Bible. It was pretty easy to honor Momma most of the time what with her bein the quiet and gentle type. Honorin Daddy was a whole 'nother matter, though.

How's a boy supposed to honor someone who drinks too much and doesn't talk much except to yell or gripe about his biscuits being too hard and such as that? I figure if your biscuits was cooked a little too long a person might as well try likin hard biscuits, but Daddy doesn't see it that way. If something isn't to his likin he just says so, and he doesn't care one bit whose feelins he steps on neither. How was I supposed to honor a man when he acted like that? That's a hard one to answer and I know it.

Momma was still hard for me to read even after Daddy had been home these last few days. It's kinda hard for me to believe that when she got up that mornin and there was Daddy sittin at the kitchen table she didn't act any different than usual. I suppose she's the one who fixed him his coffee since he didn't never do that kind of thing for himself. He didn't see it as bein a man's place to do nothin in the kitchen, not even fixin the coffee. Ever since I tried studyin Momma that mornin, I couldn't tell that she was doin anything that she didn't always do. She just went on livin life like normal.

I been thinkin a lot the last couple days about Momma. Maybe actin like normal was the only way she could keep from blowin up at Daddy for bein the way he is. But who knows, maybe she's a real saintly and forgivin person and she's not even mad at him like I am. Then again, she may be pretendin to be someone she's not. She may act like everything's okay, but it's not. That's the way I think things really are inside Momma. You know, she might have all these bad thoughts about Daddy but doesn't say so on account of bein afraid of what he might do to her. To my knowledge, he's never hit Momma, except for the time he pushed her that night he got so drunk and left. She may be afraid that he'd really belt her one if she let him have it with everything she felt.

It makes me mad at Momma for bein so lame in the way she lets Daddy get away with bein the way he is. I'd like to tell her, "Go ahead, Momma, and stand up to Daddy. Don't let him be thatta way to you." I never did, though. You know, when I go to thinkin on it, I'm really not a whole lot different than my momma in that respect. Here I am sittin here thinkin she ought to do somethin, but I hadn't done nothin either. I sure had never stood up to Daddy and told him how I felt. I didn't want to get busted in the rear end. Daddy doesn't hit Momma, but he can hit me and Cody Sue and call it a spankin or discipline or such.

Now that I ponder it, the whole family might as well all get together and tell Daddy, "Go ahead and act selfish and be as mean as you like and do whatever it is you want to do. We don't aim on standin in your way if you do." That's exactly what we were doin by toleratin his ways. Dad gum, it makes me mad when I go to thinkin like that.

I went and found Cody Sue so I could see what she was thinkin about all this. What with her comin to me awhile back and tellin me how sad she felt, maybe she'd see what I was talkin about if I told her what was runnin through my mind. "Cody Sue, why do you think we let Daddy come on back in the house and then started actin the way we always act? How come we don't do nothin about it? Don't you think it's about time we told Daddy we were tired of puttin up with his rudeness and meanness?"

Cody Sue looked at me the way only Cody Sue can look. Dad gum! It seemed like she'd been hangin around that cat of hers too much. That girl could give the blankest look of anybody I'd ever seen other than a cat. It doesn't take much to guess that I didn't get too much reaction from Cody Sue. She acted like she hadn't noticed there was somethin powerful wrong with the way our family acted. It was like she had taken them feelins she showed me the other day and stuffed them away in a drawer again so she wouldn't be bothered anymore.

I just know when I'm over to Sav's house and see his daddy put his arm around him and his momma smile at his daddy like she means it, it makes me feel kinda heartbroke that I don't have the same thing in my house. Maybe all of Cody Sue's friends has families that got along odd like we do, but I doubt it. I think it's just as convenient for Cody Sue to act ignorant about it all as it is for Momma. Don't get me wrong, I'm not sayin Momma's an ignorant person. I'm just sayin she acts that way when it comes to handlin Daddy. Same for Cody Sue.

I wanted to go talk to Woody about this whole matter and see what did he think about it, but it was too late for that. Maybe he would've told me I shouldn't be thinkin such thoughts and that I should just let things alone so they wouldn't just get worse. I doubt it, though. That isn't Woody's way. He'd probably say somethin like, "Ya cain't heps de way you feels. It's powerful hard ta know what you's gonna do wit dem feelins, ain't it?" It sure was hard. Part of me wanted to march right in to where Daddy sat and tell him what I felt and another part of me said to just shut my mouth and keep quiet.

I went to my room and started studyin history. We had a test comin up and I needed a good grade. Lord help me, I always seem to need a good grade. I know I should try harder in school, but most of the time my heart just ain't in it. I know it sure wasn't tonight what with all these thoughts about Daddy racin through my brain. Studyin about Thomas Jefferson and George Washington just didn't mean much to me at the time.

It struck me, though, as I was readin, that what if folks like Thomas Jefferson and George Washington had just sat back on their rear ends and let things go on bein the way they was back then. If that had been so, I'd be talkin with an English accent right now. Or what if Abraham Lincoln had just kept his mouth shut about the slaves bein real people just like the folks what owned them. Then people like Woody would be worse off than they are now. I doubt that my history teacher, Miss Ferguson, would want to take any credit for what I was about to do, but I felt like if folks like Jefferson and Washington and Lincoln could stand up and say what they felt, so could I. Maybe it wouldn't make much of a difference in the way our family acted, but it couldn't make things much worse than they were now. At least that's the way I looked at it.

It wasn't but a few steps from my room to the front room where Daddy was sittin. He was drinkin somethin strong and just sittin there, probably half asleep. Momma was sewin in her rockin chair, her mind no doubt a hundred miles off. Despite it wasn't but a short trip into the front room, I felt like I was walkin a long ways into virgin territory.

"Daddy, I need to say somethin to you. You got time?" I tried to sound grown-up so Daddy would know he was talkin to a man and not a little boy. He just burped. My word! Why'd he have to be thatta way? Here I was tryin to have a man-to-man talk and that's all he could do. Didn't he see the serious look on my face?

"Yeah, I ain't doin nothin. What do you want?"

"I been thinkin, Daddy. Things don't seem right around here. Nobody never talks to nobody, and it's always tense in this house. Know what I mean?" It was quickly evident to me that Daddy didn't have the foggiest notion what I was hintin at.

"What're you talkin about, Leroy? If you got somethin to say, then say it. Don't go beatin around the bush."

"What I mean, Daddy, is that everybody around here acts like they're scared to tell you what they think about your drinkin and the way you carry on and such. I been thinkin on how that keeps our family all tangled up in knots. Least, I feel tangled up in knots most all the time and I expect Momma and Cody Sue does too if they'd admit to it."

You can imagine that Momma had took quick notice to what I was sayin. If Daddy was slow to catch on to what I was tryin to communicate, she sure wasn't. She knew exactly what I meant. She also knew I had broken the biggest rule this family has, and that is to not cross Daddy by sayin nothin about his ways. She wasn't defendin Daddy when she spoke up. She was lookin out for her own worries.

"Now Leroy, what on earth are you talkin about? What's got into you?" I had done jumped in the river now, so to speak, so I had to keep on swimmin.

"You know what I'm talkin about, Momma. Nobody in this here family is ever happy with one another, least not the way we should be. Daddy got mad and throwed a fit and then left home for almost a month and then comes home and not a word's been said about it. It's been thatta way all my life, and it just ain't right!" I turned toward Daddy and kept on goin. "Daddy, you need to know that your drinkin is too much. And the way you talk hateful to everybody around here does us all a lot of harm. It's a burden on the family to live like that. You gotta quit all of this or else . . ." I didn't get to finish my "or else" because Daddy butted in. It's just as well because I don't know how I'd of finished the sentence anyhow.

"Hold on just a minute, Leroy! Who do you think you are comin in here talkin like that and threatenin me and talkin about my drinkin? I don't drink no more than the next fella, and I don't treat none of you any worse than you deserve. If you think you're ready to take charge of my house, then maybe it's time we stepped outside and took care of this the way men do! That's what me and my daddy did!"

"And you've always hated your daddy, too! Ain't that true?" I screamed. "You and your daddy fought when you was young, and you ain't hardly talked to him since! That's not what I'm wantin to do. I just want you to listen to me! I'm tired of livin the way we do!"

"Leroy!" Momma had come pretty doggone close to havin a stroke by now. She sure wanted me to hush up. That much was plain as day. Then again, maybe she wanted me to keep right on talkin because I was sayin everything she felt, too. Who knows about her. I just know she was plenty scared. So was I, but for a different reason.

Daddy was redder than I'd ever seen a man get. Daddy always has this red look to his face on account of drinkin for all them years, but I've never seen him look nothin like what he looked like now. He had dropped his bottle and it was spillin on the floor. I wanted to mock him and tell him he better pick up his bottle before all his precious liquor drained out, but I knew that bein sarcastical wouldn't be the smartest thing to do right now. I'd already said plenty to get Daddy riled up and didn't need to go gettin smart on him. I waited, expectin him to challenge me again. But he didn't say nothin. Just sat there seethin rage.

Probably only a few seconds had passed after I said what I did, but it seemed like a couple hours. By this time, Cody Sue had heard all the racket and had come runnin to the front room. She probably wanted to see if Daddy was gonna really take me outside and thrash me. I'm sure she didn't think I had any chance of holdin my own against him, despite my reputation as a fighter had improved since all that business with Bruno Lynch.

I finally spoke up again, except this time my voice was softer. In fact, I think I was about to cry. I'm not too sure if I was feelin sad or remorseful or angry or what, but my eyes was gettin wet. "Daddy, I just want us to be a regular family, that's all. I want you to quit drinkin so you can enjoy bein around us. You can't enjoy your family when you're drunk like you can when you're sober. And Momma needs you to be nicer to her. You treat her like she's a hired hand and not your wife." Momma turned white when I said that. Actually she just went a deeper shade of pale cause she was already white. She didn't know what was gonna happen next. But the odd thing is that she didn't say nothin to try and stop me. I was becomin more convinced that she wanted me to keep on talkin.

"Daddy, me and Cody Sue need you to do things with us. You know, the way Sav's daddy does things with him and his brothers. We just want you to be a regular person." I stopped talkin for just a second to take a breath. I was plumb flooded now with my feelins. Then somehow it just came outta my mouth. "Daddy, I love you. I sure hope you love all of us, too." I hadn't said nothin like that to Daddy in years. I still don't know what possessed me to get all mushy like that, but that was the feelin that just fell out of me.

Daddy was still red, but the blood that had rushed up his neck and colored his face so deep like started subsidin when I said that, just like the tide seeps back to the ocean. Boy, I'd give a hundred dollars if I could've reached inside his brain and seen his thoughts. Who knows what was rollin around in there. His face looked blank as a blackboard that had just been wiped clean. But it wasn't the same kind of empty look I had seen on Cody Sue a little while earlier. Cody Sue was just showin that her brain didn't always work, but it was plenty evident that Daddy's brain was churnin hard.

He just sat there. Didn't move at all. Didn't look at nobody nor move a muscle. He just sat. I wanted to do a lot of things right then and there. I wanted to go over and hug Daddy because I felt sorry for him. I also wanted to say I was ready to go on out into the backyard if he were ready. Then again I wanted to keep on talkin and give him a lecture the way Mr. Higgins would give students a lecture at school when he thought you needed a good blessin out. I knew, though, from listenin to my share of lectures from adults that that wouldn't do no good. To tell the truth, I didn't know what in the world to do. I just stood there with everybody else, sayin nothin.

I looked over at Momma. I don't think she realized it, but her mouth was hangin wide open. She was still dazed by what I had just done. Lord knows, she was worryin now. Despite I had said everything she probably had wanted to say all these years but couldn't, she was sure worried. You know, there's a lot of fear in worry. I know that Momma was afraid Daddy might turn into this bull and go on a rampage that might last for days. That's what had kept her shut up all these years. How long had she been married to Daddy? Probably about twenty years. For twenty years she's been thinkin and feelin all them things and never would say it. And now here I'd gone and said it all in the span of just five minutes or so.

Cody Sue almost made me mad the way she was standin there lookin dumbfounded and all. I wanted to say to her why didn't she just go on back to her room and mind her own business. She had just come in here with the rest of us because she didn't want to miss out on a good show. She didn't have no inklin of what I'd been talkin to Daddy about. She sure didn't seem to have a notion of what I meant earlier in the evenin when I had tried to talk to her. I suppose she had took Momma's lead all these years and had just pretended that what was happenin right under her own nose wasn't really happenin. I wanted to blame her for not joinin in with me and speakin up to Daddy. I felt like accusin her of makin matters worse just by actin so ignorant. Maybe that's the way she got by, though, just like that's how Momma got through twenty years of it herself. For that matter, that's what I'd been doin all my life until just a few minutes ago—actin ignorant. I suppose I shouldn't be feelin so hard against Cody Sue.

I finally spoke up again. "Daddy, you all right? I didn't mean to make you upset, I . . ."

Daddy interrupted me again and spoke gruff. At first I was offended, but then, I should've realized that the man had just been stripped of his own honor by a fifteen-year-old boy. "Yeah, I'm all right!" But then he calmed down real quick. "I'm all right."

Then it hit me like a sack of cement. Daddy *couldn't* talk about what he was feelin. He didn't know how! Here I was talkin about my feelins and all, and Daddy didn't know the language. He'd never learned it. I don't know my granddaddy much at all, but I'm for sure he isn't the kind of man who goes around talkin about how he feels all the time. Oh sure, folks would say if my granddaddy felt something, why, he wouldn't hold back from sayin it. But that ain't what I'm gettin at. That's not really talkin about your feelins. That's bowlin people over so you don't have to talk about how you really feel. My granddaddy and my daddy and a whole lot of other men just like them act like that as a way of hidin. I don't know what they're hidin from, because I had found out that when you say what you really feel inside, instead of actin like you feel different than you really do, it makes you feel a heap better. At least I was feelin better right now, despite it was so awkward bein in the front room with nobody knowin what to do next.

I found myself wonderin if Daddy was capable of ever learnin the ways of a man who could understand his feelins. Maybe not. Maybe he was too old to break out of his usual ways of lookin at things. Maybe because he hadn't learned such things as a boy it was no use for him to do any back peddlin and try to catch up now that he was grown. I didn't know what to think. I sure wish Woody had been right there by me so I could ask him all about this. I bet he'd know somethin about what my daddy was experiencin, seein that he was a grown man like Daddy. Despite how Woody grew up in a different sort of family than my daddy did, what with him bein colored and Daddy bein white and all, I bet he'd seen the same thing in some of the men in his family. Most colored folks seem to do a better job of understandin themselves than other folks does. Maybe that's because they had to put up with so much wrong all these years that they learned how to sing and shout and show what they was feelin inside instead of keepin it all hemmed up inside like Daddy and other men like him did. But still, I bet Woody would know what I was talkin about and could help me understand things.

I figured our family time, if you want to call it that, was about over. Tell you the truth, with Daddy settin there all quiet like and Momma on the verge of panic, I felt like I'd stirred the waters enough for one night.

"Well, Daddy, I've done had my say. I hope you think on what I just said. Maybe we can talk about it again sometime." Daddy kinda halfway looked at me and almost smiled. At least I think he did. He didn't say nothin, but I sure hoped he wasn't gonna toss what just happened out the window and forget about it.

I went on back to my room and just laid there. Alane Sharpe had said that just maybe I could be the one what could do somethin to make things in this family better. I kinda doubt she had in mind me doin what I had just did. Woody felt like I needed to do somethin instead of just sit back and take things the way they was. Well, what I had did was a start. Hard to say where it was gonna lead to, but it was a start to somethin. I was gonna sit back a little bit and see what happened next. But now that I had done opened up my insides, I don't reckon I was gonna close myself back up and quit speakin out. I just couldn't be that way no more. I was scared, but I felt right proud of myself at the same time, if you can follow what I mean.

Chapter 20

THINGS WAS right quiet around the house for the next couple of days. Momma went about doin what she always done. But she wasn't the same as she was even a few days earlier. You could just tell she'd been feelin different ever since I had dared to speak up to Daddy. I think she wanted to act different, too, but flat didn't know how. I reckon she was waitin to see what would I do next, bein that she sure wasn't the kind to take the bull by the horns and ride it, so to speak. Cody Sue was different, too. Every time she walked by me, it was like she had to take one more hard stare at me cause she couldn't believe I had acted like I did to Daddy and not only come out of it alive, but come out of it with maybe a little bit of respect from Daddy.

For four solid days, Daddy was halfway decent around the house. I can't say he was what you'd call the nice and friendly type of daddy, but he wasn't his usual cranky self neither. He was gone durin the day like always, but come home each night and didn't leave. I don't know that he was actin decent on account of me, but I'd like to think that maybe he was. He didn't talk none at all about what he was thinkin, but I figure his brain was churnin pretty hard. Had to be. A man like Daddy doesn't take a conversation like the one me and him had and just forget about it. If he had of forgot about it, he would've gone back to his old ways real quick like. That would've been his way of sayin it don't matter none what you think, I'm still gonna do things the way I want to. The fact that he was bein a little more respectable was his way of sayin I'm still chewin on what you said cause it's hit me pretty doggone hard.

The next Saturday I waited until late in the afternoon and headed downtown. I figured I would wind up down by Wimp's Barber Shop at about quittin time so I could walk down to the river with Woody and talk awhile with him. Downtown Cassville was a busy place on this Saturday afternoon, despite it was a right chilly day to be gettin out. Cassville doesn't have none of them tall buildins like they build in places like Birmingham. We got one or two that's pretty good size—one's an office buildin and the other's a fancy hotel. Rest of ems just regular old buildins. I like it thatta way. I wouldn't want to live no place where you was eaten up by huge buildins when you go into town. But I don't think I'd like livin in one of them little towns neither, that didn't have no place where you could go to buy things or just mosey around.

Seemed like I knew 'bout half the folks that were downtown this afternoon. One of the folks I saw was Bruno Lynch. Now there was somebody I didn't especially care to talk to. When I eyeballed his lazy body slumpin down the sidewalk, I slipped inside the five-and-dime store just so I wouldn't have to hear nothin come out of his crude mouth. Bruno wasn't exactly bein what you'd call polite to me lately, but at least he'd left me alone. No matter, I didn't want nothin to do with him and stepped out of his sight.

I kept my eye lookin out the window at him and didn't even notice that Alane Sharpe wasn't more than ten feet from me. Her and her momma was in the store buying somethin. "Leroy! Fancy meeting you here."

I wheeled around to see Alane lookin right at me, smilin big as could be. Now if that don't take your mind off of Bruno Lynch real quick like, nothin will. "Well, hey there, Alane. Hey, Mrs. Sharpe. Didn't know I'd run into you down here." It hit me while I was standing there that she probably was wonderin what in the world I was doin in the store. I didn't want to bring up Bruno's name so I come up with this lame excuse for shoppin at the five-and-dime. "Uh, I come in here to see did they have any of that Konjola medicine. You ever heard of that?"

Mrs. Sharpe told Alane she'd be right back and left me to talk by myself with her daughter. That was downright thoughtful of her to do that. I wanted to say thank you for leavin me with your daughter, but didn't know how a boy was supposed to say somethin like that so I didn't say nothin.

Alane laughed. "You're looking for what?"

"Some of that Konjola medicine. I'm not gonna get none, I just wanted to see what did it look like. I read in the paper that there was this woman who drank a bunch of bottles of that medicine and it made her into a new person. It's supposed to cure anything you got—arthritis, bad bowels, kidney problems—you name it, this stuff's supposed to cure it. Thought I might just look at it." You ever had this feelin when you're talkin to someone that you better hurry up and finish cause you sure are soundin ignorant? Well, that's how I felt right then. The more I talked about that Konjola medicine, the dumber I felt.

Thank goodness, Alane was the generous type who knew when to change the subject to keep me from embarrassin myself more than was absolutely necessary. "I haven't seen any of that before, but if I do, I'll look at it real good so I can tell you all about it. Deal?"

"Deal." And I should've added my thanks for not askin nothin more about it since I was feelin right simple at the moment. "So, Alane, what're you and your momma doin this afternoon?"

"We're just out picking up a few things. It's getting pretty close to winter and Momma says I need a new coat, so we've been out looking for one." I was wearin an old jacket that I guess had been my daddy's. I knew I wasn't gettin no new coat this winter what with us havin a hard time just payin the bills. Me and Sav had worked a little more on our fence paintin business, but I had put all the money I earned on Momma's bureau each time. She'd never said a word to me about any of that money. It's like by not sayin nothin about it, she didn't have to admit that she needed to take money from me just to help make ends meet.

"I'd like to see you in your new coat when you get it. I bet it'll look nice on you."

I think Alane embarrassed herself by drawin attention to the fact that I didn't have no money for new coats. She acted like she couldn't change the subject quick enough. Funny, though, she didn't realize she was about to ask about somethin that was even more embarrassin than me not havin no money for a new coat.

"I haven't asked you about your family lately. Are things better?"

Alane was feelin bad enough for sayin things that might bother me, so I was determined I was gonna find a way to answer her that would make her feel good about askin instead of uncomfortable. She shouldn't ought to take the blame for the fact that everything she asked me about showed up all my faults.

"Well, let's just say I think they're a little bit different. I had a talk with Daddy the other night." The way I said it, it probably sounded like I musta had this nice father to son conversation with my daddy and we had worked out all our differences.

"Tell me about it. I hope your daddy listened to what you told him." I guess I could've said that he didn't talk a whole lot so that must mean he had agreed with what I had said. But I'd felt guilty whenever I tried to come across to Alane like my family and her family weren't a whole lot different. I wasn't gonna make that mistake again.

"Well, it was one of the more unusual talks I ever been in. I guess you could say that about it. You see I got to thinkin about how by not talkin about my daddy's ways, the whole family was just tellin him to go ahead and keep on ruinin the family. So I spoke up and said what I thought. He was mad at first, but then he's been quiet the last few days. I don't rightly know what he's thinkin now."

Alane was nice and she meant well when she asked me about such things, but she was just a girl all the same. It wasn't like she was all grown-up and had all this experience that let her know what to say next. Not that I expected her to be that way, but I think she felt like she ought to of known what more to say than she did. At least she was wise enough to know that if she didn't know what to say, it was better to just say nothin. She just nodded her head and smiled this smallish smile. "I'm glad you did, Leroy. I hope that's going to make a difference in your family." We talked about nothin in particular for a minute and then her mother walked up and said it was time for them to be leavin. I said good-bye to Alane and Mrs. Sharpe, and Alane said she hoped to see me at school on Monday.

It was real nice talkin to Alane and I was glad I had told her that I had spoke up to Daddy, but sayin what little I had to her made me want even more to talk to Woody. As good as it was talkin to Alane, it did me even more good to talk with Woody. I went on back outside and made my way over a street or two to Jefferson Avenue and headed to Wimp's. I got there pretty close to closin time. Woody already had his things put away and was just about ready to leave.

"Mista Leroy," he said when he saw me, "I been thinkin 'bout you. How you been a doin?" Boy, it sure did me good to see my dark-skinned friend. He always greeted me like I was the most important person he'd ever known. My heart woke up quick when I was around him. It was like my body knew I was gonna feel better in just a few minutes.

"I'm doin all right, Woody. Thought I'd see if you was gonna walk down by the river on your way home. Might walk a spell with you."

Woody knew exactly what that meant. "Ya know, Leroy, I wuz jes sayin ta mysef, 'Woody, you needs to take a spell an walk 'long side o dat Tennessee River a little while 'fore you goes on home.' Yeah, suh, dat's jes what I wuz sayin." He grinned at me as his way of addin that he'd sure be glad to hear whatever I had to say to him just because I meant that much to him.

I didn't hardly wait until Woody and me had got down the street when I went to talkin. "Well, it's been pretty excitin around my house this week," I informed him.

"How's dat, Leroy?"

Kiddin like, I asked, "You didn't see that explosion goin off over my house the other night? I thought for sure you'd be able to see it from where you live."

Woody went along with my funnin. "Dat musta been 'bout de time I turn my back. Reckon I didn't see no 'splosion. Naw, suh, sho didn't."

I got a little more serious. "Well, Woody, I was thinkin the other night about how nobody never says nothin in my home about my daddy's ways and how he'd come home from Cow Pens and everybody went straight back to actin like normal just like Daddy had never been gone at all. You remember, that's what I was tellin you about the other day. Well, a couple nights later I just got right up from my room where I was thinkin and went in to where Daddy and Momma was sittin and told Daddy that we needed to do some changin. We needed him to start bein a Daddy and quit his drinkin and carryin on."

Woody's eyebrows was raised. "You sho got a reaction from yo daddy, I 'spect."

"Well, yes and no. At first he got all mad and said he didn't drink too much and he didn't treat us any worse than we ought to be treated. Woody, how come a man who stays drunk most all the time can set there and say his drinkin ain't gone too far? Can't he see what it's doin to everybody else?"

"Funny de way dat drinkin make you think you ain't hurtin nobody. Man's liquor can sho do sum powerful convincin when it comes ta tellin a man it ain't doin him no harm."

"I reckon. Hard for me to see, though, that he can be that blind to what all he's doin to himself and the rest of us."

"Seem like he'd see right quick dat he hurtin de whole family. Maybe he sees it but he don't do nothin 'bout it cause he figure he cain't. Hard ta say."

"You know Woody, you're right. I think he does see some of what all he's doin. I learned somethin about Daddy that night that'd never hit me before. But it hit me like a load of cement that night."

"Do tell." Woody wanted me to keep goin. We was gettin close to the river. The Tennessee River has this suspension bridge that crosses it where Stuart Avenue ends. They say it used to be the longest suspension bridge of its kind this side of the Mason-Dixie line when it was first built. I'd say that was something for a little ol town like Cassville to have a bridge that used to be famous. We headed toward that bridge. I liked to hang over the rail and look down from it into the water.

"At first when I was talkin I was pretty riled up and Daddy got riled back at me. I tell you, my feelins was runnin all over the place. I went from feelin all burned up to feelin sorry for Daddy. Then I went and got mushy and told Daddy I loved him."

"Dat's hard fo a young man ta say." Woody was tellin me I had did the right thing by sayin that.

"That's when Daddy got quiet on me. That made me think that maybe I got through to him a little bit. He didn't get mad at me no more, and he's been nice to me ever since then. I say he's been nice. It's just that he ain't been mean. You understand that for Daddy, that's bein nice."

We had stopped on the bridge and was standin there lookin out over the river. I wondered again as I watched the water pass on by underneath if the folks what lived here in this spot a long time ago went through the same kinds of troubles that we go through today. My brain chewed on whether them ol Creek Indians knew about liquor and if men used to drink back then like some men do now. If they did, I wondered would a boy stand up to his daddy and say how it hurt him.

"Somethin's botherin me about this whole thing, Woody."

"What's dat, Mista Leroy?"

"I been thinkin about God a lot lately. Don't ask me why, but that's what I been doin."

"What you think?"

"Well, if a man is supposed to be made like God is, and he made my daddy, what does that say about God? I don't aim on bein disrespectful, Woody, but if my daddy's been made to be anything like God, that don't speak too kindly of God."

I reckon Woody wanted me to do some hard thinkin on that one. He asked me, "Leroy, when you thinks o God, what do it conjure up in yo mind?"

Boy I had to think on that one a minute. I didn't want to go givin none of them answers I'd always heard in church. That was mostly folks just sayin what they'd heard somebody else say. It probably wasn't what they really thought. I wanted to tell Woody what I felt, but didn't rightly know how to say it. I gave it my best try.

"I always figured God was this big, strong type of man. You know, he's the kind what tells everything what to do and they do it. I 'spect that if God has a mind to do somethin, he just does it how he likes and he don't ask nobody else. It's his world, so he can do with it what he wants. But then I think that if God does whatever he wants to do, why'd he make it to where my daddy would act the way he does. That's the part where I have a hard time understandin God."

"You reckon dat God, he get powerful sad when he see yo daddy doin what he do?"

I'd never thought of it thatta way. I always figured God was mad whenever someone had done committed a sin and he was gonna make 'em pay for it by sendin 'em to hell or somethin. "What're you talkin about, Woody?"

"What I's sayin, Mista Leroy, is dat God, he don't make yo daddy act de way he do. It ain't like God ta jes tell folks ta go ta drinkin an sech jes so his boy gonna be angry. Dat's not like God. Dat God, he's soft." Woody leaned over to me like he was tellin me a secret. "Jes like when yo momma cry, God cry, too. He hurt jes like a woman hurt or like a boy hurt when dey husband or daddy do dem de wrong way. Dat's what I mean 'bout him bein soft."

God's the soft type who cries when my momma cries or when I do. That was a new one on me. I didn't figure God ever cried. "Then why don't he do nothin about it, Woody? Why don't he make people different so they don't act like my daddy?"

"I figure dat God, he know what he doin when he done made us de way we is. If dat's so, den we's lookin at it all wrong when we tries ta see God de same way we sees people. God, he ain't like people. He don't think like you an me. Meybe us folks down here needs ta try to think like God think, 'stead o makin it where he think like we does. Dat make sense, Leroy?" It did, but I still wanted to know more. Woody could tell, so he went on talkin. "Ya see, Leroy, if God had done made yo daddy where yo daddy don't get ta choose how he gonna act, den how yo daddy gonna be able to show you he love you? H'it's gotta be yo daddy's choosin, not God's. De way I figures it, dat's why God he stay outta de way even when us folks down here make big mistakes. He's got ta stay outta de way, else when a man like yo daddy decide he gonna straighten up, it weren't his choice."

I was gettin confused, but I was tryin to follow what Woody were sayin. "So, if God's bound to let folks like my daddy choose to drink if that's what he wants to do, what use is it for me to bother to ask God to change him?"

"Meybe dat's where you comes in. 'Member, you's got ta try ta think like God think. Ya cain't figure God think like we does." Woody smiled at me. He wasn't gonna tell me everything all at once. I think he wanted me to figure it out for myself.

"You mean, I'm the one who's got to change, not Daddy?" That didn't seem quite right to me. Daddy's the one who'd been doin all the drinkin, not me.

"You's already made some changes, Mista Leroy. You talked right up de other night when you got dis feelin inside o you. Who you 'spect might've put dat feelin in you?"

Huh? I didn't quite get it. My forehead wrinkled up. I was studyin hard on what Woody said. He gave me another hint. "De onliest person you can change, Mista Leroy, is yoself. God, he know dat. You go ta askin God to change yo daddy, he gonna say dat's sumthin yo daddy gotta do. But you go askin God ta change you an God he gonna say, now dat's sumthin we can go ta work on. If'n you go ta changin, ya never knows, meybe yo daddy take notice and he wanna change, too. Den God got sumthin he can work wit in yo daddy. See what I means, Leroy, when I says de onliest person you can change is you? An if'n you go ta changin, meybe you become a angel what heps yo daddy."

Me an angel. I'd sure never thought of that one. I can say that I liked what Woody said about me changin me and maybe that would cause something to happen in my daddy. All respect to Alane Sharpe, I don't rightly expect she had all of what Woody had just told me about in her mind when she suggested that I just might be the one to cause my family to change. When I had told Woody a couple days after that what she said, he knew that I'd understand things more in time. I'm beginnin to understand. I know I'm not through talkin to Daddy. One time ain't enough. I'm talkin some more.

Chapter 21

T HE NEXT day bein Sunday, me and Cody Sue and Momma went
to church. I got to wonderin while I was settin there did anybody
in this here church think the same way about God that Woody
did. You listen to some folks talk and they'd lead you to believe that God,
he's this man up in heaven who's the boss man over everything what
happens. Not that they mean to say that God isn't a good fella and all,
but when you go to talkin about God knowin everythin there is to know
and bein this powerful man, you lose track of what Woody was sayin
about how God is soft and cries when folks like me and Momma cry on
account of Daddy actin like he does.

I recollect hearin sermons about askin God for whatever you want and
you get it. I've asked God a bunch of times to give me a decent family, but
things never changed. Then I'd ask God to strike my daddy down and
make him feel as bad as I did, just to punish him. Daddy must feel bad
about himself, but I don't think he felt that way just cause I was mad and
asked God to go after him.

I liked the way Woody told me to try to change me and then maybe I
could be of some help to Daddy. I expect God liked that idea, too. When
you go to thinkin on it, I imagine God likes Woody quite a lot. I can just
hear him sayin from up there in the clouds, "That Woody, now there's
someone who understands what I'm gettin at when I tell folks how they
ought to be livin their lives." Woody has everythin a man is supposed to
have to be happy. He has this strange mix of features you don't see in
hardly any people. He's a bunch of things all at the same time. He's
understandin of the ways of others and don't never hold grudges against
people even when they act ugly to him. He's patient with folks who've
treated him bad, but he doesn't let folks just run over him. Somehow, he
can be mad about somethin, but still be level-headed. You don't see that

in too many folks. He can set a man to actin more polite just by treatin him the way people ought to be treated. It was like his good mood rubbed off on others. Woody can get mad and upset when he knows somethin is wrong, but he doesn't try to go out and force people to change things. He just does what he can to make things different and hopes someone takes notice.

The thing I like most about Woody is that he's soft, just like he said God is soft. Every time I talk to Woody 'bout somethin that's frettin me, it's like he steps inside me and feels the way I do just for a minute. When he does that, he don't need to go givin me all this advice. Just him understandin me helps me know what I ought to do next. 'Course, when he does tell me a thing or two about what I need to know, I sure listen. I know when Woody tries to help me out, he knows exactly what I need. Makes it awful easy for me to trust him. I figure God must be a lot like Woody, only better. Thinkin on God like that makes me feel a whole lot more religious than thinkin on him like some boss man who just runs the show from up in the sky.

The choir stood up to sing a song so I listened, seein that Momma sings in the choir. She likes to hear me and Cody Sue say how the choir sang pretty. Every Sunday while we're goin home Momma goes to commentin on who wasn't in church and who must of been sick. She even keeps track of who all went to sleep durin the sermon, too, so I never try to catch me a nap durin church like some folks do. 'Course, Mrs. Turnipseed has slept through practically every sermon a preacher's ever preached at our church. What with her insistin that she has to have some food on her big stomach all the time, it's no wonder she can drift away into her own heaven soon as she settles down in her pew. There's this man named Mr. Leaman what sits on the front row of the choir right behind the preacher that I watch a lot. Surely he ain't sleepin right under the preacher's nose, but it sure looks thatta way some Sundays. I never have sung up in the choir loft, so I don't know what it's like lookin out at everybody while church is goin on. It's plain, though, that Momma comes away from church every week with a different view of things than what I got.

Everybody was enjoyin the choir singin when right as they sung the last "Amen" this pregnant lady up on the second row of the choir loft got a little too hot and fainted. Some of the basses sittin close by carried her out to get her some fresh air. Momma's all the time talkin bout how hot it is up there in the choir loft. I reckon this lady faintin is proof that Momma's right.

A couple minutes after the pregnant lady got taken out, this other older lady got up and walked straight out of the choir loft, too, just after the preacher had started preachin. Made lots of racket leavin, too. No disrespect to older people, but when one of them gets flustered, they can sure make a lot of noise lettin other folks know about it. She was sittin right in front of where the pregnant lady had fell, so I had figured maybe she was goin out to check on things. Pretty soon, here she come walkin back in the choir loft, steppin on folks and just fussin away while she was gettin back to her seat. I know the poor old lady wasn't meanin to create a ruckus, but that's exactly what she were doin. She didn't realize how her voice was almost as loud as the preacher's. The whole choir got stirred up while payin attention to her and everybody in the congregation forgot what the preacher was sayin and went to watchin the show behind him. The preacher acted like he didn't even notice there was all this commotion goin on behind him and the choir director, he was hangin his head and shakin it back and forth outta disgust. I was glad Momma was in the choir. She could tell me later what in thunder all of that was about.

That was the first thing I asked about when we was goin home. "Momma, what happened up there in the choir with Mrs. Crowder faintin and Mrs. Pemberton goin out to see after her?"

Momma got this perturbed sound in her voice and explained, "Well, you know how the choir loft gets so hot. Mrs. Crowder got herself so worked up on account of singin so hard that she just plumb lost all the blood in her head. If you ask me, I think she held her breath too long holdin on to that last note. Her bein pregnant, you think she ought to know to stop and catch her breath durin them long notes. Well, you know how peculiar old Mrs. Pemberton is. She don't like to wear no shoes up there in the choir loft. One of the men what helped carry Mrs. Crowder outta the choir loft saw Mrs. Pemberton's shoes settin there and thought they musta falled off of Mrs. Crowder when she fainted, so he picked them up and carried them out. When Mrs. Pemberton saw that somebody had done took her shoes, she got all flustered and went out lookin for them. I couldn't believe she had the nerve to traipse right back in the choir loft and walk all over everybody after she had done got her shoes back. And to make things worse, she was just a gripin about them men takin her shoes on purpose. It's a wonder the preacher was able to keep on goin what with her makin so much racket right behind him." When Momma finished tellin the story, she shook her head like she was riddin herself of the whole ordeal seein it disgusted her so.

I didn't laugh a whole lot while Momma was talkin, seein how disgusted she was, but I have to admit that the whole thing sounded right amusin to me. I couldn't sing too good and maybe the choir director wouldn't appreciate my attitude, but I thought right then and there that I was gonna join the choir when I was an adult. Sounded like too much fun and I didn't want to miss out.

Daddy ate Sunday dinner with us, which was somethin he didn't always do. Despite money bein hard to come by, Momma always managed to fix up a good meal for Sunday dinner. We couldn't always afford a roast, but today she'd fixed one up with all the vegetables what went with it. Momma kept a garden out in the backyard and still had some summer squash she'd canned. She always planted a few fall vegetables and had cooked up some beets and turnip greens. Course, there was always biscuits to eat. We have biscuits every single meal, which is all right by me bein that I love eatin em with butter and a little sugar sprinkled on top.

We were all settin there at the kitchen table sayin our usual nothin when I got to thinkin that I was gonna find some time to talk to Daddy soon as I could. Daddy went out back after he was done eatin. I got done with my plate real quick and went out there with him. I didn't want Momma nor Cody Sue around when we talked, so I figured now was as good a time as I'd get. Pancho was standin out there by Daddy carryin that danged rubber ball around in his mouth hopin Daddy would say gimme that there ball so I can throw it for you. I knew Pancho's legs would get tired from standin a long time before Daddy ever threw him the ball, so I took it from him and went to playin catch with the old fella. I sat on the back steps by Daddy while I tossed the ball to Pancho.

I didn't know that Daddy would want to talk to me, but I figured that didn't matter. If he wouldn't talk to me, I'd talk to him. I was bound and determined I wasn't gonna act like I didn't care how he treated me.

"Daddy, I been thinkin a lot about what happened the other night. I just want you to know I wasn't bein disrespectful. I was just sayin what was on my mind. It come out a little different than I thought, but I'm glad I done said it. Least you know how I feel about things now."

Daddy looked over at me. Boy, his face was hard lookin. He wasn't even forty years old, but he looked a good fifty or more. That's what a wearisome life will do to a man. "That's for sure. You cain't say I don't know what yore thinkin now."

I couldn't tell if Daddy were gonna get mad all over again if I kept talkin, but I figured I'd just find out. "You understand what I was talkin about when I said that about your drinkin?"

Daddy shot back at me real quick. "You notice, Leroy, that I ain't had nothin to drink all this last week? I can quit any time I want to and you nor nobody else cain't say it ain't so. I ain't got no more problem drinkin than nobody else."

I tried to stay calm. What Daddy had just said was wrong and I knew it. Maybe he didn't, though. I remembered I couldn't force my thinkin on Daddy, though, so I kept myself in control. "Supposin your drinkin is a problem for me, despite it ain't no problem for you, Daddy. Would that make you wanna quit?"

"I said I ain't drank none all week!" Daddy was irritated at the fact that I didn't give him no credit for stayin dry for a few days straight. In my mind, that wasn't nothin to brag about. He's done that a lot of different times. He can't stay dry for too long, though. He's proved that. It was always just a matter of when he'd go back to the bottle, not if he'd go back. I figured I had got my point across, though, and didn't need to say no more.

I changed the subject. "Daddy, you know Judge Sharpe?"

"Yeah, I know him. What about him?" There was still this crusty sound in Daddy's voice. It was clear I had irritated him by bringin up his drinkin habits again and not givin him credit for bein able to quit whenever he liked.

"Well, his daughter, she's a girl I kinda like. I was over to her house down at the end of Stuart Avenue a good while back. They have this room in their house that they call the family room. Alane, that's the judge's daughter, says that's where they sit and act like they're a family. Why can't we have us a family room like that?"

"I expect their house is bigger than ours, Leroy. We cain't go addin no rooms to this here house." Daddy didn't understand what I was gettin at.

"I ain't sayin we got to have us a new room. We can just use the front room. It can be our family room."

Daddy still didn't follow me. "What're you talkin 'bout doin to that room? It's fine just the way it is. I ain't changin no room just because you say so."

I tried again to explain what I meant. "You don't have to change what's in the room. You just need to change what we do in the room, that's all I'm sayin." Dad gum. How could a grown man be so dense when it come to understandin somethin as simple as what I was gettin at?

"What you got in mind us doin?"

"Talkin, mostly. That and actin like we're a family."

Daddy acted like he could solve that problem real quick. "Well, if you've got somethin to say some night, then say it. Seems like that's what you've decided you're gonna do anyhow."

Daddy was sure makin it hard for me to be patient, but I wasn't gonna give up. "Daddy, do you know how long it's been since you asked me or Cody Sue how we're doin in school? It's like you don't even care. That's what I'm talkin about. That's what folks do in a family room. They act like they care about each other." The thought struck me that maybe Daddy didn't care, so I come right out and asked, "*Do* you even care any about me and Cody Sue?"

You could tell I was makin Daddy feel uncomfortable all over again, bein that I was talkin about feelins. "Course I do. Me and yore momma, we both do."

"I'd sure like to see it, Daddy. That's all I'm talkin about."

Daddy snapped at me like a rattlesnake that had been all coiled up and was waitin until he got mad enough to strike. "Wait just a minute, boy! When were the last time you done asked me about somethin except when you wanted somethin from me? Don't you go tellin me I don't act like I care about nothin around here until you can show the same attitude in yoreself."

I wanted to bite back at Daddy with my own poison, but I figured that wouldn't do no good. Just make us get in a fight and that wasn't what I was aimin at. I mean, it sure was hard to try to talk at all to my daddy. It didn't take nothin to get him riled. I sat there a minute tryin to figure what to say next. Seemed almost hopeless to keep on goin. I might as well try talkin some sense into Pancho. Least I'd probably get somewhere with that hound dog. He dropped his ball at my feet, and I threw it out in the yard for him to run fetch. Dad gum, I wasn't givin in to Daddy's stubbornness. If he wanted me to show him that I cared about what all he did, I'd just show him by askin a question.

"Well, then Daddy, if you want me to act like I care about what you're a doin, lemme ask if you've been lookin for a job lately. I figure that's somethin you probably been doin, ain't it?" I wasn't meanin to trap Daddy. Well, come to think of it, maybe I was. Might as well be honest with myself. I just wanted to let Daddy know that it doesn't do no good to ask him about what he's doin cause I know he's ashamed of the fact that he ain't got nothin to say.

Daddy sat quiet. I couldn't tell if he was about to blow up at me or if I'd shut him up by provin my point to him. Then he told me, "Leroy, I want you to know somethin. You done hurt me the other night. Hurt me real bad. I wanted to take you out here and give you the whippin of yore life and maybe I should've. But I got to thinkin that it ain't right that I went out to Cow Pens and left yore momma without no money. That's why I left in the first place. She were mad at me for not bringin in no regular paycheck."

Daddy looked me square in the eye, which was somethin he practically never did, as he continued to talk. "Then I come home and you go to sayin what you said that night. Well, I went down to the R.C. Cola plant the next day and I think I done got me a job makin R.C. Cola for folks." Then he actually smiled. He didn't look too good when he smiled cause his teeth was all dirty and crooked, but it looked good to me. "I weren't gonna tell yore momma until I brung home my first paycheck. You keep it to yoreself, you hear?"

Well I'll be dad gum! Daddy had done gone out and got himself a regular job. Look at him. He even seems excited about it all! Boy if that weren't a sight. "Oh, I promise I won't say nothin about it. Just promise me one thing, Daddy. When you tell Momma about it, do it in the front room." He nodded real slow like.

I think I was gettin through a little bit.

Chapter 22

I N THE fall, everything at Cassville High School spins around what the football team does on Fridays. In fact, every fall the whole town seems caught up in what's happenin to the football team. That's practically all anybody, least the men, want to talk about when you say how you doin to them. I mean, the fellas that sit in the chairs at Wimp Dickerson's Barber Shop can't quit talkin about the Cassville High School Tigers. It seems that if the football team wins a game by only three or four touchdowns, everybody goes to complainin about them havin a bad game. Now don't get me wrong. Football's a fun game to play, but I'll be doggone. I can't get worked up over it the way some folks around here can. Seems to me they're takin it a mite too serious.

Bruno Lynch didn't play football on the varsity team, him bein in the tenth grade, but he played for the B team. He thought that give him special privilege that wasn't allowed to students like me what didn't play football. He's already the cocky type, but bein a football player makes him even worse. One day I walked into the boy's bathroom on the second floor of the school and there was Bruno and one of his buddies, Gordon Mason, standin over this skinny fella named Kelso Read. Gordon is big and dumb lookin just like Bruno. He wears the same greasy look on his face that Bruno does and never seems to have learned what the word *manners* meant. He sure wasn't gonna learn nothin about manners hangin around Bruno, unless it was about the bad type. Ever notice how when you get two fellas together who both think rules was made for everybody but them, you got nothin but trouble? Well, that's what looked like was about to happen with Bruno and Mason as they had that poor little Kelso cornered.

I knew Kelso a little bit. He didn't live too far from me. My friend Ernie lived right around the corner from Kelso and used to play together with him when they were little bitty. Come to think of it, Kelso's still little bitty. Funny how when you're fifteen years old, some boys are already big as an ol red oak tree and some boys look like they ought to still be over to the junior high school. Kelso is one of the junior high lookin types. I doubt he's much over five foot tall and I know he can't weigh more than a hundred pounds unless he puts rocks in his pockets. That would've been a good thing for him to have done that mornin. Thatta way, he might've had some way of gettin Bruno and Mason away from him. He could've heaved rocks at them. Even a little boy can make a rock hurt if he lands it in the right spot.

Bruno asked Mason, "Hey Mase, you think ol Kelso here knows how to fly?" There was this mockin sound in Bruno's voice that I didn't like at all.

Mason had an idea what his fat, bully friend was talkin about. "I think maybe he can. He's lightweight enough that the wind could just carry him away." He laughed with Bruno as those two hogs put their hands on Kelso. "Let's toss him out the window and see can he fly to the ground. I bet he can. If he cain't, I bet he'll learn to flap them skinny wings of his a little faster."

Bruno and Mason picked Kelso up and headed over to the window. I've never seen eyes as big as the ones in Kelso's head. They were stretched wide enough to cover his whole face. Bruno opened the window while Mason stood over their prisoner. Then, as if they had been plannin to try out this new stunt for a long time, they picked up Kelso by the ankles and dangled him out the window. You talk about a bunch of racket, you've never heard such yellin and screamin goin on. Bruno and Mason was laughin like hyenas. It's a wonder they didn't drop Kelso on his head as careless as they was carryin on. As loud as they was, Kelso was screamin even louder. If you've ever heard about twenty girls scream after they all spied a big rat in the room, that's about how Kelso sounded. I really had to wonder if he was openin his mouth so wide while he was screamin that maybe his heart would drop right out and hit the ground before the rest of him did. I wanted to go over to the window and holler at him to just quit blubberin and kickin so Bruno and Mason would see that they wasn't botherin him and then they'd let him in. I was smart enough to realize, though, that Kelso wasn't in no frame of mind to be listenin to any limp advice I might want to give him.

Me and a couple other boys who was in the bathroom didn't know what to do. We hollered for the two bullies to let Kelso back in, but you can imagine how far we got with that. None of us wanted to go over and try to manhandle them two, because then they might just drop Kelso flat on his head just to get at one of us. They were dumb enough that they'd do that just to get a chance at whackin somebody who had the nerve to say what they ought not to be doin right then. Besides, if they was crazy enough to do what they was doin to Kelso, they'd do it to one of the rest of us, too.

Kelso didn't hang out the window more than maybe thirty seconds, but I doubt he'd be interested in the fact that that was all his nightmare had lasted. To him, I bet it seemed like thirty hours. Bruno and Mason finally had enough fun and let Kelso back in the bathroom. That boy went wild soon as his feet touched the floor. He didn't care that he was givin away at least a hundred pounds to each of his opponents. He was gonna give away whatever licks a boy his size could give. He landed a couple good ones, too. Danged if I wouldn't do the same thing if I'd just been dangled out a second-story window. Bruno and Mason kept on teasin him, but I think they was glad when Kelso let up and flew outta the bathroom. I don't know if he ever got around to doin his business before he left, but if he hadn't before hangin out the window, I'll bet he did while he was danglin there. I never did check to see about that.

Bruno turned around and glared at us fellas who'd seen what him and Mason had just done. "If any of you fellas tells Mr. Higgins about this, you're next. 'Cept, the only way you'll get back in this here bathroom is if you can pick yourself up off the ground out there and walk back up here." That sounded about like what you'd expect from a boy whose brain was smaller than his little toe. Like he thought Mr. Higgins wasn't gonna hear about all this from about half the school. The only one in the bathroom who believed like Bruno that they wouldn't get caught by Mr. Higgins was his lard-bellied, ignorant friend Gordon Mason.

You can imagine how quickly word spread through the school about what them two thugs had done. When Kelso ran outta the bathroom, he was still white as a bed sheet despite blood had been rushin down into his head. You wouldn't think a person could turn white when he's hangin with his head down, but that's what had done happened to Kelso. He was still rantin and ravin as he made his way down the hall to his next class. Now anybody who knows Kelso knows that if that little fella is rantin and ravin about somethin, he must be powerful upset. It isn't in his nature to go carryin on over nothin, him bein the quiet and polite type and all.

The first person to actually say somethin to Kelso about his behavior was his next teacher. Of course, any teacher is gonna say somethin if a student who is generally well-behaved comes stormin into class actin like he's just seen a bunch of monsters, which isn't too far off from what Kelso had actually seen. The teacher asked Kelso what had done happened to him, so he told her the whole story. Said Bruno and Mason was pickin on him in the bathroom and hoisted him up and hung him out the window by his feet. He told how mad that had got him and how he had swung at both boys when they finally brought him back inside. It's hard to say if he told that last part about him swingin at Bruno and Mason cause he felt the need to confess about participatin in a fight or if he said it to let the teacher know that he didn't aim on puttin up with that kind of foolishness anymore. I hope it was the second reason that made him tell on himself, but Kelso, he's such a scared type that he might have felt guilty if he didn't admit to havin ugly thoughts about them fellas.

There were a couple boys in Kelso's class who had seen all the bathroom goins on and spoke up for Kelso and said that every dad burn detail he had given was exactly how it had happened. Bruno and his buddy weren't the type who'd made a lot of friends over the years, so anybody who could help in seein to it that their rear ends got blistered by Mr. Higgins was glad to speak up. I wasn't in Kelso's class, so I wasn't one of the ones who said that yep it happened just the way Kelso said it did.

Kelso's teacher sent him straight down to Mr. Higgins office to let him in on what all had just gone on. The two other fellas was sent along with him as witnesses. Actually, I imagine the teacher sent them other boys so Kelso wouldn't get all weak in the stomach and forget to tell just how awful he'd been treated by Bruno and Mason. She wanted to make sure all the details got told so them criminals would get what they deserved. You can tell that Bruno and his buddies weren't the type that scored a lot of points with teachers any more than they did with the rest of us.

By the time Kelso and his two witnesses had got to the principal's office, Mr. Higgins had done heard about the bathroom hangin, as it was later to be called. That's what I mean when I say it doesn't take long for such as that to get back to the office. I'm not rightly sure who spilled the beans to him, but Mr. Higgins had been told. I heard some talk about Kelso in my class, too. Despite he'd just been hung out only a few minutes earlier, rumors about the hangin had done begun to fly.

This one girl asked me about it since she'd heard I was one of the eyewitnesses. "Is it true what they did to Kelso Read? I heard they took off all his clothes and hung him out the window upside down." I couldn't help but wonder how in the world could someone have made up a story like that in just a matter of five, maybe six, minutes. I set the record straight and said that yes Kelso had done been hung out the window upside down, but no he wasn't naked. I can just see what the Cassville newspaper would put in the headlines if what the girl had heard was true: "Naked Boy Seen Danglin from Bathroom Window; Said He'd Get Revenge as Soon as He

Locates Britches." Don't you know the folks at the school would have some explainin to do about that one. Anyhow, that was about as far as I went in discussin the whole thing with anybody.

Mr. Higgins did what he had to do and sent for Bruno and Mason. From what I understand they was both in Mr. Higgins office a pretty long time. The shots he gave to them two sets of hindquarters were loud enough to be heard all the way to downtown Cassville. They got kicked out of school for a whole week and what's worse they were booted off the football team for good. Mr. Higgins said that nobody with the poor judgment them two showed needed to be on a team that went around representin Cassville High School. Now that's somethin I sure could agree with. I wouldn't want folks from out of town to judge what us Cassville boys are like based on the likes of them two yahoos.

Word got around fast about what all Mr. Higgins had done to discipline Bruno and Mason. You wouldn't think the whole school would be so excited about two fella students bein whipped and kicked outta school, but that's exactly what happened. Sav said he would've paid good money to see Mr. Higgins givin them two their licks. I can say one thing and that is that the only way I'd want to experience one of Mr. Higgin's swats would be to watch someone else get it. That isn't one of them things in life I'd want to have firsthand knowledge of.

After school let out that afternoon, several of us fellas was standin under our favorite red oak tree just horsin around. We weren't payin attention when here came Bruno and Mason stompin up towards us wearin this hurt look on their faces that you can only see on bullies who have just been give a taste of justice. There was probably seven or eight of us fellas in our group. When someone spotted Bruno and Mason, somethin was said to announce their comin and the whole bunch of us just quit what we was doin and froze. When you think on it, it was probably like a scene you would've seen back when Cassville was called Shotgun Junction, 'cept that none of us had guns in our hands. Thank goodness Bruno and Mason didn't. They would've used theirs. I'm right sure of that one.

The two villians didn't exactly join our group, they just stood there about fifteen feet from us. They stared at us like they were tryin to hurt us with the ugly look that was all over their faces, which was certainly a possiblity if they were to stand there lookin long enough. Bruno spoke up for the both of em. "We just got one thing to say to you bunch of weak sisters and that is that whoever done told Mr. Higgins on us is gonna git his when we find out."

I reckon Sav was feelin brave what with us outnumberin them, but that ninny piped up and said, "What do you two boys aim on doin, flush somebody down the commode next time?"

Bruno was mad enough that he was just about to start cryin. It was enough to make you feel sorry for him if you didn't know that he meant it when he said he was gonna get whoever done told on him. "Shut up, Sav!" Then he looked straight at me and said, "Leroy Evans, I heared you was talkin after you left the bathroom. If I find out it was you that done told Mr. Higgins, you ain't gonna git outta the next fight like you done the last time!" Everybody shifted their eyes on me like they hadn't heard it were me who went straight to Mr. Higgins office after I left the bathroom.

Bruno and Mason went stompin off just like they were swingin out the barroom doors of a saloon in Shotgun Junction. Ernie said loud enough for us fellas to hear, "Look at them two limpin. Boy howdy, did they get their hams salted by Mr. Higgins." 'Course, everybody laughed, which made the two bullies turn around and remind us they were serious about their threats.

One of the boys in our group was Royce Blackwell. Royce came up to me and told me, "Say Leroy, if ol Bruno comes after you again, just head over to my house like the last time and I'll have a bunch of boys waiting to help you out." I was gettin to where I liked Royce seein as how he'd quit hangin around Alane Sharpe. Like a gentleman ought to, he backed off when he heard I had eyes for her. The more I was around that boy, the more I cottoned to him.

I laughed along with all the other fellas. Somehow Bruno's threats seemed empty to me. I think he was lookin for any excuse he could scare up to make me want to fight him. Despite he'd been ignorin me the last few weeks, I knew he was still sore about gettin in trouble when me and him tussled before. I figured I'd better set my friends straight and let them know it wasn't me that went to Mr. Higgins, not that I wouldn't have been proud to be the one to give him the news.

"You fellas all know that I went on to my next class and didn't say nothin to Mr. Higgins about Bruno and Mason. It isn't that I wouldn't have, it's just that somebody else beat me to it. You go to thinkin about it and ol Kelso could've got hurt real bad if them two had accidentally dropped him on his head. Whatever punishment Bruno and Mason got was exactly what they deserved. If you ask me, they got off light. I would've kicked em both plumb outta school for good." Sav said he would've kicked em plumb outta town. Everybody agreed with me and said they wished it had been them who got to report to Mr. Higgins about the bathroom hangin. Kind of like you would've been a hero for turnin in a couple of low-down outlaws.

We all split up and went on home. I rode in Sav's truck with him. While we were on the way home, I got to thinkin about what me and Woody had talked about before when he told me that everybody likes to have some kinda control over their piece of the world. I said to Sav, "You know, I was talkin to Woody about Bruno one other time. I was tellin him about how I didn't know why people like Bruno has to act crude and ugly to people like he does. He said that sometimes a person tries to make other people look bad so they can look good. It doesn't make sense, but that's what Bruno seems like he's all the time doin. When you go to lookin at it thatta way, it makes you feel kinda sorry for him."

"You ain't gonna hear me sayin I feel sorry for nothin that happens to Bruno Lynch, 'specially if it's bad," Sav said.

"I don't really feel sorry for him neither, but then again I do. I guess you might just say I don't want to try to control my part of the world by tryin to beat people up and make them look bad."

"What if you was to get a chance to teach somebody like Bruno a lesson and the only way you could do it were to whip him in a fight?" Sav asked.

"Don't you see, that just makes the whole thing worse. You keep fightin back at Bruno and he ain't never gonna get any higher than he already is."

"You sayin you want him to be your friend?"

"I don't think Bruno's the type that I could be friends with, but I'm not interested in feudin with him for the rest of high school. I wouldn't mind puttin him in his place if that's what were called for, but then again, I wouldn't mind helpin him out neither, just to show him that I'm not livin life down there real low like he is. That's all."

Sav thought a second on what I'd just said. "I reckon I see what you're talkin about, but I know that myself, I'd rather just put Bruno in his place and then leave him alone."

I didn't have any plan in mind on how I was gonna act to Bruno whenever it came time to either teach him a lesson or help him out. I just knew I wasn't gonna let that big lump of bad manners pull me down on to his level. I didn't know at the time, but I was gonna get a chance to show Sav just what I was tryin to tell him about.

Chapter 23

FOR THE last couple of weeks Daddy had been goin to his new job down to the R.C. Cola Bottling Company. Momma still didn't know what he done all day long between the time he left the house in the mornin and when he got home in the evenin. Least, I don't suppose she knew anything. She sure never asked him nor said nothin about it when I was around. Kinda hard to believe that a woman wouldn't even want to know where her husband was goin every day or if he had a job at all. Maybe she wanted to know but figured it wasn't her business to be askin them kind of questions. I know there was this time before when Daddy practically bit Momma's head off just 'cause she asked him what he'd done all day long. That's just the way Daddy is. He figures if you need to know somethin about him, he'll tell you what you ought to know, when he felt like you needed to know it, and none before then. I suppose with him bein like that, Momma just kept her mouth shut and wondered to herself where he must be durin the day.

I knew where Daddy had been goin what with him tellin me he had got that new job. The R.C. Cola plant wasn't that far from our house. We lived close enough so that it wasn't but maybe a ten-minute walk from our house to there. We had a car, but didn't have hardly any money to put gasoline in it, so Daddy would walk to his work instead of drive. Momma walked to the few houses she cleaned, too, but that was on account that she didn't have any other way of gettin there bein that she doesn't know how to drive. I doubt real serious like that Daddy knows about her cleanin houses. She'd started that up after he run away from home, and I'm right sure she hadn't told Daddy nothin about it. He'd for sure tell her to quit. But seein that he left the house every mornin before any of the rest of us did and didn't get home until supper time, Momma could keep it secret from him. You know good and well he wasn't gonna find out by askin her about it. I can't ever remember him askin Momma even one time how was her day or did she do anything out of the ordinary. I think about the only thing he was interested in from her was that she fix his meals, wash his clothes, look after me and Cody Sue, and take care of the house. Long as all that were done, he figured he didn't have nothin much else to ask about. That's the way it seemed to me anyhow. The whole situation is right sad.

That same night after the bathroom hangin incident had happened at school, I said somethin to Daddy when he walked in the kitchen door and plopped down in his chair to wait on his supper. "Where'd you get them holes in your good shoes, Daddy?" You got to understand that when I say good shoes, they aren't really what you'd call good. None of us had clothes that was high quality. Daddy's good shoes were the shoes that weren't so wore out like his other pair. The good shoes are the ones he'd been wearin to work the last couple weeks, but they sure looked like they'd aged more than what you'd expect to happen from two weeks worth of workin. They had holes wearin in the tops of the shoe, right through the leather. I was just askin a simple question and didn't think it was nothin that would get Daddy all steamed up. It did, though.

"They ain't nothin wrong with my shoes! Just hush up about it, Leroy!"

Momma turned around to see what else I musta done besides just ask Daddy a question. By the boomin sound in his voice, she figured I might have kicked at his shoes or spit on em while I was talkin or somethin like that. Just the fact that she turned around to look made Daddy mad.

"This don't involve you! I told Leroy they ain't nothin wrong with my shoes and that's it. That boy needs to learn to keep his mouth shut when he wants to ask about somethin what ain't none of his business!"

Dad gum. All I wanted to know was how he got them holes in the tops of his shoes. It wasn't like I'd just committed a crime or nothin. If this had happened a few years ago and Daddy had just griped at me over nothin, I probably would have gone straight to cryin. I'm the type who can get my feelins hurt pretty easy. At least, I used to be thatta way. I'm not so much anymore seein how I've learned to be a little harder on the outside than I really am on the inside. You live in this house long enough and it's for sure Daddy's gonna tell you to hush up when you go to expressin yourself. I'll wager I haven't cried at all in a good three years. I learned that it didn't do any good.

That time not long ago when Woody told me that he'd been married before and that his wife and son they died while the baby was bein born, I wanted to cry then. I don't know if Woody knew that's how I felt at the time, but I remember gettin this knot in my throat while I was listenin to him tell me all that. That's the only time I can come up with where I came close to cryin since I was twelve years old. I can still get a pretty good size knot in my throat, but I'm generally able to fight off the tears when that happens. The only reason I can remember when it was that I cried last is on account of I still remember like it was yesterday the last time Daddy gave me a real bad whippin. I've got whipped since then, but none like I did that day.

You see, it was summer and I had wanted Daddy to let me go out to Lake Cassville with Sav and his daddy to go fishin. All I did was ask Daddy could I go and he got all mad and said no. I can't say why he had got so mad, but he did. He's never needed a reason to be mad. That's just his way. Then I had to go outside on the porch and tell Sav that I couldn't go with him. I was feelin sorry for myself and said kinda loud so Daddy could hear from where he was sittin in the house that I couldn't go on account of my daddy bein mean. I'd meant for him to hear it, but soon as I walked in the house I sure wished I could've eat what I'd just told Sav. Without sayin nothin, Daddy got up from his chair and grabbed hold of me and whipped me until I could hardly stand up. He'd been drinkin, of course, and didn't like it that I had bad-mouthed him to one of my friends, as if Sav and anyone else who knew my daddy wasn't already aware that he could be pretty doggone mean. I cried harder that day than I think I've ever cried in my whole life. And I ain't cried since then.

Dad gum, it makes me get mad all over when I think on times like that. I hate feelin thatta way, but there's times that I'll get reminded of somethin from the past and then I can hardly look at Daddy for awhile until my feelins pass. All through supper that night, Daddy kept lookin over at me like he was worried about whether I was all right or not. That's somethin I wasn't used to seein. When Daddy got through puttin somebody in their right place, he didn't ever look back over his shoulder, so to speak, to make sure he hadn't done no damage. But tonight he acted like he was sorry he'd barked at me. I wish he could just learn how to say I'm sorry. You know, it don't hurt to say them two little words every now and again, but I think Daddy would choke on them if he tried to get them to come outta his mouth.

After I got finished eatin, I went to my room and got out some books to study. Miss Ferguson was a nice lady, but she sure did make us read an awful lot about history. You'd think that what's done happened has done happened and there's nothin that can be done about it, so why keep studyin it. Miss Ferguson didn't see it that way, though. She said that we were learnin about ourselves while we studied history. I never did quite figure what she meant when she said that, but she said it all the time.

"What're you doin, Leroy?" I looked up to see Daddy standin in the doorway to my room. He come walkin over to my bed and stood there like he was interested in what I had to say. Now there was somethin that didn't happen hardly any at all.

"Just studyin history. We're at the part where a bunch of British folks burned down the White House and made Dolly Madison all mad."

"When were that, pretty soon after the Pilgrims landed?" I started to laugh thinkin that Daddy was makin a joke, but I could tell real quick like that he wasn't. Let me tell you, I swallowed that laugh real quick like.

"No, sir. It says here that it was in 1814, durin the War of 1812." I had my finger placed in the book right where it gave them facts.

"Sounds to me like they made some kinda mistake in yore history book."

"What do you mean, Daddy?" I was wonderin how he could've known whether or not the history book was right. Here he'd just said he thought the White House was burned while the Pilgrims was still here, so what could he know about what I had just read out of a book written by someone who was for sure smarter than he was on the subject.

"Well, if it were burned down in the War of 1812, how could it have burned down in 1814?" I have to admit that Daddy had got me on that one. He was right. It couldn't have burned down in 1814 if the war was in 1812. Daddy told me I ought to point that out to my teacher tomorrow. Said she'd probably figure I was smart to have discovered somethin that whoever wrote this history book had overlooked.

Daddy changed the subject and let me in on the real reason he blew up at me at the supper table. "The reason I got on to you a little while ago was on account of not wantin nobody to know where I been goin the last couple weeks."

"Oh," I said. Daddy hadn't actually said I'm sorry, but what he said was good enough for me. It might as well be because that was as close as he'd ever get to them words. I figured it was safe now to ask my question all over again. "So what's wrong with your shoes that they've got holes all in them?"

Daddy explained. "You see, down at the R.C. Cola plant, I been workin some where they wash out the old bottles so's they can put some fresh R.C. Cola in them and sell it. They's this water called alkali water that they use to get all them bottles clean. It don't eat through glass, but danged if it don't eat through anything else it gets ahold of. It'll burn a hole right through leather. I didn't want to go sayin nothin in front of yore momma and Cody Sue on account of wantin to make it a surprise tomorrow when I git paid."

"How much you gettin paid?" I knew I was steppin on to thin ice again by askin Daddy about how much money did he make, but he seemed to be in a decent mood for once so I figured he might not get too mad if he told me it weren't none of my danged business. Then again, I figured he was probably gettin paid pretty doggone good workin for the R.C. Cola folks and maybe he'd like to brag a little on how much he was makin. My hunch musta been right, cause he didn't seem to mind one bit if I knew what he was gonna be gettin tommorow on his paycheck.

"I'm gettin paid for two weeks and I'm gettin twenty-eight dollars a week, so what's that, forty-eight dollars?" I didn't have the nerve to go tellin Daddy that he wasn't any smarter in arithmetic than he was in history. Besides, when he got more than he thought he was gonna get tomorrow, it would be a surprise to him.

"Somethin like that."

"I figure I can just use these here shoes for work shoes and I can buy me some new ones to wear everywhere's else. Gonna go get me a pair when I get off of work tomorrow."

I was glad Daddy was gonna get him some new shoes. Lord knows, we all needed some new things to wear, but it bein his money, I figure he ought to be the first one in the family to get somethin new. I was worried about payin the other bills too, though, and figured now would be as good a time as any to drop a big hint that Momma was sure anxious about makin it to the end of the month without lettin the bills go unpaid.

"You know, Momma's got bills she needs to be payin. I reckon some of that money will go to payin on bills, won't they?"

Daddy hung his head like I was the adult and he was the child and I'd just caught him before he was fixin to go out and do somethin he knew he ought not be doin. In this case, of course, that meant goin out drinkin. "That ain't none of yore business, Leroy. You got a roof over yore head. You don't need to go talkin about bills gittin paid. We always manage somehow. They'll get paid."

Daddy hadn't exactly fussed at me, but that was his way of sayin hush up without gettin too rude or gripey. Actually, it wasn't that he was showin me no respect, it's just that he knew that I knew that he sure wanted to go get drunk tomorrow night. I hope the look in my eye were enough to beg him please don't do it.

The next day was Friday, which is always my favorite day of the week. Even though you still have to go to school, it somehow doesn't seem as hard as all them other days of the week, knowin that you have a couple days off comin right up. Me and Sav was gonna do some fence paintin Saturday if it was warm enough, but even the thought of paintin fences didn't bother me. At least I could sleep until seven o'clock in the mornin and I'd be doin somethin different all day.

I took Daddy's advice and raised my hand while we was talkin about the burnin of the White House in history class so I could show off how smart I was. Miss Ferguson seemed right pleased that I wanted to say somethin about our class discussion and called on me. "Yes, Leroy, did you want to add something?"

I stood up like I was gonna give an important announcement. "Miss Ferguson, it says right here in the history book that the White House burned down in 1814 durin the War of 1812. I figured the fella who wrote the book must've overlooked this mistake. You see, I figure the fella meant to call it the War of 1814 or else the White House burned down in 1812, one or the other."

I was right surprised that Miss Ferguson had this disgusted look written all over her face as I sat down. Maybe she was upset on account of the fact that she hadn't discovered the mistake on her own or maybe she thought I was tryin to show her up on purpose. All she said after I had announced my discovery was, "Thank you, Leroy. You may sit down now." When I sat down I looked around the classroom and several of the other students were chokin back a giggle. Theodore Downs, who sat behind me, leaned up and whispered, "Leroy, you dope. Why'd you go and say that?"

Theodore was one of these types that thought he was better than everybody else in the school, includin the teachers. I turned around and explained to his highness, "Because I ain't interested in learnin the wrong facts about history. For your information, this stuff interests me and I aim on learnin it right. I'm sorry if you're too high and mighty to admit when you don't know everything you ought to know." Made me right mad how everyone seemed to be thinkin that I was puttin on airs when that wasn't what I was doin at all.

As we were all leavin the room after class, Miss Ferguson called me up to her desk. "Leroy, what you did today wasn't like you. Would you like to explain yourself?"

I sure would. "I don't understand what all the fuss is about, Miss Ferguson. I was studyin last night, and my daddy he's the one who discovered the mistake in the book and said I ought to tell you about it. He figured you'd think I was smart."

Miss Ferguson was this real kind type. She'd told us before that she had just graduated two years ago from Howard College down in Birmingham, so she couldn't be too old. I'd thought before that if I was about twenty-five or thirty years old, I'd sure be wearin a path over to wherever she lived so I could visit her. A pretty lady like her ought to be gettin married before she gets too old. What with me bein interested in Alane Sharpe and all, I probably shouldn't be thinkin this, but that woman had the nicest lookin kisser I've ever laid eyes on. Boy, she would've sent me straight to Mr. Higgins's office if she'd known what I was thinkin right then.

When she heard my explanation of why I'd done spoke up in class, she got this look on her face that said she felt sorry for me. Real soft like she said, "Leroy, look with me in your history book at page one hundred thirty-seven." I did. "You see here where it tells about the War of 1812?" I nodded that I did. "It tells you here that the War of 1812 began in June of 1812 and the last battle was fought in January of 1815. It was simply referred to as the War of 1812, even though it went on beyond that year. I wasn't sure if you were playing a joke or if you were serious, so that's why I didn't comment on what you said when you stood up in class."

You talk about feelin ignorant. There wasn't no way in this world I could keep from it after Miss Ferguson explained all that to me. About the only thing I could do was apologize as big as I could and then hope everybody in the history class didn't go on to their next class tellin the whole school what a danged dunce I'd made of myself. I know one thing and that is that even if Daddy's in a decent humor and tries to help me with my homework again, I ain't listenin to him no more.

That night came and Daddy got home about thirty minutes after we had done finished eatin supper. Momma had learned a long time ago that she might as well go ahead and serve supper about the same time every night whether Daddy was home or not. When he set his mind that he wasn't comin home until he got good and ready, he sure didn't send no word to Momma about it. If he wasn't there when supper was ready, Momma didn't ask no questions and just went ahead like normal. That's the way she did everything. Tried to act as normal as she could, even when it was plenty evident that things was anything but normal.

On this night, Daddy was happier than I'd seed him in a long time. It was like he was a little kid what was hidin a big surprise, which is exactly what he was doin. He walked in the back door and instead of sayin his usual nothin, he come into the front room where all of us was and told everybody to close their eyes. Instead of closin em, Momma and Cody Sue opened their eyes wider. They was probably just makin sure it was really Daddy who had said that. "Go on now, close em up. And don't peek. You too, Leroy." We all did what we were told to do. Daddy walked back through the kitchen out on the back porch and then tromped back through the kitchen into where we all set waitin. We all heard this big thud on the floor as Daddy obviously set somethin down amongst us. That all done, he told us, "All right now, open em."

You would've thought Daddy had laid down a bucket of gold in the middle of the room the way he was smilin. It wasn't gold, though, it was a gallon jug of R.C. Cola. Cody Sue got giddy real quick like. "R.C. Cola! I love R.C. Cola! Where'd you get a whole jug of it Daddy? I didn't think you had no money."

"I do now," Daddy revealed with pride. "Looky here." With that, he pulled out the money he had got from his paycheck. "I got me a job at the R.C. Cola Bottlin Company. Been there two weeks and today were payday. This here jug was give to me on account that it didn't measure up. They cain't sell it cause it don't have enough R.C. Cola in it. It's enough to satisfy me, though. Momma, go get us some glasses and let's have us some."

Momma had a hard time smilin, but I think she was tryin. She'd got so used to wearin that glum look on her face, I reckon it was hard to get it off. She went and got some glasses and put a little ice in from the icebox and poured us all up some drink. Course, we'd all had R.C. before, but somehow this jugful tasted better than usual. Maybe it was because it meant we'd be able to pay the bills that made it taste good, or maybe seein Daddy and Momma actually tryin to feel happy gave it a little extra fizz. Whatever the reason, I drunk a couple of glasses and enjoyed em both.

You know, we only sat around in the front room for maybe ten minutes, but to my recollection, them was the best ten minutes we'd had in this house since I can remember. Aside from bringin us all some R.C. Cola, Daddy had gone and bought himself a knew pair of brogans. He was gonna use them as his new shoes and the pair that had the holes burned in them would be his work shoes. For once, it seemed like maybe things was goin the right way. Maybe the front room was gonna become a family room after all. I'd be able to tell Alane Sharpe that we had one same as her family.

I was foolish for thinkin that. I hadn't stepped out of the front room more than a few minutes, but when I came back, it was just Cody Sue and Momma settin there actin like normal. "Where's Daddy?" I asked.

Momma had the usual old wore out look on her face as she answered, "He's gone out. He'll be back in a little while."

Yeah, and he'll be drunker than a skunk. Dad gum that man!

Chapter 24

THE NEXT Monday, I was flat draggin as I went to school. It wasn't simply bein a Monday that done that to me, despite that didn't help matters none. It was the fact that Daddy seemed to have been tryin and then went out and got drunk again. I don't reckon I expected he wouldn't ever drink again, it's just that he'd gone without it for a couple weeks and I had done got my hopes up. I hadn't even said this to myself before right this minute, but I think I was mad at myself for not sayin anything to Daddy when he came home after bein out drinkin. It was like I stepped back to the way I used to do things and just said to myself to leave him alone 'cause it ain't worth arguin with him over his ways. I figure he isn't never gonna change. I don't want to believe that, but the way I been actin all quiet like, a person sure would've believed I had done give up on Daddy. Maybe I had lost the fight in me. Shoot! I hate that danged alcohol of his.

I went on to school in a little while and stood under the girl's red oak tree like I had been doin lately. Alane Sharpe noticed my eyes droopin and said somethin about it. "Leroy, you sure look bad. Did you have a hard weekend?"

I put a disgusted look on my face when she said that. "I didn't have a bad weekend. My daddy did. What made it bad on me was that I thought it was gonna be good and then it went right back to the same old way it always is." I don't think Alane really understood what I was talkin about, not that I figured she could.

"What happened to your daddy?" It was an innocent question. If I didn't live with a drunk, I might've asked the same thing.

Embarrassed like, I said, "He went out and got drunk."

Alane blushed, thinkin she was the reason I was embarrassed. I wasn't embarrassed on account of what she had asked. I was embarrassed on account of the answer I had to give. "I'm sorry. I shouldn't have asked."

It was all right for me to be feelin bad over Daddy, but I didn't think it was Alane's place to be feelin rotten because of him. "Oh no, you ain't gotta feel sorry. You've got nothin to do with what my daddy did. It was his own fault."

Alane tried to straighten out what she had said. "What I mean is I'm sorry you have to feel bad for what your daddy has done."

I don't rightly know if anyone can know how humiliatin it is when someone feels sorry for you on account of having a sorry daddy that doesn't know how to stop drinkin. I haven't even hardly tasted alcohol in my whole life and here I am feelin this need to apologize for what it has done to make me into a no account boy. That isn't fair, you know.

"Thank you, Alane. You're kind. I can't tell you how kind you are, and it means a lot to me."

All a fella can do when people go to sayin they feel sorry for you is say thank you and hope they can understand all the rest. We went on in the school as soon as the bell called us in. I expect Alane had a good day of studyin. I couldn't hardly keep my head in my books, which wasn't nothin new for me.

I went home after school, but slipped on out of the house pretty soon after I'd got there. I needed to be by myself. It was the first full week in December and that meant it was startin to get a little cooler. Most days was still halfway warm, but we were havin more cool days now. Today was one of them days where it was windy and nippy outside. I warmed myself up by walkin at a pretty swift pace. It wasn't but a few minutes before I had done worked up a little sweat. I was walkin with no place in mind, but somehow I found myself strollin along the banks of the Tennessee River. There's somethin about a river that makes you feel peaceful. I haven't got no idea where the river goes to, but one day I'd kind of like to get in a boat and just let it take me on a long ride. I love livin in Cassville. To me it's kind of like what heaven must be like, but at the same time, I wonder if life might be any different somewhere else way on down the river where daddies don't drink and your momma she's happy. It's somethin to think about.

While I was walkin beside the Tennessee River, I kept lookin over to the bank on the other side, which everybody around here calls East Cassville. I don't know why it is white folks and colored folks have to keep a distance between themselves like they do, but that's the way it is. Here in Cassville, most of the colored people live either on the east side of the river or down on the deep south side of town. I've been in both areas of town before, but I didn't have a whole lot of reason for goin to either part too often since I don't really have any personal business there. I thought I knew about where Woody lived and got to wonderin if I could find his house. He didn't live too far past the river in an area where there was a little group of shanty houses. I knew pretty much where his street was and got to thinkin that maybe I'd go surprise him. It's a shame me and him is such good friends and I ain't never even set foot in the man's house. Maybe all that would change this afternoon.

On Mondays Wimp's Barber Shop is closed. That's when all the barber shops is closed bein that they work on Saturdays. I didn't know what Woody did on his day off, besides maybe fish, but I figured if he wasn't down here at the river he'd be home right now seein it was near to supper time. The white folks say you ain't supposed to be goin over to where the coloreds lived, but right now I wasn't too bothered by what everybody said you was supposed to do.

I went down to the suspension bridge and walked on across to the east side of Cassville. I kept tellin myself I shouldn't feel this way, but when I stepped off the bridge onto the dirt pathway that lead to East Cassville, I felt like I'd walked into another town. I went over one block to where Pine Street is. Pine Street is what they call Stuart Avenue on the east side of the river.

After walkin a couple blocks down Pine Street, I turned off onto one of the side streets. I couldn't help but notice that there was a lot more folks out walkin around on this side of the river than you would see in my neighborhood. I felt like a stranger ridin on his horse into Shotgun Junction. Everybody stopped their business and took a good hard look at me as I went by. I'd never felt odd bein white before, but I did right then. I didn't want to feel so out of place, but I have to admit that I was. I wondered if a colored boy my age would feel the same way I was feelin if he walked down my street. I hope I'd be the kind of fella who'd just say howdy to him and not even think twice about it, but I can't say how I'd be.

I roamed up and down a couple of streets lookin for Woody's house I remember he told me one time about havin these two big ol rockers out on his front porch where he sat on summer evenins when it was so doggone hot. When I couldn't find nothin that looked right to me, I broke down and asked this man did he know Woody Woodrow. I explained that we was friends and I just wanted to pay him a visit. He probably wondered what I was doin huntin up an old colored man, but he told me he knew Woody and directed me right to his house. I wasn't hardly a stone's throw from it.

Woody had a picket fence along the front walkway that hadn't been painted in who knows how long. "That's a job for me and Sav," I muttered to myself. If I didn't think Woody would've minded, I'd come paint his fence for him for free, but I know he wouldn't never let me. I wish I could anyway. His little front yard was practically all hard dirt. Two mulberry trees was in front of his house. Them kind of trees has roots that grow right on top of the ground, so it's no wonder nothin was growin in his yard. Right there on the short front porch was the two rockin chairs I'd heard Woody talk about. I went on up to the porch and knocked hard on the door. As I did, the door swung open and I could see Woody standin in his kitchen fixin up his supper.

"Hey there, Woody. Looky who's here! I didn't mean to knock your door open. I reckon it wasn't latched."

A broad smile stretched across Woody's warm face as he turned to see me there in the doorway. "Well bless ma soul. Mista Leroy done foun my house an come ta see ol Woody. What you doin walkin over ta dis end o town?"

I explained, "I was out walkin down by the river and figured I'd come over and see could I find your house. I thought I knew about where you lived. I was pretty doggone close, too, but this man down the street had to point me in the right direction." Woody seemed to think it was humorous that I had just up and come lookin for his house. I think he was glad to have the company, though. He told me why didn't I come on in.

"I wuz jes about to eat me sum supper. Come set down to de table wit me. I gots enough ta share if'n you's hungry."

I didn't feel it would've been right me eatin Woody's food so I told him no thank you and that I was gonna eat some when I got on home. I knew he didn't have a whole lot of money and figured he didn't need to be sharin what little he had with anybody else. "What're you eatin, anyhow?"

Woody's mouth went to waterin as he told what all he had fixed up for his nightly meal. "Made me up sum grits and sum good ol Tennessee chicken."

I looked over at the plate of food Woody had just set down on the table. The grits I recognized, but danged if that wasn't the oddest lookin chicken I'd ever seen. "What kinda chicken did you say that was, Woody?" Maybe I'd heard him wrong or maybe they grow chickens different over in Tennessee than we do in Alabama.

Woody laughed at my question. It seemed like a right practical question to me, seein as how I'd never been outside of Alabama and didn't know a whole lot about Tennessee. "Dis here ain't chicken at'all. It's fat back.

You fries it up til it's crispy and it sho taste good. Dey jes calls it chicken ta make us po folks think we's eatin like rich folks. You wanna try a bite?"

Fat back! Woody was eatin fried fat off a pig! Now I ain't been accused too often of havin good manners, but I know you're not supposed to turn somebody down if they ask you do you want to try somethin they've cooked up. You do that and you might as well come out and say you ain't eatin it because that stuff looks nasty. But I was gonna have to come up with some way to get out of eatin any of that fried fat. I went to thinkin real fast on how I could turn down Woody's invite real graceful like. Eatin that fat might have the same effect on me as chewin that tobacca did, and I sure didn't want to go through a bellyache like that again.

There's some folks I don't mind bein impolite to when it comes to eatin some of their food. One time down at the church we had this supper where they served up some pipin hot stew. I was sittin at this table right behind Mrs. Turnipseed and went to complainin too loud about how hot my stew was. Mrs. Turnipseed heard me and turned around to me holdin her bowl. I reckon she was just being neighborly when she spooned up some of her stew, blowed hard on it, and said to me, "Here, honey, try some of mine. It ain't so hot." I'm right sure I hurt that poor ol fat lady's feelins when I told her no thank you, I'd just wait a second for my stew to cool off. But that was one time I flat didn't care if I was supposed to be polite and accept her offer. I wasn't gonna do it.

Now turnin Woody down was another matter. I thought a whole lot of him and didn't want to go to bein rude right here in his own house. But I'll be dad gum if that there fat back wasn't the awfulest lookin food I'd laid eyes on in awhile. I reckon I must of waited too long to give Woody an answer 'cause he said, "You ain't used ta eatin sech rich food, is you, Leroy?" I suppose I was makin a peculiar face cause Woody couldn't help but laugh at me. I laughed along with him. Actually, I'm right sure Woody was laughin at the situation and not at me.

"No. Maybe I better wait til another time to eat a bite of that Tennessee chicken." I was glad that was over with, and I hoped Woody would understand my poor manners.

Woody asked if I'd excuse him for a minute and then he closed his eyes and offered up a prayer. "Lawd, I thank ya fo dis here food. You's done been good ta me fo one mo day an I 'preciate dat. I knows how you always takes care o ol Woody. I hope I done did sumthin fo you today dat might hep you out. Dis here Leroy settin by me, he's a fine young man, Lawd. I hopes you looks afta him de same way you done looked afta me all dese years. I'll be wit you agin soon, Lawd. Amen." I said *amen*, too. Woody raised his head and began eatin his grits and Tennessee chicken.

I sat there with my friend as he slowly ate his supper. I looked around his undersized house. It was smaller and even plainer than my house, but it had this feelin about it that made you feel right at home. The floors was wooden same as the walls, but there was a couple of throw rugs on the floor to make the wood a little easier to walk on. There weren't but three rooms in the whole place. Actually, you might say there was just two rooms because the kitchen and the front room pretty much run together. There was a bedroom off to the back and I reckon a bathroom was in the bedroom. I wasn't surprised that the place was clean and neat lookin, bein that Woody was the organized type. At Wimp's it seemed that he was always straightenin his things and cleanin up after himself.

Over in a corner of the front room was an old Franklin stove that was really crankin out the heat. A small stack of wood was right next to the black stove. A beat-up lookin couch, one stuffed chair, and two hickory rockers made up a tight circle in that room. I wondered where Woody set most of the time. I figured it was in one of them rockers. One had a little pillow in the seat, so I guessed that one was his favorite chair. There was a few cheap pictures hangin on the walls, but they helped give the place more of a homey look. Over in between the two rockers was this little pine table. A lamp was settin on it and gave the room its only light except for what come in the windows durin the day. Settin by the lamp was this small wooden box.

The kitchen where we sat was cramped. There wasn't room for any more furniture besides the plain square table and two chairs that filled the corner. The sink and stove were just a few feet away from where we set at the table. I reckon it was plenty big for just one person, but two people could hardly move around in it at the same time.

"You got a nice place here, Woody." Woody smiled through his mouthful of poor man's chicken as if to agree with me that this was a right nice little palace he had here.

It didn't take Woody too long to finish his supper. I helped him put away his things and then he said why didn't I come in the front room and set down in one of the rockers and visit a little bit before I had to get on home. Sure enough, I was right about that hickory rocker bein Woody's favorite chair seein as he went straight for it without even thinkin. I imagine it was just a habit for him to do that. I sat in the other rocker. We sat there a second without sayin nothin. I looked at the little table between us and went to admirin the little box that laid there. Curious, I commented, "This here box is right nice. What's in it?"

Woody touched the wooden box as if he were handling a fine piece of crystal glassware. As he picked it up and opened it, it was plain that it was special to him. The look in his eyes was so tender, you'd have thought the box was a real person. He paused a moment before he spoke up. In a hushed voice that somehow filled up the room, he told me, "Dis is what I gots ta remember ma wife an little boy." He carefully took out a plain silver ring, a couple of hair combs, a wore out Bible, and a piece of paper. "Dis all I kept afta my wife and boy dey die. It ain't much, but I gots a whole lot mo in my heart. We's still close, ya might say."

"You don't have nothin that used to be your little boy's?"

"Naw suh he didn't have nothin. Jes recallin his momma is 'nuf fo me ta remember him." Woody went silent like again. It was evident that he was lost in his thoughts. I figured he was pretendin his wife and son was right there next to him. The way he was smilin, he had to be feelin the presence of someone he loved a whole lot. Practically whisperin, he shared his thoughts with me. "I 'spect my boy woulda been a fine man, Leroy, jes like you's a fine young man." I could feel a knot growin in my throat. I didn't want to go gettin gushy, but it was right hard not to get a little bit on the choked up side seein the way Woody softened up soon as he started talkin about his wife and baby.

"You think about them a lot, Woody?"

He nodded his head deliberately. "I thinks about em every day, Mista Leroy. Every day." He looked over at me and must of known I was feelin sorry for him. His voice had a little more punch to it, but it was still soft. "Now, you ain't got to go feelin low on my account, Leroy. Me and God done talked all dis over, and I's okay wit it. I knows it ain't gonna be too much longer til I gets ta see my wife agin and gits ta meet my son fo de fust time. I been waitin a long time an I can wait a little bit mo."

"You ever wonder what your little boy would've looked like if he'd lived? Ever think on what trade he might have or what kinda girl he might've married?"

"Yeah, suh, I do. But, I tell ya, Mista Leroy, I thinks a whole lot mo about what dat boy woulda been like on de inside dan on de outside. I thinks to myself dat maybe he be de kind what understand hisself and understand other peoples, too. I wonders would he learn how ta look inside a man's soul and deal wit dat 'stead of dealin wit a man's outside self. I figure maybe he might've had a good humor so's he could enjoy hisself no matta what happen ta him. I think meybe he might've been de kind o man what people could respect, an what respect hisself. Dat's what I thinks on when I thinks on dat little boy."

How could the boy have helped but become all them things if he'd had Woody for a daddy? It ain't right that Woody's been without them all these years. There's some things in this world that just don't fit, and a good man like Woody losin his whole family is one of them. I looked at Woody and noticed the paper he was holdin in his hand. "What's on the paper, Woody?"

Woody compassionately unfolded the paper and told me, "Dis here be a letter my wife she wrote me. It were the onliest letter dat she ever writ to me. I wuz workin down in a cotton field away from here when she done foun out she be pregnant." And then without me even askin, he read it out loud to me, even though his readin skills wasn't so good. "Dear Woody, I hopes you feelin well. I thinks 'bout you 'most all de time. It hurt me ta be away from you. Dey's times dat life, it be's hard, but I tries to let go o worry and be calm instead, jes like you say. Woody, I's tired mos all de time. I be havin a hard time lookin up, instead o down. Den I found out jes today dat I's tired 'cause I's carryin a baby. I know you wanna know right off. I also know dat I gonna find strength from you, de strength I needs. I go ta thinkin on me havin you a little boy or girl an dat gets me ta feelin peaceful. De kinda tired I feels, all of a sudden, it be's a happy tired. I looks ahead to dat day dis little child gonna cum into de world. Dat gonna be de bes day o my life. I know it will be fo you, too. Wit all my love, Ruby."

I could tell that by the time Woody finished readin his letter, he was off somewheres with Ruby and his boy, and not here in this house. I waited a minute to let him come back whenever he was ready. When he looked over to me and smiled, I said all I could think of at the time. "I'm sure sorry the day that was supposed to be the best day of your life turned out so bad. It was the worst day you ever been through, I reckon."

"Dat's what I used ta think, Leroy, but it weren't. Ruby wuz right. It wuz de bes day o my life." Now I know Woody had done made peace over the death of his wife and son, but I was confused over how he could've said that the day his whole world died on him was the best day of his life. I asked him to tell me what he meant.

Woody's soft voice practically smiled at me as he explained, "Ya see, Leroy, on dat day my wife, she give de bes' gift she could give me. Dat woman give me my son. An she give him to me wit all de love dat were in her. She died tryin to give me all she could, jes ta show me she love me. It weren't no fault o hers she an de baby, dey die. Now if I went on bein all broke up over de sadness o dat day, I'd miss out on de love dat were give me. You see what I'm a talkin 'bout?" I nodded that I did. "Dey's a lesson in dat, Leroy. Mos o de time we looks ta take de love dat's easy to accept. De love I wuz showed, it weren't easy to take de way it were give."

You know, if that had of been me who saw my wife and child die on the same day, I'm afraid I would've got bitter and stayed thatta way a long time, maybe the rest of my life. And I would've missed out altogether on the love I could've had on account of feelin mad about the way life had done treated me.

I think Woody could see he had set me to thinkin. He took the chance to teach me another one of them lessons about life that he had already figured out. "Dey's sumthin else we needs ta admit, Mista Leroy." I raised up my eyebrows as if to ask him to tell me what he had learned, cause I wanted to know, too. "De love what's give to us, it ain't meant ta stay right dare inside o us. We's s'posed to pass it along to somebody else. But we generally gives away de goodness in us to dem what's easy ta love, not ta dem what's hard ta love." He winked at me as he folded up the letter as softly as he would've touched his wife or boy. I couldn't do nothin but shake my head showin him I understood what he was sayin. I think Woody was tryin to tell me somethin about myself.

While I was walkin on home I got to thinkin that I need to show more love to them that are hard to love and not just to them that's easy to love. Dang, that was hard to do. I had thought I was doin pretty good just tryin not to hate them folks that I had a hard time lovin. I figured that was about the best a fella could do. But tryin to love the people that's hard to love was somethin altogether different. I could think of a whole bunch of folks that fit that there category, my daddy bein at the top of the list.

Just think that right here in Cassville was a man what had more wisdom in him than you could find this side of heaven. How was I so lucky to get to hear all them things Woody said? I say lucky. When Woody showed me them lessons about life, I felt hard pressed to go out and try to be what he suggested. It wasn't easy. I still had a ways to go to be what I needed to be at home.

The Christmas season was comin up soon. That bein a time you're supposed to give, maybe I could do some practicin on what I'd just learned.

Chapter 25

"CODY SUE, we got to do somethin to make Christmas a little different this year." I was standin in the doorway to Cody Sue's room, hopin to get some help from my little sister. In the past, Christmas wasn't a time of the year where we got any too excited around our house. It's kind of hard to say why that day isn't very special to us, but a couple reasons come to mind real quick. For one thing, my family doesn't have hardly any extra money, so when it comes to buyin gifts for each other, there just isn't hardly no money to spend. I can remember one time when I was little gettin a yo-yo as a gift, but I can't think right off of any other time when I actually got a gift for Christmas. Momma usually tried to see to it that me and Cody Sue had somethin in our stockins, but all that amounted to most of the time was a couple oranges or a banana and maybe some walnuts.

The other reason Christmas doesn't mean much around our house has a lot to do with the sad shape of our family. Daddy doesn't hardly even act like he knows what day it is when December twenty-fifth rolls around every year. To him, it's just another day. He never said Merry Christmas to nobody that I know of and he sure didn't make no effort to save up and buy anybody a gift. Every now and then we'd get a tree to put in the front room, but most often, we don't have one. I remember me and Cody Sue beggin Daddy when we was little to go out to the country and cut down an old cedar tree so we could have us a Christmas tree. If he felt like it, he might get around to it, but most of the time he just didn't have the yearnin to make any effort to make Christmas special for us kids. Momma didn't act no more excited than Daddy about Christmas, but I think she'd like to. She just figured that if Daddy wasn't gonna do nothin to make it an unusual day, it wasn't no use for her to try. Oh, she'd fix a good dinner for us every year, but that was about as far as she went in doin anything out of the ordinary.

"What're you talkin about, Leroy?" Cody Sue was interested in what I had said, but I know she didn't have no ideas for what we could do.

"I mean, instead of waitin around forever for Momma and Daddy to do somethin to make Christmas a family time, maybe me and you can do somethin."

"Like what?"

"Like buyin Momma and Daddy a gift this year." I reckon I ought to take the time to admit that I ain't never made much more effort to buy gifts for anybody than Daddy did. I know I shouldn't make excuses, but it's kind of hard for a boy to buy gifts when he doesn't ever have hardly any money to spare. Besides, what with my family practically ignorin Christmas Day, it was too easy for me to do the same.

You know, it doesn't take a whole lot to get a little girl all excited when you go to talkin about buyin gifts. Cody Sue got worked up real quick like when I made the suggestion that we buy Momma and Daddy a gift. "What do you think we ought to get them, Leroy? When can we go shoppin? You got any money?" She was firin questions at me so quick, I couldn't answer them.

"Simmer down, Cody Sue! Just listen a second. And don't talk so loud. Momma's in the next room and I don't want her to hear us talkin." I let her in on my plan. "You see, I figure you and me can put our money together and maybe go downtown in just a little bit and buy somethin for each of them. I was also thinkin that maybe we could somehow get Daddy to come down to the church this year for the Christmas play. The way I figure it, maybe if we act excited about Christmas this year, maybe Momma and Daddy will get a little bit spirited up themselves. I don't want Christmas Day to be so ordinary this year. It's time me and you tried to do somethin to put a little life in this here home."

"You think Daddy will come to the Christmas play this year, Leroy? I wish he would. We're gonna do it different this year. Mrs. Simpkins says we're gonna do the Christmas play outside this year and have real animals and angels and a stable. She even told me I could be the Mother Mary and hold a real baby."

I'd heard about them plannin to make this year's Christmas play somethin different. Usually, they have the same old play where kids would dress up in bathrobes and old sheets and act out the story of the shepherds and the angels and all. "You mean they're gonna have live animals and a real baby? Who's baby they gonna use?" I was plumb curious about all this.

"Mrs. Wigginbottom has done said that if it ain't too cold that night, she'd let us use her baby girl. Even though Jesus was a boy, I don't think nobody would know no difference bein that the baby would be all wrapped up anyhow. And I'd be the one to get to hold her!" Boy wasn't that gonna be somethin. It didn't bother me none that they was gonna use a girl baby to be the baby Jesus, but I wondered what some of the deacons would say if they found out that Jesus was a girl. I guarantee you some of them would complain.

"Maybe with you bein the Mother Mary and all, we can talk Daddy into comin. Anyhow, let's get back to buyin them a gift. We can worry about the Christmas play later. I got a couple dollars. How much you got?"

Cody Sue opened a drawer in her bureau and pulled out a purse with some change in it. Countin it, she said, "I got fifty-two cents."

"Where'd you get that kinda money, Cody Sue? I didn't figure you'd have hardly any." I don't know what it is about females and money, but Cody Sue wouldn't tell me where she'd come up with fifty-two cents. She just wore this smug look on her face and said it wasn't none of my business how she goes about collectin money.

I reckon it wasn't important where Cody Sue had got her money. Between the two of us, we ought to be able to get some pretty nice gifts. I told Cody Sue why didn't we go on down to the five-and-dime in just a minute and do some lookin around. I gave Momma a lame excuse for why me and Cody Sue was goin downtown, put my jacket on and me and Cody Sue went shoppin.

It isn't that often that I do things with Cody Sue. I'm not sayin that 'cause I'm proud of it, that's just the way it works out. You'd have thought the King of England was takin that girl on an outin as excited as she appeared to be. She jabbered about nothin in particualr the whole time we was walkin to downtown. She wore me out the way she jumped around, too. I hadn't thought about it much before, but it hit me that she was fidgetin while she was walkin. You generally think of someone fidgetin when they're tryin to sit still, but danged if she wasn't squirmin while we were walkin. It was the most dogged thing you've ever seen. To tell the truth, I kinda like the way Cody Sue looks up to me and seemed to feel proud to be goin downtown with her big brother. Normally, when a fella my age is seen out with his little sister, he gets ribbed by his friends, but today it didn't matter none to me about that. Cody Sue, she needed someone she could look up to, and I was glad it was me today.

On our way down to the five-and-dime, I took Cody Sue by Cox's Department Store to see the Christmas decorations. I like the way these big department stores has them show windows out in front of the store so you could look in at them when you walk down the sidewalk. Cox's always had a show window with dummies dressed up for a snowstorm enjoyin a white Christmas. To my knowledge, we ain't never had a white Christmas here in Cassville, but that didn't keep people from dressin up a window with snow like it was a common sight around here.

Seein how excited Cody Sue was lookin around at all the decorations inside the store got me a little worked up. I was fifteen, but for a minute, I felt like I was maybe a ten-year-old boy again. It felt good. The store had tinsel all over it and red bows tied around all the cashier's desks in the store. In the middle of the store was a big Christmas tree that must of stood fifteen, maybe twenty, feet tall. It was beautiful with colorful balls and lights all over it. The store was busier than usual, which give the place this excited feel. There's somethin about bein in a crowd that can make you feel more cheery than when you're all alone.

The big hit at Cox's was the Santa Claus in the toy section of the store. This man was all dressed up like Santa and sat for hours listenin to little kids tellin him what they wanted for Christmas. Momma brought me down here a time or two when I was little to tell Santa what I wanted. I don't know why she did it because she knew right well that I wasn't gonna get nothin that I asked for. I reckon she figured it was the least a momma could do to make Christmas at least a little fun. I recall that I never did ask much for myself, probably because I had figured it wouldn't do no good. I do remember one time askin Santa Claus to get a new coat for Momma and a hat for Daddy. I was downright mad when the old goat didn't come through like I had done hoped he would. That's when I began believin Santa Claus wasn't for real, not that I ever had much faith in him anyhow.

We probably spent a half hour roamin around the department store lookin at all the decorations and expensive clothes and all. I told Cody Sue to come on and let's get on down to the five-and-dime where we could find somethin we could afford. I didn't really know what to buy either Momma or Daddy when we walked in the store. I figured it would hit me what to do when we got there. Cody Sue headed over to the counter where they sold women's makeup and right off the bat found a gift she wanted to get Momma.

"Leroy! I know what we can buy Momma. Let's get her some lipstick! Look here at this lipstick. Ain't it pretty?" She pointed to this tube of lipstick behind the counter. The red color on top of the tube was there to give you an idea of what it would look like on a woman's mouth. I tried to say somethin nice about what a fine gift it would be, but it was hard for me to think of lipstick bein somethin Momma could use a whole lot. I said why didn't we go look for somethin else, but Cody Sue wouldn't hear of it.

"Leroy, this is what I want to get for Momma. She's gonna love it. She don't never get to dress up and look all pretty. She'd love to have some lipstick to wear to church on Sundays. This is what I want for her!"

If you ever been told by a female that she's done made up her mind and there wasn't no changin it, then you know exactly how I felt right at that moment. I don't care if she's twelve years old or fifty, there's no use arguin with her. Despite I wasn't all that keen on spendin our money on lipstick, I knew that I wouldn't hear the end of it from Cody Sue if I told her we was gonna buy somethin else. Besides, lipstick was somethin that didn't cost too much. We could buy it and still have plenty left over for a gift for Daddy. I told the lady behind the counter we wanted the lipstick and in a minute, it was ours to give to Momma.

Cody Sue was bouncin all over the store, she was so dizzy over buyin Christmas gifts. I got to thinkin that maybe me and Cody Sue should've been buyin Christmas gifts for Momma and Daddy a long time before this year. It was evident that goin shoppin was doin her a lot of good. On the other hand, I wasn't too sure I could've taken all of Cody Sue's gyrations every year when it come time to goin shoppin. I reckon I should be glad she was happy, though.

We made our way over to where they sold things for men. It was kinda hard to know what to get Daddy. He didn't never wear a tie so we didn't need to look at them. We couldn't afford a new hat, so no need thinkin about that as a gift. Me and Cody Sue thought for a minute about buyin some gloves, but we decided Daddy wasn't the type who would appreciate anything like a pair of gloves. Finally we hit on the idea of some new socks. Cody Sue reminded me that Daddy had done bought some new shoes so maybe he'd like some nice clean socks to go with them. I liked the idea, so we bought a nice new pair of black socks to go with Daddy's new shoes.

After we got done with all our buyin, I still had a little money left over. I told Cody Sue why didn't she run on and look at the dolls for a minute cause I wanted to look at somethin else in private. I had this idea that I'd buy a gift and give it to Alane Sharpe. I'd never done nothin like that before, but seein as how me and her was becomin pretty good friends, I figured maybe it would be a good idea.

I headed back over to the jewelry section and looked around. This lady on the other side of the counter asked could she help me. I can't say why I was embarrassed to admit I wanted to buy a gift for a girl, but I was. I stammered around a second, tryin to think of somethin to say that didn't sound too ignorant.

"Uh, I was lookin . . . I mean I'd like to see . . . Uh, do you have anv . . ." Dang, but I couldn't think of nothin to say.

To the lady's credit, the woman behind the counter didn't laugh at me, even though it would have been appropriate for her to, seein as how I was pretty much makin an oaf of myself. "You must be lookin for something special for a young lady." How'd she know that? Maybe the look on my face give it away.

"Yes, ma'am, I am." I felt like I had just give away a big secret that there was someone in this here town I admired. I was a little bothered to admit I liked a female, but I reckon this lady wasn't gonna go around spreadin rumors about me, so it didn't hurt me to confess my feelins to her.

"Did you have anything special in mind?" Now if that wasn't the dumbest question she could've asked right then, I don't know what was. It should've been right plain that I didn't have no earthly idea what I should give to a girl. All I knew was I wanted it to look expensive, but it had to be inexpensive.

"Um, no, ma'am. I, uh, have about eighty cents. You got anything nice for that much money?" Dad gum, I was feelin foolish. I felt myself sweatin as I talked to the lady despite it wasn't especially warm in the store.

"Come over here with me. I think I have something that might interest you." The lady took me down to one end of the counter and pointed to some hair clips. "These would make a nice gift selection." I looked at them and agreed with the lady that they did look right nice. Bein that Alane was the kind what liked to keep her hair lookin all neat, I figured she'd like a new hair clip.

"That's a right good idea. I like these." I looked up at the lady and asked, "You got one I could buy?"

The lady picked one out that was gold and shaped like a long leaf. In fact, it looked pretty much like the leaf off a live oak tree. I liked them kind of trees about as good as a red oak. "What do you think of this one? It's very pretty. It would make a special gift for a young lady." She was makin me plenty nervous the way she coated her words in all her sweet soundin talk. I wanted to explain to her that it wasn't necessary to talk to me thatta way seein as how I wasn't the mushy or romantic type. I didn't want to offend the lady, though. She was just doin her job.

"It's pretty. I think I'll get it." The lady took the clip out from the display and put it in a little box for me. I could've swore she was wearin a look on her face that said she had just discovered my secret and was gonna tell everybody what wanted to know all about it as soon as I left the store. I sure hoped she'd keep her mouth shut. Even though she didn't know my name and didn't know who I was buyin a gift for, I still felt that maybe she'd go to gabbin about my romantic affairs.

I found Cody Sue and told her to come on, let's go home. Cody Sue was still all jumpy. I have to admit, though, that I had a little extra squirt in my step, too. Buyin Christmas gifts was right fun if I do say so myself. I figured I'd go over to Alane Sharpe's house in the next couple of days and give her her present. Boy, that made me all nervous thinkin about it.

Chapter 26

MOST OF the time I like goin over to Sav's house. Us bein best of friends, we spend a lot of time over to one another's place. Lots of times we just hang around doin nothin, but that's half the fun of bein good friends. You don't need to do nothin in particular to have a good time. On this day, though, I was almost dreadin walkin over to his house and tellin him what I was gonna tell. You see, we don't have no telephone at our house so when I have to call anyone I go over to his house to borrow theirs.

I was hopin to take my gift over to Alane Sharpe's house and figured it would be the right thing to call first and let her and her momma know I was comin. That's the part I'm talkin about where I dreaded goin over to Sav's house to borrow his telephone. He gets giddy at the drop of a hat and would come flat undone when he heard I had done bought Alane a hair clip for a Christmas present. I didn't care about him knowin. I just didn't want to listen to his carryin on about me buyin a girl a gift, that's all.

I walked around the corner and knocked on Sav's door. His mother answered and was her usual polite self. She was tall and skinny just like Sav. I guess I ought to say Sav was tall and skinny just like her. In fact, he had the same kinda voice as her, all high and squeaky like. I don't know what made me think about it, but when she opened the door and greeted me, I went to wonderin what her voice must of sounded like when she was fifteen years old. Maybe a high birdlike voice doesn't sound as funny comin out of a girl as it does a boy, but I bet it would've been right entertainin. I could picture in my head this skinny, awkward lookin fifteen-year-old girl with a voice that sounded like them high notes way down on the end of a piano.

"Well, hello Leroy. Come in here where it's warm. What're you doin out in the cold like that?" A big grin come across my face. I reckon she thought I was happy to see her, same as she acted happy to see me, but I was thinkin about that tall, skinny fifteen-year-old girl what made folks laugh just by openin her mouth. I was satisfied to let her go on thinkin whatever she wanted right then. I sure wasn't gonna come in her house and ask her was she just as goofy soundin when she was fifteen years old as her son is.

"Hey there, Mrs. Vickers. I was just gonna come over and see could I borrow your telephone for a minute."

"Why sure, Leroy. You go on in the hall and help yourself. I'll let Alvin know you're here. I'm sure he'd like to see you." Dang. Sav would like to see me, all right. He'd also like to hear me talkin to Alane on the telephone. I wish she'd have said go ahead and use the telephone and then she'd let Sav know I were here. But she didn't.

Before I could get out of the front room, Sav come out of the kitchen, chewin on a piece of leftover roast beef from last Sunday's dinner. "Hey, Leroy. I heard you come in. You gonna use the telephone? Who you callin?"

I thought to myself well here it comes. "I'm callin Alane Sharpe."

"You are! Boy oh boy! What're you callin her for?" He was gettin worked up already. It generally doesn't take but maybe half a second to get his motor runnin.

"I just thought I'd call and see could I come down to her house to visit for awhile. That's all."

"What're you gonna do when you go down to her house? You think I could come?" That boy didn't have no sense at all. I wasn't about to let him come with me to give Alane a Christmas gift. I can just see the scene right now. Here I'd be ready to pull the hair clip outta my pocket and Sav would be standin beside me so excited he'd be close to wettin his pants. He'd grab it from me and stick it in Alane's hand and say, "Here. Leroy done bought you a Christmas present! It's a hair clip. It's shaped like a live oak tree leaf. Leroy thinks you'd look all pretty in it. You gonna wear it next time you go to church? Can I take it and show your momma?" That's pretty doggone close to what he'd do if he was there with me, and I ain't makin all that up neither. I sure wasn't gonna put myself through that kind of torture. I was gonna be nervous enough givin a girl a Christmas present in the first place, without havin to worry about what my noodle-headed best friend might do to make it even worse.

"I think I better go by myself, Sav. I got something to give her and I better do it alone." I turned toward the hallway where the telephone was, but I didn't get to take even a step before Sav started havin his conniption.

"You didn't buy Alane Sharpe a gift, did you? You did! Where is it? Lemme look at it. What'd you get her?" He was jumpin up and down like a little boy. I knew he'd be this way, but I didn't have no other place to go to borrow a telephone. Dad gum! What is it that makes that boy the way he is?

"Simmer down, Sav. It's just a little ol hair clip. It ain't much. I just had a little extra money and thought I'd buy a small present. That's all there is to it. It ain't like I done bought her nothin expensive. Just lemme use the telephone and tell her I'm comin down to her house so's I can go on."

Sav went with me, of course, into the hallway to call Alane. I called the operator and got the Sharpe's number and dialed it. I had to knock Sav off of my shoulder several times. He wanted to listen in on our conversation in the worst way. I was afraid he was gonna drool on me a time or two. That's how aroused he was by this whole thing. There's one good thing about havin Sav act like he was and that is that I plumb forgot to be nervous when I asked Alane could I come over to her house. Said it real calm like. She said why that would be just fine and she'd be happy to see me. I told her I'd be there directly and hung up the telephone.

After peelin Sav off of my back, I told him thanks for lettin me borrow the telephone and that I better be goin. He tried to pump me for all the details of my conversation with Alane, but I was ready to move on along. Besides, I hadn't talked more than one or two minutes, so there wasn't much to tell. He was disappointed to see me leave and made me promise to come back later and tell him what all happened. While I was walkin home to get the gift, I thought to myself that I bet ol Sav's gonna be at my house when I get back so he can get a firsthand story of what I had said to Alane and what she had said back to me. You know, there's times I wonder how two people as different as me and Sav ever got to be such good pals.

I went in my bedroom and got the gift I had bought for Alane and made my way on out the back door. I had wrapped the box myself. I'm not too good at such things, but Cody Sue ain't no better so I didn't want to ask her to help me. I didn't want to ask Momma for her help cause she'd go to tellin me how I didn't need to be buyin no gift for any little ol girl. She'd worry about what Alane's momma would think about me payin good money for a gift for her daughter. It ain't like I had done bought no engagement ring or nothin, and it ain't like I meant nothin extra special by it. All I was doin was sayin thank you to Alane for bein my friend. Momma wouldn't see it that way, so I just kept the whole thing to myself.

One of the reasons I had picked today to come out to Alane's house was that it was a weekday so her Daddy would be down at the courthouse workin. Not that I minded talkin to him. He's an extra nice man. I just wanted as few people around when I give Alane her present. I figured it would be easier on me thatta way.

When it's chilly outside, you generally go to walkin faster to keep warm, which is what I did. Before you know it, I was only a block down from the end of Stuart Avenue and could see Alane's house. To me it sure was a pretty house. I'd never lived in a two story house before and wondered what would it be like to have your bedroom up over the rest of the house. For that matter, I'd never lived in any kind of house except the small type and wondered what it would feel like havin a place where you could stretch out and have a little extra room. Maybe her house wasn't as big as some of the other ones around this end of town, but with them big columns standin there on the front porch, it sure looked big. Looked comfortable, too, in a way my house didn't. My house looked small and cramped from the outside, same as it was on the inside. A person probably could tell a lot about the way our family lived just by lookin at the outside of our house. It's not that a small house can't look comfortable. Woody's house was maybe half the size of mine, but it looked plenty homey. It wasn't just that Alane's house were bigger than mine that made it look more comfortable. It's just that it looked like it was made different from mine, in more ways than one.

As I walked up the sidewalk to the front porch, I looked over next door at the Thompson's yard and saw that the fence still looked nice. Danged if I don't mind sayin so myself, but me and Sav done a good job of paintin on it. I knocked on the front door of Alane's house and waited for someone to answer.

Mrs. Sharpe opened the door and welcomed me into the house. "Hello, Leroy. It's good to see you again. I hope you're enjoying your holiday from school."

I said hello back to her and yes ma'am I am enjoyin my break from school. My momma is generally friendly to my friends when they come over to our house just like Mrs. Sharpe was bein to me right then. The difference between my momma and Alane's momma is that my momma goes right straight back to bein her droopy self practically as soon as she's done finished her greetin. I expect that Mrs. Sharpe stays on the happy side most all the time. I'm not sayin my momma is puttin on when she acts all friendly, she just has a hard time makin them feelins last.

"Come on back to the family room where Alane is. She'll be glad to see you." We walked out of the front room, through the blue room and into the family room where Alane was settin, doin somethin with a needle and thread. It did me good to see this here family room again. It looked different than I remembered it, maybe on account of the Christmas tree and all the other decorations in there. The pictures of Alane's family were still hangin on the walls, but even they looked a little different than before. Must be because I hadn't got to look at them long enough that other time I was in here.

Puttin down her needlework, Alane unfolded this warmhearted smile and said, "Hello, Leroy. Merry Christmas."

Now this might sound right strange what I'm about to confess, but it was right hard for me to say Merry Christmas back to Alane. It's not because I didn't wish her a cheerful holiday, it's just that them kind of things is hard for me to say. My family not bein the type what expresses themselves too easy, I generally just let words like that stay stuck somewheres down in my throat.

"Uh, Merry Christmas to you, too." That wasn't so bad. But just in case it appeared I was comin across too sugary, I changed the subject real quick like. "Say, what're you workin on there? That looks right nice." I pointed to the needlework Alane had set down on the divan next to her.

"Why thank you. It's just a simple little cross-stitch sampler. I usually do one every winter when I can't get outside much. As long as I don't do but one or two of these a year, I enjoy them." She held it up for me to see. She might've called it simple, but it sure looked complicated to me. I know I'd never seen such detailed stichin before and I said so to Alane. Told her she ought to enter somethin in next years's Cotton Palace exhibit.

"Momma and Daddy have framed several of the samplers I've done in the past. They're hanging in the hallway upstairs. Maybe I can show them to you sometime." Her sayin that meant that upstairs was off limits to guests, at least to boy guests who weren't in the family. I was smart enough to figure that out all by myself.

Mrs. Sharpe had done sat down in a chair, and it appeared that she wasn't goin nowhere. It looked like I was gonna have me an audience when I give Alane her Christmas present. Dad gum. I sat down on the other end of the same divan where Alane was settin and took a good look around the room. I commented to Alane's momma on how the house looked all nice and Christmaslike. "You done a lot of work, Mrs. Sharpe, makin the house look all pretty. It smells good in here, too." They had these bookshelves in the family room where Mrs. Sharpe had laid out some fresh clippins from a cedar tree and put red candles amongst them. At least I reckon it was Mrs. Sharpe what done it. I expect Alane had done helped decorate the house, too.

"Why thank you, Leroy. This year we're having some of my family over for Christmas dinner, so Alane and I have gone to a lot of effort to make the house look as festive as we can. How about you, Leroy? Is your family going to be having a big Christmas dinner with some of your relatives?"

Her askin me that question let me know Alane hadn't said nothin to her parents about how I had done confessed to her how pitiful my family is. I was grateful to her for that. I didn't think this would be the time to explain to Mrs. Sharpe that my daddy and his kinfolks don't get together on account of they generally fight and get drunk and cuss at each other. I doubt that she'd want to know that the last time Daddy was around any of his kin, him and Uncle Amos got in a bad fight and Daddy got kicked out of Cow Pens. I also figured I ought not say nothin about how Momma's family can't abide my daddy and don't have much to do with us neither. I'm right sure if I did, she'd think Alane didn't need to be takin up with the likes of me.

"No, ma'am. We generally have a quiet Christmas Day with just me and my parents and little sister. I reckon that's what we'll do again this year." I wasn't able to manage more than maybe half a smile when I said that. I don't know if I come across as awkward on the outside as I feel on the inside when folks ask me anything that concerns my family. I imagine most people can't help but tell there's somethin wrong with me when I answer family type questions the way I do. I hope they don't, but I expect they do.

I sure need to do some practicin on doin better at small talk with other people. I did my dogged best to carry on a decent conversation for a few minutes, but I don't think I did such a good job. Alane and her mother bein the gracious type, they helped me out as best they could, but it didn't keep me from sweatin. Here it was a chilly December day and I was sittin in their house sweatin. The family room had these high ceilings, so the heat went straight up to the second floor. Down where we were on the bottom floor, it was a mite cool. I say all that to point out that my sweatin was a dead giveaway that I wasn't too awful comfortable settin there tryin to act like I carried on gentlemanly conversation all the time.

I figured I might as well get about my business and give Alane her present seein as how I doubt that Alane and Mrs. Sharpe wanted me stayin around their house all day long. I reached in the pocket of my wore out jacket and pulled out the little box that had the hair clip in it. "I was down to the store the other day and figured I might get you a little Chrsitmas present. It isn't much, but I reckon you might say I got it to say thank you for bein a good friend to me." I stuck out the gift so Alane could take it from me. "Go on and open it if you like."

When I get a present, I generally rip the box open so I can find out real fast what's inside. Alane carefully unwrapped the box like the paper around it was somethin she didn't want to do no damage to. Maybe it's because I ain't never got more than maybe two or three presents in my whole life that I tear into the box so quick like. I'm right sure that Alane has got a lot of gifts in her fifteen years, so it isn't quite the same thing to her to open a present as it is for me. That plus the fact that she's got a whole lot more manners than me.

Seein the hair clip, Alane held it up to show her momma and sung out, "Oh, Momma! Look at the beautiful hair clip! Isn't it just the prettiest thing you've ever seen?" Her momma agreed and told me what a grand choice I had made in selectin a gift for Alane. She said how Alane just loves wearin pretty clips in her hair and that this one was pretty on account of it bein so unusual. Dang, I reckon I had done a better job of gift selectin than I had give myself credit for. When that lady at the five-and-dime said she knew just the thing I needed she sure was right. Whatever they're payin that lady, I think the store owner ought to give her a raise.

I told both of them thank you and I was sure glad they thought it were pretty. I pointed out how it was shaped like a live oak tree leaf and how I liked live oaks almost as much as I did red oaks. I mean, I was sure grinnin. It makes a fella like me feel downright proud to be able to make two females go on the way Alane and her momma was about that there hair clip.

When I was right in the middle of one of my big grins, Alane all of a sudden reached over to me and gave me this big ol hug. That like to made me faint just her doin that. But if that wasn't enough, she pulled on my neck and give me a peck on my cheek. Right in front of her mother, too! I hope my mouth didn't make too much of a thud when it dropped and hit the floor. I for sure wasn't expectin nothin like that to happen, especially with Mrs. Sharpe sittin right there not five or six feet away from us. If I was sweatin before, I was for sure seepin out the pores now. You talk about a way to tell a fella thank you and Merry Christmas all at the same time, Alane had sure done it for me right then.

I don't know why I looked straight over at Mrs. Sharpe when Alane smacked me, but that's what I did. You might say I just wanted her to know that it wasn't my idea for this to happen right there in her family room. Not that I was sorry it had happened. It just wasn't my idea.

Soon as Alane got herself squared away back on her side of the divan, I sprung up off my rear end real quick. I probably come close to hittin the ten foot high ceilin above me. Soon as I realized what I had done, I figured I ought to think of somethin to say, so I just said the first thing what come to mind. "Well, I'm sure glad y'all like the hair clip I done picked out. I reckon I ought to be runnin on home now." Alane and her momma both giggled when I done that. How in the world did I manage to come across so ignorant all the time? It wasn't like I tried to be that way. It just happened.

Mrs. Sharpe said I needn't rush off, but as she said it, she stood up. I said I hadn't planned on stayin too long. Besides, I knew if I sat back down, it would look too much like I was admittin to my show of ignorance. Alane thanked me again for the gift and said she hoped I had a Merry Christmas. I said the same and said I reckon I'd see her again when school started back up.

I waited until after I was walkin down the street before I let that big ol grin spread across my face again. A kiss from Alane Sharpe was about the best Christmas present I could've asked for. Boy howdy! I got a little ways down the street and made my way over to a pine tree and watered it real good. I'm glad it hadn't come out of me when Alane kissed me. Wouldn't that have been a fine thing for me to do right there in her family room.

Well, I had done give away one of the Christmas presents I had bought. On Christmas mornin me and Cody Sue could give Momma and Daddy their presents. Everything had gone better than I expected at Alane's house. I sure hope it went as well on Christmas mornin.

Chapter 27

CODY SUE was sure excited about the Christmas play down at the church. Most years they had the Christmas play on the Wednesday night before Christmas during the prayer meetin hour. This year they changed the play to Tuesday night bein that Wednesday night was Christmas Eve and nobody would want to be out much that night. To tell you the truth, I was pretty doggone enthused about the play myself. I don't exactly know why, but maybe I was just nervous for Cody Sue, seein that she was gonna be the Mother Mary and all.

Things had worked out just right to where the play was gonna be outdoors in the yard over next to the chapel. Mrs. Wigginbottom had held out until the last minute to say it was all right to let her little baby girl be used for the baby Jesus. She wanted to make sure the weather wasn't too bad so that the chances of her child gettin sick weren't too strong. Her holdin out until the last day kept Mrs. Simpkins all in a dither worryin on what would happen if the star of the show couldn't perform. To me it seemed like a pretty simple matter. If the Wigginbottom baby couldn't be there, they would just have to do what they always did and use a doll to be Jesus. You never know what makes a woman get all worked up like Mrs. Simpkins was, but she seemed bound and determined to have a real live baby this year. I think she wanted to surprise the whole church when Mary come out holdin an honest to goodness baby Jesus, but everybody knew the plan. It wasn't like it had been kept a big secret or nothin. You couldn't have convinced Mrs. Simpkins of that, though.

Once us kids got past twelve years old, you couldn't be in the Christmas play anymore. It was like when you was twelve, you had one more shot at bein a star in the play and after that your actin days at the church were over. The twelve-year-olds got all the good parts includin Mother Mary, Joseph, the wise men, the angel Gabriel, and the head shepherd who was the first one to run in and see the baby. When I was twelve I got to be one of the wise men. Sav and Ernie was the other two. That was all right, I reckon, but to be honest about it, I was disappointed that I didn't get to be Joseph. Orvil Beckham, whose father is the Sunday school superintendent, got to be Joseph that year. I can see how a boy whose daddy was important in the church would get the most noticeable job, but I remember thinkin it wasn't fair that I didn't even get a shot at bein Joseph seein that my daddy didn't never come to church. Maybe that had somethin to do with me bein excited for Cody Sue. Here she got the most important role in the whole play, next to the baby Jesus, even though her daddy was a drunk.

Cody Sue spoiled Christmas for Momma when she came out of her bedroom sayin she was all ready to go on up to the church that night of the play. She just couldn't stand the idea of that tube of lipstick we had bought for Momma's Christmas present sittin in the back of her underwear drawer bein unused. I can see how she would think that the Mother Mary ought to look as nice as she could for her big night, but it didn't dawn on her to think that Momma would ask her where in the world did she come up with that lipstick that was all over her face. She just came waltzin in the kitchen with red all over her mouth and most of the rest of her face actin like this was the way she normally looked.

Cody Sue put on her most ignorant look when Momma asked her about the lipstick and said about the dumbest thing you could think of. "What lipstick you talkin about Momma?" I was sittin in the kitchen when all this happened and had a hard time keepin myself together. It's right hard not to howl when your sister truly don't know how plumb booby she looks and is tryin hard to hide a secret that flat can't be hid. Even Momma had a hard time keepin a straight face.

You gotta hand it to Momma. She didn't want to spoil Cody Sue's night, so she didn't get on to her like she could've. She got a towel out of the drawer and wiped some of the smear off of Cody Sue's face and said, "Honey, you got lipstick all over you. It looks pretty on your lips, but you don't need it on the rest of your face." You could tell by the look in Cody Sue's eyes that that was the first time she was aware that she hadn't applied her lipstick just right. She had this shamefaced look on her that said she was about to commence cryin. Momma thought she was cryin on account of bein embarrassed, but I figure Cody Sue was afraid she was about to have to tell Momma that she borrowed some lipstick from the tube we was gonna give Momma for her only Christmas present.

At first Cody Sue's cryin made me a little irritated seein that it doesn't take nothin to turn on her faucet sometimes. But when I saw that Momma was gonna drop the subject about the lipstick to keep from ruinin Cody Sue's big night, I realized that Momma's Christmas Day surprise was still safe. For once it seemed that Cody Sue had done the right thing by blubberin.

Pretty soon after Cody Sue got all cleaned up, she was her giddy self again. She wouldn't quit talkin about how much fun it was gonna be to hold the baby Jesus for all the world to see for the first time. "I sure hope Daddy comes. You think he's comin, Momma? He said he would."

Momma did her usual job of tryin to find an excuse for Daddy and answered, "I hope he will. I reckon he had to work late tonight, so don't be none too upset if he cain't make it." I don't know if Momma figured Cody Sue was dumb enough to soak up her limp excuse for Daddy, but I know I wasn't. He had got off work a good hour ago and had probably gone to get somethin to warm himself up, as he would say. He wasn't comin to the Chrsistmas play this year same as he didn't every year, even when he didn't have no job to give him an excuse to hide behind.

Us older kids was enlisted by Mrs. Simpkins to help out with all the little details of the Christmas play. I went down to the church early when Cody Sue went so I could be around to help out. By the time I got there Mrs. Simpkins was already out of what you might call the Christmas spirit. She had made the mistake of puttin Sav and Ernie in charge of watchin the three sheep Mr. Dawkins had loaned her to be the flock over which the shepherds watched by night. She had told them to just stay out there close by them, I reckon to keep them company. They were tied to stakes in the ground and wouldn't have been a problem at all if my two friends hadn't of messed with the ropes while they were pettin the sheep. Two of the sheep got loose and took off lickety-split down Johnston Avenue. They had done rounded up the herd by the time I got there, but the whole incident had put Mrs. Simpkins in a pretty rotten mood.

Sav was mutterin to himself when I saw him, sayin somethin about how Mrs. Simpkins needed to try harder to overlook small mistakes. He didn't understand why she'd got so riled up just because two-thirds of the shepherds' flock had got in a foot race with half the men who was up at the church helpin out. I figured it wouldn't do me no good to try to explain things to Sav, so I just stood there sayin nothin while he mumbled to himself. He probably thought I agreed with him that he hadn't done nothin wrong.

Everything finally came together just in time for the play to get started. There was a crowd of folks standin out in the churchyard to watch the big event. This bein the first time for our church to have a Christmas play outside with animals and a real baby and all, we had twice the audience as normal. The angels came walkin out the way angels are supposed to and sang a couple of carols and then the head angel showed up and made the big announcement about Cody Sue havin her baby.

All the shepherds went runnin over to where Cody Sue and Joseph was to admire the female baby Jesus. I know there was some people whisperin to themselves that it just wasn't biblical for us to be havin a girl act out the part of the baby Jesus, but thankfully nobody make a big stink out of it.

I say nobody made a big stink out of it, but I reckon I ought to explain things a little further. When the shepherds got to the stable, Cody Sue and Joseph had the most gosh awful looks on their faces you'd ever seen. Cody Sue was holdin the baby out away from her and wasn't cuddlin her the way you'd think it probably really happened. When it got to the part where the angels and the shepherds sang "Silent Night" to the baby, Cody Sue was supposed to hold Jesus up for everybody in the whole church yard to see. When she did that, the shepherds that was close to Cody Sue pulled back from the baby the same as Cody Sue and Joseph was tryin to do.

Ernie poked me and Sav, laughin. "I think the baby Jesus has done filled her britches with a Christmas present for Mary. You reckon the real baby Jesus done that to his momma?" You got to keep in mind that we're fifteen-year-old boys and things like that hit us pretty hard in the funny bone. This lady standin near us heard what Ernie said and give us this real hard look that said that if she was our momma she'd take us out back of the church and teach us just what the Bible meant when it said not to spare the rod on kids like us what would laugh just because the baby Jesus had an accident in her drawers durin the Christmas play.

Soon as the play was over Mrs. Wigginbottom took her baby and relieved Cody Sue of her motherly duties. I don't think things happened the way Cody Sue thought they would. Even so, she were still excited when she found me. "Where'd Daddy go?" She asked me.

"Cody Sue, I don't think Daddy made it." I came close to doin the same thing Momma always done by thinkin up an excuse for him.

"Yes, he did! I saw him standin there watchin the play. He got here while the angels was singin. He saw me and waved over to me."

Well what do you know. I hadn't seen Daddy come up, probably because me and Sav and Ernie was too busy pokin each other in the ribs and snickerin. Despite Jesus had made the make-believe stable smell like a real one for Cody Sue and the rest of them, the play was a success just because Daddy had showed up.

My mood was pretty good when Christmas mornin rolled around and we all got up out of bed to greet the day. Me and Cody Sue made our way into the front room where our stockins was hung up and found the usual fruit and walnuts stuck in them. But down in the bottom of each stockin was a dollar bill. Cody Sue didn't know she'd got one until I pulled mine out and showed her. She dug down in her stockin and pulled out her money, too.

Lookin at Momma, she hollered out, "Where'd this come from?" Momma had this puzzled look on her face that said it was a surprise to her, too. If I had been a lot younger, I would've thought that look meant she figured that maybe Santa Claus had left it for us. It was plain, though, that she honestly didn't know the dollars was down in the stockins.

All of us looked over at Daddy, who was sittin there smilin. I can't recall that he ever give any of us a gift before. Anything we ever got, which wasn't much, always come from Momma. This was the first time Daddy had ever tried to say Merry Christmas to any of us by givin us a gift. Without sayin nothin, he pulled out an envelope and handed it to Momma. She opened it up and found a five dollar bill in it. That was enough to set her to cryin.

It isn't that we were all happy on account that we was rich now. The money we had got wasn't all that much. I ain't sayin none of us weren't glad to have the money. It's just that we all knew that gettin a gift from Daddy meant he was tryin to do things a little better than he usually did. Maybe when he said that it got to him that night that I had said we needed a daddy and Momma needed a husband, he meant it.

I was glad now that me and Cody Sue had went to the trouble of buyin Momma and Daddy gifts. Cody Sue went back to her bedroom and come runnin out holdin the two boxes me and her had wrapped our presents in. That girl could grin wider than anybody I've ever seen. She handed one box to Momma and one to Daddy and gave her instructions. "Momma opens her present first and then Daddy." Momma opened her eyes real wide and perked up like a little girl when she heard that.

When Momma gets away from that usual glum look she puts on her face, she's a right attractive woman. I don't know where they all go to, but the wrinkles that make her face look old and tired disappear. If I could give her any Christmas present I wanted, I'd give her a face that looks just like she looks right now. It would make all the difference in the world if she'd act happy more than she does. I even believe it would help Daddy quit actin the way he does if she wouldn't let him dictate to her that she was gonna go around lookin like a sourpuss all the time. I been tryin to do what Woody had suggested and do what I think is right, hopin that Daddy will notice and decide he's gonna do some changin cause I been an influence on him. The fact that Daddy had done give all of us a gift this mornin said that maybe what I had been tryin was payin off a little bit. If

Momma would just start standin up and livin her own life instead of lettin Daddy walk all over her, maybe she could make a little difference in him, too. I know I sure liked the way she looked right now and wish she'd be thatta way more often.

Openin the box and seein the tube of lipstick, Momma let go this wonderful laugh and said, "So that's where you got the lipstick you was wearin the other night for the Christmas play! I couldn't figure where it had come from." She reached over and hugged Cody Sue's neck like I hadn't seen her do in a long time.

I couldn't help but pipe in, "It's from both me and Cody Sue." I wanted a little credit, too, for makin her Christmas mornin a little brighter.

"Thank you, Leroy." She looked at me across the room to where I was settin and hugged me with her eyes, the same as she'd just squeezed Cody Sue. At least that's the way it felt to me.

Cody Sue run over to Daddy's chair and instructed him. "Now you open your present, Daddy." I know Daddy felt funny with all of us fixin our eyes on him. For one thing, he didn't like bein in the center of things, but more than that, he didn't like it when we all got mushy. Them kind of times made him feel squirmy. I could tell he felt that way right now, but I think he was tickled that we had done bought him a gift.

Maybe I was just lookin for it in Daddy since I had just got done studyin Momma, but it hit me that Daddy could put this warm look in his eyes that would set anybody at ease if they was to look right in them. I know he had grown up hard and probably didn't have much reason to go around lookin tender at folks much of the time. I wonder had he already lost that look in his eyes by the time he had reached my age. It's right difficult to imagine that he would've been as hard lookin as a little boy as he was as an adult. I'd never thought about it before, but I couldn't help but be curious as to when the look of a boy was replaced by them stony eyes he wore practically all the time now.

Daddy didn't know how to show he was pleased with the socks me and Cody Sue had got him. All he could think to do was to hold them up so everybody could get a good look at them. Cody Sue figured it was the right thing to do to hug Daddy as her way of sayin your welcome for the gift. I spoke up and said I had picked the socks out. The way I had said it, you'd think I'd gone through a hard time pickin out the color black as the color he'd like to have. Daddy just nodded. I knew that was as close as I was gonna get to hearin thank you and Merry Christmas from him, so I was satisfied.

For just a few minutes on that Christmas mornin, I was hopeful that our front room was gonna turn into a family room, same as Alane Sharpe's family had. I figured her family was havin a good time with one another in their home right now. I don't know why, but I was positive that they was all sittin in their family room enjoyin Christmas the way it ought to be enjoyed at that very moment, same as we was. If the pleasure I was experiencin would only last, it would be the best present I would've ever got. I have to tell you that I was feelin right good on the inside.

Momma fixed us up an extra good breakfast with salt-cured ham, red-eyed gravy, grits, biscuits, sausage, and fried potatoes. While we were eatin, she told us to get plenty on account of she wasn't fixin another meal until it was time for supper tonight with all the Christmas trimmins. As full as I was gonna be after this meal, I knew I'd be ready for Christmas supper once Momma said to come and get it.

That salt-cured ham was dern scrumptious, but the one thing about eatin it is that you stay thirsty for the rest of the day. I like to say that it makes your water drink good. That's about the best way I can describe what it does to you. Momma went to a lot of trouble fixin breakfast. She wasn't able to get us nothin else for a Christmas present, but I knew she'd put together two of the best meals you could eat for us that day. When your family is gettin along good, you don't need much else to make it a happy holiday.

I went walkin with Pancho that afternoon to get rid of some of that lazy feelin you get when you've eat so much. I had give Pancho a slice of ham when Momma wasn't lookin earlier this mornin. It didn't seem right for him to be left out of all the fun on Christmas Day. I even snuck a piece for Gilly, that's how merry I was feelin. Pancho was still lickin his lips from thirst like I was, but it was plenty evident he was pleased with what I had give him. We went and said Merry Christmas to Sav and Fang while we were out. When we got home, I come back in the back door like I always do and for some reason I asked where was Daddy. I figured me and him might go out back and toss the ball to Pancho for awhile seein how it wasn't so cold.

The Christmas look had left Momma's face. She turned her back to me and went to washin dishes at the kitchen sink. Before she could answer me, I already knew what she were gonna say. "He's gone out for a little bit, Leroy."

I couldn't help but scream back at Momma, "Not on Christmas Day! He ain't gonna go out and get drunk after we done had a good Christmas mornin, is he? Why didn't you tell him he couldn't go, Momma? You could've stopped him! Momma, you let him go out drinkin on the one day that I was feelin that maybe things was gonna change around here!"

Momma stopped her work and hung her head. I knew that meant she was chokin back the tears, but dang it, I wasn't gonna feel sorry for her this time. She was gonna have to help me out if we was gonna ever see this family come together like it ought to be!

Chapter 28

I FLAT refused to let Momma stand there at the kitchen sink and cry instead of talkin to me about why she lets Daddy get away with bein the way he is. I felt sorry for her and all for bein upset, but the way I figure it, if I don't never say nothin to her about bein such a limp rag to Daddy all the time, I might as well quit complainin to myself about the way she acts so chickenhearted all the time. She sure wasn't gonna see no need to change what she could if I never let her know that she was botherin me. You know, as I go to thinkin on it, she hurts me the same as Daddy does. Her way of hurtin me is different than his, but it has a way of makin my heart sink, all the same.

Daddy hurts the family by bein so shameless in the way he drinks despite he knows none of the rest of us wants him to. He ain't one bit careful to watch what he says or how his behavior affects the rest of the family. If he feels like doin somethin, then by George he just does it and the rest of us can hang for all he cares.

Momma's just the opposite. She worries all the time about doin somethin that might cause any of us to feel ill about her. She acts like she's obligated to be the slave of the whole family and that her only duty in life is to keep peace in the home, especially with Daddy. You know good and well that Daddy hasn't got one ounce of respect for his own wife. I hate to say that me and Cody Sue haven't got no respect for her neither, but if I'm gonna be honest, I've got to say that I feel thatta way a lot of the time.

Let me explain what I mean. I love Momma about as hard as a boy can love his own flesh and blood. I mean, she's the one what brought me into this here world to begin with. She'd do anything for me, and has on plenty of occasions. She doesn't think nothin of doin without just so me and Cody Sue or Daddy can have somethin that we need. I know that all I got to do if I need her is to say so and she'll drop whatever she's doin in a hound's hair and do whatever it is that needs to be done. There ain't even the leanest streak of meanness in her entire body.

That's the good side of Momma. But the peculiar thing is that her good side is also her worst side. I know that doesn't sound too intelligent when I say that, but when you ponder that thought a minute, it starts to make a bunch of sense. You see, Momma, she's so nice she doesn't take care of the most important thing she needs to watch out for—herself! I don't need a momma who just takes orders from Daddy and makes excuses for all his mistakes, which there's a bunch of. I don't need a momma who doesn't know the meanin of the word *rest* 'cause she's always on the go doin everything she can to make sure everybody in this here family is comfortable. I need a momma what takes care of all of us but takes care of herself, too. The more I stood there watchin her whimper, the more I figured now was just as good a time as any to tell her what I was thinkin. Maybe she'd listen to me for once.

I figured yellin wouldn't do no good, so I went over to the sink and took Momma by the arm and said I needed to talk to her. I guided her over to the kitchen table where we both set down. It was like I was her daddy and she were my little girl. Cody Sue was in there with us, too. She didn't want to miss nothin that she might could listen in on. I didn't mind her bein around. I started out talkin real civilized to Momma.

"Momma, I been tryin hard here lately to not be such a coward to Daddy like we're all used to bein with him. I know he hasn't done just a whole lot of changin, but the way I figure it, we're all only makin things worse than ever when we just stand there while he goes on bullyin his way around this here family. Besides, he did go out and get himself the first good job he's had in years, and he ain't been drinkin quite so much as usual. And he did come to Cody Sue's Christmas play and give us all some money this mornin. Maybe it isn't all on account of me standin up to him, but I know it hadn't hurt things around here none that I did it."

Momma was still hangin her head. Dad gum. Why did I feel like I was talkin to Cody Sue instead of my own momma? It was like she had quit growin on the inside when she reached about Cody Sue's age. I waited a second to see did she have anything to say. She didn't. It figured. I was pretty perturbed with her, that's for sure. To tell the truth, I was perturbed with just about anything you could name right at that minute. My mood wasn't so good, despite I was tryin hard to act grown up. I'm afraid I started soundin a little bit impolite as I kept on talkin.

"Momma, why didn't you ask Daddy not to go out today, this bein Christmas and us havin such a good time up until now? Maybe he'd listened if you'd spoke up."

Momma was ready to defend herself now. "Leroy, how do you know what your father would've done? He was gonna go out, and I know as good as you do that they ain't nothin that was gonna stop him. It's just easier to let him go on. I don't want to fight because I know it would be like talkin to that cat over there." She pointed to the windowsill where Gilly laid sound asleep. I wanted to say somethin smart aleck about that bein about the lowest remark she could've made about how hard it is to get through to Daddy, but I figured I'd save that one for later.

"But don't you see, Momma, that when you don't never even say one single word, Daddy hasn't got no reason to feel the need to do nothin different. You gotta start standin up for yourself!"

Momma got up in my face and practically begged me to remember that she had stood up to Daddy once. "You forgot about that night this fall when I stood up to your daddy when he wasn't puttin no bread on this table for you two children! I stood up to him all right and look what happened. Your daddy pushed me up against the wall and then left me with you two to feed all by myself for a month! And you're sayin I need to do that some more? What in thunder do you want in this house, Leroy—a daddy what goes to beatin his wife because she won't stay in her place?"

I can't exactly say how mad I was right at that time, but I was doggone close to talkin the way Daddy talks when he gets mad. I wasn't gonna act that way, though, on account of I know how much good it does when Daddy talks to people like that. You go to slingin insults and talkin like a sailor and folks drop whatever good opinion they got about you like a ton of bricks. I tried to keep my temper when I answered what Momma had just said.

I took a long, deep breath. "Momma, I ain't sayin that you gotta go to fussin and gripin at Daddy all the time. What I'm gettin at is that you don't have to go around actin like you can't say whatever it is you want to say. Take the other night when Cody Sue asked you did you think Daddy was comin to the Christmas play and you said he might not on account of maybe he was workin late. You know as good as I do that they ain't gonna keep him none too late down at the R.C. Cola plant. If you think he isn't comin to the play on account of bein out drinkin, then say so! We know just like you do what he's likely to be doin. All I'm askin you to do, Momma, is to quit hidin the way you feel from everybody, includin Daddy."

Momma was calmed down a little bit now. That isn't to say she was calm all around, but she had simmered down some. I hoped that meant she was listenin to me. "Leroy, they's a reason I do the way I do when I keep from talkin about your daddy's drinkin. I don't see that it does nobody no good to go around talkin about him. And I also don't see that it does you and Cody Sue there no good to hear me talkin bad about your daddy. You just let me handle things the way I want to handle them, Leroy."

"But Momma, you don't understand! You're already sayin what you think about the way things is around here without even usin words. Look at the way you don't hardly ever smile. You cry a whole lot more than any woman ought to. You don't never do nothin for yourself neither. And you're too quick to jump up and try to fix somethin whether it was your fault it happened or not. Everybody already knows that you ain't never happy, so why not say so? Maybe you'd go to feelin better if you'd just say what was on your mind every now and then. It sure isn't gonna make matters worse."

Momma sat still. I couldn't tell if it was on account of her thinkin real hard about what I had just said or if it were because her mind was plumb blank. I hate to say this about my own momma, but I can't imagine her agreein with the way I was talkin. She probably thought that what I had done said was pure foolishness. I knew I was takin a chance tryin to get Momma to see herself different, but what harm would it be if I tried and nothin good come from it? At least I'd have the pleasure of knowin I had give it my best try. That was a whole lot more than she were willin to do.

I looked over at Cody Sue. I don't think she had any idea what I was talkin about to Momma. She probably thought I was givin Momma the kind of fussin that a grown-up is supposed to give to a little child. Well, maybe I was. I figure it didn't do Cody Sue any harm hearin what I were sayin. Maybe when she grew up a little more, she'd understand my thinkin. I think one of the worst things that could happen would be that she would grow up and act just like Momma when she done got married. I'd hate to see the same thing happen to Cody Sue that had been happenin between Momma and Daddy all these years. You'd like to think maybe she could see some of the things Momma was doin that wasn't right and she would try to act different. If nobody pointed them things out to her, though, who knows but maybe she'd become the exact same as Momma when she's all grown up. Not meanin to be disrespectful to momma, but Lord help us if Cody Sue don't turn out different than our momma.

I felt sorry for Momma, but then again, I didn't. I know that sounds cold-blooded to say, but if I go to feelin sorry for Momma, then I know I'll just keep my mouth shut and let her go on bein miserable. That's what I'd been doin for fifteen years. If I love my momma like I'm supposed to, I reckon I ought not feel sorry for her. It sure don't do neither her nor me no good at all for me to be thatta way. I got up to leave the kitchen. I figured I'd done said enough for one Christmas Day. About the same time I got up, Momma stood up, too. I figured she was headin back over to the sink where she'd hang her head down low and be quiet for the rest of the day. Instead, she came over to me and grabbed hold of me and squeezed me like she was sayin thank you for slappin her on the face with my words the way I had just done. I reckon Cody Sue didn't know what else to do but stand up and join us. So there was the three of us all standin there huggin each other. Momma and Cody Sue were cryin and I was dern close to it.

"I don't want to be a bad momma to you two children," Momma cried. "You two are all I got to bring a little bit of happiness to me. Everything I do is for you two. Do you see that, Leroy?"

"Yes, ma'am, but what I been tryin to say, Momma, is that you can do better for me and Cody Sue if you'd think of yourself a little bit more. We'd be a heap better off if you was happier than we are with you goin around draggin the way you do. That's all I'm sayin is to think of yourself. That ain't no sin, Momma."

She didn't say nothin after I said that. I still don't think she had hardly any notion of what I was gettin at. Momma let go of me and Cody Sue and went back to the sink. I didn't know it right then, but instead of goin back to fixin our big Christmas meal, she went to puttin things away. I went in my room and laid down on the bed to just think. Sometimes I hate thinkin, especially when I feel like I'm the only one in this here house who does it. Somehow it's better to think out loud with somebody what's willin to think along with you. At least you don't feel like your head is spinnin around in circles when somebody else is there to tell you they understand exactly what you just said. Right now, though, my head wouldn't quit goin round and round.

I knew Daddy would be comin home sooner or later. I didn't know if I ought to say somethin to him when he come in about ruinin a perfectly good Christmas or not. I hated feelin this way after havin felt almost the opposite this mornin. It was gettin to where I couldn't trust my own feelins no more. The minute I went to feelin good about anything havin to do with this family, the bottom would fall in and I'd go to feelin more droopy than I thought I could feel. It got worse every time.

We didn't have no Christmas supper that night. Daddy didn't come home all afternoon and Momma stayed holed up in her room, which meant she was cryin about Daddy goin out and gettin drunk and me talkin down to her the way I had done. Part of me wanted to feel guilty for my part in the gloomy situation here in our house, but I'll be dad gum if I was gonna take the whole responsibility for this family bouncin around on every feelin you could name.

Daddy came in not long after dark set in. He done what he usually done when he come home drunk. He went straight to his chair in the front room and laid himself out so he could sleep off his booze. He stunk bad like the stuff he had done drunk had intoxicated his sweat, too. I didn't say nothin to him that night, but it isn't because I was holdin back on account of it bein Christmas night. Daddy wouldn't have remembered a dang word I would've said. It's a blame miracle that he finds our house when he comes home from drinkin as hard as he did today. But I sure was speakin my mind tomorrow.

I went back in Momma and Daddy's room and picked up the socks me and Cody Sue had give Daddy this mornin. The spirit of Christmas had done left me. I wasn't about to let my daddy have no gift of mine when he said thank you by goin out and gettin loaded that same day. If he wanted him some new socks, he could just go and get himself a pair with his own money. For that matter, I thought, he could just use the dollar he had give me to buy him some socks. I didn't want it. I went in my room and fetched the dollar he had stuffed down in my stockin and put it on the bureau in his room. Momma watched me do all this but didn't say a word at all about it. I reckon she figured it would just provoke another sermon from me.

I didn't bother to wait for the right time to come the next evenin to say what I had been thinkin. Soon as Daddy walked into the kitchen from work I went to complainin. I know it wasn't the best way to get him to take me serious, but that's what I did anyhow. "Daddy, I know you ain't gonna like what I'm fixin to say, but I'm gonna say it anyhow. It's been eatin away at me all day. I was gonna say somethin to you last night about goin out on Christmas Day and not comin home until after supper time, but you was too drunk to talk to. By the way, I don't know if Momma told you, but none of us had no supper last night on account of we was arguin about the way things is around here."

Daddy acted like he wasn't listenin to me, but I know he was. I also knew he was gettin mad, too, but I didn't let that stop me. I had been spittin mad all day. Sleepin on my feelins hadn't done me no good this time. I kept on talkin.

"You go and give all of us a Christmas present and act like you want this to be a good Christmas and then you up and leave the house so's you can get drunk. Well, that ruined whatever you was plannin on us feelin about you yesterday. If you think I appreciate the gift in my stockin yesterday, I didn't!"

That did it for Daddy. I reckon I had done stepped out a little too far. He took off his belt and come after me. "Boy, you ain't too old to get a good whippin. I'll give you the Christmas present right now that I should've give you yesterday." With that little bit of warnin, Daddy commenced to givin me the whippin of my life. Somehow, I flat didn't care that he was doin it neither. I knew in my brain that there wasn't nothin that man could do that would make me hurt worse than I felt now or that would make me feel sorry for what I had done said.

I screamed at Daddy while he was hittin me, "Go ahead and beat me like your daddy used to beat you! If you think it will do me any good, just look at yourself and look at the good it done you. It made you hate your daddy and pushed you to become a drunk!" I kept on rantin and ravin like that, but it didn't slow Daddy down, not one bit. He was takin out his feelins on me the only way he knew how. I reckon his arm got tired after awhile, so he quit hittin me. He stood me up in front of him and tried to back my feelins down.

"You had enough, Leroy? You want some more of that? My onliest mistake with you is that I ain't whipped you enough all these years! Yore gettin a mite too big for them britches you're wearin!"

I flat refused to back down. Daddy was bigger and stronger than me in his body, but I was more determined than he was to keep sayin what I thought was the right thing. I didn't care how many beatins I got while doin it neither. "Daddy, I don't care how much you beat me! I'm tellin you that the only reason I ain't lettin up is that I know that we don't have to be a low-down family! You don't have to go out drinkin like you do and Momma ain't gotta go around draggin her feelins on the floor . . ."

I slowed my voice down and finished my sentence, " . . . and I don't wanna keep on actin like I been. You acted before like things was gonna change, but I can see that they haven't. Well, I ain't givin up on makin this house a decent place for a family to live." I didn't realize it, but I was practically pantin like a dog what had been chasin wild animals, which isn't too far from what I felt like I had been doin. I added, "I'm gettin tired of everybody hatin everybody else in this here family." I looked over at Daddy and finished sayin what I had to say. "Maybe you feel like I ought to be beat for sayin the things I say, but it isn't gonna make me quit. I'm only sayin what needs to be said, and that's all I'm doin." I know I still had poison in my voice, but I was tryin to get ahold of myself again so I'd be took seriously.

Daddy looked at me like he wanted to beat me some more with that belt of his. I hoped he was thinkin back on what it musta felt like when he were a boy and his daddy whipped him like I had just got whipped. I doubt he was, though. I honestly think Daddy got beat so much when he was little he forgot how to feel. That's what I honestly believe.

While I was standin there starin at Daddy and him glaring back at me, the thought hit me like it had before that me and him was standin in a saloon in Shotgun Junction. One was waitin on the other to say come on, let's go outside and let our guns decide who's gonna win this here fight. I expect that there's been more than one time that a daddy and his boy has come down to where one of them actually killed the other on account of them bein so mad they couldn't solve matters any other way. My hands was itchin and for a split second there it felt like I was about to squeeze the trigger on a shotgun. I don't think I could've lived back in them days where arguments was decided by who could beat the other fella harder or who had the biggest gun.

"That's all I got to say. You through whippin me, Daddy?" I'm probably lucky I didn't get thrashed one more time just for bein a smart aleck. That wasn't what I was tryin to be. I just wanted Daddy to know that him beatin me hadn't made me feel no different than I had before he had whipped me.

Daddy didn't say nothin so I left the kitchen and went on in my room. I couldn't hardly lay down on my bed. My whole backside was one big whelp. I winced while I was in my room by myself, but I'll be dad gum if I was gonna give Daddy the satisfaction of knowin he had hurt me. I wasn't sorry for what I had said to Daddy, but as I laid there, I got to thinkin that there had to be a better way of gettin through to my family than I had been able to do. I didn't think it was workin too much, and I wasn't too sure my backside could take too much more of the kind of treatment I had just been give.

Chapter 29

I HAD this feelin that Woody would be out along the Tennessee River fishin that comin Monday. It bein his regular day off, I knew he wouldn't be down at Wimp Dickerson's Barber Shop. He had said somethin to me awhile back that he was gonna get in as much fishin as he could around Christmas since he'd have a couple extra days off. That afternoon I moseyed on down to the river, lookin for my friend. It didn't take me too long to find him, seein that I knew pretty much where he liked to fish. I spotted him before he saw me. He was sittin there on the bank, his line propped up on this stick. He looked about as peaceful as a man can look, like there wasn't nothin in the world what could ruffle him up. That's the way he is most all the time. I ain't never seen Woody when he was in what you'd call a bad mood. The only kind of mood I've seen him in was the good kind and the kind you're in when you're just takin care of your business.

I hollered out when I was about fifty yards from where Woody was settin. "Hey there, Woody!"

Slow like, Woody turned in the direction of my voice and saw me headed his way. I could see that big white toothy grin of his real easy from where I was walkin. He didn't holler back, but stuck up his arm to wave at me.

As I got close to him, Woody informed me, "Me and dem ol catfish is gettin along good today, Mista Leroy. How's you a doin?"

"I'm all right, I reckon. When you say them catfish is doin all right, you mean you done caught a bunch of em?" I looked down in the water, but I didn't see no stringer with any fish on it.

Woody smiled as he explained, "Well, Leroy, let's jes say dat I been talkin to dem catfish from a distance. We ain't had what you'd call no face ta face conversation." He cocked his eye at me as his way of sayin that he hadn't caught no fish, but he could've if he had just wanted to. He liked me to think he could just tell them catfish when he was ready to hook one, and they'd be pleased to oblige him right away. I knew better, though.

I plopped myself down on the bank next to Woody. Them whelps on my hind side were pretty much healed up, but I can't say the same for the inside of me. My heart was still bruised from the beatin I had got from Daddy a few days ago. The ground was a little on the damp side seein how the water doesn't dry up as fast this time of the year after a rain. It didn't especially bother me to have wet britches, although when you go to walkin in cool weather with your chops all wet, it can chap your rear end a little bit.

"You have a nice Christmas Day, Woody?"

Woody nodded his head slow and said, "Yeah, suh, I sho did. Had me a right nice Christmas Day."

"What all did you do?" I knew Woody had a few kinfolks around this area, but what with him not havin his own wife and young'uns, I wasn't real sure if he had spent any time with his relatives or what. He didn't ever suggest that he did much with his kin.

"Well, I gots me a sister over in South Cassville and she done fixed up a good meal fo everybody what want ta come, so I went over dare fo de day."

"What all did she fix?" I was right sure the food Woody ate was plenty different from what my momma generally served at my house. You could see Woody's mouth water up soon as I asked him that question.

"Umm mmm. It sho were good. We had us sum chittlins an Tennessee chicken—you remember what dat is—an sweet potatoes an beets an fried onions an some fried tomatoes an cornbread wit sorgum syrup. Had banana puddin fo dessert." He set there for a second eatin all that imaginary food all over again in his mind. "How 'bout you, Mista Leroy? You have you a good Christmas Day?"

"Well, part of it was good, but it turned out to be a danged awful day before it was over with."

"Dat so?" Woody knew I would want to talk more, so he waited on me to keep on goin with my thoughts.

"Yeah, this was the first time since I can hardly remember that Daddy gave everybody in the family a present. He give me and Cody Sue a dollar bill each and he give Momma a five-dollar bill. Me and Cody Sue had bought both of them a present, too, so everybody got a gift that mornin."

"Dat mus be de good part."

"Yeah. The bad part came later when Daddy went out and got plenty drunk. He was just about as bad off when he come in that night as he was the night him and Momma got into that real bad fight and he run away from home."

It didn't take much for Woody to guess that things had got worse real fast on account of Daddy's drinkin. "Musta been a whole lotta arguin 'bout dat," he guessed.

"There wasn't any arguin with Daddy that night. He was too drunk to even know I was talkin to him, so I waited until the next day, then we got into it pretty bad. Me and Momma had us a bad round on Christmas Day."

"You and yo momma?" I reckon it surprised Woody to hear that me and Momma had squabbled with each other.

"Yeah. You see, I figured Momma didn't have to let Daddy go out that afternoon when she knew good and well what he was gonna go do. I reckon I lost my temper and let her have it for bein so lame with Daddy. She didn't take it none too good. We didn't have no Christmas supper that night on account of all the arguin."

I noticed that I was hangin my head when I said all that. It wasn't that I minded tellin Woody about it all. I reckon I felt shameful for goin and fightin with Momma and didn't have nothin good to show for it. Woody must of realized what I was feelin cause he said, "Makes ya wonder jes how much you ought ta say ta yo momma 'bout de way she handle yo daddy."

Woody had hit the nail right flat on the head. "I do, Woody! I never know when to speak up and say what's on my mind and when to just keep my mouth shut. My brain gets all jumbled up sometimes. Take the other day, for instance. I told Momma I had been tryin to act different to Daddy because I wasn't gonna be a part of his drinkin habit. I told her she needed to start standin up to him, too, if we was ever gonna get through to him. She said that she didn't want to go bumpin up against Daddy on account of she figured he'd go to beatin her if she did."

Woody sat there and thought with me for a minute before he said anything. I knew that meant he was picturin in his brain what all must of happened that day. He was tryin to figure out what he would've thought if he'd been me at that time. You talk about feelin relieved that someone was tryin their dead level best to put themselves in your shoes, that's just what I was feelin right then. Somehow, I already had this feelin that between me and Woody we'd figure somethin out.

He shook his head and said, "She jes don't see it de way you does, do she?" I shook my head back at him. He looked me square in the eye and said, "You wants everything ta be jes right in yo home, don't cha, Mista Leroy?"

"More than anything. You already know how I feel about that one. That's all I want is to live in a regular ol home with a family what gets along with everybody else."

"Things jes ain't right in dis ol world, is dey?"

"No, they sure ain't." We sat there for another minute. I figured Woody was fixin to say somethin else, then it hit me. He was wantin me to bite on what he had just said about things not bein right in this here world. I took the worm. "What do you mean by that, Woody? I mean, I know things ain't right in this world, but what're you gettin at?"

Woody let this real slight smile creep across his mouth and into his eyes. I could tell we was about to do us some powerful thinkin. "What you done said 'bout yo momma an yo daddy set me ta chewin on my cud. We all wants everythin ta be jes so in dis life, but it ain't never gonna be dat way. Dat hurts. It seem dat no matta how hard you tries, you jes cain't have dat nice family life dat you wants." Woody looked me right in the eye again and added, "An you deserves what you wants, too. I knows dat."

"I reckon I ought to quit tryin to make things perfect, huh?"

"If you quits tryin ta make things perfect, what you gonna do? Ya cain't jes do nuttin 'cause if you do dat, den things gonna get worser. Jes seem like ya cain't get caught up." Woody shook his head back and forth.

"Woody, you think everything it's gonna work out for the best? That's what you hear some folks say."

"Dat's a hard one, Leroy. Think on it wit me. If ya say dat things is gonna work out fo de best, den meybe dat mean dat dem bad things what comes yo way happens so's dat good could grow out of it. Now somehow dat don't seem to be de way it is. But if ya go an say dat when sumthin bad happen, good could come out of it, den dat dare is sumthin else altogether. Ya see de difference, Leroy?"

"Yeah, I think so." I thought about my family and said, "I got to admit, though, that sometimes I think that can't no good come out of my family. I mean, it ain't never gonna change, least not the way I want it to. I been tryin to do what we talked about before and do what I think is right so's that maybe I can help my folks change. Maybe it works a little bit, but I don't think that me actin all different is gonna amount to much. That's what I was thinkin when I got in that fight with Momma and told her she needs to start talkin up more, just like I been tryin to do."

Woody could feel me wantin to give up. "It be's hard ta keep on tryin. It sho take a long time fo change ta happen. Sho do. It be's easier ta jes give it up an say, well dey ain't nuttin I can do ta make things none better, so's I's jes gonna quit."

I quickly took up for myself. "But I ain't gonna do that! If I did, I'd be just like the rest of all my kinfolks when I'm grown-up and on my own, and I don't aim on livin like they do." There was this sound to my voice that was almost defiant. I looked over at Woody and saw that same little smile curl over his lip.

"Dat's what I means when I says dat maybe everything ain't fo de best, but dat good can come out of it noway." I couldn't help but smile a litle bit myself. I saw Woody's point.

"You reckon I was wrong to get on to my momma the way I done on Christmas Day?" I wanted Woody's opinion on that one.

He just answered me with a question. That meant he had his own ideas, but he figured we needed to take a look at my ideas first. "What were de reason you done what you done?"

"I reckon I wanted my momma to go to standin up for herself more than she's been doin. I figure if all of us acts the same way, maybe we could get Daddy's attention."

"Den what you done were good. Is dat what you'd say?"

"I reckon."

"But what happen when you say dat to yo momma?"

"We got in this big fight, and then she didn't fix no supper, and we all just sat by ourselves the rest of the day poutin."

"Den dat mus mean what you done wuz bad."

"I reckon it must. Is that what you think, Woody?"

"Maybe not." Now I was gettin confused. At first Woody says that what I done was the right thing and then he says it was bad and then he says that maybe it weren't all that bad after all.

"I don't get what you're sayin, Woody. You think what I done was good or bad?"

"It's right confusin ain't it, Mista Leroy?" He sat there with his head in his hands. We had both done forgot all about them catfish. I got to wonderin if there was some catfish down there in the river starin at the worm Woody had on his hook. If there was, they was probably talkin to themselves wonderin if it was safe to nibble away at the bait. They might be thinkin that they better stay clear of it or else they might risk gettin snagged. I had this urge to holler out to them to go ahead and chew on that there bait all they liked cause nobody up here was payin any attention.

Woody brought my mind back up to the riverbank with a comment that made me think. "Leroy, you think you too close to yo momma an daddy?"

"What do you mean too close? We sure ain't what you'd call a close family. That's for sure. I'd like to be closer to them if that's what you're gettin at, but I don't reckon I can be seein as how they won't never spend the right kind of time doin anything with me. 'Bout the only time either of my parents spends any time with me, it's to argue with me or give me a whippin or some such as that."

I could tell by the way Woody reacted that I had done missed the point he was tryin to get across. He was kind enough to explain what he meant. "Dis here's what I's thinkin. Ya see, when a young man get too close ta his family meybe he can see de damage what's been did, but he cain't hardly see what ta do next, cause he be's too close to de way everybody feel. But de young man, he figure he got ta do sumthin, so he do what he think be's de best thing. Now some young men, dey jes curl up like an ol turtle an don't let nobody get near dem. Anotha young man, he might jes go ta feelin sorry fo everybody an try to be de one what gonna save de day like he de big strong eagle. Den dey's one mo young man," he continued as he eyeballed me, "he jes attack like what dem lions does."

I liked the way Woody had done put that. I knew real quick like which one of them animals I was. "So I'm like a dad gum lion, huh?" I kinda laughed at myself when I said that. Woody laughed along with me. I know that he had said what he did to help me see myself different. He wasn't tryin to be disrespectful to me or nothin like that. That's about the last thing he would let himself be.

Now Woody was ready to give me a piece of advice. I know I was ready to hear it. "Ya see, Leroy, sumtimes ya gots ta stand back a little bit." He held up his hands and pulled himself away from me to show me what he meant. "Dat don't mean ya gots to act likes ya don't care 'bout yo momma an daddy. But when you acts like yo family is de people what live next doe to ya instead o wit you, den what dey do, it don't crawl under yo skin quite so bad like."

I understood what Woody was gettin at, but I was havin a hard time puttin it together with what me and him had talked about before. "But then they might go and think that I don't care nothin about what happens. I'm tryin to show that I do care when I get all mad. I don't think they can see that, but that's what I'm aimin to do."

"You jes said sumthin what be's impotant." I got that ignorant look on my face. I try not to look like that, but I always know when that expression is all over me. Woody didn't act like he thought I was ignorant, which I appreciated.

"What did I say that was so important?"

"Why, you done said dat you cares what happen, but yo momma an yo daddy, dey probly don't see it dat way! Ya see how it work, Mista Leroy? A young man, he can stand back, but dat don't mean he don't care. It mean he do care! It's jes dat ya ain't lettin nobody control de way you feels but yoself."

"And that's what we was talkin about before! I can't control nobody but myself." Now it was all makin a little more sense to me.

"Dat be's an impotant word, Leroy. Control. Jes think 'bout it. All us folks likes ta be in control o sumthin. 'Member yo friend, Mista Bruno and how he like ta be in control o his world? We all does. Sum of us jes do it in a different way, dat's all. Meybe you's still tryin too hard ta make all de decisions fo yo family. 'Member ya . . ."

"Ya cain't control nobody but yourself," I said, finishin the sentence for him. Woody smiled at me like I was a student what just done passed the test. Maybe I had. "I just need to keep tellin myself that."

Woody pulled his line up out of the water. Nothin was on that ol hook. "Why, dem catfish done took ol Woody's bait." Somehow Woody sounded plumb surprised to see an empty hook. I reckon them fish took my advice after all and stole Woody's bait while we was talkin.

I kidded Woody. "Them fish ain't ignorant. They could hear us settin up here talkin and not payin no attention to them. They recognized a free meal when they seen one." My friend chuckled as he hooked another worm and spat on it. "You didn't bring no chewin tobacca today?"

Woody looked shamed and said, "Dat's why I ain't caught me no catfish." Without lookin at me, he smiled while he kept on workin at hookin his bait.

We set there a good while longer talkin about nothin in particular. I had done enough hard thinkin for one afternoon, and I think Woody knew it. It hit me after a while that I had plumb left out one important detail about my Christmas gifts.

"Hey Woody, I almost forgot to tell you somethin! I got me the best Christmas present you could ask for. At least it was the best present I'd ask for." You know, there's lots of times I wish I was somebody else and could see the way my face looks. All I can do is watch the way the other person inspects me to try and figure out how I must appear on the outside. The way Woody looked, I must of looked like a giddy little boy. Or maybe I looked like Cody Sue looks when she gets all full of bubbles.

"Well, you's keepin me all tied up! Go 'head an tell ol Woody what did ya get?"

"I got me a kiss from Alane Sharpe! Right here." I pointed to the exact spot on my face where Alane had pecked me. I could still feel it, just like she was just now pullin her mouth away from me.

"Do tell!" Woody couldn't help but laugh. I hoped it was one of them laughs what meant he was glad for what I had done got. But more than likely, he was laughin on account of how red I had just turned when I give away my secret.

Despite I had embarrassed myself a little bit, I went ahead and told him all about it. "You see, I had done bought her this hair clip for a Christmas gift and went over to her house to give it to her. Me and her was in the room that they call the family room. Her momma was in there with us. Well, I give Alane the gift and she just reached over to where I was sittin on the divan and smacked me real good. And her momma didn't say nothin at all about it neither!"

Woody had got all excited while I was tellin him about my good fortune and was laughin pretty hard by now. I couldn't help but laugh with him. I can't really explain what was so funny about me tellin Woody that Alane Sharpe had done kissed me, but we both hurt our sides from whoopin it up right there on the riverbank. I bet if them catfish looked up from where they was, they'd of thought we was the two looniest fellas they'd ever seen. And they was right.

Dad gum. All that talkin about Alane Sharpe made me want to see her again. I couldn't wait for school to get goin next week. I told Woody I was gonna go home cause my ribs was gonna get sore if I didn't. Besides, I wanted to get on home and let Momma and Daddy see that I could be a happy person despite how nobody could get along in our house.

Chapter 30

MY GEOMETRY teacher, Mr. Montgomery, walked into the room on our first day back to school after Christmas and told the class, "I want you to pay attention because I'm going to take you through a mental activity that requires your concentration." The class moaned, figurin that this was another one of them tricky arithmetic problems that was practically impossible to solve. He liked to give them to us just to see if any of us had learned how to think up these creative solutions to odd situations. At least that's the reason he gave for tossin us them kind of problems. As for me, I was right certain that the old man was bound and determined to drive as many of us students crazy as he could. It probably doesn't take a whole lot to guess that I didn't never come up with the answers to them tricky problems, at least not the right answers. If you talk to someone like Rufus Elderbee, who solves every dad gum one of Mr. Montgomery's problems, he might give a different opinion than me.

"I'd like each of you to pick a number between one and ten and remember that number. Keep it to yourself. Now, in your head, multiply that number by nine." So far I was doin real good. He hadn't lost me yet. "Now take the two digits in that number and add them. For example, if your number is fifty-seven, you would add the five and the seven and have the number twelve. Does everybody still understand what we're doing?" Everybody shook their head, even Sav. If Sav knew what was goin on, then that meant everybody else understood.

"Next, subtract the number five from whatever your current number is. Now count through the letters of the alphabet until you reach the letter that corresponds with your number. For example, if your number is one, the letter A corresponds with it. The number two corresponds with B, and so on " That almost throwed me off, but I was still followin the directions.

"Now then, I'd like you to think of a country that begins with your letter and keep that in mind. You may pick any country you like. Once you've done that, go to the next letter of the alphabet and think of a mammal that begins with that letter. Pick any mammal you'd like." Now that everybody had done picked a country and a mammal, Mr. Montgomery said, "There's one thing I'd like you students to understand before we go any further. There are no elephants in Denmark."

When Mr. Montgomery said that, the whole dang class got in an uproar. Sav hollered out what the rest of us was thinkin, "How'd you know that's what I was thinkin? What is this, some kinda trick you done pulled on us?" I didn't tell Sav, but I figured out what Mr. Montgomery had did to us. I don't think Sav ever got it, and I sure wasn't gonna tell him. For once, I felt like maybe I had a little bit of a brain in my head. You get a teacher who pulls a joke like that on you and somehow it makes the rest of the class go all right. I wasn't all that happy about havin to go back to studyin, but I was kinda glad school had started back.

I saw Alane Sharpe for awhile before school, but I didn't get to talk to her much. After school was done, I run out to where she usually stood around for a little bit before goin on home. We got to talkin about what we had did durin the Christmas break. Of course, she asked me did I enjoy the time I got to spend at home. I didn't want to go and tell her about my daddy gettin drunk on Christmas Day and how he whopped me the next day when I told him what I thought of him. I also didn't want to say how I had done told Momma how she needed to quit bein such a do-nothing around Daddy. I didn't want to lie to Alane none, but I for sure didn't want to go embarrassin myself neither.

"Well, let's say I done learned somethin useful about the way me and my family gets along." I think Alane liked when I said that. She probably figured me and my momma and daddy was all gettin along better now.

"That's good! What did you learn?"

"Well, I was talkin to my colored friend, Woody. He's the fella what shines shoes down at Wimp Dickerson's Barber Shop. I reckon your daddy knows him. Anyhow, we was talkin about how my momma makes things worse around the house on account of how she doesn't never say nothin to Daddy when he goes to actin the way he does. Woody told me that I don't have to get all upset when they decide that they're gonna do whatever it is they're gonna do. You see, when I go to gettin upset and fuss at them, then I start to feelin that it's my job to fix everything in my family, and I just flat can't do that."

Bein from a different kind of family than mine Alane probably didn't understand all I was gettin at, but she was tryin her best to see it. "That's sad, Leroy. You don't think there's anything at all you can do to make things better?"

"The way I look at it, maybe the best I can do to make things better is to not make it worse by arguin and frettin over what my momma and daddy does. That make any sense to you, Alane?"

I don't think it did. She asked, "But if you just let it go on, aren't you also just letting things get worse?"

"That's what I used to think, but Woody and me done figured that about the only thing I can control is me. And it doesn't do me any good to get all tangled up in Momma and Daddy's ways, 'cause if I do I got the same problems they got. Maybe all I can do to make things better is to figure that I ain't gonna act the way they acts. Thatta way when I get grown up and have me my own family, that's when things will be different. You see what I'm gettin at?"

Alane shook her head that she did, but then she added, "It just seems that maybe there is something you can do to help your parents get along better." She was thinkin that maybe if I tried hard enough, I could figure something out and be the one what would save my family. I just flat wasn't gonna try that no more. I had, and it hadn't worked none at all. She asked, "Is there something maybe I could do to help out?" I don't know what all she had in mind, but I knew they wasn't no other solutions. I had done tried all I could think of and I know she couldn't come up with nothin new. I did appreciate her askin though.

"There is one thing you could do, Alane."

Her eyes lit up. She thought I was gonna ask her a favor or somethin like that, I reckon. In a way that's what I did when I said, "You can keep on lettin me know that you don't think less of me on account of how my daddy's a drunk and my momma she don't do nothin about it. That's about the only thing a person could do for me."

You go to thinkin about it, and it *is* the only thing anybody could've did for me. About all I had left in my life that hadn't been stepped on and squashed was the way I felt about myself. I know they didn't mean it this way, but Momma and Daddy had done plenty to give me reason to just give up on myself. There was plenty of times I've been about ready to, too. It was people like Alane and Sav and Ernie and, most of all, Woody that kept me from wantin to just quit tryin to make somethin of myself.

I don't know if Alane understood how big a favor it was that I had just asked her for, but she said, "That's something I'd be happy to do."

I wasn't in no hurry to go home and it didn't appear that Alane was in no hurry neither, so I figured I'd just go right ahead and ask her a thing or two and see exactly where did I stand with her. I had been wantin to have this conversation with her for a good while, but never could seem to find the right time. Well, now seemed like as good a time as any. "Alane, there's somethin about you that I ain't figured out yet."

Most girls like it when a boy says that to them. It makes them feel all mysterious like. But I don't think Alane wanted to be thatta way with me. "What's that, Leroy?"

I took a long draw of air and give her my real feelins. "You see, Alane, me and you aren't alike in a whole bunch of ways. You come from a nice family and my family, it hasn't got nothin but characters in it. Your daddy makes a good livin and my daddy doesn't act like he hardly likes to work at all. You talk all sophisticated and I sound all ignorant like the way I talk. You wear nice clothes and I wear whatever I can find that'll keep me warm. I mean, with all them differences between us, I never have figured out why you been actin so nice to me the last few months."

Alane looked like she was fixin to let me in on how she really felt about me, and I was a little scared she might say that she felt sorry for me and that's how come she'd been so nice. That's honestly what I was thinkin. "Leroy, I have to admit that before that Saturday that you came over to my house right after school started this fall, I didn't think at all about having any kind of close friendship with you. In fact, after you went on home that day, my daddy asked what I saw in you that encouraged me to have you come over to study with me. At the time I had a hard time giving him a good answer, other than to say you were nice and I just wanted to be nice in return."

My heart got five or ten pounds heavier when she said that about her daddy not thinkin too high of me. Funny how your heart does that when you get this feelin that you've heard somethin you didn't want to hear, and that you was probably fixin to hear more. "Your daddy didn't think I was good enough, I reckon. That's what I was afraid of."

Alane was nice enough to change my words around a little bit. "I wouldn't say that he felt you weren't good enough. He commented on your good manners. It's just that, like you just said, we come from two different worlds. That's what he meant by that."

I still didn't know all I wanted to know about where I stood with Alane, so now that we was talkin about these kind of things, I brung up another matter. "I don't know if you recollect this or not, but not long after I had done been down to your house that time, I noticed Royce Blackwell was actin all friendly to you. I figured you'd start likin him, seein how he's more like you than I am."

Alane looked like she felt a little sorry for me. I didn't want that. But what she said surprised me. "I think you and I are a lot more alike than

Royce and I are. Royce was interested in us getting to know one another better, but I wasn't as interested as he was. He's nice, but I like the way you talk about things. I also like how honest you are with me about your family. That time we were at the Cotton Palace grounds and you told me what your family was like, that's when I realized that you weren't at all like what a lot of boys would be if they had been through the same family troubles you have. I mean that as a compliment, too."

I appreciated what Alane had done said, and to tell you the truth I was surprised. "Thank you." I stalled around another second. "You know what I'd like more than anything in the whole world, Alane?"

"What's that?"

"I'd like to have me a family room like you and your parents got. Where'd you come up with the name family room anyhow?"

Alane explained kind of proud like, "I was actually the one who named it that. When I was a little girl, we lived in a different house. My favorite room was the front room where we had all the photographs of our family members, so I started calling it a family room. My parents picked up on the idea and that's what we called it. When we moved to our new house about two years ago, I didn't know what to call the room where we always sit in the evenings, so I just said it would be our new family room. We had the same photographs in it, so it just made sense."

I didn't know what it was like havin a family what all sits down in the evenins and does things together, so I asked Alane, "Tell me, what all do y'all do in the evenins at your house? Me and my family, we don't hardly ever even talk to each other. Do y'all?"

Alane seemed excited to tell me. "Momma has always insisted that I learn to appreciate fine literature, so most evenings she reads a novel aloud to me and Daddy. Some nights, she'll read for as long as two hours without stopping. Other nights, I sew on needlework or help Momma with some of the chores around the house. I keep a journal, so I write in it several times a week. Daddy is constantly studying for his work, but he takes time to be with me and Mother. Some evenings we simply sit in there and talk about whatever comes to mind."

Boy, that sure was different than what we do in my house. "Shoot, my Momma and Daddy can't hardly read, I don't think. We just sit around and do nothin. I bet there's a bunch of nights where we don't say five words amongst the whole bunch of us. Me and Cody Sue usually just sit in there and sometimes talk to each other or we lay by ourselves in our own rooms. It isn't a whole lot of fun bein in my family."

You know, whenever I said anything bad about my family, Alane didn't never agree with me that they were no count. She could've said somethin about how my momma and daddy ain't no good, but she never did that. That's somethin I appreciate about her.

Alane asked me to explain somethin about myself. "What is it that makes you different than the rest of your family, Leroy? I know you don't like the way your family is, but what keeps you from acting just the same as they do?"

Now that was a hard one to answer. "I hadn't never really give it that much thought. All I know is that a person hasn't got to keep on makin the same mistakes he's seen his momma and daddy make. Havin Woody as a friend all these years has helped me learn that. Me and him talk a lot about that kind of thing. I tell you who I worry about and that's my sister, Cody Sue. She's the excited type and acts thatta way a lot of the time, but there's a whole lot of times she acts just like my momma. She doesn't never do nothin to try to get anybody to act different. She just acts like it's okay by her however anybody wants to be. I just can't be thatta way. Maybe you could just say I'm stubborn and that's how come I try to act different. I just don't wanna go around unhappy all the time like the rest of em does."

Alane had a different opinion than me. "I don't think I'd call it stubborn. I'd call that being wise. You just see things a lot deeper than most people. That's what attracted me to you that first time you came to my house and that's what still attracts me to you now."

I just about said somethin else, but my words stopped before they could come out of my mouth. It registered with me that Alane had done said she was attracted to me back in the fall and she was still attracted to me now. Dad gum! That was right nice to hear. If that don't get a fifteen-year-old boy's heart to pumpin blood, they might as well start diggin his grave. I figured I better not let the chance get away to say somethin about that. I tried to think of a comment that would make me sound like the smart person Alane had just said she thought I was, but all I could think to say was, "You ain't joshin me, are you?"

So much for me bein smart. I was glad Alane had said that she thought I was the smart type, but I wasn't too convinced she were right. "No, I'm serious, Leroy. I think you're one of the most wonderful boys I've ever known. I'm just glad we're . . . well, friends."

Shoot, as good as this was goin, I figured I might as well take our talk a step further. "Um, Alane, when you say friends, are you talkin about bein just a friend or girlfriend to me?"

Alane blushed. She looked doggone pretty with her face turnin all red like that. I'm right sure I had done caught her with her guns unloaded, so to speak, when I asked that there question. She said in a kinda whispery voice, "The second type." I say she whispered, she might as well have shouted it as loud as she could from the roof of the school. I know her words come in real clear to my ears. My heart was just about to start showin through my skin, seein that it was probably wearin a hole in my chest. I wanted to be polite and not go to whoopin like I were one of them rough Shotgun Junction yahoos like my ancestors probably was.

I reckon I had gone to blushin, too. Alane said, "Your face is red." Then she felt the warmth of her own face and added, "I suppose mine is, too."

One of these days I'm gonna find somebody who knows what to do in situations like I was in right there and ask him to give me some lessons on how to not come across so simple like. Here I was standin there all beet-faced after Alane had done told me she liked me in a girlfriend sort of way, and I couldn't for the life of me think of nothin to say that was past your average, ignorant statement. Them lover boys in books would've come out with some perfect soundin answer that would make the girl of their dreams faint on account of bein so touched. I remember readin about Romeo and Juliet in English class and wonderin how in thunder did Romeo always manage to come across so romantic like. 'Course, things didn't turn out so good for him, but I think you can see what I'm gettin at.

About the best thing that would come outta my mouth right then was, "You know, Alane, I don't rightly know what to say now." That isn't what Romeo would've said and I'm plenty aware of it. Then I started to giggle. It made me feel better that she done the same. I didn't feel quite as foolish what with both of us standin there feelin all awkward like.

I figured the best thing to do next was to change the subject. Maybe if I did, my face would go back to bein its regular color. Hers, too. I was still thinkin about what Alane said about her daddy not takin a shinin to me the first time we met and was wonderin if things had changed any since then. I sure hoped so. "Say, Alane, let me ask you this. You know how your daddy didn't like me a whole lot the first time around, well is it still the same way with him?"

Alane were nice to say, "I didn't mean to make you feel he didn't like you. He just thought you were different than me, that's all. I think he sees you differently now. Momma's the one who thinks well of you. Each time she's talked with you, she seems to think more of you. She's even told Daddy as much. I know, I heard her say so myself."

I found myself wonderin what would my momma and daddy say if they met Alane. It seems for sure they'd like her. Who wouldn't? Then again, maybe they'd think she was the uppity type and wouldn't like her on account of how she dressed nice and talked all proper. I'll tell you somethin that makes me wonder even more than that is what would Alane think if she was to talk for a little while with Momma and Daddy. I suppose she'd like Momma all right, seein as how she can be right mannerly and hold a decent conversation with somebody. I sure can't imagine her takin a likin to Daddy, though. He probably wouldn't even say nothin to her or if he did, he'd cuss or say somethin to embarrass himself—and me. I figured I'd worry about that one when the time come. I didn't want to ruin what good feelins I was havin right then.

In a way, I was wantin this moment to be over with. I mean, knowin that Alane likes me for more than just a friend is wonderful, but I sure wanted to get over this clumsy feelin. She musta felt the same way, cause she said she agreed that it was probably about that time to get home herself.

I don't know what it's like to be a bird, but I come pretty close to flyin to my house. I had started out the school year wantin to get to know if Alane would be the kind of girl I'd be interested in. That was why I had done gone down to her house to begin with that first time. I reckon I done found out the answer to that question. Yes, sir, I sure did.

Chapter 31

"YES, SIR, Mr. Higgins. You wanted to see me?" I stood in the doorway to Mr. Higgins's office waitin to see why he had done called for me. He had sent word up to my English teacher, Mrs. Lemming, that he wanted me to come by before I left the buildin for the afternoon. Now I have a pretty hard time keepin my mind on my studies anyhow, but when I've been told in front of the whole class that I'm wanted in The Office as soon as school is out, that pretty much sends my mind right off the rails. I didn't do nothin but stretch my brain the rest of the class tryin to figure out what in the world Mr. Higgins might want from me this time. I couldn't come up with any good reasons, only bad.

"Have a seat, Leroy. I wanted to talk to you about a thing or two."

Before we went any further, I figured I may as well ask what had been botherin me the last hour. "Um, Mr. Higgins, am I in some sort of trouble or somethin like that?"

Mr. Higgins couldn't help but laugh. At first I couldn't tell if that laugh was the wicked type that a man cuts loose of right before he goes to torturin his victim, or if it was just a plain and simple ol laugh like any normal person would let go of if he'd just heard somethin funny. "No, no, you're not in any trouble. Why do you always seem to think that when you come to my office, anyway, Leroy? You know I don't think of you as a troublemaker. Least you ought to know that." He was still grinnin pretty big.

I felt a ton more comfortable now and could even join Mr. Higgins in laughin a little myself. "Don't you know, Mr. Higgins, what everybody says about you and what they say happens when they come in your office?" With him bein in a good mood, I figured I could have a little fun with him.

Surely he did, but he acted like he didn't. "No, I don't. I'd like to hear what all the students say about me. You feel like tellin me, Leroy?"

I guessed I wasn't givin away no secrets, so I went ahead and opened up my mouth and told him. "Everybody says you give the hardest licks of anybody they've ever been around. So you see, when a fella like me gets called in here, I'm always afraid I'm gonna get to find out just how hard them licks really are. And with my hind side bein on the skinny side, I'm not so sure I could take it."

Mr. Higgins throwed back his head and really howled this time. What I just said about how hard he gives licks sure sounded funny to him. I laughed along with him, but I can tell you he was laughin harder than I was. "I've heard that's what students say." Still smilin, he leaned up on his desk and looked me in the eyeballs. "Leroy, what've you been up to that you're hidin from me? You've got this look on your face that suggests you know plenty more than I do about some of the things that go on around this school."

Soon as he asked me that question, I thought I had done figured out now why I was brung into his office. Mr. Higgins wanted me to go to tattlin on some of my friends and tell as many bad things about them as I could think of. If that's what he wanted, I'd just have to say I couldn't do that. I'd be marked for death for sure if I told everything I knew. "Honest, Mr. Higgins, I ain't done nothin I wasn't supposed to be doin. And that's the truth." At least it was doggone close to the truth.

Still smilin like he was enjoyin our little game, Mr. Higgins challenged me. "Let's do this, Leroy. Why don't you tell me about one single incident you know about that I don't know about. I promise that whatever you tell me will stay in this office. No one else will ever know about it but me and you. I want to prove to you that you can trust me."

"You promise?"

"Promise." He sat there smilin, ready to hear any juicy gossip I might like to give him.

Kinda nervous like I said, "All right, how about this one. You remember how last week, some boys got in the girl's dressin room durin one of the gym periods and stole all the girls' stockins?" He nodded that he did. "Well, I know who done it."

"Go ahead and tell me what you know." Mr. Higgins had this friendly look on his face that said I could trust him, but him bein in the position of power he's in, I wasn't real sure if I was doin the right thing. I went ahead and unbuttoned my lip anyhow.

"It was my friend Ernie Chambers and this other fella, Rayford Berry-hill. We all call him Berry, ya know." Boy, ol Ernie would let me have it good if he knew that I was sittin in the pricipal's office spillin the beans about what him and Berry did.

"Right, I know both of them. Nice boys."

I still didn't know why I was tellin Mr. Higgins all about the dressin room incident, but I kept goin. All the while Mr. Higgins was smilin like he was sure enjoyin this conversation with me. "You see, Ernie and Berry figured it would be right funny to see how all the girls acted when they had to go around school the rest of the day wearin no stockins. Them fellas had *wanted* to round up all the girls' drawers, but, of course, the girls was still wearin them. The next best thing they could do was take their stockins, which they did." There. I had told Mr. Higgins about somethin he didn't know all about. Now I just had to wait and see was he gonna hold up his end of the deal and keep it between me and him.

"See, Leroy. That wasn't so hard, was it?"

"Actually, it was. I ain't used to tellin on my friends like that. I don't mind tellin you things that folks like Bruno and his buddies are doin, but I feel kind of bad tellin on folks like Ernie and some of my other friends."

Mr. Higgins acted like he didn't hear all I said. He wanted to go back to talkin about the dressin room incident. "All those girls were certainly mad the rest of the day. You can sure believe I heard about it from more than one of them." Then he laughed again. "You got to admit, it would be uncomfortable going around with no stockings on for the rest of the day. But I guess the girls can be thankful it was just their stockings that turned up missing." He laughed some more. Of course, I laughed with him. It seemed like the right thing to do. While we was settin there havin our jollies, I couldn't help but think that I bet Mr. Higgins was the kind of boy what got into plenty of mischief just like me and my friends like to do. I bet if he weren't the pricipal of this here school, he would've been right down there in the girl's dressin room stealin stockins with ol Ernie and Berry.

Figurin we were done with our business, I asked, "That all you want from me, Mr. Higgins? Can I go now?"

"I haven't even talked to you about what I wanted to discuss with you. You got a few more minutes?" I said I did. Mr. Higgins continued. "I simply haven't talked with you in awhile and wanted to see how you were doing, that's all. I've still been checking up on you and I've noticed your grades have improved lately. Does that mean things are better for you at home?"

"Not really. Actually, maybe they's some better."

"I just thought I'd tell you your teachers have said they've seen a change in you for the better. How long's it been now since your daddy's been home?" I counted the months. Here it was the middle of February now and Daddy come home about the first part of November.

"About three months now, I reckon."

"What's caused the change in you, Leroy? Are you happier?"

I didn't mind tellin Mr. Higgins what all had been goin on in my home since the last time me and him talked. "I'm tryin to be. You see, the last few weeks I been doin a lot of thinkin about how it ain't doin me no good to go around gettin all mad at my momma and daddy for actin like they do. They still act pretty much the same, except I try to stay out of the way now when I can see it isn't gonna do me no good to jump in the middle of things. I had been tryin to do too much to make my momma and daddy quit doin like they do. I still try to just do what all I can to make things decent around the house, but I try to help myself out at the same time. I don't want to be a grown-up what stays all tied up in knots all the time. I figure I ought to start practicin that now while I can."

Mr. Higgins had this look of surprise on his face when he said, "Leroy, that's the kind of talk you hear comin from an adult, not a fifteen-year-old boy. Where'd you learn all this? You figure it out by yourself?"

"Not really. You know Woody that shines shoes down at Wimp Dickerson's Barber Shop?"

"Yeah, I go in there. I don't really know the fella, but I know who he is."

"Well, Woody and me is good friends. Have been all my life. Sav's my best friend, but Woody's my very best friend, even though he's old and colored and all. Him and his daddy used to pick cotton for my momma's daddy a long time ago, and I've known Woody since I was born. Anyhow, he teaches me these things. I talk to him about everything."

I don't imagine Mr. Higgins knew Woody was as smart as he is. I know Woody hasn't got all the formal education of someone like Mr. Higgins, but he's the smartest man I know, that's for sure. I didn't figure I ought to say that out loud to Mr. Higgins right here, though. I didn't want him to think I was sayin that it doesn't matter if a fella finshes school.

"You're a fortunate young man, Leroy. Not everyone knows someone who can teach them things the way you've been taught." I nodded my head that I agreed.

I was about to get up again, when Mr. Higgins spoke up again. He still wasn't through talkin with me. "Leroy, I saw your daddy in town last Saturday and had the chance to talk to him. He asked me how you were doing in school, and I told him you had been doing much better the last few weeks. I took the liberty of telling him I thought it would be good for you if he would try to show a little more interest in you. I was tactful the way I said it, so I don't think he was offended. He said something kinda curious that I thought I'd run by you and see what you thought."

"What'd he say?" I couldn't hardly imagine my daddy tellin anybody nothin about what he thought, but maybe what with Mr. Higgins bein a principal and all, Daddy would say more to him than he would other folks.

"He said he thought that was a good idea, but he wasn't too sure if that's what you wanted. I said that I couldn't imagine a boy not wantin more time from his daddy, but he didn't see it that way. I asked him if he minded me talkin with you about all this and he said that would be fine. Leroy, I think that somehow your father is a bit intimidated by you."

"What do you mean intimidated?" I hated askin that question. Here Mr. Higgins had just told me how I was doin better in school, and then I go and ask him what he's talkin about when he uses a word I can't define.

"What I mean is that I think your father doesn't know quite what to do to approach you and make things better with you. He told me that you've been more outspoken the last few months than you ever have before. That's not exactly how he put it, but that's what he meant." I give this sheepish grin seein how I figured Daddy had told Mr. Higgins how I had made it my job to go to dressin him and Momma down when I just couldn't stand things no more. I bet he used some pretty colorful language in doin it, too. "This is just a hunch, Leroy, but I think you've hit a nerve in your daddy. I believe he's waiting for you to give him a sign that you want things to be better with him."

What Mr. Higgins was sayin kind of confused me. I thought I had give Daddy plenty of signs that I wanted things better. He sure couldn't say that I hadn't told him what I felt about things. After that time around Christmas when I told him to go ahead and keep on whippin me if that's what he felt like he had to do, he hadn't challenged me no more. Then there was that time I talked to him about us makin the front room into a family room where we set around and talk and do things together like Alane Sharpe's family does. And I've done told him how he needs to quit drinkin and pay more attention to me and Momma and Cody Sue. What more kinda sign would he want from me?

"You got any suggestions on what I ought to do?" Seein that Mr. Higgins had gone and talked to my daddy about how me and him get along, I figured it wouldn't hurt none to get his opinion on what I could do. After all, Mr. Higgins was a daddy, too, so maybe he could tell me what he'd sure appreciate from his son if things were the same between them as they are with me and my daddy.

"What do you think would happen if you went in to your daddy tonight and brought up the subject of maybe you and him gettin along better?"

"You think my daddy would wanna talk to me about somethin like that?"

"You never know. I think he'd like it if you made that sort of gesture to him. He talked like he wished things were better."

"I don't know. Don't you think it would be better if I waited on Daddy to be the one to say he wants to make things better at home? After all, he's the daddy, not me."

"Probably that would be the ideal thing, but we're not dealing with an ideal situation. I agree with you that it would be best for your daddy to take the first step, but I don't think he can. You're able to do that, though."

Mr. Higgins was right. We sure weren't dealin with no ideal situation all right. Maybe what he was sayin was somethin I ought to consider. "I'll think on it, Mr. Higgins. I reckon it's somethin I could do. I appreciate you lettin me know all this."

As I left the office, Mr. Higgins said one more thing. "Leroy?"

"Yes, sir?"

"Thought you might like to know that I already knew about what Ernie and Rayford did. But since you've told me all about it, I'm going to treat it as an unsolved crime. I don't want you to get the blame for getting them into trouble." He smiled as he added, "But I'm gonna watch those two rascals pretty close now that I know." I shot a grin back at Mr. Higgins. I reckon I could trust him.

I got to thinkin some about what all Mr. Higgins had done told me while I walked home. The more I thought about it, the more I believed I should try and do somethin other than grumblin and complainin about my family. What he had said to me set me to thinkin more about some of the talks Woody and me had had about how I can't change nothin but myself. I didn't know quite how to take Mr. Higgins, but for the most part, I felt like he was a pretty good man. Maybe he snooped around in my family's business a little more than I'd like, but I had to admit that he done what he did to help me out. Seein as how he had talked to Daddy some about me, I thought I'd just bring up the subject when I got the chance this evenin.

Things was just like they always are at our house that night. Momma fixed supper and we all ate without sayin a whole lot and then everybody did whatever it was they wanted after supper. Cody Sue went off to herself in her room and Momma and Daddy was sittin in the front room. Momma had somethin she was sewin on and Daddy set in his chair with a bottle on the floor next to him while he shelled some pecans that had been give to us some time back.

I got me a pecan cracker out of the drawer in the kitchen and set down on the floor by Daddy's chair. "Mind if I shell some of these here pecans?" I asked. Daddy grunted that that was fine by him and to help myself. I cracked open a couple and took the meat out and set it in the bowl where Daddy was puttin his pecan halves. After a couple minutes I spoke up. "I talked to Mr. Higgins today after school."

"You not in any trouble are ya?" Daddy answered. I wish he wouldn't automatically assume I was in trouble just because I had been in Mr. Higgins's office this afternoon. Of course, that's what I had thought about myself when I got called into the man's office, so I reckon I ought not blame Daddy for thinkin the same thing.

"No, sir. He just wanted to see how I was doin in school. He keeps up with my teachers, ya know. He says I'm doin better than I was earlier."

"That's good." Boy, ol Daddy don't have much to say most of the time, that's for sure. It's right hard to talk to someone who don't like to talk much.

"You like Mr. Higgins, Daddy?"

"I'd say he's a right decent man." That was Daddy's way of sayin he thought that Mr. Higgins was a splendid fella. It's just that Daddy ain't much for makin over how nice people is. I put another pair of pecan halves into the bowl. Daddy had done cracked two pecans in the time it took me to shell one. That's one thing he's right good at.

I figured I'd get on down to the point of what I wanted to say to Daddy. "Um, Daddy, Mr. Higgins suggested that maybe I ought to do more around here to help us all get along better. I been thinkin on what he says and figure maybe I could do more. I know I done my share of gripin and complainin around here lately. I don't aim on makin things harder on everybody. I know I get mad pretty easy when it doesn't work out the way I'd like."

Daddy shook his head slightly. I supose that meant he heard what all I had said and it was okay by him if I done whatever I could to keep things all peaceful around here.

"What's that supposed to mean, Daddy?"

"What's what supposed ta mean?"

"I mean when you just nod your head." I didn't wait to give Daddy a chance to answer. I blurted out with another question. I say question, it was really an accusation in question form. I reckon I shouldn't be ashamed to admit that's what it was. "Why don't you never talk, Daddy?" I didn't even have to look at where Momma was settin to know that her eyes was gettin bigger by the second.

Daddy sat hushed for a minute and then barely smiled. "I reckon I ain't got much to say." You couldn't hear it, but he give out a little chuckle.

"Why do you reckon you're thatta way?"

Silence again. I wasn't gonna be the one to break the silence though. After a spell he said, "Just am."

I knew exactly why he was thatta way. His daddy never took the time to talk to him and my granddaddy's daddy probably had did the same before him. "I aim on breakin the way men talk in this family," I vowed.

I hope I wasn't soundin defiant, but I bet I was. I thought I had better watch myself seein as how I didn't want no big ruckus again tonight. Through the back of my head I could feel Momma starin at me, practically beggin me to stop before things got worse. I wanted to turn around and say why don't you quit worryin 'cause I ain't gonna do what you think I'm gonna do. "What do you think about that?" My voice was softer when I asked that question.

This time the silence was pretty long. I couldn't read Daddy's face. He would've made a good poker player back in Shotgun Junction days. Mine and his ancestors probably was. I bet they were the kind that always set with their back up against the wall, too, just in case someone come huntin them down. Then the least smile came on Daddy's mouth again, and he quiet like said, "I'd like that. I want you to be a happy young man." Daddy then reached down and gripped the back of my neck hard with his whole hand. I could feel the callouses on his fingers and palms, but somehow the way he squeezed me made his hands feel soft.

This time I was the one what went silent. Just like Daddy had did a couple minutes ago, I barely nodded my head. Even though he didn't say hardly more than a couple words, Daddy had spoken more to me just then than I can recall him doin in years. In a few words and with a grip of the hand he had told me, "I ain't so happy bein the way I am. I know you're different than me and that's good. I believe in you and I'm right sure you're gonna do yourself better when you're growed up than I've done did." Maybe some folks would've had a hard time knowin that that's what Daddy was sayin to me then, but it was plain as day to me. I could even feel Momma givin a sigh of relief from where she set over on the divan. I think she agreed with Daddy that maybe I was gonna break them dern chains what shackled the heart of every man in my daddy's family for as far back as you'd care to go.

"Thank you, Daddy." Lemme tell you somethin, I slept better that night than I have in a powerful long time.

Chapter 32

I HAD got to talkin to Alane after school one afternoon about how this would be a right good day to be goin fishin and that's where I wished I was right then and there. She said she thought that sounded like fun and suggested that maybe we could go out to Fish Pond some Saturday soon so I could show her how to catch a big ol fish. Next thing you know we had made these plans for me and her and Sav and Virginia Bledsoe to go on an outin to Fish Pond the first Saturday we got a chance. Her daddy bein a member of the private fishin club, she said it would be all right for all of us to go out there.

When that day came, I was in the kitchen tellin Momma about our plans when she commented on how me and Alane was gettin sweet on one another. "That Sharpe girl must think right well of you to invite you to go out there to Fish Pond with her. Her daddy gonna take y'all out there?"

"No, ma'am. Sav's gonna borrow his daddy's car so's we can all have room to sit and then we're gonna pick up Alane and Virginia Bledsoe and take them out there. There wouldn't be enough room for all of us in his truck. Virginia's this friend of Alane's who's kinda taken up with Sav," I explained. "You ought to see the way Sav acts around Virginia. He's actin like he's got a little more sense about him than when he first met her, but sometimes that boy gets so jittery he doesn't know what to say. It's like the words just won't come outta his mouth right." I laughed and so did Momma. I loved to see her smile, not only because of the way it made her look prettier than usual, but because she didn't hardly ever seem to feel no reason to smile. I felt like I had give her a gift when I made her smile.

I wondered did she ever used to smile a lot when she was a little girl or was she the unhappy sort back then, too. Somehow it was hard for me to picture Momma as a girl. When you've never seen a person when they were young, it's hard to imagine what they were like way back then. We don't have hardly any photographs in our house so I don't think I've ever even seen a picture of Momma as a child. Daddy doesn't hardly ever call her by her first name of Martha so it was even hard for me to imagine her goin by a name other than Momma.

What with Momma talkin about me bein sweet on Alane, and me thinkin about Momma as a child named Martha, it made me wonder about what it was like when she first met up with Daddy. I asked, "Momma, tell me what it was like when you and Daddy first got to goin together. There must of been somethin about him that made you want to be with him. Was things different back then?"

Momma don't like talkin about them kind of things and I know it, but that hadn't kept me from wantin to ask her, so I just jumped out with my question. This one time, she didn't seem to mind tellin me a little bit about her younger days. "Your daddy was rough back then, same as he is now, but it didn't show all the time. You wouldn't know it, Leroy, but your daddy's got this soft side to him that most folks don't know about. He showed it to you the other night, you know."

"I know. I wish he were like that a lot more of the time."

Just like she was talkin to nobody in particular, Momma kept on explainin. "Knowin that he's got that other side to him is probably what keeps me goin. Lord knows, I got little other reason to keep pushin on." She caught herself and looked at me with the kind of look I thought a mother should always have for her child and added, "'Cept I got you and Cody Sue to help keep my heart runnin."

Then she fell back into her past and went to daydreamin out loud again. "I think your Granddady Evans done took all the life outta your daddy. We used to see a lot of him before me and your daddy married and for the first year or two after. Them two men had one fight too many, though, and your daddy ain't wanted nothin to do with his family since. I think his daddy feels the same way. Your daddy ain't been the same since right before you was born. He used to not even drink liquor at all, but once he got started he didn't stop. Like I say, he's always been on the rough side, but used to I could get him to show me that other part of him every now and then. Now I cain't."

"Momma, you think Daddy's ever gonna be different?"

All Momma could do was shake her head. "I don't know, Leroy. I just cain't say." I don't mean to speak for Momma, but I'm right sure she was meanin to say no she didn't think Daddy would ever go back to bein the way he used to be, however much better that was than what he is now.

"You know, Momma, I done decided that I'm not gonna try to change

Daddy no more. He can drink himself to his grave and I don't aim to stop him." Momma give me this look that asked how could I dare say a thing like that. I answered her, "I don't mean I'm gonna open his mouth and pour the stuff in there for him. I'm just sayin that I got no control over Daddy and I'm gonna quit worryin about what he does. It's his business."

Momma probably thought I was bein hard by sayin that. I wasn't. I was just tryin to get her to see that I had figured out that waitin on Daddy to make me happy by changin his ways wasn't what was gonna give me any satisfaction in life. That's all.

Momma got quiet like. I think she was afraid that if she kept talkin to me like she had been, it would mean that she was turnin her back on Daddy. She didn't see it as bein a woman's privilege to badmouth her husband. I figured our conversation was over, so I stepped on outside to wait on Sav to come pick me up. As I went out, Momma followed me. "Leroy, you'll need this." She stuck out an old quilt she had got out of the closet.

"I don't think I'll need a quilt, Momma. Alane said her momma was gonna fix us a sack lunch, and I expect she'll have somethin we can all sit on."

Momma insisted. "Just take it, Leroy. I feel bad enough about someone else fixin your lunch. The least you can do is take a quilt that y'all can set on." I took the quilt figurin it wouldn't hurt to have it along. At least it would make Momma feel better. If nothin else, I could just lay it on the floorboard of Sav's car and then when we got home I could bring it back in the house and say it had been a real handy thing for us to have along.

Sav came along in just a minute drivin his daddy's car. His daddy has this big ol long Ford sedan. I mean, it was a fine lookin car. Made me feel kinda proud when me and him came drivin up to Alane's house to pick her up. Virginia had already come over to Alane's house, seein as how she was a little embarrassed to have a couple of boys come pick her up at her own house. I ribbed Sav and told him I reckon I'd be on the embarrassed side, too, if I was a girl and he was gonna come by for me. He shot back and said it was on account of havin my ugly mug in the car with him that kept Virginia from wantin him anywheres near her neighborhood. He said maybe we could drop her off when we went home later in the afternoon, seein as how he'd like to see what her house looked like and all.

Mrs. Sharpe had packed us up some fried chicken and some leftover cornbread and potato salad for a picnic lunch. She also made us up a gallon jar full of lemonade for drinkin. Soon as we headed out toward Fish Pond, I commented on how I was gettin both hungry and thirsty just thinkin about what all Alane had brought for lunch. We laughed and carried on and had us a good time drivin out to our afternoon getaway spot. It only took maybe ten or twelve minutes to get there.

Fish Pond is right out north of town hardly a stone's throw from Lake Cassville. I'd say Fish Pond's about two or three acres in size and it has the most beautiful grounds around it that there is in this part of the country. Me feelin the way I do about red oak trees, this here place is like dyin and goin to red oak heaven. Just away from the pond, maybe a couple hundred yards off, was a grove of red oaks. But dominatin the whole grounds was that one red oak with about four trunks growed together that Alane had told me about one time last fall when we had got to talkin about trees. Before we went down to the pond, I told Sav let's go over to that huge live oak and see could the four of us fit our arms around it. We tried, but we needed one more person to make a full circle. I can't say how impressed I was at a tree that grand. If we didn't catch not one single fish this afternoon, I can honestly say it had done me good to come out here just so I could see that tree and hug it for a minute.

Makin our way down to the pond, we pulled out all our fishin tackle. Sav announced to the rest of us that he was ready to catch a whale, or at least a good size bass. I could see it happenin as soon as he started to talkin about how he was gonna catch himself a big fish. Sav was workin himself into one of his peppy moods where he goes to runnin around on his toes, so to speak, and his high-pitched voice gets even higher. Just like it was his duty to get Virginia as worked up as he was, he commenced to showin her how to hook a worm on a fishin line.

"Looky here, Virginia," he said as he pulled a fat juicy worm outta the bucket of bait me and him had brought, "you gotta get a fat one like this so's it'll make the ol bass's mouth water." Then as if he'd just thought of the funniest joke ever told, his eyes got real big and he throwed back his head and hollered out, "Wait a minute! It won't do no good to make a fish's mouth go to waterin what with him bein all soakin wet down there in the pond anyhow!" He died laughin and so did the rest of us. I wasn't gonna be the one to tell him, but I know I wasn't laughin as much at what he had said as I was at him. You can bet that's what them two girls was laughin at, too.

Sav continued to give Virginia a lesson in puttin bait on a hook. "You take this ol worm and stick him through the hook about four or five times, like this." He jabbed his poor little victim and made worm juice squirt out on Virginia which caused her to have a conniption fit. There's nothin funnier to a boy than seein a girl scream over somethin like gettin a little worm juice sprayed on her. "It ain't gonna hurt you none," Sav assured Virginia. "Just think of it as a little bit of water. That's all it is."

Virginia didn't see it thatta way. "Well, I sure wouldn't put any of what just came out of him in a glass and drink it! You can't make me think that what just got on me isn't anything more than just a little bit of water." She grabbed the towel Sav had stuck in his belt and wiped her arm down real good. I thought about tellin Virginia about how that towel was Sav's fishin towel and that it not only had dried worm squirtins on it, but dried fish juice as well. Don't you know she would've gotten all behind like a fat woman if she had known that?

We all got our lines baited and throwed out into the pond and settled back to wait for the Big One to grab ahold. Alane was sittin maybe twenty feet from me and I commented to her on how today was a perfect day for catchin us some good fish. We had us an overcast sky without hardly any breeze in the air. It was warm, but not too warm so as to talk the fish into takin a nap on us. I told Alane, "If it would only go to rainin, I know exactly where we could catch all the fish we could carry home."

"Where would that be?"

Real serious like I told her, "Why under the dock over there! Them fish don't like gettin rained on any more than people do."

Alane nodded her head as if I'd just let her in on a good fishin tip that she was gonna try and remember. Then it hit her that maybe I was joshin her. "What? Under the dock! Why would a fish care if it was raining?"

That set me to laughin as I acted like I was reelin in a big one on my line. "Gotcha!" She laughed right along with me. Boy did that Alane ever look pretty when she smiled big like that. She looked pretty whatever expression she drew on her face, but when she laughed and smiled, she looked extra beautiful.

Me mentionin rain made Alane look upward to the sky. "You know, the way those clouds look, I think it might rain, don't you?"

I looked at the sky, too, but said, "Naw. Maybe it'll rain tonight, but I don't think we're gonna get us any this afternoon. I don't think them clouds are heavy enough yet to rain." There was this confident sound in my voice that hopefully made Alane feel a little better, but all the same she suggested we eat our lunch before too long, just in case I might have missed on my prediction.

I said that suited me just fine and hollered over to Sav and Virginia, who were farther around to one end of the pond that maybe we'd eat our picnic lunch in just a little while. Sav hollered back and said that before we did, he was gonna go on around a little farther to the other side and throw out his line a few times because he thought the fish might be bitin over there. When he said that, I told Alane, "I think ol Sav thinks he can talk them fish onto his line." Thinkin about that I added with a laugh, "I'll say this, if anyone can, that boy can. He can sure jabber."

It took Sav several minutes to work his way over to this spot where there was some rotted logs and old branches that had fallen in the water a good while back. As I saw him castin out his line, I found myself thinkin that just maybe he had found the right spot to catch him a good-sized bass. No sooner had I thought that thought, Sav hooked one and went to screamin, "Leroy! Leroy! I got me a big one! This here one is huge!" I got all excited watchin his pole bend deep down to the water and pulled in my line so I could run around to a spot where I could get a better look at what he might've snagged. Alane came with me. Virginia had stayed where her and Sav was first fishin, but ran over to join us.

It isn't good enough for me to try to describe what Sav looked like tryin to haul in his big catch. For one thing, that boy's eyes was the type that got big anytime he got jumpy. If I had to say what one thing stood out about him right that minute, I'd say it was them big white eyeballs of his. His mouth was right funny lookin, too. I didn't know a fella could move his mouth around in so many different positions, but just like that was an important part of pullin in a big bass, he was makin every face a guy could make. I can tell you, he was jerkin and strainin hard so as not to let that bass win this here fight. He was strainin so hard, he lost his footin on the slick bank and slid right down into the water. As if I wasn't already enjoyin Sav's splendid little show, I went to hootin and howlin when he did that. So did Alane and Virginia. I looked over at them and asked, "I'll bet you didn't know fishin could be so entertainin, did you?" They said they had no idea it was this much fun. It ain't when you go with someone besides Sav.

Sav heard all the racket we were makin and held up his line, hollerin out, "See? I ain't lost him yet. I still got him on the line. I think I'm wearin him out! Get us a fire goin, Leroy, so's we can fry this fella up. There's gonna be plenty for us to eat all we want!" He enjoyed braggin on how big that fish on the end of the line was, that was for sure. I know he was gettin a big kick out of landin a prize catch right here in front of a couple of girls. Somehow he managed to pull himself back up without losin his pole and went to strainin and tuggin again.

After a long battle, he pulled his big catch out of the water onto the bank. About that time, the three of us just about lost our senses on account of laughin at the great fisherman. "It's a danged ol turtle!" Sav yelled. He then kicked the poor thing off the hook about twenty feet out into the pond. After all that fightin and fallin in the water and all, Sav had caught himself a turtle.

"I gotta hand it to ya, Sav!" I hollered out, "That's about the prettiest derned turtle I've ever seen. Why'd you go and kick him back in the pond for? We could've cooked him up for our picnic lunch."

We commenced to laughin again. I had already been whoopin pretty good, but when he hollered that he'd caught himself a turtle, I about fell out on the ground. Poor ol boy had hoped to come out lookin like a great fisherman, but ended up lookin like a wet-legged turtle chaser instead. I honestly don't think he minded, though, on account of how we was all havin such a good time. It's a good thing ol Sav's the kind that can take a good ribbin, 'cause I was givin him a hard time. I knew it'd be my turn to be laughed at sooner or later.

We got all our picnic goods out of the car and had us a nice spread for lunch. Virginia had brought a quilt for all of us to set on. I figured it would be better for us to use it instead of the one I brought, so she'd feel like she was makin a contribution to our picnic. I had to remind Sav to stick his slimy legs off of the quilt so he wouldn't get it wet and stinky and make Virginia's momma all mad. While we ate on our chicken and potato salad and cornbread, the wind began to pick up. It wasn't bad enough to blow away everything we had brought, but it was a nuisance. That's one thing about Alabama that I wish was a little different. There ain't nothin north of here to stop the wind from pickin up steam and rollin right through the state fast as it cared to go. There's not much I don't like about where I live, but that's one thing I'd change if I could.

I laid back and shut my eyes after eatin my fill of food for lunch. A nice little snooze would feel good about now. Sav joined me in stretchin out and I think we both could've rested real good, but real sudden like, the wind changed from bein just a nuisance to bein a concern. I stood up and looked north and could see some lightnin in the clouds that was headed our way. Them clouds was plenty dark, too. "Looks like our little picnic is gonna get washed out," I said. "We better start gettin our things together and get on back home." I wanted to stay around and show Alane how the fish hide under the dock when it rains so they won't get wet, but figured that would have to wait until another time. Besides, whatever was packed in them clouds had decided to hit us all at once. It looked like we weren't gonna have any time to waste gettin outta here.

Chapter 33

SOMEHOW IT wasn't near as fun gettin in the car to ride back to town as it was when we had headed out to Fish Pond. That storm had done blowed up on us so fast that we didn't hardly have enough time to get all our things together. Sav lost one of his fishin poles cause it got gulped into the pond. You watch, a few days from now he's gonna tell everybody that while we was at Fish Pond he was fixin to pull in a seven-pound bass when the storm come up and helped that ol fish yank the line right outta his hands. I know he ain't gonna mention to nobody that all he really caught was a turtle.

"I mean, when it decided it was gonna rain, it didn't fool around none, did it?" I was hopin to help everybody have a little fun and laugh at what we were goin through. The way I figured it, we might as well try to have a good time despite we were gonna get washed out. No need of lettin a little storm give our good spirits the heave-ho, too. The others tried to appreciate my good humor, but to tell the truth, I think they were all gettin worried. In fact, I might as well admit that I was gettin a little shaky on the inside myself. It looked like we were gonna get us more than just a good soakin.

Virginia pointed over to the north where I had spotted lightnin a few minutes earlier and said, "I don't like the way those clouds look over there." We all followed her eyes and looked at where she was pointin. Sure enough, the clouds had taken on this deep green kind of tint. They was dark as night and looked like a bully who was ready to jump in on a good fight. Just seein that was enough to keep all of us from talkin. Odd how you don't say nothin once you've got this scare in you. I know I had gone past bein just perturbed that our fishin trip had been cut short. This here storm was gonna be a bad one and I was gettin downright concerned. By the time we got too far down Fish Pond Road, the wind was so strong

I honestly felt like it might pick up our car and sling us off the road. It sure didn't take long for that wind to get all lathered up. I've never seen such a tantrum as this storm was throwin at us. We didn't get more than a mile away from the pond before the rain got so hard you could hardly see the road ahead of us. Sav had the windshield wipers goin, but they weren't doin much good.

"Can you even see where you're drivin, Sav?" I asked.

I do believe Sav was just about to panic. With that high voice of his, he hollered like I was a hundred yards away from him. "Not hardly! Leroy, I don't think we're gonna even make it back into town! What do you think we ought to do? This here rain, it's bad. I ain't never seen nothin like it!" I think if Sav had of been calmer about all this, my nerves would have settled down a mite, but calm was about the only thing Sav wasn't. Him bein plumb terrified by what we was goin through put me in a frenzy right along with him. I can tell you my heart was thumpin ninety to nothin.

Alane was tryin to stay composed, but I'm right sure she was havin just as hard a time as the rest of us keepin her heart from beatin right through her chest. There wasn't a whole lot of steadiness in her voice when she asked, "Do you think we ought to find a place to pull over?"

I didn't know exactly what we ought to do, but I knew we didn't need to stop if we didn't have to. We needed to get somewhere else as fast as we could and shouldn't give in to that storm. Sav must of agreed with me, since he yelled out, "I'd like to keep on drivin if we could. I'm afraid if we stopped, I might not get this here car goin again. Then what would we do? Why don't we try making it over to your house, Alane, and if it's still bad, we'll just stay there until this thing blows over." Despite he was screamin at the top of his lungs, we could hardly even hear Sav. It was that loud now. Sav's eyes was huge. His face was wet, but I can't really say if it was rain or sweat runnin down from his forehead. I know I didn't have no control over my body and Sav probably didn't neither. I was pretty doggone close to havin me a nervous conniption. We sat in silence while we crawled on through the wind and flood. I doubt we was even goin five, maybe ten, miles an hour. I bet it took more than half an hour to make it three miles. It seemed like forever. We finally hit Cassville Drive and turned on it, givin us a straight shot back into town.

Now here's where things get almost eerie. We hadn't hardly turned on Cassville Drive when the storm all of a sudden lightened up on us. It was like we had drove to the end of the sheet of rain right on out into broad daylight. I ain't never been lost in a cave or a tunnel, but now I know how it must feel to all of a sudden walk out of somethin like that after you've done convinced yourself you ain't never gettin out alive. The wind was still blowin hard, but believe me it was a danged relief to get out of that rain.

"What the . . ." Sav's words got stuck in his throat. I think he about wrecked the car on account of bein so shocked that the suffocatin rain what had been chokin us all that time had just quit all of a sudden like. I mean, every one of us started breathin again, all at the same time. Until that second, I didn't realize that I hadn't taken a breath in awhile. I turned around and looked out the back window and could see the storm still kickin and screamin behind us. It looked fearsome, but it looked a heap better from where we was now than it did just a minute ago. It's hard to explain how happy a fella feels when he realizes he has just got loose from that kind of stranglehold, but I was feelin a heap better. So was Sav and the two girls. I thought we were out of danger now.

Tryin to let everybody know we were for sure safe now, I said, "I think we've outrun that storm. Look at them rain clouds back there. It's like they're mad that we got away from em." I was hopin we could laugh, but a weak smile was about the best any of us could muster. Like a big brother tellin a little sister that she didn't have nothin to worry about no more, I told everybody, "I think we'll have time to get everyone on home and then let this thing pass us on by." I wanted to believe that the worst was done behind us, but I was beginning to get this sick feelin that this storm wasn't done with us yet. It was like it had a mind of its own and had decided it wasn't through fightin yet. I could just see that bully cloud starin us down, darin us to try and get away from him.

We made it real easy from there to Alane's house, seein that where she lived wasn't but maybe a mile from where we turned on to Cassville Drive. When Sav stopped in front of Alane's house to let her out, she and Virginia grabbed their things, bolted out of the car, and sprinted straight for the front porch, despite it was hardly rainin right then. When Virginia jumped out with Alane, Sav called behind her, "Wait, Virginia! We can take you home, too!"

She didn't even turn around as she yelled back, "Thank you, but I'll call my daddy to come pick me up after the storm's past. I don't want to stay in that car one more minute. I'm scared!" Sav slumped down in his seat like he'd just been rejected. I know Virginia hadn't meant for her words to sound the way Sav took it. He thought Virginia was rejectin him personally. Instead, she was just showin how bad that storm had unnerved her, that's all. Soon as the girls got up on the front porch, they turned around and hollered for us to come on in with them to wait out the storm. They had this concerned look on their faces.

Knowin what Sav had thought when Virginia leaped out of the car with

Alane, I assured him, "See, they had a good time. Virginia run outta the car 'cause she's afraid that storm's fixin to hit again. They're worried about us makin it home. You think we ought to go in with them?"

I think Sav believed what I said about why Virginia didn't want him carryin her home, but all the same he said kind of disappointed like, "Naw, we can make it on home. I don't think we need to be gettin in the Sharpes' way." I felt pretty much the same as Sav. I figured we had outrun the storm by now, and I wasn't no more anxious than Sav to go in Alane's house all drippin wet and smelly. That wouldn't go over too good with the judge and his wife. We hollered out at the girls that we was goin on home and told them we'd see them at school Monday.

Sav headed down Stuart Avenue toward downtown. Our plan was for him to stop off at my house and then maybe he'd come in with me so we could see if the storm would hit hard again. We figured we could watch it from inside my house and not have to worry about it drenchin us again. That was the plan. We made it into the downtown area before the storm caught up with us one more time, blastin us with such force that we might near got throwed off the road. Sav and I both immediately went speechless again. I thought the rain we had drove through just a few minutes earlier was awful, but this was even worse. You don't think of things like a storm havin a will of its own, but I swear this here one seemed to have this dogged desire to do some hurt to us. The rain was comin down so hard now that we didn't have no choice this time but to stop the car. You couldn't even see the hood of the car, it was that thick outside. I heard this queer hissin sound and asked Sav did he hear it, too. He did. We was yellin just to hear one another, despite we weren't but two or three feet from each other. I was within an inch of havin an instant heart attack and thought that maybe Sav had done had one.

"What do you reckon that sound is, Sav?" I yelled.

"I . . . " Before he could get out another word, that hiss turned into a roar, just like a train. I ain't never experienced fear like I did right then in all of my life. If my body coulda jumped outta my skin, it would've. Sav screamed, "I think it's a tornado!"

"Hit the floorboard, Sav!" I don't know why I thought to do that, but it seemed the only safe option we had, not that we had too many to choose from. I grabbed that old quilt Momma had insisted we take with us and pulled it on top of us. We both laid on the floor of his car listenin to that bully of a storm thrash and beat everything around us. The windows of the car broke out, sprayin glass all around us. The quilt was thick enough to shield us from gettin cut. This wasn't the way Momma had intended for us to use it, but I was for dern sure glad we had it.

The car rocked like we was a small boat out on the water. For all we knew, that may have been exactly where we was, too—out in the middle of a river. I could feel us movin and was afraid we was about to turn over. The ground couldn't soak up the water as fast as it was comin down and it had begun to flood real quick like. I found myself thinkin how we would manage to get out of the car if it did dump over. To tell the truth, I wasn't sure we *could* get out if we had to. The storm was made louder by hail which about made our eardrums bust the way it was wallopin the car. I was as close to havin a seizure as a boy can come without havin the real thing.

While me and Sav laid there on the floorboard, thoughts flashed through my head so fast I couldn't hardly keep up with them. I worried about Momma and Daddy and Cody Sue wonderin where I was at. They was bound to be plumb sick thinkin about what might be happenin to me and Sav right this minute. I know I was about to get nauseated worryin about them. Our house wasn't all that far from where we was, so they was probably goin through the same horror that we was, the only difference bein that they was inside while we were right out in the middle of this here eruption. I wondered if this tornado had done touched down and if it did, did it hit my house where they was. I know Sav must of been thinkin the same about his family.

The thought struck me that we might die right here and now. Funny, I wasn't so bothered about dying. I just didn't want it to be painful. I was right positive that any minute now somethin was gonna happen and that would be the end of me and Sav. I could just see me all laid out at my funeral with folks comin by to look at my stiff body sayin that I had been a good boy and all. I looked over at Sav and could tell he was even worse off than me. If I was scared, he was plumb mortified. If this had been any other situation, I might have found a way to laugh. Sav had this way of puttin on a face that was like nobody else could do. Only this time, he wasn't horsin around. That look he was wearin was for real.

Dang, we shoulda got out and went in Alane's house with her and Virginia. Virginia was smart enough to see that this here storm was still runnin fast—too fast for us to shake off. I don't know why we thought we could make it on home before the bottom fell out again. When we passed through that sheet of rain, I thought the worst part was done over with. I can't believe I'm that ignorant.

"Leroy. Listen!" Sav had come back to life and was brave enough to throw off the quilt and sit up on his knees. "I think it's done moved away." It was still rainin hard, but not nothin like what it had been. The hail had quit and the roarin sound wasn't there no more. I got up on my knees next to Sav, almost too scared to look outside. The inside of the car was just about destroyed. Glass was everywhere and had ripped up the car seats. The whole car was soaked like it had been dunked in a huge tub. I peeked out the window to see what was out there. I was right about us maybe settin in a river. Water was gushin down the streets. We were up on the sidewalk off of Stuart Avenue. I reckon the buildin we was up against had kept us from getin throwed upside down. I tried, but couldn't open my door on account of the water floodin up against it.

Downtown was a wreck. Glass and trash was all over the place. I couldn't see any buildins that had blowed over, so I reckon the tornado hadn't hit ground around where we were. The street had this eerie quiet about it. There had to be people around seein that it was still afternoon, but everybody was hidin out, I suppose. It was like we was all waitin for this here outlaw to leave Shotgun Junction. The rain slowed to a regular ol shower right fast, just like the storm had decided it had done finished its temper tantrum and was ready to go back to behavin like a spring rain was supposed to behave. I bet the worst of it hadn't lasted more than three or four minutes.

Sav knocked the glass off the seat and said he was gonna try to crawl out his window. He did and got up on top of the roof. I climbed out my side and joined him up on top of our heap. The car was battered. His daddy wasn't gonna be none too happy about that, but somehow neither one of us was too worried about them kind of matters right then. "What do you think we ought to do, Sav?" I don't know why I asked him that question. He didn't have no more experience knowin what to do once a tornado's passed than I did. Sometimes you just open your mouth and let whatever words wants to fall on out to come out. "You think we ought to go see if the tornado hit down somewhere's near here?"

Sav just stood there, dumbfounded. His eyes was glazed. Mine probably was, too. I doubt there was a whole lotta difference between how him and me looked at the time. He climbed down off the roof of the car and sloshed through the streamin water over to the middle of the street where it wasn't floodin. I followed.

"Let's walk over thatta way and see can we maybe walk on home," he suggested as he pointed over to the next street over, which was Jefferson Avenue. We hadn't walked more than two or three blocks when we saw a car what had been turned over by the torando winds. A man was tryin to get another fella out, so me and Sav run over to see could we help out.

Seein us comin, the man said, "Thank God you boys is here. My son here got his leg hurt. I think it's done broke. If'n you fellas can help me get him out we can take him in that store over yonder and see what's the matter." There's somethin about a time like this that makes you glad to help anybody what needs it, even if you don't even know them. We reached in the car to help out the man's son.

"Bruno! Is that you? You all right?" That big brute had this hurt look all over his face and looked right pitiful.

I don't think Bruno would've cared one bit who helped him right now. His leg was in bad pain and he'd accept charity from anybody, even me. "Leroy Evans and Sav. Boy am I ever glad to see you fellas. My leg hurts bad and Daddy cain't get me outta here by hisself." I didn't know Bruno could even pretend to be nice, much less actually sound like he meant what he had just said. Real quick like he added, "I'm glad you fellas come along. Hope you ain't hurt. You fellas all right? What're you doin out here anyhow?"

Imagine that. Bruno showin concern for me. Here he was with a hurt leg, and he's sayin he hoped me and Sav were doin okay. "Me and Sav got caught in the storm a couple blocks away. His car ain't in no position to be drivin, so we was just walkin home. I sure hate that you got turned over. I reckon it could've been worse, huh?"

Bruno winced as we pulled him up out of the car. His daddy held him up on one side and me and Sav held him on the other. I mean, he's a big ol boy. Bruno couldn't hardly help us move him, so we practically dragged him through the flooded street over to the five-and-dime store where people were already waitin with a comfortable place for him to lay down. I was right sure his leg was broke. The thought hit me that just a few months ago I had ducked in this very store just to avoid maybe gettin slugged by Bruno and here I was now pullin him in here to be nursed on.

One of the men in the five-and-dime was talkin about what all the storm had done on down Jefferson Avenue a few blocks away. "The tornado touched down maybe three blocks down. I just been down there. Everybody thinks they's some folks in some of them buildins that may've got hurt."

I looked over at Sav and told him, "C'mon, let's go down there and see can we help out." We made sure Bruno was all right and he stuck out his big ol hand and squeezed mine like we were best of pals. I told his daddy we were gonna go down the street and see if there was any way we might could be useful.

Before we left, Mr. Lynch said, "You boys has already been a big help. I cain't thank you enough. You fellas friends of Donald's?"

"Yes, sir," I said. "We're friends of his from school." No use tellin the man anything else. I sure wasn't gonna tell Mr. Lynch right then that his son didn't hardly have no friends, except the kind that were just as mean as he was. Maybe there'd be another time when I could ask Mr. Lynch would he mind workin a little harder at teachin his boy some better manners, but for right now I was actually feelin that maybe Bruno was my friend.

The rain picked up a little as we headed on down Jefferson Avenue. The dark green clouds was gone now so I wasn't worried that the storm was gonna come back and whop us again. I had a sick feelin as I looked at what the tornado had done. There wasn't hardly a window on this part of Jefferson Avenue that hadn't got splintered. Cars was laid out along the street like they were all dead. Trash was scattered all over the place like you wouldn't believe. But that was nothin compared to seein that the roofs of several buildins had just been plumb blowed off. I'd heard that when a tornado hits, it'll suck the air right out from a buildin and then make it just blow up like a bomb has been let off inside it. That's sure what looked like had happened here. This place had for certain been hit by some kind of bomb.

Men and women were swarmin the streets and buildins by this time, lookin to see was there anybody what needed help. I told Sav I was gonna go look through some of the stores that you could still get into and see what I could see. I roamed through one store and looked all around at the destruction inside it. Half the roof was gone so I could see pretty good despite there weren't no lights. It was a furniture store and a lot of the fine things in it was nothin more than junk now. It all happened in just a few short minutes, too. That's the scary part. I went back in the alley behind the store and looked up and down it. Water was still runnin hard along the buildins. It was nothin but a junk pile back there. The dark hadn't left the alley yet, bein that the clouds were castin pretty heavy shadows between the buildins. It give me the creeps just bein back there all by myself. I was just about to turn around and go back in when I barely heard this voice crying out.

"Help! I cain't move." My heart sunk a foot down into my stomach. I knew that voice. Followin it to a shed behind the next buildin over I looked in and saw a man curled up under a bunch of rubble, all pitiful and dirty lookin. It was Woody.

Chapter 34

WOODY, IT'S me, Leroy! I'm gonna help you get outta here."
"Mista Leroy. Is I ever glad ta see you. I knowed God he gonna send me a angel an I's glad it wuz you he send. You's a sight fo my so eyes. I got in dis here shed when de rain git bad. De roof fall down on me an I cain't git mysef up. I cain't say what's done wrong wit me, but my ches, it hurt pretty bad." He grabbed at his heart with one hand and stretched out the other one to touch me. Even though Woody was obviously in pretty bad pain, he still sounded peaceful like he always did. I knocked away the trash and scraps of junk that covered Woody and bent down to sit by my dark friend and took the hand he held out to me.

"Maybe we ought to just sit here a minute to see if it's all right to be movin you. I don't want to get you up just yet if that's gonna make you worse." Woody nodded at me. His breath was short and he was sweatin pretty bad. Despite he was weakened from the roof fallin on him, his grip on my hand was strong. He seemed to relax when I set down by him. I knew that would do him good. We didn't need to try and move him until he was over the shock of what had hit him. This may sound odd, but I enjoyed settin there for a few quiet minutes just waitin to decide what we was gonna do next. I didn't say nothin, but looked down at Woody and give him my best look to let him know everything was gonna be all right. Somehow, I knew it would be.

I tried to figure out what had happened here. I looked up above me and saw that the corner of the roof to this shed was blowed off. Some of the bricks off the side of the shed had caved in with it. This was a storage room for a hardware store where the store owner kept a bunch of old tools and other junk that I reckon he didn't want to get rid of. It was hard to tell if this shed were damaged real bad by the storm or if it looked messy all the time anyway and the storm just added to it. I kind of think the storm just made this shed more of a junk pile than it already was. The door that opened to it wasn't nowhere near here. It must of come unhinged and got carried down the way by the waters. It was wet in here, but there wasn't no water standin on the cement floor, so we were able to stay about as dry as you could given the situation.

After a couple of minutes, Woody almost whispered, "You all right, Mista Leroy? You ain't hurt none by dis here tornado is you?" I shook my head to let him know I was fine. He smiled that tender smile and bobbed his head up and down to say "Dat's good." Another few seconds later Woody whispered to me again. "I feels real good right now." I looked at his eyes when he said that to me, and could see that there was somethin in them that went beyond his usual look. He always looked peaceful, but he was more than that right now. It was almost like he'd been through the best experience of his life, he was so satisfied lookin. I couldn't put my finger on it, but there was somethin peculiar about how calm he was right then.

I stayed quiet for a couple more minutes, but then I asked Woody, "You feel like maybe tryin to get outta here? It ain't hardly rainin now. We need to get you over to Dr. Warren's clinic and see can he tell how bad off you are."

Woody nodded, "Dat be a good idea. I thinks I can git up." He put his hand on my shoulder and tried to hoist himself up with my help. I didn't lift him up hardly at'all when he fell back down. I don't reckon a colored man can turn white, but Woody just about did. He was hurtin worser than I had thought. I wasn't quite sure what to do next. I hated to leave Woody here by himself, but I knew for sure now that he needed medical attention and needed it fast.

"Let's put you back down here, Woody. I don't think me and you can get out of here by ourselves. I'm gonna go and try to find some help. You think it would be all right to leave you for a few minutes? You gonna be okay?"

"I be's jes fine, Mista Leroy, jes fine." His voice was weak, but the color was already comin back to Woody's face once we got him laid back down. I looked around for somethin I could use to prop under his head to make him feel a little more comfortable, but there wasn't nothin of the sort in the shed. I did what I could to help him get laid out in a good position. For a minute I thought about takin Woody's jacket off of him and usin it for a pillow, but then I figured he needed it to keep him from catchin cold.

Nervous like, I told him I'd be right back with some folks what could help him. I sure hated leavin him there, but I didn't have no choice. It did help me to feel a little more at ease to see him lookin so rested. He assured me as I left, "I be here when you gits back, Mista Leroy. I's all right. You don't go frettin 'bout me."

I run through the furniture store back onto Jefferson Avenue lookin around frantically for anyone I knew who could help out. I spotted Sav down the way helpin to clean up broke glass out in front of some store. I went sprintin down his way to get him to come help me out. When I got there, I saw his daddy and my daddy there helpin clean up, too. This was one time I was mighty glad to see Daddy.

"Daddy, Sav, Mr. Vickers! Y'all gotta come help me real quick! It's Woody! He got caught in the tornado in this shed in the alley and he's hurt somethin awful. I can't lift him up by myself!"

Mr. Vickers had better control of himself than I did and tried to find out from me exactly what the situation was. "Calm down, Leroy. What seems to be wrong with Woody? Can you tell if he has any broken bones or is he cut real bad?"

"It ain't nothin like that! He says his chest hurts and he's so weak he can't even stand up." I saw this worried look come over the faces of both Mr. Vickers and Daddy.

Mr. Vickers turned to Sav and said, "Alvin, you run on up to Dr. Warren's clinic and let him know we're bringin Woody down there. Tell him it sounds like he might've had a heart attack. Let him know it's Woody we're bringin. Be sure to tell him that." Sav took off runnin. It wasn't but a few blocks over to Dr. Warren's place. Before he got too far away, his daddy hollered out again, "Call yore momma, Alvin, and tell her you and Leroy's all right." Sav waved that he would and kept on runnin.

Everybody in town knew who Woody was, least most of the men did. Him bein the shoe shine man at Wimp's where practically everybody I know got their hair cut, he'd made friends with a lot of folks. There wasn't a man I know that didn't like him. Even the men that normally talked bad about colored folks didn't say nothin too bad about Woody. I thought to myself right then that even though it wasn't right to treat one man different than another, I was glad Woody was gonna get a little extra attention. Dr. Warren was one of Woody's regular customers, and I imagine he thought pretty kindly of him.

Me and Daddy and Mr. Vickers run back to the alley and I showed them where Woody was layin. He hadn't moved a muscle since I'd left. It struck me hard right then how much of a difference there was between Woody and the other three of us. Here we was practically panicked and Woody was as calm as you'd expect a man to be while he was settin in a church pew. Didn't nothin seem to disturb him. The three of us figured that Woody didn't need to be movin around any more than he had to, so we lifted him up and carried him down the alley out to the street.

Once we got him there, we stopped and Mr. Vickers said, "I got the truck parked a little ways over. Why don't I run over there and get it and we can drive over to Dr. Warren's place." We propped Woody up against a wall, and Mr. Vickers left while me and Daddy stayed with Woody.

I felt kinda funny settin there with my daddy and Woody, seein that I had told Woody before about all the bad things what had happened to me in my home. I don't think it bothered Woody none at all, though. He reached up and touched my daddy's arm and with his weak voice said, "You gots you a mighty fine son dare, Mista Evans. He mighty fine."

My daddy looked at him and answered Woody, "Thank ya. That Leroy's a pretty good boy. I'll agree with you there." My teeth almost dropped out when I heard him say that. Daddy didn't never say nothin nice about me that I was aware of and here he'd gone and told Woody that he agreed that I were a fine boy. What do you know about that.

Woody asked my Daddy, "Yo place get hit by dat dare tornado?"

"Naw, it rained and blowed hard, but we didn't get none of what hit here. We heard it, though, and me and Vickers figured we'd come on out and see what we could do to help out." Lookin over to me, Daddy added, "Yore momma is home worried sick that you boys got stuck out in this here tornado. We need to let her know y'all are all right. Alvin told us about the car and how y'all heard the tornado pass right over you." He shook his head and dang near looked like he was chokin on a lump in his throat.

I tried to pretend I didn't notice that Daddy was gettin a little emotional. "Maybe Sav'll think to have his momma go over to our house and let Momma and Cody Sue know what all happened."

I couldn't help but wonder what Woody thought of my daddy. I know they was around each other a little bit when Daddy would go into Wimp's to get his hair cut, but I'm right sure they hadn't talked hardly none to each other before. Daddy didn't have any shoes that was worth shinin and wouldn't have paid nobody to polish them up for him even if he did. Woody was always the friendly type, but he didn't go around strikin up a conversation with just every man what come into the barber shop. He generally waited for the other fella to show that he wanted to talk before speakin up. That's the way most colored men acted when they worked around white folks. I ain't sayin that's the way it ought to be or that I think it's right. It's just the way things is around here. I know my daddy ain't the type to go strikin up a conversation with hardly anybody and especially not with colored folks, so I doubt the two of them had exchanged too many words before now.

I was right sure Woody didn't hold no judgment against my daddy. He wasn't the type. Whatever he knew about Daddy, he still had this belief that it was my daddy's business and nobody else's what kind of person he chose to be. I think if Daddy were to give Woody the chance, Woody could even make friends with him. I wish that was possible cause one thing Daddy didn't have hardly any of was friends. It would do Daddy good to hear some of Woody's wisdom. I knew for sure, though, that wouldn't never happen. For one thing, Daddy don't like to think about things the way Woody and me do. For another thing, Daddy don't seem to feel this need to have a friend he could talk to, especially not a colored man. Still, I wish Daddy could have some of what I've got in my friendship with Woody.

Mr. Vickers pulled up in Sav's truck. I wondered how much Sav had told his daddy about the shape his car was in. I reckon Mr. Vickers hadn't seen it yet, seein as how they was workin on helpin to clean up down on Jefferson Avenue where the tornado had hit and probably hadn't gone over to Stuart Avenue where his car was sittin up on the sidewalk.

We put Woody up in the front seat by Mr. Vickers and me and Daddy sat in the bed of the truck to ride back there. By the time we got to Dr. Warren's clinic, there was some folks there ready to help us out. Dr. Warren and a couple other doctors had this little hospital downtown that could only hold a few people. I guess you could call it a hospital. Most folks called it a clinic and not a hospital. It wasn't like the big hospital on the north side of town, but it bein the closest place where Woody could get help, it seemed the best thing to do to bring him here.

I don't think folks give nurses enough credit for what all they do to help people out, so I'm gonna say right here that them nurses who took charge of Woody was the danged nicest women I've ever seen. They took Woody on in to a room where Dr. Warren could see him in a minute and treated him like he was their own flesh and blood. One of the nurses went right to takin his wet clothes off of him and put a dry gown and a warm blanket around him. I stayed in there a few minutes with my daddy and Mr. Vickers until the nurse told us they would take care of things from here.

We went out in the waitin area and found Sav. I asked him was his momma gonna go around to my house and let my momma and Cody Sue know we was okay. He said she was and that his momma said we ought to get on home pretty soon. I think she just wanted him there so she could put her hands on him and give him a big hug. Hearin Sav tell about how upset soundin his momma had been on the telephone made me realize all of a sudden just how close we'd come to makin it to heaven a little earlier than I had planned on gettin there. A cold chill run down my back when I thought of that. I reckon that thought had hit Daddy, too, and that's why he'd said them nice things about me back there a few minutes ago.

After a few minutes, I spotted this one nurse who'd helped us get Woody into the clinic. I went over to her and asked how he was doin. She made me feel good the way she said, "I think he's gonna be fine. He's resting right now. Dr. Warren is busy with some other patients, but he'll be in to see Mr. Woodrow soon. He's in good hands."

I asked her, "You reckon I could go back there and set with him? Me and him are pretty good friends."

She smiled at me like she hated to tell me what she had to say. "I'm afraid you need to stay out here. He needs to rest. Maybe tomorrow Dr. Warren will have him out on the ward, and you can visit him then."

That wasn't what I was wantin to hear, but I know the nurse was just doin what she thought were best for her patient. I went back to where the rest of them was and told them, "I think I'd like to get on home. It's been a long afternoon."

Mr. Vickers and Daddy got in the front of the truck and me and Sav sat in the back. I hadn't noticed it so much earlier, but the wind was still blowin pretty hard. I was cold and shiverin. I needed to get out of these wet clothes and take me a hot bath. Me and Sav got out at my house while the two men went back to downtown to see could they help out any more. I didn't feel none like talkin much and told Sav I'd see him tomorrow.

Cody Sue had heard the truck pull up in front of the house and met me on the front porch before I could open the door. Momma was right behind her. They both give me a hug like I was a hero that had just come home from the Great War. I didn't feel like no hero, seein that I had only just come back from Fish Pond. I did feel like I had been through a war, though. Them hugs from Momma and Cody Sue felt right good. Even though we don't go around showin it none too much, I was glad to know that they loved me. I was sorry that I didn't feel like doin much huggin in return, but I have to tell you I was more wore out than I can say, both on the inside and outside of me.

I peeled off my clothes and took a hot bath. Momma had done cooked up some good ol chili and served it to me like I was the king of this house. I do have to admit, I liked bein treated the way I was, but I don't want to have to go through what I did today to get this kind of tendin to again any time too soon.

Daddy stayed gone until well past dark. I was right proud that he was one of the men what took it on themselves to do a good deed even though they didn't get nothin in return. It helped me to see that maybe there was this good side to Daddy and that I need to think more of him as that kind of person instead of always lookin on him as nothin more than a no good drunk what don't care about nobody at all.

I hear folks pray when I'm in church and sometimes I even pray myself. But that night while I was layin in bed, I felt this urge to talk to God like I ain't never felt before. You might say it was on account of me feelin all overwhelmed by the events of the day and maybe it was, but I did my best to tell God what I was feelin right then and there.

"God, it's right hard for me to let you know what's runnin through me, but I reckon you can just imagine what it's like to go through a tornado and to feel like you was about to die. For a little while, God, I was thinkin that maybe me and you was gonna have to share a bedroom tonight, but I made it back here to my own room instead.

"A lot's been passin through me, God, about what's done happened today. I was right surprised to see Bruno all hurt in his car. He was friendlier to me than I thought he knew how to be. I almost hate to say this, but I suppose I can tell you I'm almost glad that happened to him. Now maybe me and him can get along all right.

"Another thing that happened today that's gone and set me to spinnin inside is the way my family has done acted to me. I can't remember Daddy ever showin no emotion about me like he done this afternoon. Maybe there's a side to him that I don't give him enough credit for havin. Or, maybe he don't know he's even got that side to him. Whatever it is, I'm glad things happened to me the way they did so I could see that side of him. It give me a right nice feelin inside, if you know what I mean, and I'm sure you do.

"The main thing that's worryin me right now, God, is Woody. I didn't hear it from no doctor, but Mr. Vickers thinks he must of had him a heart attack. That's what's got me worried. Them heart attacks are bad and I worry about him, despite that nurse sayin he's gonna be fine. I don't want to go askin you to do nothin you don't want to do, but I sure do wish you'd let Woody be all right. He's the best thing that's ever happened to me. I know it ain't your fault that I got me a family that don't know how to talk to each other and that Daddy drinks the way he does. All I'm sayin is that since things are the way they are around here, it sure has done me good to have Woody around. It seems like I'm almost talkin to you when I'm talkin to him. I don't mean no disrespect to you when I say that. I'm just sayin you done a good job when you made Woody and I need him, that's all."

I stopped for a minute and thought some more before I continued.

"God, I hope you don't mind, but I got a whole lotta questions to ask you when I get up there. One of them is gonna be why did you make it to where we have things like tornados? It doesn't seem that much good comes out of them."

As soon as I had done said that, it hit me that some good had come outta this tornado, at least it had for me. I had helped Bruno out, and maybe we was gonna get along better now because of it. My daddy had told Woody that I was a good son and had showed me he's got this good side to him. And Momma and Cody Sue had treated me like I was company tonight.

"Let me change that last thing up a little bit, God. Maybe good comes out of things like tornados, but I still want you to explain to me why you made them like you done. The main thing is that I wanted to let you know that I'm worried about Woody and I hope you'll keep your eye out on him. And whatever way you do things like this, if you could let him know I was askin about him, I'd appreciate that. Amen."

I laid there and tried to go on to sleep, but it wasn't easy for me despite I was dog-tired. I just couldn't get my mind off of Woody.

Chapter 35

ODD THAT after a horrible day like yesterday the sun would be shinin bright and the sky would holler out good mornin like it was sorry for what it had done the day before. I told Momma not to count on me goin with her and Cody Sue to church. I was gonna go down to Dr. Warren's clinic and see could I get in to talk to Woody. Sleep hadn't come too easy for me on account of how I kept dreamin about Woody and the tornado and all that had happened on Saturday. I was plenty disturbed the whole night and couldn't wait for mornin to come so I could check on Woody to make sure he was all right. I generally eat a big breakfast, but this mornin I had other things on my mind. Usually it takes me maybe fifteen minutes to walk as far as it is over to the clinic, but today I walked so fast it didn't take me but maybe seven or eight minutes.

There was a different bunch of nurses workin the floor than the ones I had talked with yesterday. I wished them same nurses had of been there because they would've known who I was. I hoped I could just walk right on in like I owned the place and find Woody, but this one nurse stopped me as I headed into the men's open ward where I figured he would be.

The nurse asked me with this bossy type sound in her voice, "And may I help you find what you're looking for, young man?" It was plenty obvious to me that she meant she'd be happy to show me the way back to the front door so I could get myself on home. She talked like I was a student who had done broke a major school rule and she was Mr. Higgins, tryin to decide did I need two licks or three.

As polite as I could I answered her, "Uh, I'm sorry, ma'am, but I'm lookin for a colored man named Woody. You see, we're . . . " I didn't have a chance to end my sentence. The nurse butted right in.

"Oh, and what is your name, young man?" Boy, there sure was a change in her tone of voice. She sounded like a lady now, one who couldn't possibly have talked down to me the way she had did just five seconds ago.

"Uh, it's Leroy, ma'am. Leroy Evans. You see . . . " I was gonna explain that I was right positive Woody would like to see me, but I didn't get that out neither.

"Dr. Warren said that Woody would want to see you and that I should look for you this morning. If you'll let me step over here to the nurses' station, I'll put my things down and take you to his bed."

I mean, this lady was fallin all over herself tryin to help me now. I can tell you she was a lot nicer to be around when she acted this way than she was when we first met. Soon as she finished her nursin business, she walked me to the back ward where Woody was laid up at the end of a row of maybe six beds. She put her hand on my shoulder as she pointed to his bed and smiled as she turned to leave me.

I thanked the lady real mannerly like. Whatever she had heard about me must of been nice, judgin from the way she changed her attitude and become a different person once she knew who it was she was talkin to.

Woody was half asleep when I first walked up. He seemed to perk up a little when he saw I was standin there. His voice was weak, but he wanted to talk. "Mista Leroy. How you doin today, suh? I tole the doc you'd be lookin in on me dis monin and ast did he mine if you sets a spell wit me. He said dat be right fine and say he tell de nuss to look out fo ya." He reached his hand out for mine and grabbed it. "I's glad you's here."

I looked down at Woody's hand holdin mine. Actually, I kept my eyes goin on down to the floor so I wouldn't get teary-eyed. I can tell you it makes you feel pretty low to see a good friend all weak and laid up in the bed like he was. As I gazed a second at his hand, I couldn't help but notice the stains on his palms and fingers from the shoe polish he spread on folk's shoes. I reckon them stains wouldn't come clean on account of spreadin on all that polish for so many years. That stuff was sure hard to get off, I know that. I also couldn't help but notice how white my skin looked up against his. It made me think how in a lot of ways me and Woody are right different. He's dark-skinned and I'm light-skinned. He was a country boy and I've lived in town all my life. He's an old man and I'm just fixin to turn sixteen years old. We live on different sides of the river in different worlds. I'm privileged just because I was born into a different colored family than he was.

Then again, me and Woody is alike in a bunch of ways, too, ways that I think makes us a whole lot more kin to one another than what most folks would realize. You ain't gotta be just alike on the outside if your heart and soul is made the same way. And I know one thing's for sure and that's the fact that Woody and me think and feel a whole lot alike, despite the fact that nobody else is real aware of it.

I looked into Woody's eyes and tried to work up a smile. It's hard to smile when you're lookin at someone who's all sick, but I tried. "How you feelin, Woody? I didn't sleep a whole bunch last night thinkin about you. I was afraid you didn't have a good night bein how you're sick an all."

Woody gave me this contented look and said, "I knowed you wuz thinkin about me. Somethin jes tole me so." I remembered my prayer from last night and said thank you in my heart to God right there. "I's doin jes fine. I slep pretty good. Dese here nusses takes good care o you. De doc, he say I had a heart attack durin dat tornado. He sez I's a sick man. I sez I ain't. I's feelin right good, Mista Leroy."

I didn't want Woody to go to thinkin he could do more than Dr. Warren said he ought to, so I warned Woody, "You best listen to the doctor. He probably has his reason for saying you ain't doin so good." I probably sounded like a momma the way I was talkin.

Woody smiled like he knew somethin I didn't. "I may not feels good in ma body, but de res' o me, it feel good."

Hearin Woody say that made me think back on how he had seemed so calm yesterday while he was layin in that shed in pain. I just had to ask him about that. "Woody, there was somethin kinda odd you said yesterday that I was gonna ask you about. You remember how when you was layin there in that shed you told me that you felt good?" Woody nodded that he remembered. "Well, it was plain to me that you couldn't have felt good and I couldn't help but wonder what you meant. And now here you done said the same thing again."

Woody couldn't hardly talk above a whisper, he was so weak. But his eyes was glowin. That's about the only way I can describe them. The rest of him looked awful, but his eyes was strong. "I wuz feelin good on account o seein Miss Ruby. I still feels good jes thinkin on dat visit me an her done had."

When he said that, I wasn't exactly sure what he meant. The only woman named Ruby he could've been talkin about was his dead wife. Surely he couldn't mean he'd been talkin to her, unless he had maybe been dreamin. "Which Ruby you talkin about, Woody?"

"Why ma wife, dat's who. Ma little boy wuz wit her, too, 'cept he weren't little no mo. He wuz all growed up. I knowed who he wuz nohow."

I was plumb confused, and I was beginin to think Woody was too. "I

ain't followin ya, Woody. You sure we're talkin about the same thing?"
I was beginnin to wonder if maybe Woody's mind was slippin a little.
That'll happen to a fella sometimes when he's done had a heart attack.

"Sho we is. Ya see, Mista Leroy, I went ta heaven fo a spell. It wuz
sumthin else, too. Like nothin you ain't ever seed befo in yo life."

Now some folks may say my brain had gone soft, but it hit me right
there that Woody was tellin me the truth. Somethin was odd about the
way he was talkin, but it was this type of oddness that was somehow
believable. You know, sometimes you just get this feelin that a person ain't
makin up the story he's tellin you, no matter how peculiar it sounds.

"What happened? How'd you get there?"

Woody told me his story in a low voice, but it was full of life. He didn't
have no physical energy in him, but his voice was sure alive. "Ya see,
Leroy, de wind wuz blowin hard an it started to rain, so's I said I better
fine me a place to git dry. I run up ta dat dare shed where you done found
me an I figure I ought to stay put til de rain it git done. While I wuz standin
in dat shed, I hear dis buzz and den dis engine roarin and I knowed it wuz
a tornado. I ain't never seed a tornado befo, but dat's what I heared it wuz
like. I got back down in de corner o dat shed an crouch down. All o a
sudden, I hear dat dare tornado rush over like it wanna take me along wit
it. De roof fall in some and ma heart it give a jerk an de next thing I knows,
I wuz floatin up in de air, all above de storm an de shed. I even seed ma
body layin down dare all crouch down."

To me Woody's words sounded like a dream, but to him, it was for
real. "Could you feel anything, Woody? What happened to ya then?"

He continued. "I feel two different kinda things, Leroy. One wuz de
way ma body feel an de other wuz de way ma soul feel. You see what I
means?" I said I thought so. "I didn't feel no pain. I feel like I wuz yo age
agin, all young an strong like. Dat wuz de way ma body it feel."

"What about the other part of you? How did it feel?"

"De onliest word I can say is peace. Dat's what I feel right den. Peace.
You cain't know what it wuz like 'cause you never been dare, so's I cain't
describe it to ya any better. Den I feel mysef movin down dis long dark
tunnel, but I weren't scairt at'all. Dey wuz dis hummin sound in dat tunnel.
Dat what make me know I wuz movin. When I come out o de tunnel, I
come in dis bright place. At fust, it wuz jes a sof light, but den it git brighter
an brighter, and surroun me. It wuz brighter dan de sun. Dat's how bright
it wuz, but it didn't hurt de eyes an it weren't hot, jes warm. Real warm,
jes like a momma's womb. I cain't tell ya how I know dis nex part, but I
know dat de light, it wuz God. He wuz de one holdin me in dis light. He
know who I wuz an he tell me welcome. He talk ta me, but I cain't say

what he said. I ain't never felt mo better in ma whole life. I ast him could I stay wit him, but he say no. I hadda go back to ma body an finish what I need ta do befo I can come back."

I was spellbound. That's all I can say about how I was feelin while Woody was talkin to me tellin me about his trip into heaven. "I wish I could've been there with you, Woody. Why did God have to say you had to come back?"

It was like Woody knew what God had done told him, but had to keep it a secret. All he would say was, "You'll see, Mista Leroy. An I tells ya anotha thing. You gonna be dare one o dese days, too."

Hearin him say I was gonna be there, too, one of these days give me a lift. If that's what dyin were like, then I wasn't gonna be afraid of it. I wanted to hear more about Woody's experience and urged him to keep on talkin. "Tell me more, Woody. You ain't told me about Ruby and your boy."

A smile stretched across Woody's sickly face. "Dat be's de bes part. When God he tell me I gotta go, I ast agin can I stay, but befo he can answer, I see Miss Ruby wit ma boy standin dere next to her." He stopped talkin and got lost in his thoughts for a minute. I didn't say nothin, but waited on him to continue. "She don't talk ta me, but sumhow she let me know dat she doin all right. Ma boy he don't say nothin neither, but he have dis look on him dat he glad ta see his daddy. Dat when I look at God an tell him thank you an den when I look back over ta where Ruby an ma boy wuz standin, dey be gone."

"Was that the end of it all?" I hated for his story to be done.

"Jes about. God tell me agin I got ta go back cause I gots mo ta do befo he ready fo me. Den de nex thing I knows, I wuz back in ma body an I call out and dere you come ta hep me." Woody was tuckered out after tellin me all that. Even talkin was a chore for him right then.

The look in Woody's eye right then was one of thanks to me. He was sayin thank you for bein his friend. I knew that was what he was thinkin. I felt embarrassed. I wanted to let him know he didn't have to say thank you to me, 'cause he had did more as a friend for me than I could ever do for him. I couldn't make no words come outta my mouth, though. I stood there quiet for several minutes lookin back and forth between Woody and the floor. Woody's expression never changed at all. If I could have a photograph of Woody, it would be of him lookin thatta way. He was the most handsomest man you would want to see, despite he looked so pitiful and weak in that bed.

I fought off the lump in my throat and managed to speak a little bit more to Woody. I told him I had went on home yesterday after we carried him up here to the clinic and how Momma and Cody Sue treated me like I was somebody special. Woody asked about my daddy, and I told him how Daddy had gone back downtown and helped out with a bunch of other men who was cleanin up after the tornado.

"Yo daddy, he wuz kind ta hep me out. Tell him I say thank you. Same ta yo friend an his daddy."

"I will. They'll appreciate that."

"I thinks what you done been doin ta try an change de way you acts in yo home be's workin, Mista Leroy. You keep it up, ya hear?"

The nurse what let me in come up to Woody's bed and told me real quiet like, "Leroy, honey, it's time for you to be going. You can come back tomorrow if you'd like."

I looked up at the clock. It was nine o'clock. I hadn't realized I had been there for almost an hour. I know Woody must of been tired out from our visit. He sure looked weak. Funny how your body gets wore out so easy just from talkin when you're as bad off as Woody was. I reached down to shake Woody's hand and squeezed tight. He gripped my hand as hard as he could, too.

Not carin to fight back the tears any longer, I reached down to hug Woody's neck and told him, "I'll see you tomorrow. I hope you're gonna feel fine."

Woody hugged me back as best he could. "I's jes fine Mista Leroy, jes fine. I'll look ta see ya tomorrow when it git here."

I turned around to walk away with the nurse, but before I took more than a few steps, Woody whispered out as loud as he could, "Mista Leroy! One mo thing befo ya go." I looked at the nurse, and she nodded for me to go back to Woody's bedside. She walked on down the way to give us a moment by ourselves.

Standin by Woody's bedside, he grabbed my hand again and told me, "Dey wuz one thing else I wuz gonna tell ya about ma trip ta heaven. When my son wuz standin dare by Ruby, he wuz about yo size an yo age. When I tole God thank you fo lettin me see dem two, I also say ta him, 'Ya kno, dat boy o mine, he a lot like dat Leroy, ain't he?' God, he agree wit me." Woody's eyes got wet, but he kept that same gentle smile on him. "I jes want ta say thank ya fo takin de place o ma boy, Mista Leroy." He paused and looked at me for a minute with them soft eyes of his. "Thank ya."

Words wasn't able to come outta my mouth. I don't know why, but I couldn't hardly even look Woody in the eye. Maybe I felt too undeservin of what he had just said All I could do was look at the floor, shake my head up and down, and turn and walk quickly out. My throat hurt like I had just swallowed a grapefruit and my heart was achin worse than I thought it could. At the same time, I felt like I had been give the grandest compliment a boy could ever want to be give. I just couldn't hold my feelins.

By the time I got to the door leadin outside, I was pretty broke up. The nurse put her arm around me and said with a voice that made me sure she was somebody's momma, "You and Woody have a special relationship, don't you? Don't you feel ashamed one bit for crying like that. It takes someone special to feel the way you feel right now. You come back tomorrow and ask for me again. I'll be here in the afternoon about the time school is out. My name is Sally. You ask for me and I'll take you back to see your friend again." I thanked Sally and told her I'd come directly after school was out tomorrow.

All anybody wanted to talk about the next day was Saturday's tornado. Alane acted like she was real glad to see me when I walked up under the girl's red oak tree before school that mornin. Said somethin about how her daddy went downtown and had heard about me and Sav gettin stalled on Jefferson Avenue. Thankfully, she didn't say nothin about us not comin on in her house like her and Virginia had suggested. She said she fretted the rest of the weekend about what all had happened to us. I made the story sound plenty spooky when I explained all that we had been through, which wasn't tellin a lie. I have to admit, though, that I was doin my dead level best to get a little sympathy, which I think I did.

I found out that Bruno had done broke that big bone in the top part of his leg. I know I was supposed to have learned the name of that bone in my biology class, but I 'spect that was one of the days when I wasn't payin attention the way I ought to have. Anyhow, he was gonna be laid up at home for awhile, but would eventually be out bein his usual self again. I hope he manages to keep the part of him what come out when me and Sav helped his daddy pull him out of his car. I don't think he knows it, but he could be a halfway decent fella if he'd just try. I wouldn't say that out loud, 'cause folks would think I had done turned soft. But then again, they weren't all there in the middle of that storm and don't know how bein right there underneath a tornado can change the way you see things.

That day dragged by. I kept lookin at the clock durin every one of my classes, as if that would make it go any faster. It didn't. When my last class was finally over, I headed straight over to Dr. Warren's clinic. I was sure Woody would be doin better today and was anxious to see him. I planned to stay around as long as the nurse would let me before goin home for supper.

I walked in the clinic door and stopped the first nurse I seen. "My name is Leroy Evans. This nurse named Sally told me to ask for her. She knows who I am."

The lady I was talkin to didn't even say nothin, but just motioned for me to wait where I was while she went and got Sally. Directly, Sally come walkin down the hall lookin at me. She wasn't wearin the same friendly face she had on when I left yesterday. It was more like the one I had seen on her when I first walked in the clinic yesterday mornin. I figured she must of had a rough day and that was why she looked kind of hard.

"Come on in here with me, Leroy," she said as she walked into a room behind the nurses' station. "Have a seat." She motioned to a chair and set down in the one next to it.

"How's Woody doin today? He all right?"

That compassionate look came right back into Sally's eyes. "Leroy, I don't know how to tell you this," she said, drawin a deep breath as she spoke, "but your friend Woody passed away yesterday. I hate to be the one to tell you. I've felt sick all day knowing we would have to have this talk. I know you thought an awful lot of him and it was apparent he thought the same of you." Then she hugged me like I was her own. "I'm sorry, Leroy."

Woody dead. I flat didn't know how to act. I buried my head deep in Sally's chest and wept like a baby, not even carin that me and her was practically stangers to one another. I found myself holdin on to her, hopin that she could somehow make Woody come back. Maybe there was somethin she could do as a nurse to make them words she just told me into a lie. I knew she couldn't do nothin to make Woody come alive again, but I couldn't help but wish for a miracle.

After hangin on to the nurse for several minutes, I lifted my head up and told her thank you for tellin me and for bein kind to both me and Woody. I told her I knew Woody would want to make sure she knew he appreciated all that had been did for him. I wanted to get up and leave, but I couldn't. Knowin that this was the buildin where Woody had been last, it was hard for me to walk away.

Through my tears I asked, "When did he die yesterday?" I couldn't hardly believe I was askin questions about Woody dyin. Maybe I was havin another of them bad dreams like I had night before last and I'd wake up in a minute.

Sally quietly explained, "It wasn't more than maybe ten minutes after you left. He just closed his eyes and passed on quietly, just like he fell asleep."

Ten minutes after I left. My first thought was to wish I had stayed there until he passed, but then it hit me. He wasn't gonna die anyhow until I had done come and gone. That's why God had told him he had to come back—to thank me that I had took the place of the son he never knew. That was his way of tellin me good-bye. My English teacher, Mrs. Lemming, would say that was his way of puttin a period at the end of his life. God was waitin until that time before he let Woody into heaven for good. When that thought went through my head, suddenly it wasn't quite so hard to work up a smile. It wasn't a big one that spread across my mouth, but it was a smile anyhow.

Sally noticed it on me. "You feel better, Leroy? It makes you feel good to think about Woody, doesn't it? I'll bet that's what you're doing."

"Yes, ma'am, it is." I had another question for the nurse. "Um, ma'am, could you tell me did Woody have anything more to say after I had done left yesterday?"

Sally put her arm around me again and told me, "He told me after you left that he had done all he needed to do and now he was ready to go when God was ready. Isn't that a sweet thought? I suppose he meant he had finished a full life's work and he knew his time was up." I liked the way Sally had treated me. She wasn't too old, so whatever kids she had must of been little. One thing's for dern sure, and that is that they're lucky.

"I reckon that must be what he meant when he told you that," I answered. Sally was part right, but she didn't know all I knew about where Woody had been a couple days ago durin the tornado. I didn't need to tell her, seein that it wouldn't mean the same to her as it done to me. It's one of them things you just want to keep to yourself, it bein of the personal nature and all.

I had one last question for the nurse. "Do you know anything at all about when they're gonna bury Woody? I'd kinda like to go if I knew where it was gonna be and all."

Sally told me she had heard Dr. Warren talkin to Woody's sister later in the day Sunday. The buryin was gonna be down in the pauper's graveyard in South Cassville the next Sunday afternoon at two o'clock. They weren't gonna have no church service, just a preacher sayin some words over the body for Woody and his family. I hoped they didn't mind me bein there along with them. I know Woody would've wanted it thatta way and figured his sister would understand.

Chapter 36

I COULDN'T hardly stand havin to wait until the next Sunday for them to bury Woody. Them six days was the longest six days of my entire life, I do believe. Momma told me that colored folks hate to give up one of their family when they've done passed, so they wait a good while to have the buryin, sometimes even longer than they was waitin to have Woody's buryin. All I can say is that it sure seemed like a long time from one Sunday to the next. I went on about my business and tried to act as normal as I could, but I didn't do such a good job of hidin my grief. I flat couldn't hide it even though I sure tried. You know, I've done said how I'm the kind that doesn't like to go to cryin about things. I know that isn't right, but I reckon livin with a daddy that acts like mine does, will turn a boy against bein soft. There's times I wish it was easier for me to let loose with my emotions of the tender sort, but it's right hard for me to do. This is one time I might not've minded bein a girl seein how girls have it easier when they go to showin how they feel about somethin. That tells you how low I had done sunk down when I admit that I wished I could be a girl even for a little bit. It sure would've helped if Sunday would hurry up and get here just so we could get the buryin behind us and I'd know for sure that everything havin to do with Woody was over. I don't mean no disrespect for Woody by sayin that, it's just that waitin to tell him good-bye that one last time was about to drive me around the bend.

When Sunday afternoon finally showed up, I put on my best clothes and started walkin down to the pauper's graveyard. When I say I put on my best clothes, about all I mean is that I put on a clean white shirt that Momma had ironed special for me. I wore the same old pants and brogans that I wear every day. The graveyard was down on First Street only about two blocks over from the Tennessee River. Seein as how I had left the house plenty early, I figured I'd walk on down by the river on my way to the graveyard.

Now you might think I'm a little touched in the head when I admit what I did while I was walkin, but I pretended Woody was walkin alongside of me and I had me a nice little talk with him. "Woody," I told him, "I can't tell you how hard it is for me to be goin down to the graveyard to see you this one last time. I figure that when I get to the hole where they're gonna drop you, I'll be so choked up I can't speak, so I'm just gonna let you know right now how powerful bad I miss you."

I had this feelin that Woody was talkin back to me right there while I was walkin, "Dat's all right, Mista Leroy. If'n you cain't talk when you get's ta where I is, I'll understan. Ya know, Leroy, you does a whole lotta talkin wit yo eyes anyhow, an I knows jes what be's in yo heart de minute I look in dem two eyes of yores. You ain't gotta talk ta me fo me to know what you feels." I swear I could see him smilin at me the way only Woody smiles. I tried to smile back at him.

I kept on goin with my talkin. "Woody, I done figured out why God he told you to come on back here and take care of some more business before he'd let you into heaven for good. I was choked up last Sunday when you told me thank you for takin the place of that boy of yours what done died. I'm sorry I walked out on you without sayin nothin, but I flat couldn't talk. Woody, I ain't never got an award or nothin like that, but you sayin that to me was like I had done been crowned king of the world, at least my part of it. I want to thank you for that fine compliment." I saw Woody noddin his head slowly to say I was sure welcome and that he had meant every word of it.

Walkin on down the riverbank a little farther near to where I needed to get on back up to First Street, I stopped and stood there lookin out onto the water, still pretendin Woody was by my side. I told him how my daddy had said that was right nice of him to tell me how he appreciated that he helped out durin the tornado. Said that I had this feelin that I'd done turned the corner, so to speak, with Daddy and that things were for sure gonna be better at home.

I also let him know about me goin down to Wimp Dickerson's Barber Shop and how the place seemed empty what with him not bein there and all. All the fellas that came into the barber shop said somethin about how they was gonna miss him. It wouldn't be near as bad as how I was already missin him, though. Then I told him how I could just see it when Wimp walked into heaven when it was his turn to get there. He'd come in with his ears freshly lowered and that perfumy smellin tonic on his hair and he'd walk straight up to God and say, "Howdy, pal." I pretended that Woody got a kick outta how I said that.

Even if he was just a memory, I hated to leave Woody there and stood for a minute more with him right there next to me. "Remember the way you liked to come down here to the river and say you was fishin?" I asked. "You gotta admit that half the time, you didn't even keep a worm on your hook. Ain't that right, Woody?"

I heard Woody chuckle as he 'fessed up, "Dat's right, Leroy. Let's jes keep dat mine and yo secret." He was still grinnin when he told me, "Besides dat, Mista Leroy, meybe I wuzn't tryin to catch no catfish sum o de time. Meybe I wuz tryin ta catch me a little peace o mind. Ya gots ta admit, I catched a lot o dat." He laughed quietly again and I laughed with him. I could've swore I felt his arm around my shoulder. Dad gum, that Woody was a better fisherman than I'd been givin him credit for all this time. I reckon he caught what he had went after. There's a bunch of folks that can't say that.

I was the only white person at the graveside service. Woody attended the Dogwood Bloom Baptist Church. I liked the name they had given their church. The whole church, about fifty people in all, had turned out for the funeral. I reckon most of them were common folks just like Woody and me, but let me tell you somethin. Just because folks are common doesn't mean they can't have plenty of heart and soul. Them folks sure knew how to send a man off into heaven in grand style. That funeral was powerful. They let loose of their feelins in a way I can't do. At first I was right taken back by the way they carried on, but when you hold them feelins in they don't do nothin much but cause you a bunch of trouble. Woody's friends were probably helpin themselves out when they turned up them feelins the way they did.

I'd never been to a colored man's funeral before. For that matter, I haven't been to but one buryin in my whole life, that bein that uncle of Momma's that I didn't hardly even know. When one of my kind gets buried at the pauper's graveyard, the dead person is lucky just to have a couple family members around and a minister to read a few verses from the Bible, like the poor fella had died in shame. Colored folks don't see it thatta way. It doesn't matter one lick what a man was like when he was livin. When he died, it was the right thing to do to make sure Jesus and God knew he was comin their way.

An old man drove up in a beat-up lookin truck with Woody's body in the back end of it. Six men picked up the box Woody's corpse laid in and carried it over to the hole that was to be his body's bed for the rest of time. It wasn't even a real casket he was laid in. A pine box had been made by some of the men in the church. I was right positive that suited Woody just fine. The men walked in unison one half step at a time, paused, and then took another half-step as they slowly made their way over to where the rest of us stood. While they were walkin a choir of eight or ten folks started singin,

> *Ma Lawd, what a mornin*
> *Ma Lawd, what a mornin*
> *Ma Lawd, what a mornin*
> *When de stars begin to fall!*

The preacher took the lead role as he sung the verses with the choir chimin in behind him. I haven't been to heaven like Woody has, but I can't imagine the choir up there singin any better than these folks did. I was moved. Everybody started singin in with the preacher and the choir and went to swayin and clappin their hands. I wanted to join in the singin, but the knot in my throat was so big, no sound could've got through my windpipe if I had wanted it to. I tried to sway and clap with the rest of them, but I know I didn't do it right. It didn't seem to bother anybody.

About the time the pallbearers got Woody to the hole and started lowerin him down in the ground with ropes, this one huge colored woman dropped down to the ground and started jerkin around like she was havin a convulsion or some such. Another woman next to her lifted her up and hollered, "Gloree, Sister Louise done seed God's mercy fall down on Mista Woodrow!" I was the only one there that worried about the poor woman faintin again.

The preacher then stared straight up into the sky and gave out a prayer that almost sang like the song he just finished. "Dear Lawd, we's come here ta give you dis here frien' o ours. Dis man, Woody, he been one o ours all dese here years. Now he belong up dare wit you, Lawd. He be one o yo's fo good now. Lawd, Woody done give us all he got. He give us peace in our heart. He give us his friendship. He give kindness ta dem what he don't even know. He give folks a reason ta believe in deyself. He give honor ta what it mean ta be called a man, Lawd. Dat's what dat man who up dare wit you right now done give all us down here." He lowered his head and collected his thoughts while the choir began softly singin "Swing Low Sweet Chariot."

When he sang out the words *comin for ta carry me home* I couldn't help but be happy that Woody was home for good now, home with Ruby and his boy. It also hit me that Woody had carried me home with him by the way he showed what it means to live at peace with yourself. I'd always be grateful to my black-skinned friend for that.

Lookin up after a minute, the preacher kept on with his prayer while the choir was still singin. "Lawd, we's scaired down here. We gots troubles. Brother Woody, he ain't got no trouble now. He see past dis here life. He see what none o us can see. Lawd, I want, and all dese here brothers an sisters wants what he done gots. We wants a strong heart like dat dare Woody gots. Lawd, we wants you standin right dare beside us, jes like you's standin dare right by our frien."

My heart was dern near ready to break in two. I wanted to jump down in the hole and lay there right next to ol Woody. I wanted to be in that home where he was. The preacher had made it sound so invitin to be up in heaven that I wanted to go right then and there.

Composin myself, I looked around the crowd to see if I could figure out which one of these folks was Woody's family. Everybody there was actin like they were tore up the way only family could be tore up when a man dies. I thought I could tell which one of the women was Woody's sister because folks seemed to be comfortin her more than the rest. She looked pretty much like Woody, kinda tall and thin with those same eyes he had. She was cryin, but at the same time she had this peace about her that said she had some of the same character that Woody had. I figured she had to be his kin. I hoped I could talk to her once the funeral was done.

This man who the preacher called Deacon Wilkerson stepped up to tell some about Woody. "We's here today ta lay ta rest Herbert Henderson Woodrow. Us folks knows him as Woody." Lookin upward he asked, "Dat's what you calls him, ain't it Lawd?" I imagine God shook his head about then, lettin the deacon know he was right. Until right then I didn't even know what Woody's real name was and I've known him all my life. I bet God didn't know his name was nothin other than Woody neither.

The deacon kept going, "Woody was borned in 1868, son of a free man in Richmond County, Georgia. He come out here ta Alabama when he weren't but a boy an been here ever since den. He had him a wife, Ruby, who die when she give him his boy, Willie Mayso. He die, too, but dey's all together now wit de family of God up dare in de sky." All the while as he was talkin, the deacon was encouraged by everybody there with loud shouts of "Amen!" and "Dat's right!" and "Tell me mo!" Them colored folks were feelin everything that man said as if it had come right outta them. I was feelin the same way, too.

The deacon curled up his forehead and got this serious sound in his voice as he boomed out, "Dis here man he been through a lot o pain! He know, jes like I know, what de word heartache mean. He know what it

mean ta be down at de bottom o de heap! He been treated wrong by dem
folks what think dey de one what give a man his worth!"

Then his voice grew curiously quiet. "But what did Woody do? He
show de world what it mean ta be gentle. He show de man what treat him
wrong dat he gots patience in his heart. He treat every man de way a man
oughta be treated. He show he can talk de language of a king. Woody he
trust hisself. He tell hisself what it like ta be a good man. He don't listen
ta de world and do what de world tell him ta do. He do what he done
been put here by God ta do. Woody he wuz jes what God made him ta
be, nothin mo."

Then scarin me half to death, the deacon screamed out with a voice that
was louder than a clap of thunder as he beat on his chest and fell to his
knees, hollerin and wailin out in a sing-song chant,

Good God! *I* wants ta be like dat man!
I wants ta be what I wuz made ta be!
I wants ta love life!
I wants ta love ma brotha and sista!
I wants ta listen ta mysef an not everybody else!
Good Lawd up in heaven, give us *all* what dis here angel done got!
Give it to us! Give it to us! Please, Lawd, give it to us!

The deacon bent his whole body down to the ground, beggin and
weepin as the entire crowd of folks joined him in a grand show of every
feelin in them. I thought Woody was gonna rise up out of his box and join
us right then and there. I stood by watchin not knowin whether to join in
with them or what. My feelins were aroused, but I wasn't able to go to
showin them the way these folks were. It did me good to be there, though.
Just watchin the singin and clappin and cryin and wailin made it seem like
they were doin for me all the things I couldn't do for myself. It was like I
was livin through them folks.

Directly, some of the men commenced to shovelin dirt over Woody's
box and the whole crowd quieted down as if they were told to. The
preacher and the choir sung "There is a Balm in Gilead" while everybody
else hummed along, cryin that Woody was bein covered up never to be
seen this side of the ground no more.

Once the men had filled up the grave with dirt, the preacher looked
straight up to the sky again and offered up a final prayer. His voice was
quiet and he wasn't chantin like the deacon did, but his prayer sounded
like music just the same. "Lawd, we cain't see right now. We's blind. We
don't know why you takes away a man's life when ya do. We's hurtin,

We's grievin. But Lawd, we knows you's hurtin, too. You hurts ta see us hurt. We needs yo hep right now cause we cain't find no man what can take dis man's place in de world. Give us peace. Give us de same spirit dat you give to ol Woody. Our hand it be's in yo hand, Lawd, every step o de rest of de way. God bless dis man, Woody . . . Amen."

A wooden marker with Woody's name and the years he lived carved into it was pounded into the ground at the head of his grave. Just like that it was over. Woody's life was done. There was still some singin and cryin goin on, but it wasn't an organized sort of thing. The woman I thought was Woody's sister came up to me and pulled my head down onto her shoulder and said, "You mus' be Leroy. Woody he done told me 'bout you." She hugged me like a baby for a long time, just holdin onto me like she didn't want to let go. I hugged her back as a way of lettin her know what I thought of her brother. She then grabbed hold of each of my shoulders and with her arms holdin me out so she could get a good look at me, she stared at me and told me, "Mista Leroy, Woody done said you's gonna be somebody what gonna make a difference in dis here world. Ma brother he tell me you and him talks a lot. Dat can only mean one thing, an dat be's dat Woody he think you got de touch o one dat can carry on what wuz in his heart. He say you different dan other folks. You's a thinker. Mista Leroy, I want you ta know dat Woody he feel a whole lot fo you. You don't let him down. Jes remember what ol Woody he teach you. He want you ta teach all dem things ta somebody else. Dat what he want you ta do." Then she squeezed me again like I was one of her own and cried hard as she said, "Mista Leroy, keep dat spirit dat wuz in ma brother alive! You keep it alive an give it ta somebody what you loves! You do dat fo me?"

I wasn't able to talk. I hoped Woody's sister didn't take offense that all I could do was shake my head up and down. But in my heart I was sayin, "If I don't do another thing for all the rest of my life, I'm gonna take what all I've learned from Woody and give it away to anybody that will let me. That's a promise to you and to Woody and to God above." I couldn't say them words, but I hope she knew that's what I was thinkin.

I couldn't go home right then bein that I was too doggone spent. Who knows what was happenin at my house. I couldn't bear the thought of walkin in the back door and bein swallowed up by all the stone-faced dullness of my momma and daddy. I didn't want to be there in case this was one of those days where Daddy decided he was gonna gripe about any little thing that came to his mind. I didn't want to see Momma all droopy and spiritless. I needed to be by myself so I could get some strength that I just can't find in my own home.

I went back down to the banks of the Tennessee River, only this time I was by myself. Woody wasn't nowhere around. He was gone for good now. My mind was mostly mush. I do believe I was too numb to think straight. Without any special order, thoughts just went spinnin as they pleased right through my head. I thought first about me and Woody fishin and how I had tried some of his Taylor Made and got all sick. I remembered that time I sat in his house listenin to him read me that letter from his wife and him tellin me about how she and his boy died. Then my thoughts moved over to Alane Sharpe and her family room and how I'd die to have a family room in my house. I mulled over the goings on at the graveyard and how I was sure different than them colored folks. I thought about how maybe I could save Cody Sue from bein just like Momma when she grows up.

I went back to thinkin on Alane. What with Woody bein gone, I sure hoped she could be someone I could lean on to maybe fill in some of that empty feelin that was in me on account of not havin Woody any more. She was different than Woody, that's for sure, but then again she liked to think, just like me. She had just turned sixteen and I was pretty near sixteen. Maybe as we both grew up she'd be the one who could help me talk things out so I could make sense out of my feelins. I know I'd sure like to do the same for her. Maybe we could help each other out thatta way.

I stayed out by the river until near dark. The time finally came when I figured I better get on home, but right as I stood up from where I was sittin, I got swallowed up by a sack full of feelins that dragged me down so low I couldn't hardly bear it. Them feelins just attacked me like they were bound to come rippin out sometime and now was when they had decided to come. I've felt lonesome before, but for just a few minutes I felt more closed off from the rest of the world than I ever remember feelin. Everything I had been tryin to hold in for the last week came spillin outta me all at the same time. I couldn't do anythin but lay my head down on the riverbank and let the water faucet go to gushin. And there wasn't nobody out there to comfort me.

Chapter 37

I FELT Cody Sue's hand on my shoulder as she shook me. "Leroy! Leroy, wake up!" I didn't know quite what time it was, but I can tell you for dern sure it was earlier than I wanted to be gettin outta bed. This bein a Saturday, I wanted to get my usual extra hour or so of sleep. Didn't appear I was goin to this mornin. Through my fuzzy eyes, I could see this frazzled look on Cody Sue's face that let me know real quick that she wasn't gonna listen if I told her to leave me alone cause I wasn't interested in what she had to tell me. I could tell that much even though I wasn't hardly awake.

"What're you doin in here so early, Cody Sue? What's wrong with you? Can't you see I'm still sleepin?" I should know it doesn't do one bit of good to go askin Cody Sue them kinda questions, but I did anyhow.

"It's Gilly, Leroy. He needs you powerful bad!"

That was the last dad gum thing I needed to be hearin right then. I was about as excited to be gettin outta bed early on a Saturday mornin for that danged cat as I was to go into Daddy's room and ask him would he mind givin me a good beatin. I wanted to suggest that Cody Sue go hike around the block a few times just so she could walk off some of her heebie-jeebies, but I knew I'd be wastin my breath if I said that. I sat up in bed and rubbed my eyes so I could at least see straight.

"What in thunder has that cat done now?"

"I can't tell you, Leroy. It's a surprise! But you gotta come outside right now. He needs you real bad."

Figurin that I may as well give in and get up seein as how Cody Sue wasn't gonna let me alone until I did, I crawled outta bed, pulled on some britches, and pretty unenthused said, "Take me to that dumb ol cat of yours and let's see what all he needs."

Cody Sue grabbed my arm and dragged me out into the backyard and pointed to Gilly, who was standin right under the edge of the back porch. Pancho was standin right next to him. I sure hated seein Pancho chum up with that cat, but I reckon he didn't have much choice, seein as how they shared the same backyard. "See, there he is."

"So, he looks just fine to me. What're you all worked up about?" Just as I said them words, Gilly slipped back underneath the porch and vanished. Pancho disappeared with him like he was in on Gilly's little game. That dog was disappointin me.

"You gotta go under there with him, Leroy! That's what he wants you to do!" Cody Sue was all of a doodah again, jumpin up and down like she was about to wet her pants.

"Cody Sue, I'm not gonna crawl under there and get Gilly out! He just showed you he can come out by himself. He doesn't need me to go pullin him out from under there." I was about to get mad at Cody Sue for gettin me outta bed all for nothin. In fact, I reckon I was already more than just a little bit peeved.

"Gilly don't need you to pull him out. He needs you to get his baby kittens out from under there. That's why I come and got you." Havin made her grand announcement that Gilly had baby kittens, Cody Sue stood there beamin at me broader than day.

"Kittens? I thought Gilly was a boy cat. You mean . . ."

"Yep. I reckon he's a girl cat."

"Well I'll be . . . Have you looked under there to see how many of em there is?"

"Cain't tell for sure, but I could hear a bunch of em cryin like there's maybe ten or twelve of em. Please hurry and pull em out! I wanna see em."

Tryin to think on what all we might need for our rescue project, I told Cody Sue to run in the house and get an old sheet outta the hall closet so we could have somethin to lay the little critters in once I got them out from under the porch. They didn't really need any milk seein as how they could get that from Gilly, but I told her to pour up a little anyhow. I figured she'd like wettin her finger with the stuff and lettin the little cats lick it off of her. Girls like to do that sort of thing, you know.

Once she got back, I told her to come on to the edge of the porch and I'd bring the kittens out to her. There wasn't a whole lot of crawl space under the porch for me to get around, but I scooted along on my belly until I got back to where Gilly and Pancho and the kittens was. At first, it was hard to even see, but my eyes adjusted pretty quick like. "Mornin fellas," I said to the animals. Pancho looked almost as worked up about this whole matter as Gilly was. "You ain't the daddy of these here kittens are you, Pancho?" I laughed at my own joke. Might as well try and laugh seein as how it wouldn't do me any good to be any other way.

Them little cats went to whinin and cryin real big once I got to them. I know they couldn't see me bein that their eyes wouldn't be opened all the way yet. I reckon they could tell, though, when somethin other than one of their own had come along. Pickin up the first little fella, I crawled back out to where Cody Sue was waitin. Gilly and Pancho crawled alongside of me. Handin the kitten to her, Cody Sue squeeled and told me to hurry up and get the rest of em out. I left her there actin all excited, kissin her new pet and rubbin her face up against its fur. One by one, I pulled each of Gilly's newborns out into the backyard, handin them over to Nurse Cody Sue, who gave them a grand welcome into their new world. There was eight of em altogether.

One of the kittens was the spittin image of Gilly. I mean, that little thing was Gilly made all over. The one that was the runt of the litter was nothin but ugly. I hate to say that about a freshly born cat, but his fur was all different colors, makin him look like he'd been born with the mange. Two of the kittens were nuzzled up next to each other. One was coal black and the other was snow white. It hit me that it ought to be thatta way with people just like it was with them two kittens. Here they were different colors and it didn't make a hill of beans difference to them. Peculiar how people can take things like the color of a person's skin and make such a big to-do about it.

Seein them two kittens made me think on how they was like Woody and me, and how much I missed him. It's been three or four weeks since he was buried, but I've thought of him every single day. It was little things that reminded me of him. That's probably the way it should be, too, since Woody was the kind who could set a person to thinkin over somethin that would've passed right by an ordinary fella.

My job done, I took a seat on the porch step and watched Cody Sue and Gilly take care of their babies. Pancho set right by me and seemed to be right proud of our new family members. I know he couldn't be the daddy of them young 'uns, but I figured he could be their honorary uncle. Scratchin the hound dog's neck, I said, "Uncle Pancho. I'd say that has a nice ring to it, wouldn't you?" I think he agreed. I can't be too sure if this is what Gilly meant, but even he, I mean she, come up to me and set in my lap for a little bit as if to say thanks for helpin her out when she needed me.

I smelled the coffee brewin in the kitchen, which meant Momma was up. As I went in the kitchen, I sat down by Daddy as he waited for Momma to serve him.

"Gilly had himself eight little kittens," I informed him.

"Thought that boy was gettin fat." Daddy wasn't too excited that we had some new life around here. I didn't care that he was unimpressed with Gilly's feat, I was gonna tell him about it anyway.

"Cody Sue come and got me outta bed. I was put out with her at first, but I reckon it was worth it when I saw how she looked when I pulled the first one out from under the porch and handed it to her. Why don't you come out and look at em with me."

Daddy looked over at Momma and seein that the coffee wouldn't be ready for another minute agreed to follow me out. Kinda sad that a daddy won't agree to take part in what his children are doin unless he's got nothin else to do. Actually, I shouldn't be quite so hard on Daddy. I've got to hand it to him that he's been tryin a little harder to be more of a father and husband over the last few weeks since me and him talked that time. For that matter, I been doin a better job of not stayin so mad at him and Momma for their ways. It ain't like I've grown to like things any better than I ever did. I've just quit fightin so hard to force them two to change, that's all.

I pointed to the white kitten and the black one he was nuzzled up against. "Look at them two over there. Reminds me of Woody and me."

As if that was the first time Daddy had thought about Woody since his passin, which it probably was, Daddy said, "How long's it been since that nigger friend of yore's died?"

"He wasn't no nigger, Daddy! He was colored." I wanted to get mad, but I caught myself real quick. The fact that Daddy asked me anything at all about Woody was his way of showin that he was tryin to show an interest in me. I know he doesn't have the best way in the world to say he wants to know how I'm doin in my grievin, but him askin me that question was better than the usual grunt he would've given just a few months ago.

"I didn't mean it thatta way."

"Woody has done more to help me out than any man could do."

Daddy didn't seem offended that I had suggested that Woody had been more of a daddy to me than he had been. He looked at me and said, "I'm grateful to him for that."

How 'bout that. Daddy sayin that was the same as sayin he knows he doesn't have in him whatever it takes to be a lovin daddy and he's glad I had someone else to lean on while growin up. I do believe Daddy is beginnin to see himself a little clearer now than before.

I took care of a few chores that needed to be done around the house that mornin and then told Momma I was gonna go up to Alane Sharpe's house for a visit. I had got to where I called on her sometimes on Saturday afternoons. Her momma and daddy didn't seem to mind, and I know it sure did me good to see her more than what I did on school days. I hope it did Alane some good, too.

It was May, which I'd probably say is my favorite month of the year. Around here it generally gets pretty warm on May afternoons, but it's not so bad that you can't stand it. July and August can be downright miserable on account of the heat, but in May the weather is almost always just about right. It took near to thirty minutes to walk from my house all the way out to the end of Stuart Avenue, but I sure didn't mind it bein it were so nice to be outside. The trees was all leafed out by now, but still had that fresh lookin green color to them. Out where Alane lived a good many folks have flower gardens in their front yards or vegetable gardens around back. My momma always plants a vegetable garden in the spring, same as a bunch of other folks. Alane's daddy planted one, too. In fact, I had gone down to their house a few Saturdays ago and helped him plant black-eyed peas. That was just about all that man wanted in his garden. That and a few tomato plants. He said he grew up eatin black-eyed peas and loved them better than anything else what come from the ground. I feel the same way about black-eyes.

As I walked up Stuart Avenue, I could see Alane's house from a good half mile off. It and the Thompson's house were about the only ones that far out. I expect I picked up my pace a little as soon as I saw her place, but I don't think I was aware of it at the time. Alane and her momma was out in front of the house plantin flowers when I walked up.

"Hey there Alane! Mrs. Sharpe. Y'all all right today?"

Alane stood up and shot me a broad smile. Boy did that do me some good to see her actin all happy to see me. "Hello Leroy! We were just about to finish up. Don't you think the flower bed looks pretty?" I had to admit it did and said so. I think I even impressed Mrs. Sharpe by tellin her that periwinkles was one of my favorite flowers. It helps to say things like that to let your best girl's momma know you've got a little bit of knowledge about such things as flowers.

Mrs. Sharpe stood up alongside her daughter. I realize this sounds right sappy to say, but Alane and her momma sure did look pretty standin there together like they were. I almost said so out loud, but I stopped myself on account of not wantin to appear to be too flattering. A boy can overdo them kinda compliments, you know. But both of them had that pretty dark hair and dark complexion that made them look like a queen and her princess. At least that's what they looked like to me.

Mrs. Sharpe said why didn't she go in and get us all somethin to drink. I helped Alane pick up their work things and put them in the storage shed around back behind of the house. When I came back to the front porch where Alane was sittin, she had poured me a glass of cold water from the pitcher her momma had left with her. Mrs. Sharpe had went back in the house to get herself cleaned up. I suggested to Alane that we take our drinks across the road so we could sit under the shade of the red oak tree over there.

We hadn't talked more than just a few minutes when I commented to Alane, "You know I been feelin right odd the last few weeks."

"Something been wrong with you, Leroy?"

"It ain't that there's somethin wrong with me. It's just that it feels funny not havin Woody around no more. I wonder what he's doin right now up in heaven and if he can see me down here. I know he's happy bein with his wife and boy and Jesus and everybody else up there. I'm glad for that."

I paused for a moment and let my mind wander off and thought about the best friend I had ever known. My heart went to hurtin pretty fast when I did that. I hadn't cried a whole lot since I laid on the riverbank after Woody's funeral and bawled like a baby. I had got teary-eyed every now and then thinkin about him, but I hadn't broke down anymore like that day. At the time it didn't seem that life would go on without Woody. Life's gone on all right, I suppose, but it hasn't been the same, that's for sure. It's hard to say how it's been different since Woody's passin, but I know the world seems a whole lot emptier than it used to.

"You really miss Woody, don't you?" Alane had this comfortin sound to her voice that I sure liked. She wasn't sayin that just because she felt sorry for me. I think she was tryin to feel my feelins along with me. I liked that, too.

"I just can't say how much. I know that folks like Woody don't come along very often and I'll never know another man what can take his place. They threw away the mold when they finished makin him." We sat for a minute and that lump in my throat started growin again. "I sure miss the old fella," I whispered.

Alane looked me in the eye and asked, "Could you tell me more about Woody? I never got to meet him." Her lookin at me thatta way made me kinda nervous. Lord, it's hard for a fella like me to understand all his feelins.

"Tell you the truth, Woody's kinda hard to describe. I reckon it's because he's so different than most anybody else you'd meet. He was the best of what you'd want to see in any man. All at the same time he was full of fun and yet he was the most serious man I'd ever talked to. He could see deeper down into a fella's heart than you'd think was possible. The only way I can describe it is that he was able to become you while he was listenin to you talk. That make any sense when I say that?"

"I see what you're saying. I wonder how a man can do that so naturally."

I pondered on what Alane said and gave my thoughts on the matter. "The way I figure it, he was plenty satisfied with himself and so he didn't see no need to spend all his time thinkin about what all he needed outta life. That left him plenty of room to think about other people."

I think Alane liked the thought of a man bein thatta way. Not enough men are, you know. It ain't that I'm proud to admit it. That's just the way things are, unfortunately. "It had to make a person feel good to know he was so interested in listening."

"I can tell you this, he knew how to make me feel better than I could ever feel when I was with anyone else. It does somethin to you when you know a man is willin to become you for awhile. Makes you feel all important. I know I sure felt important when I was around him."

I thought back on the funeral service at the graveyard and how all the people there didn't have nothin but good to say about Woody's ways. Course, folks say mostly good things about anybody what done just died, but I'm for certain they meant everything they said about Woody.

"You should've been at Woody's funeral, Alane. It was like nothin you've never seen before in your whole life. Colored folks has this way of showin what they feel that I don't know how to do. It did me a heap of good just bein around them. But I'll tell you what else hits me when I go back to thinkin on that service. Every single person there kept shoutin and sayin how they wanted what Woody had. They wanted to be just like he was. Everybody felt thatta way. I sure been thinkin a lot about that since then."

"You mean you want to be just like Woody?" I shook my head that I did. Alane asked, "What exactly do you mean, Leroy?"

I studied her question for a second before I spoke up. "Woody used to say that I'm a thinker like him. I'm not near as good as he is, but that's what I aim to become. I want to learn to look at things the way he did. That's what I mean."

"I don't see any reason why that can't happen. You're already halfway there." Alane talked like she had confidence in me. Then she said somethin that kinda took me back. "Leroy, do you realize how lucky a person you are?"

I'm right sure I had a confused look on me when she said them words. "Lucky? I don't think I'd call myself lucky. I ain't had it so good in life. I'd call you lucky, but not me. Look at what all you got. You got a family what knows how to show that they love each other and you got a momma and daddy what gets along good and is respected by folks all over town. I'd call that lucky, but I wouldn't say that about me."

Alane disagreed. "But look at you. You've had a friendship with Woody that most people go all their life looking for. I've got lots of friends, but I've never had a friend that understands me the way Woody understood you. That's something rare. You're so far ahead of most boys your age in the things you understand. You've taken some of the unfortunate situations you've been in and learned something from them. And you give what you've learned to people like me. I learn a lot just from talking to you. It makes me wish I had more of what's inside you."

Now lemme tell you, when you hear a special girl like Alane say them kind of flowery things about you, it's pretty doggone hard not to grin real wide. "I reckon I hadn't never thought of it thatta way before. Maybe I am lucky."

Then Alane said, "Someday you could teach me all the things Woody has taught you. That way maybe both of us could have the same kind of happiness he had." Her sayin that made me think I could do just what Woody's sister had asked me to do when she told me to share what I had learned from her brother.

Without no forewarnin this thought shot straight into my head and I acted on it. Leanin over to Alane, I smacked her square on the mouth. I ain't got a lot of experience in these kind of things, but I know that when a boy plants one on a girl, she can either just let him do it and then it's over with, or else she can kiss him back. The second thing is what Alane done to me.

Well I'll be dad gum.